PRAISE FOR *UNSPOKEN*

"A sexy and sinful new adult read you don't want to miss!"
—Katy Evans, *New York Times* bestselling author

PRAISE FOR *UNDECLARED*

"[I] can't wait to read the next installment in the Woodlands series, the characters, storyline and gushing romance were all wonderfully written and Jen Frederick's writing is extremely engaging—she is definitely an author to remember and this is a book I'm more than happy to add to my favourites list!"
—Obsession with Books

"Noah Jackson was perfect in every way! He was compassionate, considerate and sexy as hell! His old school values mixed with his slight debauchery made him a perfect alpha male and you can't help but adore every part of his character."
—Craves the Angst

Titles by Jen Frederick

The Woodlands

UNDECLARED
UNSPOKEN

UNSPOKEN

Jen Frederick

UNSPOKEN

PEAR TREE LLC
100 N. Pleasant Hill Road
Warner Robins, GA 31093

jen@jenfrederick.com

Cover Photo Cover Photo © Per Winbladh/Corbis
Cover Design by Meljean Brook

ISBN-13: 978-0989247955

First Edition: September 2013
CreateSpace Independent Publishing Platform

www.jenfrederick.com

To all the girls in this world
who feel that they are alone.
You are not. We stand with you.

To my family, I love you.
Your support makes all of this happen.

ACKNOWLEDGEMENTS

It's hard for me to believe that this is my second book. I think people who know me are just as surprised, and I couldn't have accomplished this achievement without the help of so many people.

There are amazing bloggers who supported *Undeclared* such as Karen from BookCrushReviews who coordinated the first blog tour, Ena from SwoonWorthyBooks who championed my debut, and Lisa and Milasy from The RockStars of Romance who are ceaseless supporters of romance novelists, particularly indie authors. I will always treasure the first reviews I received from bloggers like Sharon at Obsession with Books and Karina at Nocturnal Book Reviews.

I have two really core beta readers—Brie Clementine and Kati Dancy —without you two I don't think I'd get a word written.

To the authors who inspire me and encourage me, I want to thank you for sharing your knowledge, spurring me to write, and commiserating with me when I'm feeling discouraged. Meljean Brook, Jessica Clare, Katy Evans, and Elyssa Patrick, thank you for holding my hand through this journey.

For AW, you are kind of an idiot savant at the editing gig, aren't you? I'm so lucky to have you as a friend and a professional colleague.

Daphne, our weekly talks really mean the world to me and you continually help me get better as a writer.

Finally, thank you to all the readers out there who have taken a chance on this newbie author. You will never know how much I appreciate your Facebook posts, your emails, and your tweets.

UNSPOKEN

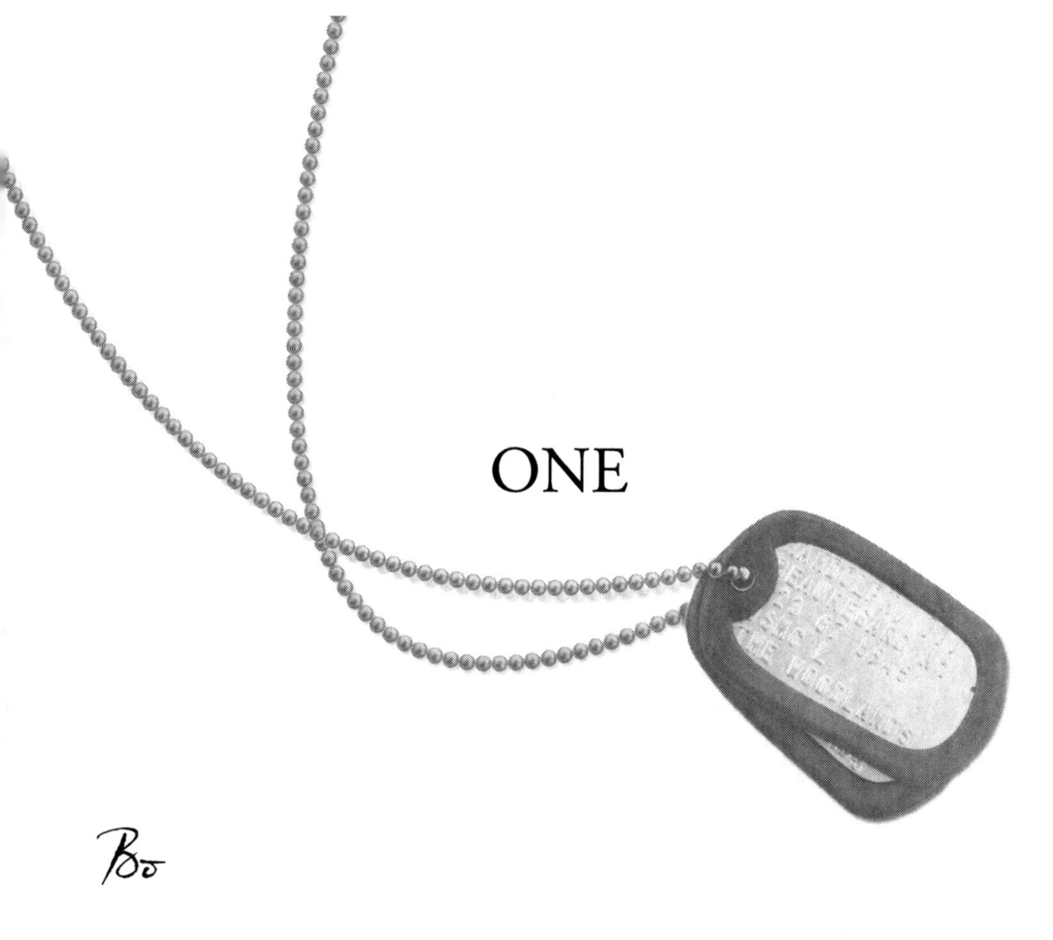

ONE

Bo

"TAMPONS SLOWING YOU DOWN THIS morning?" I taunted the young businessman who'd volunteered to spar with me this morning. We'd been dancing around each other for the last five minutes. I wasn't here to carefully gauge the length of his reach or the power of his jab. I wanted him to hit me, and I wanted to hit him back.

My smear on his manhood worked better than a fist to his gut. He jerked out of whatever fantasy he was concocting of being the next king of the Octagon and rushed me. I waited, slid slightly to the side, and then kneed him in the ribs. As he was bending over from the impact, I brought up a left uppercut and then a right punch. He crumpled like a tin can at a recycling center.

As he lay face down at my feet, it occurred to me I'd made a big strategic error. My third of the morning. I was a slow learner. I looked up to see Noah Jackson shaking his head at me. Noah was my best friend, Marine battle buddy, and roommate. He knew me better than anyone else.

He knew the lightbulb had just gone off over my head. There would be no more hitting in the Spartan Gym today, which meant my hope for a good match was as sunk as the guy at my feet.

With a groan, yuppie number three rolled over. I pulled off a glove and offered him a hand up. He looked at it for a couple of heartbeats like I might punch him again. Christ, I wasn't a jackass. I didn't mind fighting dirty if the situation called for it, but I wasn't going to hit someone who was weaker than I was, who couldn't fight back. You got smacked around here at the Spartan Gym. That was the whole point.

At least that was why I was here. I woke up every morning with an itch under my skin. I could work out that irritation a couple of ways. My preferred method was fighting. But the downed businessman with the soft hands was my third opponent this morning and not one of them had laid a hand on me outside of a few glancing blows that slid off my protective headgear.

I pulled back my hand and walked over to the corner, shaking my head in disgust. Paulie Generoli, the owner of the gym, climbed into the ring and glared at me. I wasn't supposed to damage the merchandise. These rich guys were the way he paid for his gym and when they weren't given enough opportunity to feel like conquerors, they didn't want to come back. I ignored his summons to come over and jumped down off the platform. Noah was on the mats to the side, practicing some Brazilian jiu-jitsu moves.

Noah used to partner with me. Or actually, I sparred with him to ready him for a world of professional fighting. I wasn't allowed to do this anymore, as Noah had been invited to be part of the UFC, the officially sanctioned group of mixed martial arts fighters.

Paulie, who trained Noah, said I was too dangerous and undisciplined to fight Noah. I thought it was better for Noah to face down dangerous and unpredictable in the safety of a gym setting before facing it inside the Octagon, where the UFC fighters battled for fame and money, but I never voiced any opposition.

If it were anyone other than Noah, I wouldn't have kept quiet, but I wasn't going screw up Noah's opportunities here. Even if I wanted to because Noah could put a beatdown on me like none other, and we both felt better after. None of the other amateur fighters could get in enough blows to make a difference and my fight instinct was too strong to just stand there and take it.

I pushed open the door to the locker room, and the stifling smell of ball sweat and ass swept over me. Stripping out of my shorts and jock strap, I leaned into one of the two tiled shower stalls at the back to turn the water on. Paulie was not a generous owner. Complain about the cold water and he'd tell you it was called Spartan Gym for a fucking reason and that if we wanted some goddamned hot water we could go to the meatbars out west. Didn't seem like much of a difference these days, with the infiltration of yuppies thinking they could grow a bigger dick by putting on a pair of boxing gloves.

The cold water washed away what little sweat I'd generated, but the excess energy inside me still pulsed just under the surface. The tension I'd woken up with hadn't been pounded out of me, and I felt as agitated now as I had at the start of my workout. With all the good fighters off limits because I wasn't supposed to hurt anyone while they were training, I was left with few options.

I dried off quickly and pulled on my underwear.

Throwing my towel on the metal bench, I sat down and scrolled through my phone's contacts until I hit the right one.

Fight tonight? The response was immediate but disappointing. Too early in the week for an actual match.

Thursday. Casino. Real fight. Want in?

The reservations held the human version of cockfights because they weren't bound by state laws. This could be awesome or I could go home on a backboard. Either one looked good to me right now.

In.

The locker-room door creaked on its hinges as Noah pushed his way in.

"Already done for the morning?" I asked in surprise.

"Just wanted to put my two cents in," Noah said.

"How so?"

"Figure you're trying to set up some fight this week because this morning's rounds were so disappointing."

I just shrugged in return. I wasn't exaggerating about Noah's familiarity with my behavior. More than a decade of friendship and four years of military service deployed together to Afghanistan made us tighter than an ass in spandex.

"Look, I don't want to be the heavy, but one of these days you're going to come out of these fights a vegetable."

I scratched the back of my neck and took a deep breath to gather some patience. I didn't want to say something that would end up pissing us both off. "Okay, Grandma. You're one to talk."

"It's sort of a 'do as I say, not as I do' type of lecture," he admitted sheepishly.

"You have other suggestions?"

"Not really. Just be careful. I think the crew back in San Diego would spit on your hospital bed if you ended up in a coma after you'd come back hale and hearty from deployment."

He wasn't wrong. No one liked to hear the news about a brother who survived the war only to come home and get fucked up in some random accident. It seemed pointless, a total waste of a good man, but I wouldn't ever put myself in the "good man" category. "Yeah, got it."

I stood and pulled the rest of my clothes from the locker. Jeans, ratty T-shirt, boots, and a heavy winter coat that weighed about ten pounds. I hated the cold. As I threw my clothes on the bench, the clink of metal sounded loud against the concrete floor.

Noah walked over and picked up the heavy coin that had fallen. "What do you think this guy would say about your fighting?"

The heavy coin with the emblem of the Medal of Honor stared up at me, almost as if it looked disappointed. *Do the Corps proud, both in uniform and out.*

I rubbed both hands over my face. "You're a dirty fighter, Noah Jackson." I snatched the coin from his hand and curled my fist around it until the rope-finished edges bit into my skin.

His response was to wrap his hand around my shoulder and squeeze it tight. "*Semper Fi,* brother."

AM

YOU'RE GOING TO REGRET NOT *being in biology with me,* I texted Ellie Martin, my best friend since kindergarten and now college roommate. We were taking the dreaded science elective that every other student took their freshman year, but Ellie and I'd managed to duck the requirement until our second year. Our advisor, Dr. Highsmith, told us to get it over with or he would drop us. I thought it was an empty threat, but we both loved him as our academic advisor—hideous sweaters, tendency to spit, and all. Dr. Highsmith was considered one of the foremost economic thinkers in the country, and his chair was endowed by some bigwig alum who credited his post-college success to theories that Dr. Highsmith taught. I planned to be the CEO of my own insurance company someday and endow my own chair. The AM West Chair of Economics. That had a nice ring to it.

You'll be the one with regrets when you have nightmares about flying monkeys.

Ellie had been afraid of tornadoes since she watched *The Wizard of Oz* when we were seven. She'd heard from someone that they watched storm chaser footage during biology class and she changed her science elective that same day. No amount of arguing with her about how biology had nothing to do with the weather could convince her otherwise, which was why I was walking into class by myself. I sent her a picture of the flying monkeys that I'd saved to my phone this morning for just such an occasion, grinning at her immediate curse in response. Getting the finger through text just has no power.

"You're gonna run into that stage."

My texting conversation with Ellie came to a halt at the softly drawled warning. About five inches from my shin was the front of the lecture stage in my Biology 101 class. The warning had saved me from sure embarrassment, but my cheeks heated anyway as I turned to see the person behind the voice. I'd an idea who it was, but I was two parts dismayed and two parts enthralled by the sight of *him.* Bo Randolph.

I knew of Beauregard Randolph. Everyone at Central did. Central College was one of the best liberal arts colleges in the nation, nestled in an urban area in the Midwest, but it was smaller than some city high schools. Gossip whispered at the start of morning classes at one end of campus was heard at the other by noon in the cafeteria. Or some version of the gossip, anyway.

I'd never envisioned attending any other college than Central, but one drunken party later and I wished for the anonymity of those public universities and their enormous student populations. So while I'd heard many rumors about Bo, I didn't know how many of them were true. The rumors about me—that I was a slutty girl who'd banged the entire lacrosse team—had only a grain of truth. I'd given up my virginity after one fraternity party to some lacrosse player, who then bragged about it to his teammates.

Somehow that one encounter became the entire team. Once a field bunny, always a field bunny. The lacrosse squad made it their goal to see that everyone believed I was fair game, prey to be chased down and taken at any opportunity. Sober, not sober. Willing, not willing. I wished there had been an informational sheet in my freshman welcome packet warning that hooking up with a lacrosse player resulted in social ruination.

The rumors about Bo ran the gamut from him being a professional fighter to having killed some guy on the east side of campus for looking at him wrong. Oh, and don't forget the women. Bo's name was linked to every sort of girl here at Central. It didn't matter if a girl was sporty, artsy, quiet, or popular, Bo seemed have hooked up with them all. Naturally, this only served to heighten Bo's reputation with both sexes. If you were a guy, your conquests made you a god. If you were a girl, you were the conquered, no better than a toy.

I'd sat directly behind him in Advanced Economy Theory last semester and spent months battling twin emotions of lust and resentment. Resentment because of the unfairness of how differently our actions painted us in the eyes of our classmates, and lust because Bo made it exciting to go to class. It wasn't because price discrimination was a fascinating topic or that economics was my actual major. No, the highlight of those days was staring at the interplay of muscles and skin and tendons when Bo wrote, stretched, or reached behind him to pull his backpack over his shoulder. He looked like the live model for a Rodin sculpture. Even the tinkling of what I assumed to be his dog tags striking each other when he moved generated a Pavlovian response of craving in me. About the only flaw I could see in Bo was his messy dirty blond hair, but even that just invited me to sink my fingers in it and smooth it down.

Ellie told me the only way to exorcise those conflicted feelings was to engage in a long bout of angry sex with Bo. But all I did was fantasize. Like most things I enjoyed about Central, my pleasure in Bo Randolph was taken surreptitiously and privately. Only Ellie knew.

"Miss, in the yellow sweater, if you'll sit down, I can start my lecture," the professor barked out.

I turned to look to the side to see if anyone else was standing, but Bo just shook his head sadly and leaned forward to whisper, "He's talking about you."

If my cheeks were hot before, it was nothing like the five-alarm fire blazing this time. Bo stood and waved me into the empty space beside him and I had no choice but to sit down. I rushed and tossed my messenger bag on the empty table space. If I had taken one second more, I could have moved down five seats or even farther before I bumped into another student, but in my panic I didn't notice.

None of these things were like me. I tried to draw as little attention to myself as possible on campus. I sat in the back of the classroom. I did *not* make a spectacle of myself in front of an entire classroom of one hundred students. I could only be grateful that these were freshmen and hope that whatever rumors swam through the college artery system about me couldn't be immediately attached to my rarely-seen face.

I pretended I wasn't sitting next to Bo, that I hadn't been called out by the professor, and that a hundred pairs of eyes weren't pinned on my back. Instead, I pulled out my laptop and opened my IM screen to ping Ellie. Humiliation had to be shared in order to be endured.

AM_1906: *Bo Randolph is in my bio class.*

Eggs_Martini: *What? Why is he not in Rocks for Jocks?*

AM_1906: *Dunno.*

Rocks for Jocks was Geology 101 and was so nicknamed because all the athletes took it to pad their GPAs. It was commonly known that Bio 101 was harder, but at least you avoided spitballs hurled across the room and suffocation from the smell of gym socks and sweaty jerseys.

Before I could reply to Ellie, the professor began telling us how a typhoon would swallow us up eventually or that the sea level would rise gradually, so that all the land would be eroded. Nice. I could see Bio 101 was going to be swell.

Out of the corner of my eye, I heard the rustling of paper and then the scratch of a cheap pen. Bo was a lefty, and he took notes the old-school way. By hand. With a pen and paper. Insane.

AM_1906: *Good call on changing science class. Apparently we're all going to die soon. From a natural disaster.*

Eggs_Martini: *Escape now.*

AM_1906: *Like rocks for jocks will be better? You can die from a mudslide or avalanche or other geological disasters. Global warming, anyone?*

Eggs_Martini: *Rocks do not cause or are not related to global warming.*

AM_1906: *I'm pretty sure the class is more than about rocks.*

Eggs_Martini: *Clearly not or it wouldn't be rocks for jocks.*

I was so intent on my IM conversation with Ellie, I hadn't noticed that Bo had angled himself to view my screen until I felt the brush of his arm against mine.

"Nosy much?" I hissed, turning the laptop away, my anger and surprise overcoming my initial nervousness.

"Sorry, couldn't resist," drawled Bo. The rumor about Bo being a southerner? True. His drawl was as recognizable as the shocking blue eyes he sported. They were so blue I wondered if they were fake. I stared at them for a moment too long, looking for the outline of a contact lens, but saw nothing but pure ocean blue, like the waves you see in the spring break pamphlets of the Caribbean Sea lapping against the white sand beaches. Who needed Cancún when you could stare at Bo Randolph's eyes for a week?

I wrenched my gaze away. Bo was the poster child for every disaster that female singers warbled about. He'd break your heart and do it smiling. Worse, he'd make you think you were better off for having your heart broken because it was done in by *him*.

"Why are you even here? Aren't you a senior?" I said, anger at myself making me sound peevish. At least I kept my voice low enough to avoid getting us in trouble. The professor was on the other end of the stage, making sure everyone in the room was sufficiently depressed with their dim prospects for survival.

"No, I'm a junior college transfer and I'll be a junior forever unless I get my science prerequisite out of the way," Bo said, unperturbed. His reportedly quick trigger was apparently not set off by snippy girls. "Why are *you* here? You seem like a responsible person who would've taken her science elective in her first year."

His gaze swept me like a scanning machine and I felt so thoroughly examined I wondered if he was planning to make a 3D model of me later.

Probably wishful thinking, but it didn't stop a thrill from shooting up my spine at the thought of Bo pulling up a mental picture of me during a private moment.

"How do you know I'm not a first year?" I whispered.

He looked at me disbelievingly. "Because you were a sophomore when you sat behind me last semester in advanced economic theory, *AnnMarie West.*" He emphasized my name. It was my turn to be disbelieving. I could not believe that he knew both my name and that I sat behind him in class last semester.

I didn't have a chance to respond because the professor had strolled back to our side of the auditorium and was instructing us on how to sign up for a lab partner.

"The TA will hand out sign-up sheets. If you know someone and have arranged to be their lab partner, please indicate that on the sheets. If you don't have one, one will be assigned for you at the end of the day, randomly. Thirty-five percent of your grade will depend on your lab work. Choose your partner wisely."

My heart sank into my feet. With Ellie in geology, I would be assigned to some random freshman. It could be some guy who would think he could make obscene passes at me because I was *that* girl, or a girl who thought I'd try to steal her man. This was part of the reason I'd put off my science requirement.

The teacher's assistant handed Bo, who was sitting at the end of our table, a sheet and he scribbled his name and another. I wondered who he was partnering with and why he wasn't sitting next to that person. I didn't know what to write down, given that I avoided all the other students and knew only a few names, none of whom were sitting in this room. But Bo didn't hand me the sheet when he was done. Instead, he leaned past me and laid it on the far side of the empty table, where another student grabbed it and started writing.

"Hey," I said, trying to reach for the paper, but Bo covered my hand and jerked his chin at the first-year to go ahead.

I rounded on Bo. "I didn't get to write my name down."

"You don't have to," Bo said, still holding my hand in his. His large hand made me feel tiny and fragile and, briefly, I allowed myself to enjoy the feeling of being protected, like Bo was the shell of my frail turtle body.

I shook it off and reminded myself I had my own protective casing called self-reliance. I tugged gently, but he refused to let me go. "We're going to be lab partners."

"We? As in you and I?"

"That would be the correct composition of individuals making up the 'we' in my sentence."

"But…" I wasn't sure whether I was secretly indignant or relieved.

"You don't want to be stuck with a first-year. You're smart, given that you were in advanced theory last semester. You'll be a good lab partner."

"But are you a good lab partner for me? You're taking a first-year elective in your third year. You were in advanced economic theory with me, a sophomore."

Bo laughed but then grew serious. "Fair enough. Yes. I have good grades, and I never let a teammate down."

A tremor shot through me at Bo's words. I didn't have many people on my team, and this guy, this much-wanted guy, was suggesting he was going to stand beside me? *It's for the class*, I cautioned myself. But the part that crushed on Bo all last semester? That small, secret part was whispering things I knew I should not allow myself to believe. Like that Bo wanted to be on *my* team.

I looked down at my hand, still engulfed in Bo's, and knew that *want* was winning the battle against *fear*.

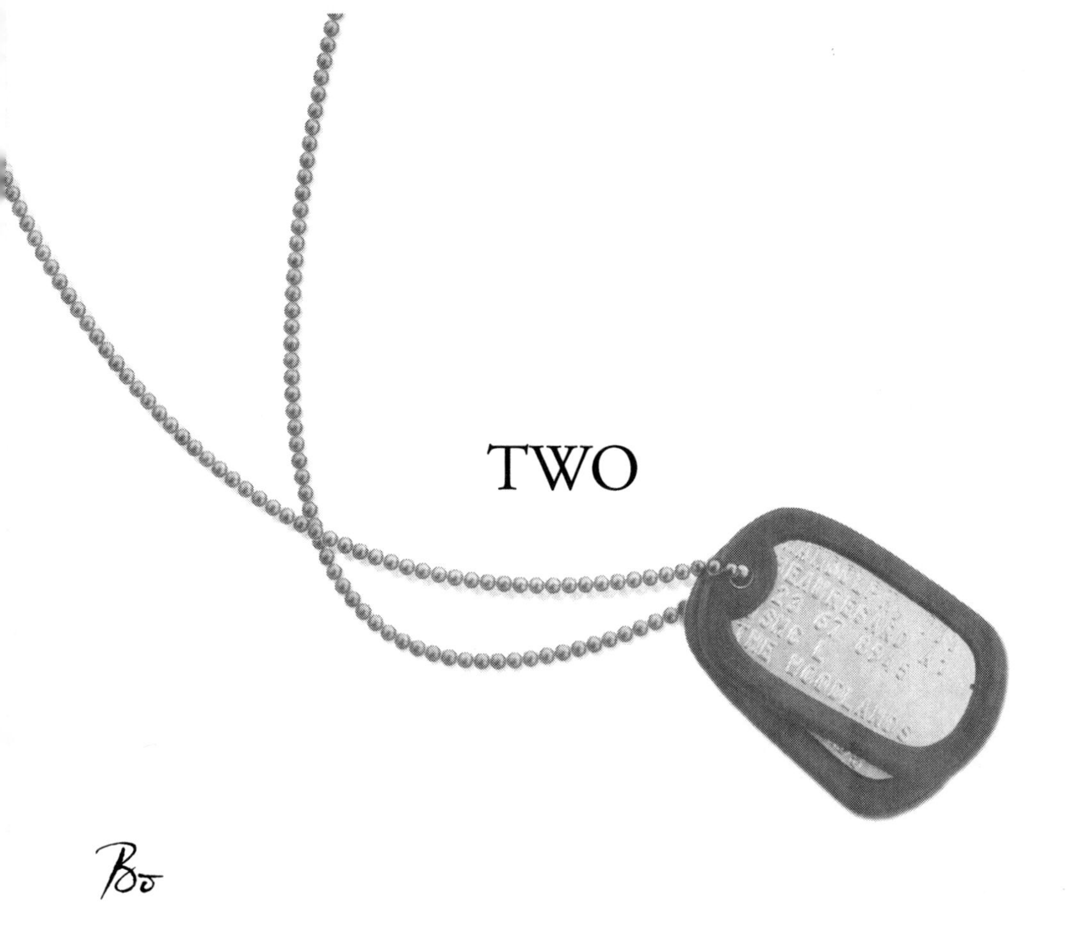

TWO

Bo

AnnMarie West. I'd sat in front of her for an entire semester and chick didn't say two words to me. She didn't say two words to anyone, though, if I recalled correctly, other than to her friend who sat next to her. Her friend called her AM, like the radio or the time. My first glance at AM last fall made me think that she'd look good in the morning with her hair spread out on my pillow and her long legs wrapped around my waist. AM's hair looked like the color of a melted Hershey's kiss, and, sitting close to her, I realized it smelled just about as good. Not chocolatey, though, but like a hard candy. Maybe lemon. It made me want to lick her neck to see how she'd taste.

I had winked at her once, to test out the temperature, but received a frightened glare in return. Or maybe it was a frozen look. Either way, it wasn't an encouraging response. I wasn't going to pursue someone who was afraid of me.

Over the course of the semester, though, her frightened look faded and sometimes I thought I caught a glimpse of interest. But if I'd smiled at her, she'd recoil. Frustrated, I gave up and went for the easier hookups.

But now she was in biology with me. What were the chances? It was like fate had dropped her in my lap and instinct told me I shouldn't allow this chance to go by unwasted.

The female population had always been attentive to me, from old ladies to little babies and every age in between. The Randolph men were born with something that drew women in. Maybe "lured" was the better word, because we Randolphs rarely ended up being good for women. I tried to reduce the wreckage by limiting myself to women who were interested in short-term encounters. It meant that my liaisons were shallow, but no one got hurt. I should just leave AnnMarie alone. And I would've if she'd looked scared again, but fear wasn't evident in any of her responses. Instead, she looked at me like I was a tasty treat and talked back like we were equals. *I'm delicious, AnnMarie, take a bite.*

Still juiced after a lackluster workout, I found myself pushing at her limits. It was the college version of dipping her pigtails into the inkwell or pushing her off the swing in hopes she'd chase me back.

AM spent this class, like the economics class of last semester, looking intently at the teacher, disregarding the TA's attempts to catch her attention, and typing studiously into her laptop. I doodled on my paper and watched her the entire time. Her fingers flew over the keyboard, switching quickly between her IM chat screen and a note-taking application. There was a tiny muscle in her biceps that flexed when she clenched her fingers to release the tension built up through typing and from holding her body rigidly away from mine. I'd have offered to rub her tension away, but based on our earlier interaction, I guessed the offer wouldn't be welcome.

I could hear the professor droning in the background but preferred reading AnnMarie's recitation of the lecture.

Global disasters. Too far from anything interesting to die. Cells, molecules, plants. Disgusting lab things with THAT guy.

I know you're watching me type but I'm not sharing my notes with you.

I snorted out loud. She had my number. And then I realized that the ball in the pit of my stomach that I hadn't managed to work out this morning had dissolved. While watching AnnMarie, from sparring with her, even a little, I'd somehow, miraculously, calmed down. I closed my eyes and envisioned my failed fights this morning. Nope, still felt good.

At the end of class, AnnMarie pulled her phone out of her bag and set it on the table while she packed up her laptop and pen. Her phone lay forlornly on the side of the table, as if were waiting for me, so I seized the opportunity that had presented itself. Pressing the home button and accessing the dial pad, I entered my phone number and pressed send.

"What are you doing?" she asked, grabbing the phone out of my hands.

"You know, you should really use a passcode on your phone," I chastised. "Anyone could use it."

She looked at the screen. "What did you do?" Her voice rose, nearing the screechy, dog whistle octave.

"As your lab partner, I think we should exchange phone numbers." I looked as placid and nonthreatening as possible, angling my body toward her but pulling my hands out of her space. She might bite my fingers off if they were too close to her mouth. I didn't mind taking chances, but I wasn't stupid. I also knew I needed to spend more time with her. If a man in a desert finds a pool of water, he doesn't leave until he's lapped that fucker dry.

"You could have asked me first," she bit out.

"I could have, but you'd have said no." My reasoned responses were only making her angrier, but she was trying to fight it back. She had a lot of control. I admired that. I possessed little myself. It was one of the many shitty things I inherited from my dad. Maybe biology would teach me how to excise the bad genes from the good ones. I think that's what they teach in the molecular biology section.

"We can communicate via e-mail," AnnMarie replied evenly. Her color was high, but she'd subdued the high notes in her voice.

In just fifty minutes, I'd learned several important things about AM. She had cute, tiny, girl muscles; she took great notes; she smelled good; and she had a great deal of self-control. And in no way was she afraid of me.

"Come on. No one uses e-mail but professors." I nodded toward the front stage, which now held only an abandoned lectern and a desk. The good thing about us having this extended post-class discussion was that the aisles weren't crowded and the TA had gotten fed up waiting for AnnMarie to break from the herd so he could inappropriately offer her private tutoring sessions.

"You look like you're going to blow up. It's a good thing class is over," I added. Something perverse inside me wanted to needle her some more just to see how good her self-control really was.

Her eyebrows shot up, but instead of the expected high-pitched yelp, her voice got lower. "Oh my God," she said in clipped, low tones. "It's a good thing there are still people in here because, I swear, if we were alone, I would stab you through the eye with a pen."

"You know, a lot of people say that they'd do those things, but I've found few can actually follow through." I tried for contemplative but could feel my facial muscles moving into a grin, and probably an unrepentant one at that, because the more she talked, the more interested I became. She was actually turning me on. I might have to sit in the chair for a few minutes before I could walk out.

"Don't test me," she replied coolly, now completely in control, as if a moment ago she hadn't threatened me with bodily harm. "You're deliberately goading me, and I don't understand why."

I didn't think "because it turns me on" was a good response. She was right, though; I *was* deliberately goading her and I felt a tiny twinge of guilt at using her to make myself feel better. But it was so small that I squashed it without remorse.

"Boundaries. Girls are always putting up boundaries." I sighed dramatically.

"I can't believe you're my lab partner. Would you just stand up and let me out." She threw her backpack over her shoulder and gestured for me to move, but I couldn't. I had a little wood in my pants and I needed her to be about fifteen degrees less cute in order for me to be able to obey her commands.

"I'm feeling kind of hungry. Are you hungry?" I stalled for time.

"You have got to be kidding. Do you dye your hair? Has too much peroxide use damaged your brain function?" She shook her head. I was blond, and unlike many a fair-haired lass I'd spent time with, mine was all natural.

"So that's a no? I couldn't tell because I didn't hear a no in those words."

"Yeah, that's a no," she hissed at me. Then she leapt onto the table like a puma, jumped down, and hustled out of the classroom. My eyes followed her jean-clad ass all the way up the stairs and out of the classroom.

Pulling out my phone, I looked down at her number and tapped a button to add her as a contact. I thought I'd found a good way to spend my time before Thursday. Helping AnnMarie learn how to say "yes."

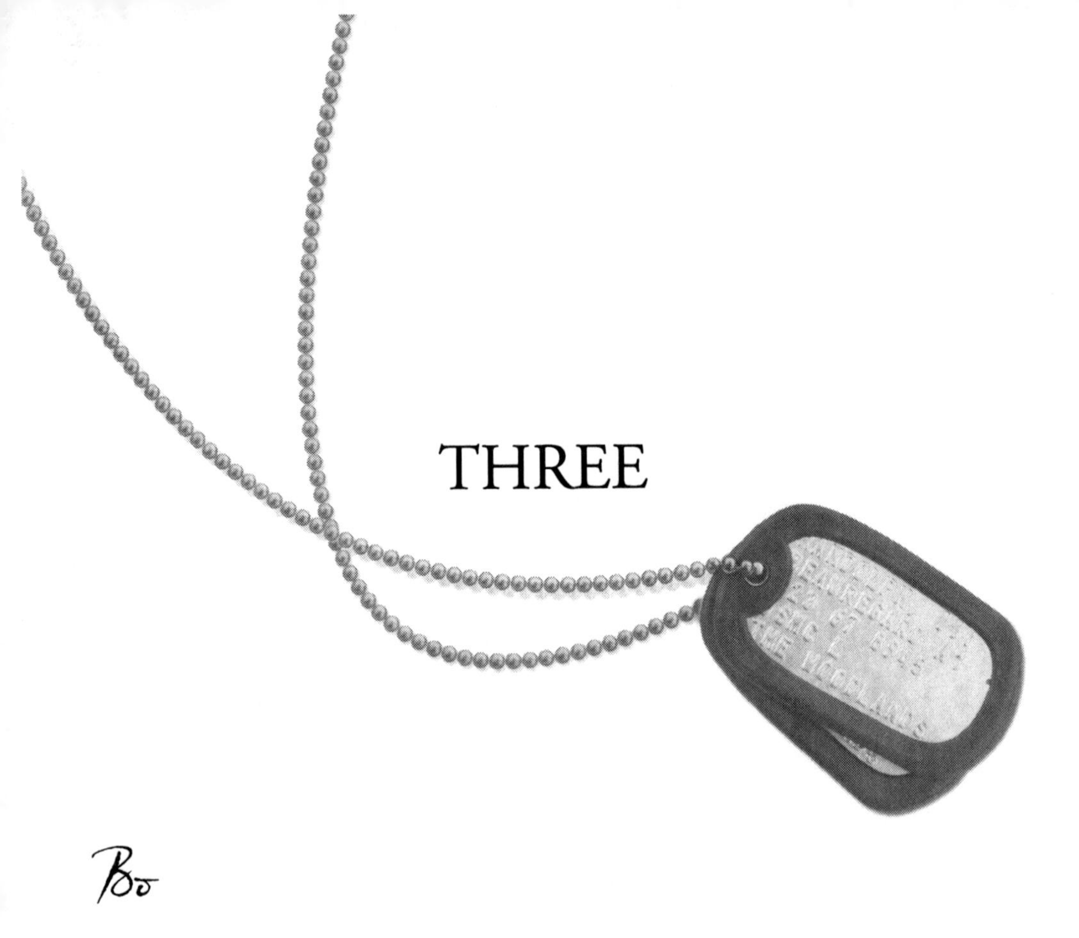

THREE

Bo

BY THE TIME I'D EXITED the classroom, AM was gone. I didn't know much about her, but I knew one person who would.

Noah's girlfriend worked at the library, and the library was the source of all gossip and rumor at Central, primarily because the student supervisor, Mike Hanover, served as a kind of oral historian of Central College… if by historian you meant someone who traded in gossip and rumor.

A certain amount of bullshit weighted Mike's commentary, but he seemed to know a shitload about everyone and wasn't shy about sharing it. I headed to the floor where Mike held court.

My prey sat behind the circulation desk pretending to read a textbook. Mike owed me one since I'd orchestrated a little love connection between him and the object of his unrequited lust. Basically he'd just needed to nut up and ask the chick out. But he was too weak-kneed, and I'd had to act as the third-grade go-between. Now he owed me a favor. Noah thought the world ran on money, but Mal, another roommate, said it runs on favors. I didn't need money, so I gathered favors. Mike owed me about ten for hooking him up with the love o' his life.

"Michael Hanover, my man, what is up today?" I knocked fists with him. Some guys like a more complicated greeting, like two back slaps and a finger grip, but Mike was a one knock to the knuckles sort of guy. I'd tried a more detailed greet one time and the poor guy looked so confused I'd just pretended we were giving each other high fives.

"Hey, Bo. No fights lately?"

"Got one this Thursday at the Casino."

Looking like a kid whose toy was snatched from him, Mike moaned, "Nothing closer?" The Casino was a forty-five-minute drive from here. It didn't seem all that far away to me, but Central kids liked to stick close to campus. Maybe they thought they'd turn into pumpkins or something.

"Nah, I'm trying to be a good boy. Apparently Central admin doesn't like it to be known that its students are engaging in brutality against others, even if it is mutually agreed-upon brutality."

Mike nodded his agreement, although I wasn't sure if he was agreeing with Central admin's uptight staff or agreeing we should be able to beat the shit out of each other without interference.

"So, Mike, I have Bio 101 this semester." I got straight to the point.

"Dude, why?"

"I wouldn't reveal this to everyone, Mike, but I have a weak stomach," I lied.

Mike's eyes grew huge, as if I'd shared some deep dark secret even though the untruth was obvious. If I had a weak stomach I'd have chosen geology as my science elective over biology. Mike traded in confidences like Mal and I gathered favors. Everyone had their own currency. For Mike, you had to share one to gain one and the easiest way to trade with Mike was to just make shit up so long as you didn't care that the rest of the campus knew about it by the end of the day.

"Are you asking me how to get out of Bio labs?" Mike asked, nearly breathless with this new gossip he'd broadcast to the next dozen people he came into contact with.

"No, I don't mind the labs. I want to know more about my lab partner."

Mike looked relieved. "That's a good thing, man, because I couldn't get you out of the lab. Who's your lab partner?"

"AnnMarie West."

At the sound of her name Mike's eyebrows shot into his forehead. "Typhoid Mary?"

"Typhoid Mary?" I repeated dumbly.

"Yeah." His eyes were bright with excitement and he leaned over the counter, motioning me closer. I tilted my head forward but didn't move. I only got that close to another person if it was a woman and she was going to stick her tongue in my mouth. "You're new, so you weren't here last year when she slept with the entire lacrosse team. She gets around a lot. A lot." Mike repeated the last part as if I hadn't understood his insinuation the first time.

I bit down on my tongue hard, hoping the pain would prevent me from punching Mike in his smug little mouth. Few girls ever banged an entire team. They usually slept with one or maybe three and that was enough for people to label her a groupie. Noah and I'd seen it happen in high school to a girl I'd slept with. We spent one night together, and the next day talk was she'd slept with the entire football team. Noah and I had tried to put out the fire the best we could, but the whispers persisted when we weren't around. Pack attention didn't shift until the girl transferred schools.

I waited to hear the rest of the rumor, measure the extent of the damage for myself. At my encouragement Mike spilled the rest.

"I heard she's a recruiting perk. Like when they bring new recruits on campus, they get a visit from AnnMarie." He wiggled his eyebrows so I understood "visit" was a euphemism for some type of sexual service. I guess Mike thought everyone was stuck in third grade, like him. "They call her Typhoid Mary because she slept around so much you could get a disease just standing next to her."

"I don't think STIs work that way."

"Right," Mike said, not understanding. "Um, but that's her nickname."

"Seems like it would be a bad recruiting perk to have a new student come in contact with someone who's so disease-infected." I pointed out the obvious contradiction in his rumor but, like the handshake, it only confused him. Mike looked at me as if I'd asked him to find the square root of some four-digit number.

Some guys felt their reputation was enhanced by bragging about the number of women they slept with. You could always divide that number by about ten to get to the accurate one. It also never made much sense to me to brag about sleeping with a girl deemed easy. Where was the challenge if the girl would sleep with anyone? The sex conquest currency was irrational.

"So Typhoid Mary is your lab partner? Dude, you're going to see so much action this semester." Mike smiled at me as if we were sharing some kind of great joke.

"I'm not even on the lacrosse team," I said.

"I don't think you have to be on the lacrosse team," Mike reassured me.

"This girl not play your game?" Mike's gossip wasn't usually so barbed.

"I tried her out, but she's too stuck up for me. I'm not an athlete, I guess," he admitted. "But you shouldn't have a problem getting into her pants."

"Why'd you want to hook up with a girl who's got the Health Clinic on speed dial?"

Mike cocked his head. "Wow, I really dodged a bullet there."

Irrational. Bug fucking nuts. Nothing I was saying was getting through, so I gave up. "You see her around the library much?"

"Not really. She hangs out with another chick, tiny girl, braids, and some theater people. They don't come into the library much. I probably should have reserved my game for after class or at the commons."

I tilted my head back and exhaled heavily. *No, dickhead, she would have turned you down no matter what.* That girl could smell rotten from a mile away after being exposed to so much of it, which was probably why she never talked to me in class last semester. But there was no educating Mike. She'd turned him down, so her bad reputation was fair game. He'd probably console himself with the thought that he was lucky to have gotten turned down by a skank. "Thanks for the info, man," I said.

"No problem, Bo," Mike said cheerfully, totally unaware I wanted to drag him over the counter and beat him bloody.

"Grace and Noah around?" I needed to move on from Mike and this topic.

"Ah, yeah, in the stacks." Mike pointed to the center of the library, which held old and uncirculated books. It was a dank, dusty, low-lit place with rows of metal shelves. Perfect for on-campus making out.

I'd used it a few times since Noah showed me where he and Grace "studied." I always made a big show of banging on the shelves when I entered. I was pretty sure Grace and Noah did very little studying in there.

Every time I'd seen them in their nook they were disheveled, and Grace's lips looked like they'd been chewed on by a big, bad dog.

It was fun breaking up their nookie time.

AM

A PAPER WAS WAVING FROM my car window when I got to my apartment building, which was situated a block off the eastern end of campus. The scrap looked like a pinned butterfly with two edges fluttering in the wind on either side of the windshield wiper. It could have been a flyer, an invitation to see a band downtown, or a coupon. It could have been anything innocuous or innocent, but I knew it wasn't.

Dread was a cold feeling. It swept over a body like a blanket of ice and immobilized you. I forced my hand up to the windshield and pulled it off. I already knew what it would say, or at least some variation.

Saw your "dad" over break. Does he know what a slut you are?

I crumpled the note in my gloved fist, thinking that if Clay Howard III was standing in front of me right now I'd have no problem driving a pen directly into his eye—no matter what Bo Randolph said I was or wasn't capable of. I wanted to throw the page away but didn't. Instead, I carried it upstairs to put it with the other notes from Clay. I wasn't sure why I kept them, other than to remind myself that staying off Clay Howard III's radar and off Central's campus was the best thing I could do for the next two years.

And that I didn't date Central College guys. Ever. Not even ones that looked like Bo Randolph.

That was one of my immutable life rules, along with no wearing of white pants during *that* time of the month and no reading Stephen King before going to sleep.

"I have terrible news," Ellie announced as she walked into the apartment. I was making us sandwiches and soup, the meal of poor college students and old ladies, the note tucked safely away in my drawer.

"Mayo?" I held up the jar and Ellie nodded. She pulled out a bar stool and propped her elbows on the counter to watch my culinary efforts. I gestured with my mayo-laden knife for her to continue. "What's the drama?" I piled meat, lettuce, and tomato between the bread slices.

"There's a very cute freshman who could be my lab partner." She groaned and put her head on top of the counter.

Ellie was a math major and smarter than 99 percent of the students at Central, including me, but she looked like a cheerleader, her dark, coarse hair pulled up into two low ponytails. She also had the habit of sleeping with her study partners. Her last boyfriend, Tim, was our economics tutor. We had set up the tutoring session, not because we were failing, but because we wanted to get As. Unfortunately, after their sex life petered out around midterms, Ellie lost interest, and I ended up attending the remaining awkward sessions trying to duck Tim's inquiries about the missing part of our once merry triad.

"So don't sleep with him." I plated our sandwiches and poured the microwaved cans of soup into bowls Ellie and I'd picked up at a garage sale. Our apartment was filled with secondhand goods. Ellie was a scholarship student and while my tuition, books, and this apartment were paid for by my father, neither of our families could afford to furnish the apartment in anything but castoffs and hand-me-downs.

"You say that like you haven't known me since I played with Barbies." Ellie's voice was muffled since she was currently speaking into the counter, but I could still make out her lame protest.

I shoved the bowl and plate into her head. "Will I like him?"

Ellie had pretty good taste in guys. Most of the ones she'd dated since freshman year had been nice, but she'd never stuck with one longer than a semester. I doubted this latest one would last past finals. Ellie's attention span was too short.

"Yes, he's adorable. I wanted to shove him into my pocket and bring him home," Ellie lamented.

"Good thing you didn't. Our lease only allows for two occupants."

Before Ellie could respond, our apartment door opened and our neighbor waltzed in, looking amazing, as always. Sasha had lightly bronzed skin and high cheekbones, a gift from her Native American grandmother, and they gave her face an elegant and almost regal look. I'm pretty sure the straight male guys on campus held a wake the day it got around that Sasha liked girls.

Sasha and I had bonded immediately over a late-night talk shortly after Ellie and I'd moved in. She'd asked me why she never saw me around campus, and after some prodding, I shared my story with her.

"It's either the Garden or house parties. Seems like most guys here still think that saying you're a lesbian is just a flirtatious challenge," she'd agreed.

There was no judgment or pity from Sasha, only understanding.

"I'll take what you're having," Sasha announced. I handed her the second bowl of soup and dug in the cabinet for another can. "How's your mom?"

"Okay. Roger and I pretended we didn't hate each other for the three days we spent together, but other than that it was good." I made a face. Roger was my mother's lover and, unfortunately, my father, but I've never called him Dad and he hasn't ever invited it. Clay's father was a friend of Roger's and knew all about my family's dirty business. "I can't wait until I'm out of here and my mom can live with me and not depend on Roger."

"Is she thinking about leaving him finally?" Ellie asked.

I thought back to the note Clay had left for me. "No, but she really doesn't have any options, given that she doesn't work and Roger completely supports her. When I'm done with college, she'll be able to live with me." Not wanting to discuss it further, I turned to Sasha. "How was your break?"

"Good. Had to take a vacation from Victoria. She is *so* needy. You two are lucky not to be lesbians." Sasha pointed at us one at a time with her spoon to punctuate her point.

"Eh, men are just as hormonal." Ellie sniffed. She'd had her own share of relationship drama. Tim hadn't taken their breakup well, and Ellie had had to turn off her phone for two weeks after she'd stopped attending tutoring sessions with me.

"She texted me about ten times on New Year's Eve, wanting to know if I was going to kiss someone," Sasha complained.

"Did you?"

"Yes, but that's not the point."

I quirked a brow at her. Sasha just shrugged. "It was New Year's Eve, and it was just a little tongue and lip action. Nothing below the belt."

"Why are you with her if she's too hormonal for you?" Ellie asked.

"Have you seen Victoria?"

We all fell silent. Victoria looked like she was a fembot from an Austin Powers movie, complete with the glorious afro, killer rack, retro seventies dresses, and high kneesocks. Sasha and Victoria were a striking couple, a sight that probably caused a few car accidents along College Avenue.

"God, I wish I could pull off her look," Ellie moaned.

Sasha looked her over. "You've got cute nailed, but you're too short for the afro."

"I know." Ellie pulled the sides of her mouth down into a mock frown.

"She tried it one night and it made her look like a chia pet. It was bad," I revealed and then had to duck when Ellie threw a napkin at me.

"I'm proud of my lustrous hair." Ellie patted her head. "But yeah, it took an entire bottle of vitamin E to take my hair back to normal. Braids are simpler."

Sasha patted Ellie's now-straightened locks. "I think this is a better look for you. But Victoria is really good with her—"

The door banged open, and Sasha's roommate rushed in. "Wait, you can't tell lesbian sex stories without me," Brian panted. I sighed and dug out another bowl.

"You guys are going to owe us lunch tomorrow." I shook a spoon at Brian. Brian's family was pretty well off, so he could afford to take us all to lunch sometimes.

"Fine." He shrugged and pulled out the last stool at our counter. He looked reprovingly at Sasha. "I thought we made a deal. I pay the rent and you pay me in stories."

Brian, like Sasha, was a theater arts major. He declared he was straight, but we all had our doubts. I pegged him as bi-curious. He liked hearing stories about the boys far too much for a straight guy.

"Victoria. Tongue. Needy." Sasha summarized for him.

"I'm going to need more details," Brian said, picking up my sandwich and eating half of it in one gulp. He had a guy's appetite, that's for sure.

"What'd you do over break, Brian?" I got the soup out of the microwave, poured it into the two bowls, and started to eat.

"Skied. Tried to reclaim as much stuff from the little shit as I could." Brian's little brother was apparently enjoying Brian's absence at college by taking everything of Brian's—from his baseball card collection to his high-school girlfriend. Brian only cared about the card collection.

I'd thought I wanted siblings until I heard horror stories from Brian and Sasha. It seems younger siblings were the very devil. My two older half-siblings didn't mix with my mother and me, so I never got to be the annoying younger sister. And after me, my mother never made another of *those* mistakes again.

"Catch me up. I had to stay late after class because I was busy sucking up to the TA," Brian confessed.

"Ellie has a cute freshman lab partner, Sasha's tired of Victoria, and I sat next to Bo Randolph in biology." I conveniently left out mention of the note.

Three sighs of delight reverberated through the room at the mention of Bo's name.

"Bo looks like he's sculpted from stone by some master and skin was stretched over the form. Unreal," Sasha declared. "I'd love to see him in a life drawing class."

"The guns on that guy," Brian concurred.

"Where are all of you seeing him?" I asked, surprised at their distinct recall of Bo's body.

"I see him in the gym, lifting," Brian said.

"Yoga," Sasha offered.

"He does yoga?" My eyebrows shot up in surprise.

"No, while I'm doing yoga, I see him working out. He's like all muscle. Last semester's yoga class at 5 P.M. was packed once word got out that he and his buddy Noah lifted weights there before dinner. It's like a burlesque show. They start out with their shirts on and then slowly unveil the package as they get sweatier and sweatier," Sasha explained. "Then, when they're super hot and super sweaty, they'll run their discarded shirts over their chests. Bo's got this huge tattoo of a bird on his back and Noah's got some tree up the side. It's indecent and delicious and ovary-clenching good," she concluded. "See the things you're missing out on with your Central campus exile?"

"I think my ovaries aren't prepared for those kinds of scenes," I replied dryly, but inwardly those private parts tightened at the visual of a nearly naked and sweaty Bo. Sasha regularly tried to entice me back onto campus, whereas Ellie was content to join me in my self-imposed exile. Unfortunately, being with me meant no lunch in the commons or the QC Café. No studying in the library. No hanging out at the campus Starbucks. And no group yoga classes where you tried to do downward-facing dog while still sneaking peaks at the jocks working out in the weight room next door.

Sasha just shook her head. "What's your project for biology?" she asked.

"Don't know," I admitted. "It hasn't been shared yet."

"He must be rotating," Brian said. "My bio project was determining which natural disaster would be most likely to result in the apocalypse here in the Midwest."

"See!" Ellie shouted. We all jumped at the sharp bark of her voice. "I *told* you this was all about death and weather. He probably has flying monkey costumes in his office, the sadist."

"Brian, were there any monkeys in your class course?" I asked.

He rubbed his chin, feigning thoughtfulness. "There was this one time when he mentioned that tornadoes were the result of monkey farts."

Ellie, Sasha, and I groaned, and Ellie responded by pushing Brian off the stool. I threw a paper towel at him.

"How can you live with him?" I asked Sasha semi-seriously.

"We don't share a bathroom," Sasha said.

"And I pay the rent." Brian looked piously into the distance.

"There is that." Sasha sighed.

"Let's talk about the most important topic of the semester," I said. My audience perked up. "Where are we gonna spend spring break?"

We argued raucously about the merits of going north to ski or south to the beach for the rest of the afternoon. And I tried hard to push all thoughts of Bo, Clay, and Roger to the very back recesses of my mind.

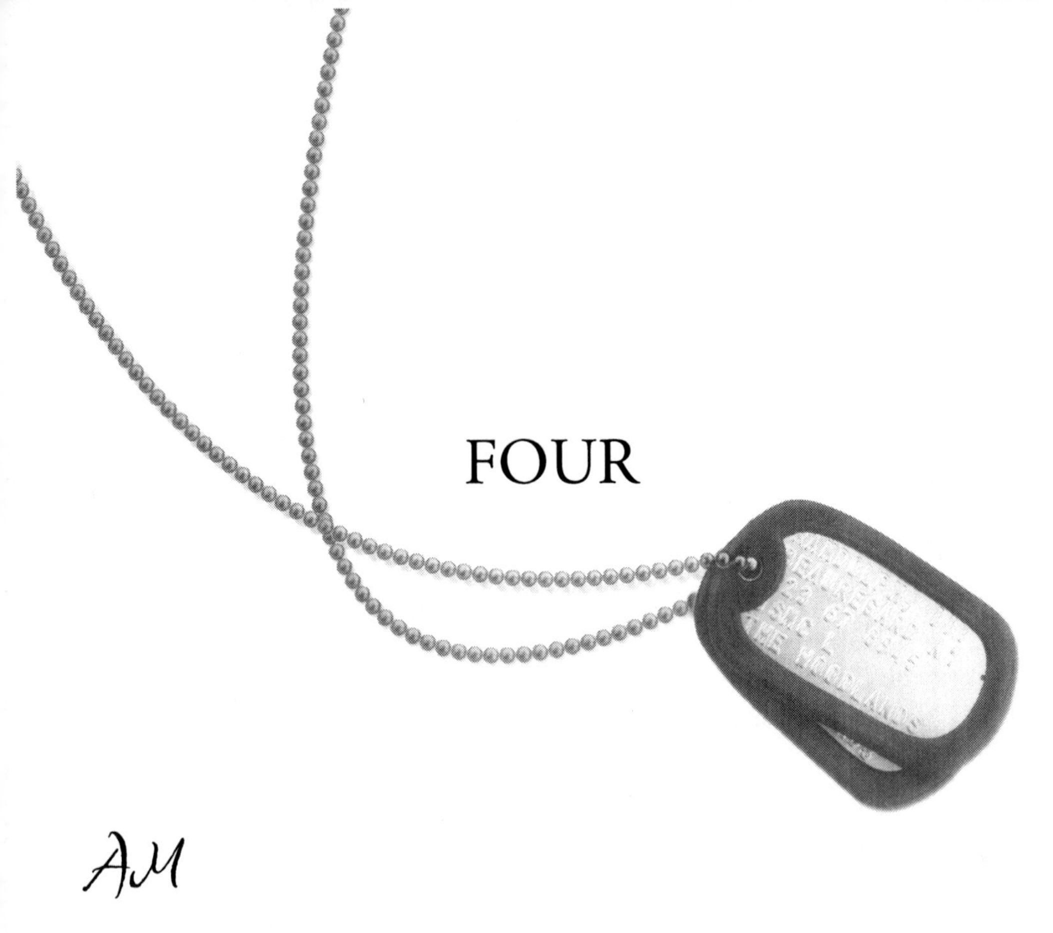

FOUR

AM

WHEN MY PHONE ALERTED ME to a text message just before I was getting ready to go to bed, I figured it was my mother. Two weeks spent at home had made me ready to flee back to school. For my mother, time spent together at Christmas break only made her more melancholy when I departed. But the message wasn't from my mother.

I'm going to put this number to good use. Bo Randolph.

What was he doing sending me a text message at nine on a Monday night? I debated deleting the message.

"Bo Randolph just texted me," I yelled down the hall to Ellie. She appeared like a witch at my door a second later, scaring me half to death.

"My God, where were you?" I yelped.

"Looking for my hoops." Ellie held up large gold earrings. Just outside my bedroom door, our front hall held a mirror and dresser, courtesy of the thrift store, and it had become a repository for all of our jewelry and half our makeup as we dumped things coming and going from the apartment. Most of the time it looked like the sale counter at the mall after the prom rush swept through.

"Should I reply?"

Ellie shrugged and pulled her pearl studs out of her ears. "What'd he say?"

I read her the text.

"He's flirting. No guy texts at nine at night with just friendly intent." Her eyes were bright with interest. I wondered what mine looked like. Probably full of stars.

"Replying would be encouragement I don't want to give." If I told myself that I wasn't interested enough times maybe I could make it true.

"Why not?" she challenged.

I ticked off the negatives. "He's really good looking. He doesn't care what anyone thinks of him. He took advanced econ theory apparently just for the hell of it." *Because Clay Howard has a hard-on about me being on campus and is threatening me.* I didn't list the last one out loud.

Ellie's mouth hung open. "These are his bad attributes? Give me the phone. I'll text him back!" She lunged for the phone, but I turned on my side and held it away from her. Ellie's pixie-sized, and I'm like a horse compared to her. There was no contest.

"Fine," I huffed. Now that I'd told Ellie, I'd have to text Bo back or she'd take the phone from me somehow. Ellie didn't make idle threats. She told you what she was going to do, and then she followed through.

How? You going to send duck-faced selfies? I shot back.

What? Came the immediate reply, like he had nothing better to do than send me texts.

I searched the Internet and then selected an appropriate picture of three young girls making the V with their fingers pointing to their overly pronounced lips pursed and pressed into little fleshy duck bills.

I now know why we're sitting next to each other in bio. We need to find a cure for the disease those young ladies are suffering around their oral cavities before it spreads to others.

An inadvertent huff of laughter escaped me, and Ellie demanded to see the reply, which I showed to her.

"You're toast." She rolled off the bed and exited the room.

"I know it," I told the empty space. Bo was funny, smart, and showing an inordinate amount of interest in me. I was *so* screwed.

OTHER THAN THAT LATE MONDAY night text, I didn't hear from Bo again. On Wednesday, though, he met me outside of class.

"Cutting it a little short, aren't you?" He checked his watch, a big black thing with many dials.

"Class hasn't started yet." I tapped his watch, which showed we had about two minutes to find a seat. "Besides, I like to sit in the back."

"Since when?"

Since the rumors regarding my supposed sexcapades had infiltrated the classroom and people behind me felt bold enough to lean forward and whisper things like, "Leave your panties at the Delts last night?" I didn't know whose panties were waving from the fraternity flag; they weren't mine, but protests were only met with knowing smirks.

"Since Thor decided to hog the front row."

"I'm Thor?" he asked, sounding a bit too pleased.

I guess being compared to a Viking war god was a compliment. I cringed inwardly at revealing that I sometimes envisioned him standing on the prow of a longboat with a horned helmet and a spear. In my fantasies he was shirtless even in the long, cold, Icelandic nights. Real Vikings, I theorized, would be immune to the cold. Or at least they were in my dreams.

Adopting my best uncaring attitude, I waved a hand down his body. "You add a spear and a helmet and you look like you should be standing at the prow of a longboat."

Too busy rifling through my mental images of Bo, it wasn't until he maneuvered me sideways that I realized I had walked all the way to the front again where we had sat on Monday.

"Just because we're lab partners doesn't mean we have to sit next to each other in class." I frowned.

"I know." Bo just grinned and pulled out my chair. "It's a perk."

Remaining immune to his infectious charm was going to be near impossible. I was given a momentary reprieve when the professor greeted us with an announcement about our lab studies. "You'll have two primary lab projects this year. The first is to test the hypothesis of nature over nurture by examining whether there are innate differences between males and females. The second is to create a crossbred plant or animal that can survive here in the Midwest and combines whatever traits are perceived to be lacking in the other."

I tried to pay attention to the details of our lab project, but as hard as I was attempting to ignore Bo, every shift of his body that brushed up against mine sent little prickles of electricity shooting throughout me. I felt his jean-clad thigh press against mine when he let his legs fall open. He stretched his right arm across the back of my chair. The smell of his cologne or aftershave or shampoo released into the air with each movement.

By the end of class, I felt like I was drunk on Bo Randolph. How in the world was I going to make it through a five-credit course with Bo Randolph as my lab partner and not become totally obsessed with him? *Get a grip,* I scolded myself. So what that he was so good looking he belonged on a movie poster? So what that he sent cute text messages? So what that every time I inhaled, I could smell a warm, inviting masculine scent? None of these were things I couldn't find in some other guy. Okay, maybe not as good looking or as funny, but there had to be hundreds of non-Central College guys who smelled good.

And had big hands and broad muscular chests. And tousled blond hair with a thousand different colors that would take me a year to catalog, with a matching scruff around his chin and upper lip. I wondered what that felt like if it was close to your skin. Would it feel scratchy or soft?

"Something on my face?" Bo asked, his long fingers coming up to wipe at his cheek.

"Uh, no, why?" I said, still staring.

"Because you're rubbing your cheek and staring at me like I have parts of my breakfast hanging off my chin."

Heat burned my cheeks as I realized I was stroking my face as I fantasized about the texture of Bo's stubbled cheek against my skin.

"Ah, no, just a scratch," I lied, turning my nails inward, wincing at the pain as I scraped my skin too hard in compensation. "Don't you type?" I tried to distract him. He was about the only one in class without a laptop.

"I can, but I also have impulse control problems." He shrugged. At my questioning look, he went on, "I'd want to play a game or something. But I do get them typed up. Want to share?"

Why not. "Sure, text me your e-mail address and I'll shoot you my notes."

The indent on the left side of his mouth deepened as he smiled with approval. Was it wrong that I wanted to stick my tongue into that groove? I shifted uncomfortably in my seat, a movement that caught Bo's attention. His eyes shifted down to my lap and then up to my face again. My breath stopped, or maybe it was just time that froze, as he leaned toward me, his ocean-blue eyes now the color of water at midnight. All thoughts of my immutable rules, the reasons why to avoid him, were gone, replaced by the shape of his lips, the hot, dark hue of his eyes, and the warmth of his breath as his face came ever closer.

His mouth brushed lightly across my cheek and I felt him inhale, his nose an infinitesimal space away from my jaw. His chest contracted, and he let out a waft of warm air that lifted my hair away from my neck. "You smell good, AnnMarie. It's hard to concentrate, so I need my pen and paper to keep me on track."

I was still shuddering when he drew back. An earthquake had happened inside my body. He was going to utterly ruin me.

TO: annmarie.west@central.edu
FROM: beauregard.randolph@central.edu
SUBJECT: Class notes
ATTACHMENT: Notes*Day*2

AM—

Did I ever tell you I actually hate texting? My fingers are way too big for those tiny little squares. I might not be in class on Friday. Have something going on the night before. May be too sore to show up. I know it makes me sound like a lazy jackass, but can I borrow your notes if I don't make it?

Bo

Sore? My God, was he telling me he was going to be having sex all night and would be too worn out to show up for class? This was probably the reason he asked for us to exchange notes. The balls of this guy. He *knew* he wasn't going to show up and was planning ahead. Affronted, jealous, and upset with myself for even caring, my return message was terse.

TO: beauregard.randolph@central.edu
FROM: annmarie.west@central.edu
SUBJECT: RE: Class notes

Really? Sore. Whatever, but don't make this a habit.

AM

TO: annmarie.west@central.edu
FROM: beauregard.randolph@central.edu
SUBJECT: RE: RE: Class notes

AM—

Promise not to do this often. Have plans this weekend? Let's go talk to some plant experts and get our lab project out of the way.

Bo

What kind of *ass* was he? Bo was going to screw some girl so hard on Thursday night that he wouldn't be able to make it to class, but he wanted to go to do our "lab" project this weekend? And I'd already planned on going to the Natural History Museum this weekend to look up indigenous plants and talk to a staff member. I tried to remember if I'd mentioned this in class because I couldn't believe he'd come up with this on his own. I was totally going to call him on this bullshit.

TO: beauregard.randolph@central.edu
FROM: annmarie.west@central.edu
SUBJECT: RE: RE: RE: Class notes

Sure. When, where, etc.

AM

I slammed my laptop shut before I could read any response but couldn't turn off my thoughts. *How could he flirt so blatantly with me one day and then give me the kiss-off the next?* I fumed. The rest of the week I was testier than a five-year-old stuck inside because of rain for a week.

"WHAT'S YOUR PROBLEM?" ELLIE ASKED me Friday morning as we were getting ready for class.

Not wanting to admit that it was thoughts of Bo making me act unbearably, I held up my birth control case. "Why do I take these when I haven't had sex in months?"

"Because you're in college and you might have sex?"

"Why not just use condoms?"

"Because you're smart and thrifty."

"Thrifty?"

"Yes, birth control is free from the health center. Condoms fail. Abortions cost money and having a baby is like eighty thousand times more expensive than that. Birth control is an economically sound decision." Ellie spoke in calming tones, as if she knew one wrong word would send my head spinning around on my neck.

After my less-than-stellar first time here at Central, I'd tried out two more guys. One was a local, a gorgeous guy who introduced me to good sex. I followed him around like a stray puppy, which annoyed him, and he dumped me after a few weeks. My second try at the dating scene was last semester. I hooked up with an osteopath student from the College of Osteopathy across town, but we never clicked. He'd take time describing each bone in my body like I was an anatomy exam, and while he might have thought he sounded sexy, it came off like he wanted to dissect my cadaver. I ended things with him, but his sigh of relief when I suggested it wasn't working out was telling. My lust for Bo was probably just a product of a long dry spell.

"Right, economically sound." I popped my pill in my mouth and swallowed. "Maybe we should go out this weekend and put this pill to good use."

Ellie's face lit up. "Sounds like a great idea. I'm going to do some recon at class today to figure out where my future boyfriend will be partying."

"Does future boyfriend have a name?"

"Ryan Collins."

"Can't wait to accidentally run into him at a bar this weekend." I winked at her.

"Me either." Ellie smiled wryly at me. "It's okay to crush on Bo. Nothing to be embarrassed about."

Despite my attempts at diverting her attention, Ellie had accurately identified the source of my bad mood. I gave her a tiny shrug. "It'll be forgotten this weekend."

Being the good friend she was, Ellie didn't laugh in my face at this bald-faced lie.

To my surprise, when I arrived at class on Friday, Bo was already there, leaning against the door, waiting for me. He had a black eye and a puffy lip. There was a bruise over one of his cheekbones and his hands were scabbed and swollen. He could barely hold the pen in his left hand, yet he looked happier than I'd seen him all week.

I rewound my memory of the e-mail he'd sent. Sore? *Something* going on? My mind had jumped immediately to the bedroom because that's where Bo spent most of his time in my imagination, but I'd apparently interpreted the whole thing wrong.

After I'd stared at him for what seemed like five minutes, he broke out in a huge grin and held out his hand. "Stop looking at me. I'm not supposed to smile."

"What the hell, Bo?"

"The other guy looks worse?" he offered as some kind of half-baked explanation, leading me down to our now customary seats in the front.

I shook my head. "Were you fighting?" I whispered, not wanting anyone else to hear me, particularly not the two freshman girls who sat behind Bo and me and had clued in to what a magnificent addition he was to the homo sapiens species. I actually saw one of them give the thumbs-up toward heaven the other day in class after Bo leaned over the table to pick up a piece of paper that had floated off. You could bounce a quarter off that ass.

Bo leaned close to whisper back, "Yes. Why are we whispering?"

"Isn't it illegal?"

"The Casino," Bo explained in a normal tone, not caring who heard him. "Different regs there."

"Like no regulations?"

"Pretty much." He nodded and started to cross his arms but winced when he realized his hands were too tender to be tucked into his body.

I bit my lip to keep from asking a bunch of nosy questions. "Do you need me to take notes for you today?"

"Yeah. Do you mind?"

I shook my head. "When you e-mailed me and said you would be too sore for class today, I thought it might be something else."

Bo gave a hoot of laughter. "Nope, but it *was* all consensual. You jealous?"

Yes, I was, I thought sourly, but I didn't want to admit it. For some reason, now that Bo was my lab partner, I'd begun assigning other ownership thoughts to him. What a crazy thing to do. I kept my mouth shut because I didn't have a good comeback other than the truth, which I certainly was *not* going to share. Conveniently, the professor began his lecture, but Bo leaned over and whispered, "Nothing to be jealous about, Sunshine."

Sunshine? Bo slouched against his chair and spread his legs wide, brushing up against mine. He slung his right arm over the back of my chair. If I leaned backward, I could have pretended he was hugging me. Concentrating for fifty minutes was a bitch. At the end of class, I quickly packed my belongings, afraid that if I spent one more minute with him, I'd throw him down on the table and see what bruises he had hiding under his shirt today. And if I could kiss them to make them better. If I spent even one more minute with him, I would be, as Ellie had put it, toast.

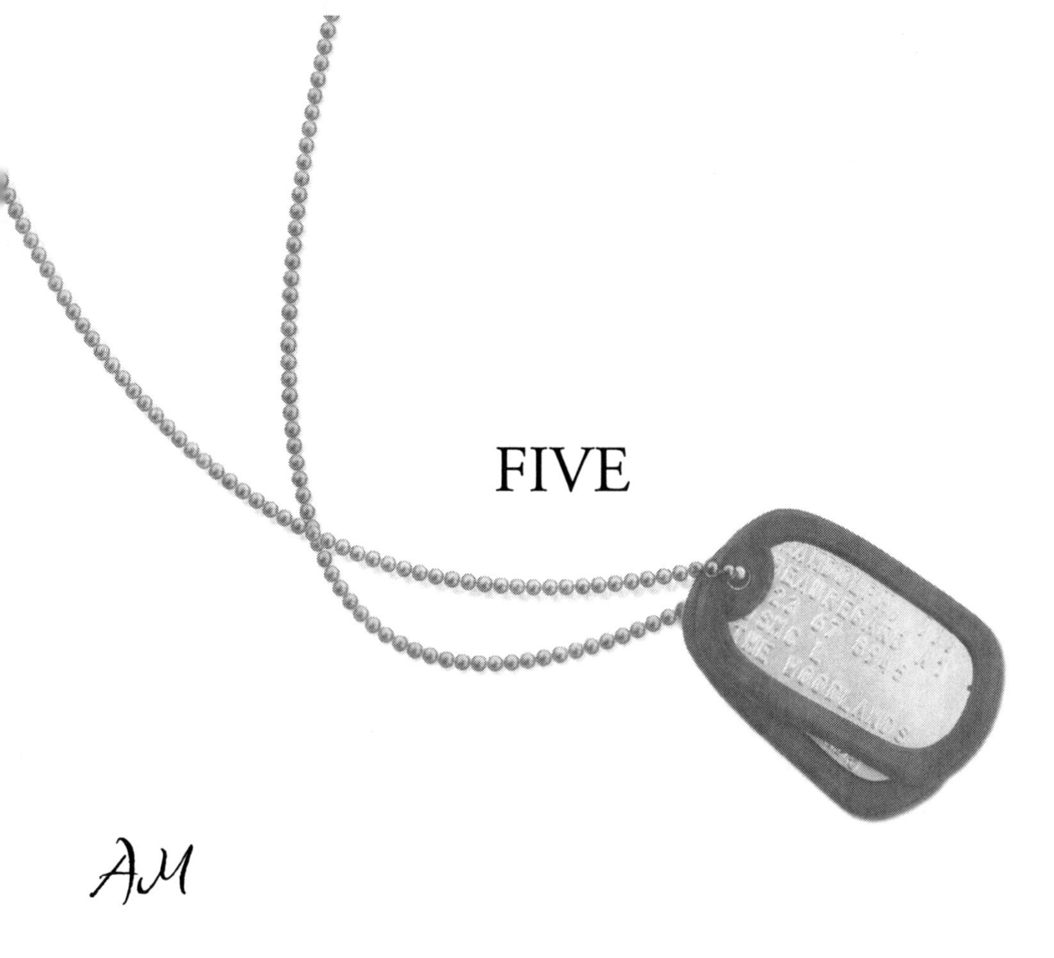

FIVE

AM

DESPITE OUR BIG TALK OF partying all week, Ellie and I stayed in and watched movies when the weekend rolled around. While we watched actresses drum songs on the bottoms of cups, I shored up my anti-Bo defenses. I made a new list of excuses why I shouldn't be crushing on him and ran through them each morning. None of them were very good, but that wasn't the point. If I could make it through this semester without tearing my clothes off in biology class, the little white lies I told myself would be worth it. When Monday rolled around, I intentionally arrived late to class and sat in the back. I didn't remember much of the lecture, as I spent the whole time staring at Bo's head and wishing I was sitting right next to him. Bo turned around once and found me in the first pass. We stared at each other for what felt like an eon but was probably seconds. I couldn't read his emotions but I knew what I was feeling. *Regret.*

On Tuesday, I met up with Ellie back at the apartment after classes were over. When I came through the door, she shot me a pleading glance.

"What's up with the puppy eyes?" I peered at Ellie, who was standing with her hands clasped in front of her next to the paisley sofa we'd bought from a garage sale on the west side. It was so hideous—blue with red floral paisley designs all over looking like grotesque snails—that we both agreed it had circled around to awesome. Plus, it was super comfortable. We theorized the person who'd bought it was colorblind and sat on it and felt as if he was lying in marshmallows. Then he fell in love and his new partner made him throw it out. At least that's the story that Ellie and I made up.

"I need to ask you for a huge favor." Ellie looked pitiful and hopeful at the same time. Like I would ever say no to her. Ellie had been my rock since we were kids. Half my courage in sticking it out here at Central came from knowing she was standing right beside me.

"Sure, buttercup. What do you need?" I flopped down on the sofa, tossing my phone on the coffee table.

"Willyougotodinneroncampustoday?" Ellie spilled out her request so fast that it was like one long word. I thought she was joking at first because Ellie knew I never ate meals on campus. Not since about midterms of my freshman year. Not since the unspoken words and low murmured whispers turned to actions. But when she didn't laugh or give me a verbal cue that it was just a prank, I turned to look at her.

She gave me a pained, wry smile. "It was a stupid idea." Unlocking her hands, Ellie came to rest on her side of the diseased-looking marshmallow.

"Tell me about it," I said quietly. The invitation was all she needed. Turning to me, Ellie hitched one leg up on the sofa. As I looked at her glowing face and her sparkling eyes, I knew I was going to be eating on campus tonight.

"I'm totally in lust with that guy, Ryan, that I told you about from my Rocks for Jocks class. I need to know more about him," Ellie babbled. "I'm pretty sure he's a freshman. Maybe on the baseball team? I mean, I assume he's a jock because why else is he taking that course?"

"So he's eating where tonight?"

"Oh, um, I overheard him say he was meeting 'the guys' at the Quad Commons Café." She blushed and said, "I don't know what it is about him that I find so adorable, but he's all dorky cuteness."

"We need to do a little covert stalking is what you're saying," I finished for her.

She nodded. "I know I'm asking for something big here."

"Nah." I shrugged. "I've been thinking that my self-imposed exile is kind of dumb. How am I supposed to crush on Bo Randolph if I avoid campus?"

"You really want to go?" Ellie looked skeptical.

"And miss the opportunity to stalk this guy with you?" I grabbed her hand. "Tell me more."

As Ellie described his mini Mohawk and retro cool eyeglasses, I mentally assured myself that everyone had moved on from my sex life. There had to be other scandals, other bits of gossip that people were exchanging. By the time Ellie had finished giving me an exhaustive rundown of this guy's entire physical appearance from his eyebrow piercing to his dark wash jeans and plaid button-down shirt, I'd convinced myself that I had nothing at all to fear. What could anyone say that they hadn't already said? Clay Howard's threats were probably hollow. He couldn't be on campus all the time, and the likelihood of running into him in the QC Café was very low.

Still, I spent an inordinate amount of time later that day wondering if my jeans were too tight or my T-shirt showed too much cleavage. In a fit of uncertainty, I changed into a pair of loose fitting khakis and a white button-down shirt and left the room to find Ellie inserting earrings in front of the hall closet dresser. Ellie looked me over and almost stabbed herself through the cheek with the earring post.

"Are you going to work as a clerk in a shoe store?" Ellie asked with a heavy amount of disdain.

I looked down at my clothes. "Too bland?"

"Girl, even the people at the Dockers store would be embarrassed to be seen in that outfit." Ellie frowned. She was right. Ordinarily I had no problems picking out the right outfit, including for class, but for some reason tonight I was a mass of nerves and indecision.

"We don't have to go," Ellie said in a rush, measuring my anxiety by the hideousness of my outfit. She met my gaze in the mirror and her eyes softened in sympathy. That look sent a steel rod up my spine.

I hated pity more than I hated the gossip. Maybe she gave me that look on purpose, to help me find my courage. I turned on my foot and went into the bedroom, where I picked up a pair of discarded skinny jeans and a loose silky top. I pulled on a pair of heavy socks and a battered pair of riding boots. My heavy felt, navy-blue peacoat completed the outfit. I looked a lot less like Dockers layaway and more like hip young person. I felt better, too.

The past year had taught me that sometimes the best defense in the world was a stony glare and the right attire. Going into the lion's den dressed like I was dressed for church was bound to create even worse talk than looking like a prostitute. The latter they expected, the former said I was trying too hard. The vultures never liked anything more than cutting down people who set themselves up.

I picked up my phone and ID card and headed out to meet Ellie. She was putting on the last touches of makeup. The au natural look required as much effort as the heavily made-up look. Guys never knew the difference, but the cosmetic industry didn't have fifty shades of natural and blush lipstick because girls could run around with bee-stung lips just by biting them heavily. Biting led to chapped lips and teeth marks.

We didn't talk as we walked toward the commons. Ellie seemed to instinctively understand that I didn't have much to say. The campus looked magical in the evening light. The snow sparkled where it was illuminated by the lampposts that marched along the sidewalks, intersecting the campus lawns. Central was an old campus, over one hundred years old, and even though it had been modernized, the feel of it was nostalgic. The streetlights were made of wrought iron instead of hard steel. The callboxes looked like old-fashioned telephone booths. Even the sculptures positioned throughout had an old-world charm to them.

Maybe the student body took cues from it. For all the modern, liberal thinking that was preached from the professors' podiums, the men and women who took classes here had some deep-seated, old-fashioned views. Girls who hooked up a lot were sluts. Guys who did the same were studs. Girls who wore their hair short and their pants long were lesbians. Guys who used too much product and cared too much about their appearance were gay. And those who didn't conform were weirdos and easy objects of scorn.

During my freshman year, I'd have given anything to be thought of as a weirdo or gay. Being deemed a slut meant that you were fair game to every asshole on campus. They could slap your ass or casually grab your boob during the sober, daylight hours. Once the sun went down and the beer came out, the groping was more obvious. Then it was a full body press, trying to corner you in a dark spot and stick their hand up your skirt. If you said no at any time, you were a bitch or cock tease or cunt. And because no one wanted to admit being turned down by the class bicycle, rumors started anew.

I remember one guy whom I'd never met, never talked to, bragging in the library to a few others in his study group about how he had to force me off his dick so he could get another beer, that I was just *so* hungry for him. Another guy regaled the group with how he'd poured beer on his penis and then forced me to suck him off. They all laughed when he described, graphically, how he had held my hair in place and how the gagging noises I made only made him harder.

None of it had ever happened, but it didn't stop me from feeling violated, used, and dirty. It wasn't one thing that drove me off campus, but a hundred wounds both large and small. I felt that if I spent one minute more than necessary there, I would be nothing more than a dried honeycomb, all the life sucked out of me, exposed and used.

As Ellie and I walked down the sidewalk, no one stared at me. The cement at our feet didn't crack in half. We were just two students in a big crowd, some moving toward the commons and some away. I felt anonymous for a moment, and I almost stumbled when relief poured through me.

The commons looked the same. It was a squatty brick building, one of the uglier structures on campus, built into the side of the hill. When you approached from the south side, it looked like Bag End, or some other building from the Shire, only without the cute circular doors. On the north side, it was all windows, so that when you were here in the morning you could catch the sunrise through the two-story foyer. Whoever decorated the interior must have used a focus group study from the '80s. It was full of dark browns and blues with neon light tubes twisted into waves and circles. The café housed in the lower level served up a mix of salad bar fresh foods and mystery plates. You could hear the cacophony of the slap of forks and plates and trays against tables from the balcony that overlooked the seating area.

Ellie and I paused at the railing and looked down. "Do you see him?" I asked quietly. First rule of crush stalking was to ensure that you weren't obvious. You can't alert your prey that you're observing his every move.

Ellie scanned the crowd and checked her watch. "No, but we're about five minutes early. Should we wait?"

I didn't want to wait. I wanted to eat and get the hell out. Even though nothing bad had happened, it was early yet. I wanted to ease back onto campus instead of jumping headfirst into an unknown body of water. Who knew how close the rocks were to the surface? I took a deep breath. I was here for Ellie, just as she'd been there for me all those times before. "Sure, let's walk through the Bookstore for a few," I suggested.

The commons had a lounge area with pool tables and a quiet study place upstairs, along with rooms that local high schools sometimes rented out to hold a prom. The bottom level was a major arterial vein of the campus. Lots of activity flowed in and out of QC Café and Central Bookstore, a small store where students could come and buy sodas, snacks, and Central attire. Ellie started forward, but I stopped her. I'd walk down those steps first just to prove to myself I could, even if I was trembling inside.

Students passed me by and still nothing. Not a sideways glance, not a smirk, not a whisper behind a hand to a companion. By the time we had reached the Bookstore, I felt nearly serene and not a little chagrined. I should have braved the masses last semester. A summer away from Central had probably dimmed my reputation in everyone's memory. What a self-important asshole I was, thinking that I was so important that people were *still* talking about me. I gave a half laugh and Ellie turned to me with a lifted eyebrow. "Sorry," I said, "just swallowed wrong."

Ellie nodded and looked toward the door, trying to keep an eye on the crowd streaming through entrance of the café while not being obvious about it. I didn't know who I was looking for despite her exhaustive description earlier.

A loud group came in, commanding everyone's attention. It was a group of guys barking loudly to one another, like a flock of geese. At the light in Ellie's eyes, I knew that her new man was in this group. Showtime.

We waited another ten minutes in the store, pretending to admire the variety of sweatshirts, T-shirts, and sleep pants adorned with one big C on them. When we judged that the boisterous man crew had made their way through the cashier, we went and gathered our food. Salad bar for both of us because that was the only fresh food served in the café, that and deli sandwiches. Anything else and you were just asking for a bout of food poisoning.

Exiting the cash line, I stood with my tray in hand while Ellie surveyed the crowd, trying to find exactly the right table where we could sit and observe and maybe even eavesdrop on the table that held the object of her crush.

She started forward and then stopped and I nearly dumped the contents of my tray on her back. I followed her gaze to a table in the center of the room filled with guys wearing their trucker caps backward, mid-calf socks, and Flow Society shorts even in winter. The lacrosse team. Or laxers, as they liked to call themselves.

The hottie from Rocks for Jocks was a lacrosse player. Ellie turned and looked at me with dismay, and I briefly closed my eyes in silent supplication, praying that the team would not look at us. I abruptly walked to a table as far away as I could get.

"I'm so sorry. I didn't know he was a lacrosse player," Ellie whispered as we settled into our seats. I barely heard her because I was too busy internally debating the safest way to sit. Should I position myself so I could see them coming or with my back to them? I compromised and sat at an angle from their table, making myself the smallest target possible. The giant salad I'd assembled looked like the least appetizing bowl of food ever. I moved my fork around, pushing the cherry tomatoes to the side and rearranging the mushrooms into an ordered pattern, one slice lying next to the other in a circle around the bowl. I was so intent on repositioning my food, I missed the signs of an approaching classmate.

"Hey, uh, aren't you in my geology class?" I heard a voice slightly above me say. Out of the corner of my eye, I could see the lacrosse table laughing behind their hands and some were not so furtively pointing in our direction.

Ellie looked at the object of her crush with contempt and gave him a short, no-nonsense answer. "Yes." It was not an invitation to start a conversation. This must be some kind of hazing, although I thought that started at the beginning of school, not halfway through the semester. Why else would this poor kid be forced over to our table to start up a conversation?

I kept my head down and averted, which I knew was rude, but I didn't want to be here and definitely did not want to participate. Two months into college, I'd had my fill of lacrosse guys. I didn't need to make the acquaintance of any more.

Ellie's dismissive answer didn't drive the freshman away. Instead, he pulled out a chair, flipped it around, and sat down so he could lean his arms on the back. "Thought I recognized you. I'm Ryan Collins." He held out his hand to Ellie. She stared at it like it was diseased. He held it out for a couple of beats and then awkwardly brought his hand down to his side, to wipe it on his pants.

No one spoke a word. Ellie stared at Ryan with hostility and Ryan returned the look with puzzlement. Maybe he didn't mean to come over and make some rude come-on. Maybe he really did mean to introduce himself to Ellie.

I felt reluctant admiration for this guy who was bucking normal rules of engagement and putting himself out there for public rejection, in front of his teammates and other classmates. I knew what it felt like to be the subject of unwanted scrutiny. Almost against my will, I spoke up. "Nice to meet you." My voice sounded raspy, as if it hadn't been used for a week. I cleared my throat. "I'm AnnMarie and that's Ellie."

She shot me a shocked glance as if I'd engaged the enemy in direct combat. I gave her a tiny shrug. The introductions shook loose Ryan's mute button. "Ladies." He smiled and two dimples appeared on either side of his mouth. The dimples, the short hair with the slight Mohawk styling, retro black plastic glasses, and brow piercing all bespoke a guy who was making his own way in life. He didn't look like a stereotypical laxer. There was no STX lanyard with his keys and ID. No hat, not even an old tournament jersey.

"So you play lacrosse?" I asked when Ellie remained silent.

Ryan nodded, seeming relieved that I included him in a question. "I do. We're gearing up for our season to start in a couple of months."

"Where's your pinnie?" Ellie asked, sneering slightly. I was surprised at her overt hostility. Shouldn't asshole girl be my role?

Ryan shifted uncomfortably in his chair. "I just like to play the game. It's fun, a good way to keep in shape, and why am I defending myself to you?"

"You came to sit with us," Ellie pointed out.

"I'm guessing you had a bad experience with a laxer?" Ryan suggested.

"You might say that." I was grateful that Ellie didn't turn to look at me when she replied, insinuating that it was her problem and not mine.

Ryan scrubbed a hand through his shorn hair, destroying his mini

Mohawk and making the short hair on his head stick out in different directions.

"So I'm guessing my suggestion that we be lab partners is going to be shot down?" Ryan said, giving an adorable half smile. Even though I had a hate boner for all laxers, Ryan's smile was potent. It looked like it might be affecting Ellie as well.

Ryan took her hesitation as a maybe he could turn to a yes. "I'm just a dumb freshman. Take pity on me."

That was smooth. He was all dimples and self-deprecation. Ellie resisted, though. "I've had a *really* bad experience with laxers."

At that, Ryan turned to look to his table. There was no avoiding it. The table of lacrosse players had seen us and identified at least me. I could see the shit-eating grin of one Clay Howard III from a hundred feet away. I shrank back. Never had a grin ever looked so menacing.

I wondered if Clay even knew my real name anymore, or if the nickname he'd given me was my only source of identification. I wasn't convinced Clay even thought of me as a real person. Maybe I was some imaginary punching doll he'd created and trotted out for jokes to his pals.

Ryan's eyes moved around from Ellie to me to his table. He stood then, and I noticed Clay had also risen from his seat and was making his way toward us. I looked wide-eyed at Ellie and my anger and trepidation were reflected in her face. And then I felt my backbone stiffen as my fight instinct kicked in.

Why was I allowing one douche bag to dictate my life on campus? I wondered how many other girls who sat in the café right now had turned down Clay, only to be branded a slut in exchange. I watched in wretched fascination as he swaggered over to our table. As he walked toward us, each section he passed seemed to quiet, as if they knew something was about to happen.

Ryan had positioned himself slightly in front of our table, as if to intercept Clay, a move I couldn't comprehend at that moment. I inhaled, taking breaths as deep as I could make them without being obvious about it. *I'm going to own you one day,* I mentally told Clay. *You'll be broken at my feet, and I'll laugh as the world pisses on your head.*

"Bro." Clay's greeting to Ryan sounded like a shotgun in an empty range. He held out his fist for a bump. Ryan obliged but said nothing.

"You looking for some action?" Clay asked.

Ryan shook his head. "No, just catching up with Ellie about a class we have together."

"These girls, particularly Mary here, probably have a lot they'll be willing to put out." Clay smirked at his own really bad pun.

"It's AnnMarie," I said quietly but loud enough that I knew Clay could hear.

"What's that?" Clay asked, obviously hoping to set me up or hoping I'd shut up.

"It's AnnMarie," I repeated and stood up next to the table. Ellie got to her feet and picked up her tray. She was ready to go. I wasn't going to run out like a scaredy cat, but I also wasn't going to sit there and be the butt of the innumerable lies that Clay would enjoy regaling young Ryan with.

As I bent down to pick up my tray, Clay remarked on the nearly uneaten contents. "Did you eat too much before you came to dinner tonight, *Mary*?" He emphasized the name so I wouldn't miss that he'd intentionally called me the wrong name again.

"I was afraid if I ate something, I might have to ingest the same air you breathed. Plants die when you're around," I told him. Rumor was that Clay had nearly flunked biology, failing to grow his seed into a plantable seedling. High color flared in his cheeks. Rumor must have been correct, and this spurred my feet into motion. I knew I was needling an angry animal now, but I couldn't resist another poke, and as I walked by him I said in a low tone, "Heard you had problems germinating seeds."

He grabbed my arm, causing the tray to tip precariously. Ryan reached out and steadied the tray and looked questioningly at Clay's hand on my biceps. Out of the corner of my eye, I saw a tall, dark-haired guy rise to his feet. Noah, Bo's weight-room buddy. His thickly muscled arms and toned body caught Clay's attention, too. He dropped his hand and then shook it in the air. "Damn, I'm going need to some sanitizer so I don't catch one of your friends." His words rang out loudly in the now-silent cafeteria. This time I was the one who couldn't keep the blood from rising and coloring my cheeks.

Now we both looked like angry animé characters with red spots denoting our anger and embarrassment. "You aren't good enough to touch me, and you know it," I told him.

"I'm no OB, but I know a cunt when I see one." Maybe he'd meant to whisper it to me, but everyone was so quiet, so intent on getting the details of the drama, that the insult carried on the waves of silence through to the entrance of the dining hall as clearly as the Main Hall bell that rang at noon. The entire room sucked in their collective breaths and even Clay, as dim as he was, realized he might have gone one step too far with the putdowns.

"It's gynecologist," I said, leaving him behind. I heard him say, "What?" and Ryan answered slowly, as if he could barely believe what had just transpired. "An OB delivers babies. Gynecologists examine women in the way you were suggesting."

"What's the difference?" Clay asked.

Ryan's response was filled with disgust so transparent that I think even Clay must have noticed. "There's a difference."

By the time we reached the conveyor belt that took the dirty trays and plates back to where I assumed everything would be washed, I was shaking like a leaf. The contents of my tray were clinking together, and Ellie took my tray from me before the contents spilled onto the floor.

She looked miserable. "I'm so, so sorry."

"Are you kidding?" I said, trying to breathe normally instead of in little frightened pants. "How is this your fault? You're not responsible for him." I couldn't bring myself to say his name.

"I'm not going to recount the obvious timeline that brought you here," Ellie said, reaching up and slinging an arm around my shoulders, "but just know that I'm taking responsibility whether you like it or not."

"If it makes you feel better." I tried to joke but I felt nothing but gratitude that she was holding me.

"It does," was her firm reply. The steadiness in Ellie's body and the lighthearted tone she was using helped me walk out of the commons instead of crawl out.

"I wouldn't still be here without you, Ellie."

"That's kind of what scares me," Ellie admitted.

"What?" I turned at the top of the stairs. "Why would you say that?"

She shrugged. "Because maybe you shouldn't be here anymore."

That only made me stand up straighter. "I'm not running away."

"I know. You don't like to quit, but maybe that's kind of an outdated slogan. I mean, it's not like you're Braveheart trying to stand up for the right to wear kilts against the British."

"Is that really what Mel Gibson died for?"

"That's what I got out of it," Ellie said.

We had made it to the door. No one had stopped us. I hadn't heard any more jeers or taunts. I was going to survive this day, just like I'd survived all the past ones. And tomorrow would be better. It had to be. We bundled up and wrapped our scarves around our faces, protecting ourselves from the wind. Too bad there wasn't a scarf I could wear indoors to protect my heart.

As I pushed on the door, I saw one more obstacle. *Damn.*

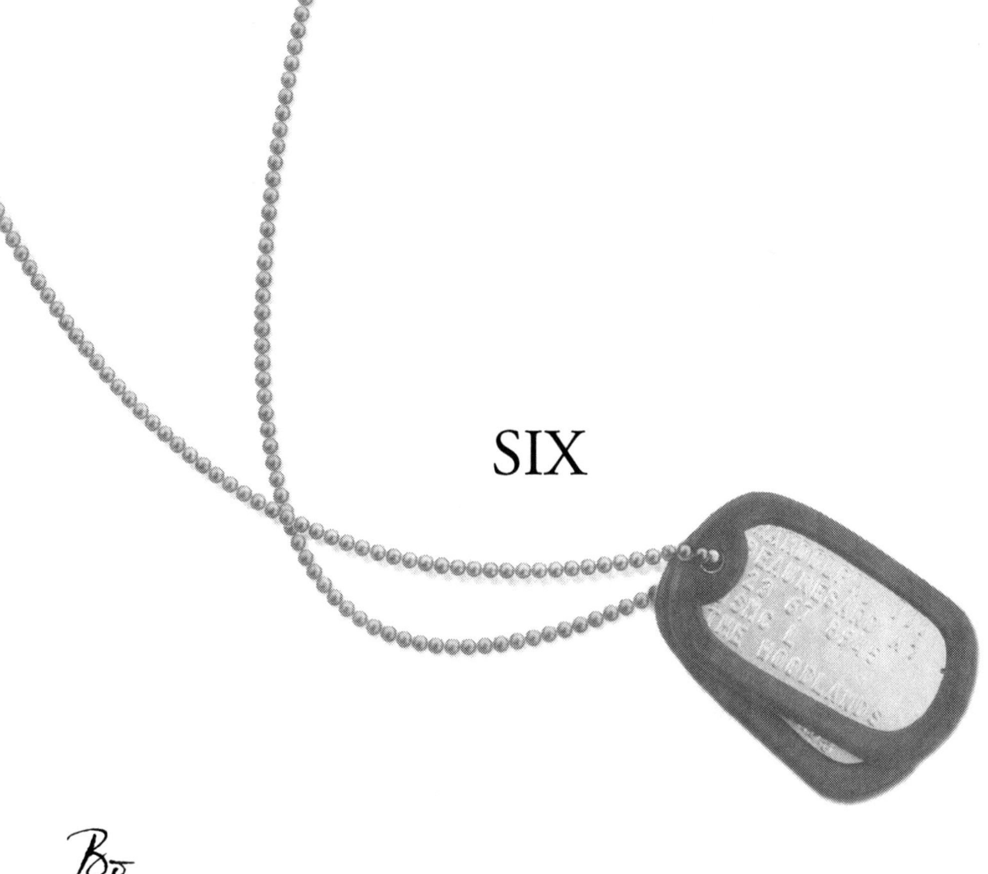

SIX

Bo

"Hey, Sunshine," I said, holding the door as AM and her roommate rushed out. Ellie gave me a small smile, but AM didn't turn toward me at all. As she passed by me, I could see something glistening on the ends of her eyelashes. I tightened my grip on the door, not liking what that meant.

"Hey," I repeated forcefully. When she looked at me, the pain I saw reflected hit me harder than an unexpected blow to the jaw. I knew AnnMarie only a tiny bit, but my guess was that this girl who tried to appear even-keeled in the face of minor ribbing by a classmate would prefer that her agony wasn't riding so close to the surface.

"Here for the show?" she said, her voice brittle as an icicle. I moved to hold her, thaw her out, and pass on whatever warmth I could, but she held up her hand. I stayed my impulse because I didn't want to be the one to break her as she stood there trying to hold it all together.

"No, just for dinner." I smiled benignly, simulating normalcy as best as I could, but anger rose up from my gut. No girl looked like AnnMarie did right now, bruised around the eyes and the mouth, just from having a simple meal. The urge to storm in and rain down retribution like hellfire sawed at my nerves. My entire body tensed up with the unrelieved desire to deliver a beatdown to *someone,* but I managed to eke out a normal sounding response. "Meeting Noah and his girl Grace for dinner. See you in class tomorrow, right?"

AM looked confused for a minute, then nodded. She took a deep breath and said, "Tomorrow." With that last word, she allowed her friend to lead her away.

I walked slowly so it didn't appear like I was trying to chase down and enjoy the last remnants of whatever show AM was referring to. When I got to the stairs, however, I jogged down and bypassed the food line to look for Noah and Grace. The two of them were seated at a table against the window, talking seriously. I went over and sat down. "So did something just happen here?"

Noah grimaced and Grace looked away. "Just some guys being assholes," Noah said.

"No big deal?"

"Yeah," Noah said unconvincingly, looking over at Grace.

"So if it's no big deal then why can't Grace even look at me?" I pointed at her turned face. She heaved a big sigh and turned toward me, scrunching up her nose as if something smelled terrible. I was pretty sure it wasn't me, the shower being the reason I was late to meet the two of them for dinner.

"Just a lacrosse guy trying to prove the size of his dick," Noah interjected before Grace could open her mouth. Grace and I weren't great friends despite our mutual connection with Noah. I wasn't entirely convinced that she was good enough for him, and she thought I was a bad influence. I tried to tell her that Noah wasn't influenced by anyone but her, and she was slowly coming to realize that. But I wanted to hear how Grace had seen the events.

"Grace?" I asked, as gently as possible. Noah, ever protective, jumped in before Grace could say a word.

"It was ugly, just leave it alone," Noah commanded.

"It involve a girl named AnnMarie?" I asked Grace, ignoring Noah. She nodded. "Tell me," I asked, tacking on "please" so she didn't think I was a peremptory jerk even though I was, kind of.

"Do you know her?" Grace asked.

"She's my biology lab partner." A day ago I'd have said that maybe we were on the road to a hookup, but based on the look she'd shot me on her way out of the commons, I was guessing less than nothing.

Grace frowned. Maybe she thought I was bad news for everyone, not just Noah. "I don't want to spread rumors," Grace said, casting a glance over at a table full of lacrosse guys, a table that was abnormally subdued. Usually these guys dominated the classroom, the lunchroom, everything with their loud talk. They were always acting jacked up, like a newbie at boot who thought he was ready to join Marine Force Recon because he achieved level sixty-five in *Call of Duty*. They annoyed the hell out of me. Noah met my gaze and rolled his eyes in agreement. Jackasses, all of them. Or, as we called all persons not infantry Marine, fucking POGs.

"I've heard all the rumors about AnnMarie, Grace," I said impatiently. "Your pal Mike was a fountain of information. I couldn't shut him up about it."

Grace pressed her lips flat in clear distaste. Great thing about Grace was that every emotion she had you could read on her face. I couldn't understand why she was such a mystery to Noah, unless love truly did make you blind.

I knew love made you stupid, which was why I shied away from it, but I had a feeling I was in too deep with AnnMarie already for either of us to come out of it unscathed.

"Mike's wrong," Grace said. "AnnMarie is a nice girl."

"I don't care if she's slept with a platoon of Marines, Grace," I said. "I just want to know what happened so that when I see her in the morning I don't make her feel worse than she already does."

"How do you know how she feels?" Grace tipped her head to the side.

"Because I ran into her as she was leaving and she looked like someone took out her insides, stomped the shit out of them, and tried to make her eat them." What little patience I had was quickly eroding.

Noah sighed and leaned forward, speaking softly, "Some lacrosse guy grabbed her by the arm, called her a cunt, and implied she had a venereal disease."

Noah clamped a fist around my arm as I half rose out of my seat to go and annihilate the entire table. I resisted for a moment.

"Think, man," Noah said, pressing down. "Do you want to make this worse for her? For once in your life, use your head before you follow your gut. You destroying that table of jerkwads will only provide fuel for whatever rumors are going to spill out tonight. It'll make it harder for her to forget about what happened."

"I think Noah broke the table trying to prevent himself from adding to the scene." Grace pointed to the edge of the table where the black plastic edging was crumpled and separated from the side of the wood.

I bit my tongue hard until the pain overrode the desire to go turn someone into a pretzel. Nodding at Noah to let him know that I'd gotten it under control, I asked, "The entire room heard this?"

Noah nodded and let me go. "Affirmative."

I turned to Grace. "What do you know of this?"

She shrugged helplessly. "I don't know much. AnnMarie rushed our freshman year, but I don't think she joined a sorority. She lived in a different hall than I did. About two months into our freshman year, rumors started that she had a thing for lacrosse players. She dropped out of campus activities and moved off campus with her friend Ellie after Christmas break. You never see either of them anymore. I think her showing up at the café surprised everyone. She always seemed nice."

"She is nice. Niceness doesn't change depending on how many people you sleep with. Assholes are assholes regardless of the number of their sexual partners," I said sarcastically. Noah shot me a warning glare but I ignored it. "Take, for example, our lacrosse table. They only talk shit like that because they're a club sport. They don't get the recognition they think they deserve, so they bray like jackasses in hopes that people will look their way. Guys who're getting it regular never act like that."

Grace looked surprised, as if this had never occurred to her, but Noah just grunted an agreement. "Act like you've been here before and that you'll be there again."

Grace smiled at Noah like he'd said the most amazing thing. "Homer?" she asked him.

"No, Barry Sanders," I said.

"Barry who?" She looked at me with some confusion.

"Running back. Detroit Lions. The quote is from him." I rubbed a hand down my face. "Noah, let's take the guy out back and beat the shit out of him. You know you want to."

"Don't tempt me. You know I can't do that." Which was his unspoken way of saying he'd hold the towel while I pummeled the guy. I just had to arrange it.

"So basically this one douche bag and his friends have driven AM off campus into some kind of self-imposed exile?" I concluded.

"I don't think it's so much self-imposed," Grace said with a shudder. "I wouldn't want to face that kind of confrontation."

Why didn't you do anything, then? I wanted to ask but I knew that question would only cause friction between Noah and me. Noah thought Grace was perfect and wouldn't tolerate anyone questioning her behavior. I looked at her hard, though, and hoped she read the message.

I stood to leave, but Noah stopped me. "You can't save everyone."

"Tell me something I don't know," I said and threw off his hand. I didn't want to save everyone. I wanted to save AnnMarie. I wanted to save myself. Somehow it seemed the same thing at that moment and surely that wasn't asking for too much.

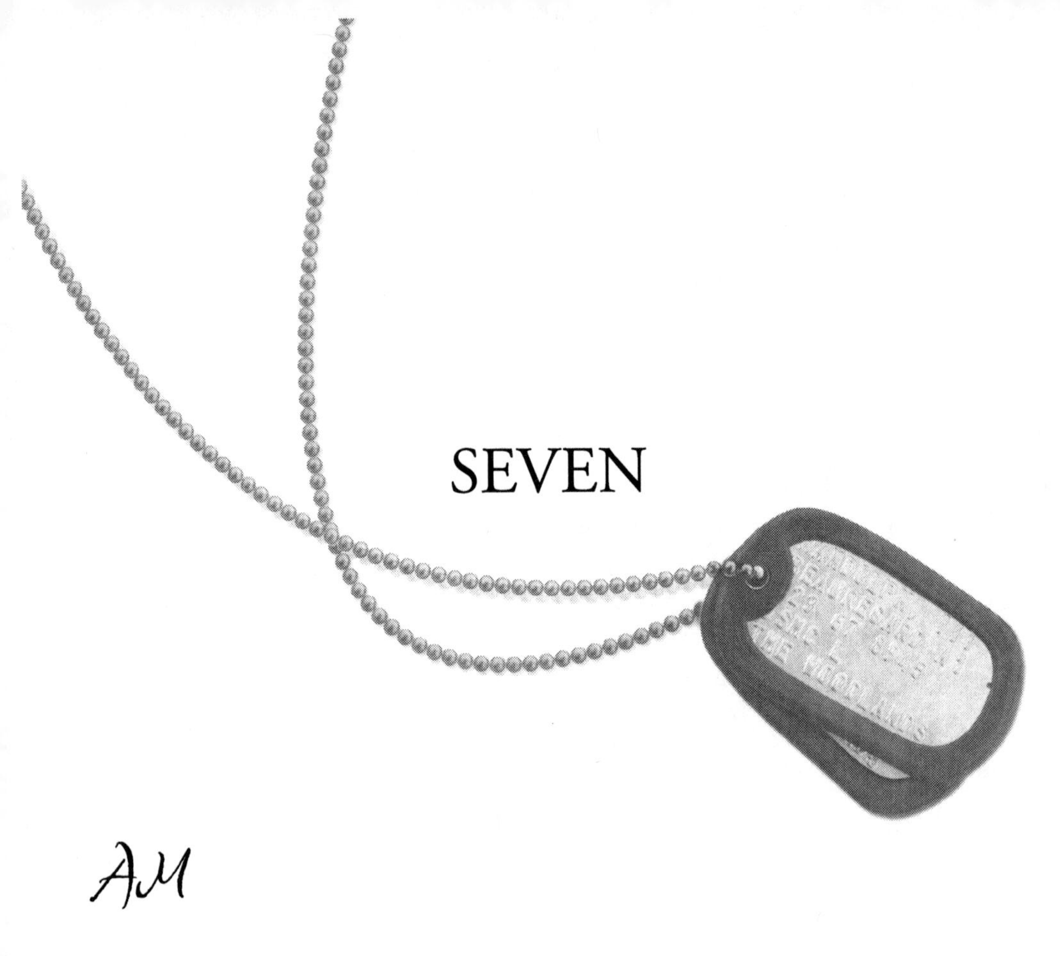

SEVEN

AM

Ellie looked at me as if I were a recently cracked windshield, just waiting for me to collapse into a million broken pieces. But I'd survived Central campus and its rumor mill for months. I was still standing even if I was still shaking from the encounter with Clay.

"I wish I could come up with better insults on the fly," I complained. My heart was bruised, and I was pissed off that I shook like a frightened kitten facing a bathtub filled with water. I'm not sure if it was his size or just the confrontation, but I never felt like I got the better of Clay. "You'd think that I would've rehearsed one. All I can think of is 'You're an asshole.'"

"That's because he *is* an asshole," Ellie replied.

"True." Then I added tentatively, feeling Ellie out on the subject, "But Ryan seemed to be bothered by Clay's comments."

"I would never date a laxer!" Ellie cried. She sounded like I'd inflicted a mortal wound or insulted her mother.

"He seems different than the other guys," I pointed out. I didn't want *my* issues to be infringing on Ellie's interests. She'd already taken on far too much of my drama as her own, and it wasn't necessary.

She strongly believed in the "an enemy of yours is an enemy of mine" theory, which made her a great friend but also made me feel guilty. Ellie murmured something unintelligible into her scarf that I mentally translated into "don't be an idiot," so I just changed the subject. "Do you really think taking Rocks for Jocks is going to be better than biology?"

Ellie merely shrugged her shoulders, dipping her face deep inside the well of her jacket. "I think math should serve as a science requirement. I mean, it's more important to know how derivatives function than it is to know what rocks come from what region."

"You should know that I got the syllabus and there's very little about natural disasters in biology," I urged. I could kill two birds with one stone. Bo would be forced to partner with someone else, and I would get a best friend back. "Come back and we can be lab partners."

Ellie peered at me from behind her scarf. "No, I'm stuck now. I went and changed my schedule at the admin office and the lady there gave me an angry glare like I was asking for a grade change or something."

"Given that nearly everyone in the class gets a B or above, it kind of is," I pointed out.

Ellie huffed. "I'm a *math* major. I deserve one cake class."

"Maybe I should switch, then." It didn't matter to me what science class I took.

She didn't reply immediately and when she did her voice showed strain. "Yeah, I don't think you'd like it."

Translated: there were too many jocks there, and I'd be miserable.

"Plus," Ellie added, "even if you wanted to, I don't think Dr. Highsmith would allow it. He told me he was only approving the transfer because he didn't think it was healthy that we were joined at the hip."

"Fucking Highsmith. Who does he think he is, our advisor?" I joked. It was weak, but I felt better for making the effort.

By the time we had arrived at the apartment, hunger was overriding anger. "Should we order a pizza?" I suggested.

Ellie hadn't eaten much of anything either. She nodded her agreement, and I ordered while Ellie sank into our couch and flicked on the television. The entrance buzzer sounded thirty minutes later to announce the arrival of the pizza delivery person.

By the time I'd returned with the pizza, Ellie had pulled out napkins and forks and laid them on our coffee table. It was one of those oak things that had curved edges and was designed, I think, for families with small children. Ugly but functional, the table was safe for toddlers and drunken college students. Ellie and I'd spent more than one night passed out in our living room, and never once had we suffered a coffee table-induced injury.

"What was it that Clay said as you walked by him?" I asked her, remembering hearing an odd murmur behind me.

"He called me a carpet muncher," Ellie said, pizza slice halfway to her mouth.

"He's so original. Like eating pussy is some kind of insult," I scoffed.

"It is for him. He's probably the most selfish lover ever. Girls start thinking about being a lesbian because their sexual experience with him was so horrible, they can't stomach the idea of being with another man." Ellie waved her pizza at me, a pineapple cube flipping dangerously on the end.

I sat back. "It's a good thing I turned him down, then, or I'd be after you hard."

"You should seduce Bo and then when he's in your thrall, point him toward the laxer house. By the look of him, he'd be able to take down at least five of them in the first go around. Yum." Ellie licked her lips and I knew it wasn't because the pizza tasted so good.

I avoided the Bo topic and told her instead, "I wish we were lesbians. We'd make a great couple."

Ellie gave a genuine shout of laughter. "Would we take turns wearing the strap-on?"

"No, I'd be the top," I insisted sternly. This only made her laugh harder.

When she finally stopped rolling on the ground, she sat up and wiped the tears from her face. She rearranged her expression into a faux serious look and leaned toward me. "You know what might suck as a lesbian?"

"Your mouth?" I smirked.

"You wish!" Ellie shook her head. "Seriously, though, you know how in *When Harry Met Sally*, Harry says that men and women can't be friends because of the sexual attraction? Well, if you were a lesbian, you couldn't be friends with girls because of the sexual attraction you had toward women and you couldn't be friends with guys because they had the hots for you."

"It's amazing, then, that Sasha has friends," I pointed out.

"Just saying that the natural extension of Harry's theory is that friendship is prohibited between people who could potentially have a sexual attraction toward each other."

"I've seen you puking in the toilet after drinking. That pretty much killed any budding desire I had for you."

"Dude, I wouldn't want to be your girlfriend if you're all judge-y like that," Ellie pouted.

"You don't want to be my girlfriend because you like dick too much," I retorted.

"You, too," Ellie exclaimed and threw a hot pepper flake packet at my head. It struck me right in the forehead and stung for a moment and then we started laughing again. The hurt inflicted by Clay was cleansed by the support of my friend. Ellie never failed to make me laugh at just the right moment.

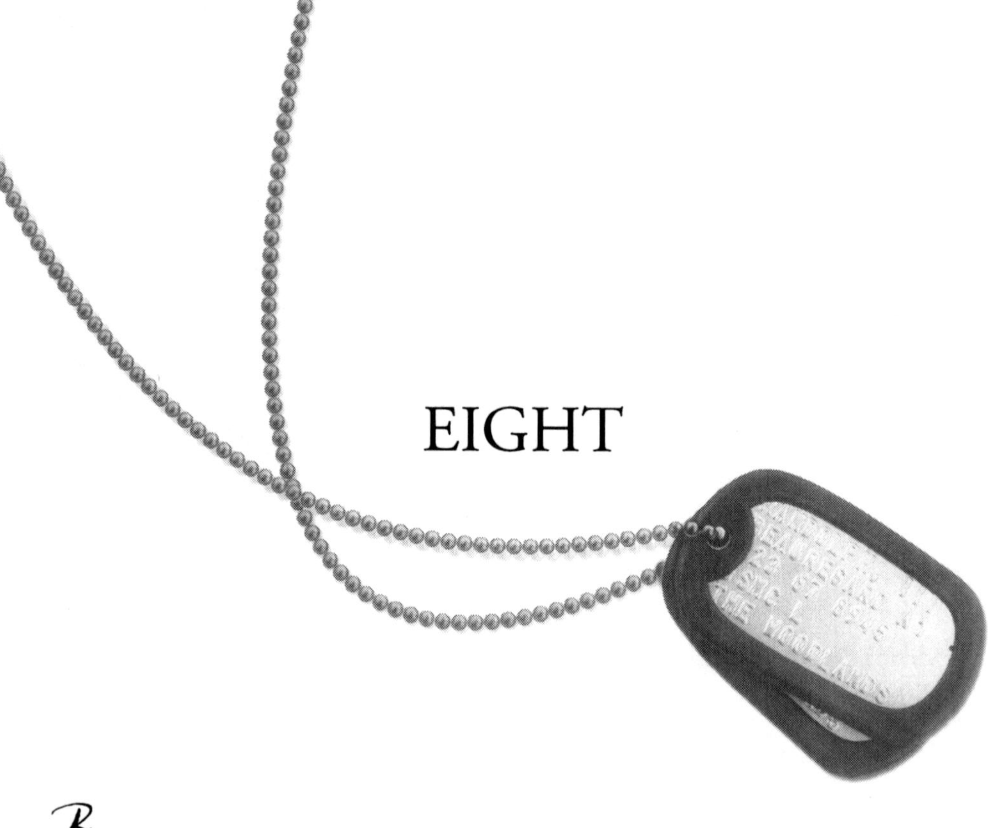

EIGHT

Bo

"So AnnMarie West?" Noah said as we started our run. "Not your usual type." He'd decided to do a predawn run before going over to the gym, leaving Grace asleep in his room. She was starting to be like a sixth roommate with as much time as she was spending at our house. I tried not to be a dick about it, as this was Noah, and he'd spent years pining for this girl.

"I have a type?" I dodged his question.

"Mike Anderson describes your type as 'prime'."

"That guy needs to get laid. Or get a new hobby."

"Apparently you've never transacted business with him before. He was excited to share with Grace." Noah sped up, and we ran as fast as we could for five minutes, and then slowed to a jog. Interval training sucks. I'm not sure why I do it other than it seems like a thing Noah enjoys. "Mike says she has issues."

"Mike says she has issues?" It took Noah about a minute before he realized I'd stopped running.

"What the hell, man?" Noah asked, jogging back to me.

"Since when do you take Mike's word on a woman? Consider the source," I fumed.

"Wow, okay, that was probably not well done of me."

"Not well done? Not well done is drinking the last Shiner Bock and not replacing it."

Noah clapped a hand on my shoulder. "Say no more. You like her; I like her."

"Sorry, just on edge." I rubbed a hand down my face and launched into a pace too fast for either of us to talk.

Noah didn't let it go, because when we arrived back at the house, panting and sweating like pigs, he asked, "So you like this girl or what?"

"Or what," I muttered. I didn't know what I was doing with AM. At first, I thought she'd be a good way for me to pass the time this semester, but after hearing Mike's story and learning about the showdown at the commons, I knew that I didn't want to be one more shitbag in a long line of shitbags she'd encountered at Central.

When I saw her in biology, I noticed things about her I'd missed all last semester. She was careful to walk without touching another person. She didn't acknowledge anyone, not the other students, not the TA, not the professor. She looked straight ahead, focused on one thing, and pretended that the world around her didn't exist.

AM deserved a guy who could act like a grown-up, and I wasn't sure that was me.

But the more time I spent with AM, the more intrigued I became. She was reserved, but as she talked, I could see *her*—her humor and her willingness to challenge me. My "type" were girls who couldn't remember my name the next day. Who were looking for one night of feeling good. Hell, one of the girls I hooked up with over the summer used some other guy's name in bed and cried after she came. She was suffering through a bad breakup, and I didn't mind being rebound guy. We had spent more than a few nights with each other until she kindly told me that while I was the best she ever had, she was looking for something serious and it couldn't be with a guy who made her cry while she orgasmed. I didn't let it bother me. After all, the goal was to feel good, and she did when she left me.

AM was so different than the rest of those girls. She wasn't going to fall into bed for a one-night stand. I had a feeling she'd be reluctant to get involved with me for reasons having nothing to do with my fighting, my past history, or my propensity for hookups. Hell, reluctant was too mild. Scared shitless would be more appropriate.

I had to figure out what exactly I wanted from AM before I spent any more time with her. For both our sakes.

Finn was in the kitchen throwing something together as we walked in.

"Why are you always up so early?" I asked him, waving Noah into the shower. He was heading upstairs, presumably to wake up Grace and take her back to campus. I headed straight for the sink and drank a gallon of water.

"Got shit to do," Finn replied, his mouth half full of scrambled eggs that he must have prepared for himself. Noah and I couldn't cook for shit and if it wasn't for our other roommates—Finn, Adam, and even Mal—occasionally cooking us a meal, we'd eat microwaved foods and take-out only. Actually, I take that back. I could make a mean dessert out of MREs, but other than cereal breakfast escaped me. "Every morning?" I asked Finn, wondering if he would make me some eggs if I asked.

"Yes, every morning. That's what working stiffs do. Get up every morning and work." Finn wiped his mouth with a dishtowel and carried his dishes to the sink.

"But at the asscrack of dawn?" I'd lived with Finn for nearly a year now but didn't know much about him other than that he drove a truck, had a lot of tools, and came home covered in dust and grime. He seemed to work nonstop, kind of like Noah. They both made me tired just listening to their twenty-minute recap at the end of the day.

Mine could fill two minutes, maybe five, if I took the time to describe a few of the chicks in class.

Quickly cleaning the dishes, Finn dodged my question with a repeat of his own, "What's your problem this morning?"

"Are you trying to use the Socratic Method on me? Usually I only allow girls to grill me this hard." I lobbed back a nonsense answer. Finn just shook his head.

"Fine, if you don't want to talk about it, I've got plenty of other shit to do." He wiped his hands and threw the used towel in the laundry room.

"What kind of shit?"

"I'm demoing a house today. Want to come? You can be in charge of knocking down three walls with a sledgehammer," Finn offered.

"That's the lamest come-on I've ever heard," I said, but given that I wasn't allowed to fight anyone decent in Noah's gym, wielding a sledgehammer did sound like a good invitation.

"Ladies like my sledgehammer," Finn replied.

"It's too early for dick jokes." I ran upstairs and threw on some clothes. When I returned, I gestured for Finn to lead us, but he just stood still, looking me up and down. "What's wrong? I'm not pretty enough for you to take to bed?"

"Just wondering if you were going to class in those clothes?"

I looked down at my sweatpants and T-shirt. "Sure, it's not like I'm trying out for best dressed or I'm going to have some points deducted by my frat bros for not wearing the right stuff."

Finn shrugged. "Your funeral, but this stuff gets messy."

Messy sounded good at that moment.

"Hold up," I heard Noah call, followed by thunder on the stairs. He jumped the last four steps and handed me a gym bag. "You can shower at Grace's if you want. There's a key in there."

"Thanks." I took the bag. It was Noah's unspoken apology for earlier.

Finn drove us to the north side of town where a dozen tiny houses looked like the builder had gotten his plans from the Monopoly game. The only thing different about these cookie-cutter buildings was that they weren't all green. We swung into the driveway of one that had been painted white at one time. Nearly every exterior board was peeling and the paint still clinging to the wood was a dingy gray. Shingles hung drunkenly off the side of the roof.

"This house looks like it was fucked six ways from Sunday by the other houses on the street and then left to molder," I observed, unbuckling my seatbelt and hopping out of Finn's truck.

"She looks gorgeous to me," was his reply. I shook my head.

Inside didn't look much better. The kitchen was dirty and the smell of the house was rank. The floor was some kind of plastic that stuck to my feet.

"Smell that?" Finn said, taking a deep whiff. Guy was obviously insane.

"Yeah, it smells like someone was slaughtering animals in here and left the carcasses to rot." I pulled up my sweatshirt to cover my mouth.

"Nope. It smells like money." Finn handed me a sledgehammer and a face mask. The iron hammer was heavy and made me feel like I could knock down the entire structure with one well-placed blow. *AM, Thor here. I'm coming over and bringing my hammer.*

"How's this work?"

"The sledgehammer? You knock shit down with it, like a baseball bat."

"No, dumbass, your house flipping."

"Oh." Finn laughed. "You buy an unrenovated house in good neighborhood for low amounts of money, put a lot of sweat equity into it and not a lot of materials, and sell it for a sweet profit four weeks later."

"Like what kind of profit?"

"I bought this crackerjack box of a house for fifty grand and most of the houses along this road sell for ninety or more. I'll put maybe fourteen grand in upgrades into this place and pocket the rest."

I gaped at him. I had no idea it was so profitable. "You have to pay anyone?"

"Yeah. My crew and my realtor." Finn placed a round white bucket on the floor and pulled out a tool belt, buckling it around his waist. "I used to have a great one, but then Adam slept with her. Now she won't talk to me."

"Ouch." When he shook his head at me, I asked, "What?"

"You and Adam are a lot alike."

"How so?"

"You both have a hard time keeping it in your pants. I know what Adam's problem is. He's trying to live up to his father's legacy. What's yours?"

What was I doing with all those women? I hardly knew anymore. "Trying to forget my father's legacy." That was the best truth I could come up with. Sunk deep in the soft embrace of a woman or feeling the sick give of a man's flesh against my fist were the best ways to forget that I spawned from the gene pool disaster that was my dad. I didn't want to talk to Finn about the fact that the only way I knew how to cope was to fight or fuck. It sounded bad enough when I thought about it. Verbalizing it would only make me look like a two-dimensional caricature.

"You do one a month?" I asked, changing the subject.

Finn cocked his head and eyed me curiously, but answered my question. "Right now, but I hope to be doing four or more a month once I get a few crews running for me. No one else will show up before nine, so for the next three hours, it's just you and me."

Finn showed me the supports he'd jacked into place to hold the ceiling up when the walls came down. "Take the tip of the sledgehammer and poke it through the sheetrock carefully, like you're doing a virgin. Look for wires or ducts. If there's something there, leave it alone. If it's all clear, bang the shit out of it."

"The walls are female?"

"Anything you push a long hammer into is a female," Finn replied, his voice fading at the end as he went down the hall.

When I swung the sledgehammer into the walls, the impact and resulting destruction felt awesome. Almost as good as hitting someone in the face. Definitely not as good as sex. I made quick work of the wall and bellowed for Finn.

"Geez, aggression much?" He inspected my work from the other side. I could see directly into the opposite room, only vertical slats of wood separated the two of us.

"Now what?"

"Now you knock down that wall."

"The boards?"

"Yup."

This demo was the shit. After knocking down the wall, I realized how much larger the house seemed. Before, it was a rabbit warren, with tiny closed-off spaces. Now, I could envision relaxing and having a beer without feeling as if I was going to be crushed like a can in garbage compactor.

We took down one more wall, which required the both of us because on the other side were appliances and stuff that had to be moved first.

"Are some of the houses you flip totally rotten? Like nothing can be salvaged?" I asked him as we wrestled a refrigerator away from the wall.

"No, most houses just need cosmetic work. A new bathroom. A new kitchen. Sometimes new flooring."

"But sometimes the house's foundations are destroyed?"

"Some homes have termites or mold or stuff and require some structural work, but there are few that can't be salvaged."

"But some of them, right, should just be razed to the ground?" I pressed.

"No, Bo, most of them can be salvaged," Finn said quietly, seriously.

"Almost all of them can. They may have been put together by shoddy builders, but they can almost always be saved."

That was in Finn's estimation, but I heard what he was trying to say, just as he had accurately interpreted the meaning of my question. *Am I salvageable?*

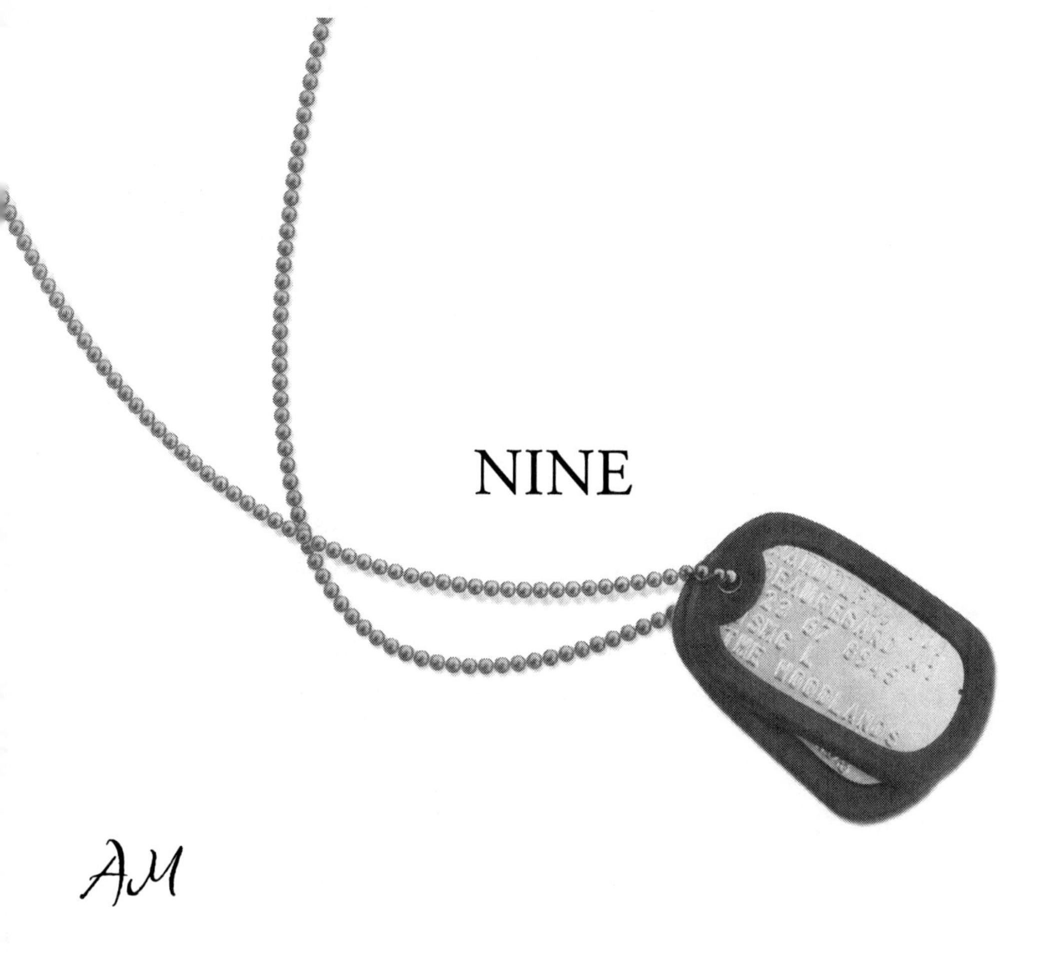

NINE

AM

I RECEIVED ANOTHER NASTY HATE note from Clay and avoided campus for the rest of the week. The commons confrontation left me feeling uncertain and a little afraid, which I absolutely hated. My only solace turned out to be biology. Bo acted as if nothing out of the ordinary had happened. I was still acutely aware of his presence next to me in the classroom, but his broad shoulders acted like a buffer between me and the rest of the students. No whispers reached us. No cutting remarks were cast my way. He waited for me outside the classroom and walked me down to our shared table. After class, he escorted me out.

Never once did he bring up the commons incident and other than his watchfulness before, during, and after class, his treatment of me was quite ordinary. Whatever rumors he'd heard about me, he seemed to be saying silently, mattered not at all.

I could feel myself thawing toward him, yearning for him. I knew it was dangerous, but I needed something sweet in my life. If I didn't act on my longings then I'd be safe. When he turned to share a smile at me over the nonstop innuendos during the discussion of fertilization and pollination, I felt hot and prickly. During the discussion of common parasites, we both grimaced. Bo whispered that there wasn't a lot that put him off his feed, but tapeworms in the stomach might be it. He was charming and *decent*, and I could feel myself weakening with every minute that passed. But he also didn't flirt with me, smell my hair, or make a suggestive comment, as he had in the past. More than once, I caught him staring hard at the lecture stage as if he were engaged in some internal struggle.

At the end of the week, Ellie met me for lunch at our usual place off campus with breathless news. "You want to see Bo fight?"

My eyes must have gotten as big as saucers because Ellie laughed. "I'll take that as a yes."

As we stood in line to order, Ellie whispered the details to me. "I heard there's a fight tonight in the warehouse district. Someone is supposed to text me directions."

"Do you have to pay to get in?"

"When Tim and I went, the cover was twenty-five dollars per person and then there are bets made inside. I didn't bet, but Tim did."

I whistled. "Wow. That seems steep. No one complains?"

"Not yet, I guess. Who wants to be the person that shuts something like this down? It would be worse than your ordeal."

"Worse than me?" I grimaced. "Thanks."

"You know what I mean." She lightly punched me on the shoulder. I did. No one welcomed that type of treatment. The guys on campus would be particularly rough. I think fight night was responsible for at least fifty percent of them getting laid.

"So I take it Bo said nothing about it in class yesterday?"

"No. We haven't really talked about anything other than class stuff lately."

"Like?"

"What's more gross—tapeworms in the stomach or parasites in the ear?"

Ellie shuddered. "So glad I took Rocks for Jocks."

"Yeah, that might have been a good decision."

"So you and Bo, in class?"

"There just isn't a ton of time to talk. Plus, he's got more moods than a preteen who just got her period."

"Really? I would never have guessed that."

"I've decided that flirtatious is Bo's default mode and his other setting is broody."

"Still want to go?"

"Hell yeah." When I was a kid, I'd asked my mom why the moths kept moving in droves toward the light, almost hugging the exterior despite witnessing the death of their fellow insects. Mom said that sometimes temptation was just too great to resist. *Zzzzap.* That was me. Bo was the light and I was the dumb moth.

Ellie was prattling about the details of the fight she'd gone to with Tim. We had to stick together, she said, because mini fights could break out in the crowd.

"Do you bring something to drink?"

"They don't sell it, and Tim brought a flask when we went. No one's doing a bag check there."

I'M NOT SURE HOW BO spotted Ellie and me in the crowd. People were packed into the space. I had a hard time believing something this well attended could remain a secret, but we were told nothing illegal was going on here. This was private property, and we were all invited to the party. The cover was actually a donation, per the bouncer's instructions.

A stamp in the form of a clenched fist was slapped on the backs of our hands, but we were warned that if we left, we would have to repay the money if we wanted to come back inside. The point of the stamp was never explained, but I wasn't going to ask anyone with arms the size of my thighs and no apparent neck why I needed a mark on my hand.

The fight was being held in the basement of a restaurant in the East Village. The owner was a friend of the guy who set up the fight and more than one underground shindig took place here, although never more than once in a month or even once every six months. The fights required some luck and coordination. Or at least that was what I gleaned from listening to the crowd around me.

I didn't know when Bo was fighting or even if he was fighting. It was only rumor. Even tonight, inside the building, there were just hopeful mutterings. But rumor became reality when he walked in and his name was carried on a wave of whispers from one end of the long narrow room to the other. I saw him almost immediately, the bangs of his messy blond hair peeking out from the front of his sweatshirt hood. The basement was lit by a string of bare lightbulbs strung like hormonally enhanced Christmas lights along the sides of the rock walls. Toward one end, a number of what looked like halogen lights hung from the ceiling, brightly illuminating a single space. That must be the fight ring.

It smelled musty and earthy, as if we were in a cave rather than underneath a ritzy establishment. I wondered what the patrons upstairs, in their pearls and worsted wool, would think if they knew that behind the wine racks and cheese rounds, two guys planned to beat each other bloody. Probably they'd be thrilled. Maybe everyone knew and this was part of the cachet?

Ellie had found a barrel we could share against the wall. While it was farther away from the center where the fight would take place, the barrel allowed us elevation and a heightened sight line. Or, in simpler terms, we could just see a heck of a lot better by standing on the barrel. I tracked that blond head moving in and out of the crowd until it stopped right before me and the barrel. My legs gave out and I sat down before I fell off.

Bo had on a zipped hoodie with the hood flipped up. The sketchy lighting and hood made his appearance seem nefarious. Maybe that was the point, though. For some reason, I felt compelled to reach up and push his hood off. It was a brazen, forward act. He looked at me with surprise I'm sure was echoed in my own eyes. I'd never initiated any contact with him, I realized, not physical or emotional. I was always reacting to him, and he was always pushing me.

He raised his hand to capture mine, but not because he wanted me to stop pushing off the hood. No, he held my hand in his and used it to draw me down from the barrel. I didn't see who was with him or how Ellie was reacting. In spite of the crowd, with him only inches away, we seemed cocooned from everyone else.

"I didn't know you were into this sort of thing," he murmured. He placed my hand on his chest and leaned toward me, one hand bracing against the top of the barrel right next to my thigh and another against the wall. The vibrations of his words teased me. The heat of his body warmed me. Desire took control of my body and I watched as my fingers clasped his sweatshirt zipper and pulled downward, just a bit. Just enough so that my hand could touch his shirt, so I could feel the flex of his muscular pectorals against my fingers. I ran my fingertips over the ridged cotton of his tank. His muscles flexed and released when I kneaded my fingers against his chest.

"I don't know if I am into this sort of thing," I said hoarsely, looking at my hand as it followed the rise and fall of his chest. I was mesmerized, enthralled, by his simple act of breathing. A cough sounded, and I was jolted out of my mini trance. Snatching my hand away, I noticed Ellie staring at me, her mouth forming a comic little *O*.

I pulled my hands together and clenched them front of me, grateful the darkness hid the heat in my cheeks. Bo leaned down to my ear. His breath was warm and his voice, deep and strong, raised the hair on my neck. "We'll have to test the hypothesis. I'll ask again when it's over."

As he drew back, it felt like his lips dragged across the top of my lobe, and a shiver shook me from head to toe. He removed himself slowly, one arm pushing upward and off the barrel. I looked at him and bit my lip, trying to suppress any dumb statements. He grinned and brought his thumb up to draw my lower lip out of my teeth and rubbed his thumb over the abused area. My lip plumped up under his ministrations.

I wondered for a breathless, endless second whether he was going to kiss me, here in front of all these people, but he didn't. Instead, he motioned for Ellie to get down from the barrel. Bo introduced us to his two male friends, whom I'd barely noticed. Finn, whose hair looked black as tar, and Mal, dark and serious, both gave us chin nods of acknowledgment.

Bo pulled me behind him through the crowd. Ellie grabbed the belt loop on my jeans and we proceeded forward like a mini conga line.

Bo's progress was unimpeded as person after person stepped aside. We reached the makeshift ring that was simply movie theater metal stands at four corners with rope tied between them. The posts were unstable, which was probably why there was a large guy stationed at each one to shove the crowd back. Bo led us over to one corner manned by a bald man with a dark goatee.

The two executed a complicated hand exchange before Bo introduced us. "Phil, this is AnnMarie and Ellie. Okay that they stand here tonight?"

Phil nodded. Bo turned to me. "Stay close to Phil. The crowd can get rowdy. I don't want you punching anyone out."

"Ha ha. What about Phil? I could hurt him. Who'll protect him?"

"Ellie?" Bo looked at my friend. She flung her arm up and around my shoulders.

"Dude, we girls stick together. Phil is toast if this thing goes sideways."

"Well, Phil, you're on notice then." Bo slapped Phil on the back. Phil just grunted, obviously unamused by our banter. Bo and his friends went down to another corner. Finn peeled away from the group and crossed diagonally to speak with two others, one Bo's opponent. There was nodding, talking, and a shaking of hands.

"What was that about?" Ellie hissed at me.

"I don't know." I raised my palms and shrugged. I couldn't explain what had just happened, neither my actions nor Bo's.

"Want to bet something?" a person at my elbow asked. I turned and a guy about my height waved a pen at me. He had a wad of cash stacked behind a little notebook. I shook my head, but Ellie pulled a twenty out of her pocket and handed it to the bookie.

"Twenty dollars on Bo Randolph."

"Three to one odds there. Other guy's more lucrative."

Ellie shook her head. "Why bet against the house?"

"Fine. Name?"

"AnnMarie West."

"What?" I protested, but the bookie was already moving on to the next set of people.

Ellie just grinned and shrugged. Phil looked stoically ahead. I wondered how he, instead of the guy opposite him, got stuck babysitting us. I didn't have much time to ruminate because the bookie went out into the middle of the ring. For a small guy, he had a booming voice. He twirled around, as if he was emceeing a big Vegas fight. His arms were outspread as he spoke.

"We're about to begin. Book is closed. There are no rules. Fight until the other taps out."

As if by practice or rote, the crowd roared back in unison, "There are no tap outs."

I looked to Ellie for an explanation. "Tapping out means surrender, like the white flag," she whispered to me.

"So they aren't allowed to tap out."

"I think so. I mean, at the fight I went to, the other guy waved his hand or something, and Bo climbed off and the bookie guy announced him the winner. I didn't see the tap out but I guess someone signaled something."

I was worried now. "Does it mean that someone could die down here? Like from a blow to the head?"

"Technically, I guess."

We both looked to Phil. As if it took more effort than he had inside of him, Phil expelled a sigh and said, "Guys in the corner will tap out for the fighter if he can't or won't tap out."

"Like Finn or Mal?" I asked

I received a short nod in return. My chest tightened as I stared into the well-lit square that was waiting for the fighters. There were stains in the concrete. I wondered if it was blood from previous fights. I didn't want to see Bo get hurt. What was I doing here? It's not like I was a pacifist, but I'd never watched anyone fight. Ever. And I'd never seen anyone hit in real life. I put my hand to my stomach, as if that could quell the queasiness. In Bo's corner, Mal stood off to the side using his body to create some space between Bo and the pressing members of the crowd, who looked like they wanted to be in the fight, not just watch it. Finn was wrapping Bo's hands in white tape or wraps.

"Will they wear gloves?" I asked.

Ellie shrugged. "I don't think so." We both looked to Phil, who pretended he didn't hear us.

Bo looked up, as if he could sense me watching, and winked. He unzipped his hoodie the rest of the way, exposing his tank and well-defined biceps. Even from across the square, I could see the veins in his arms standing proud of his muscles, as if there were barely room for the arteries under his skin. He flung his arms out, crossing them in front of him, stretching his back and chest and arm muscles. Each movement accentuated the sculpted perfection of his body. He had jeans on and some weird soft shoes. My eyes swung to the opposite corner.

Bo's opponent's head, like Phil's, was bald, with a tattoo of a skull encompassing the sides and top. The pain from getting a head tattoo seemed to me like it would be unbearable. My eyes watered when I was just brushing my hair. Bo was in for a tough time with this guy. Skull Man, as I'd mentally dubbed him, was shirtless and wore jeans as well. His feet were bare.

"Do they have to wear shoes?" I asked Phil, despite his previous attempts to ignore us entirely.

"No, you can wear whatever you want."

Right, of course. This was no-holds-barred, no-rules fighting. Wear what you want. Don't tap out, even if you are going to die. Mal ran down the line toward us and handed me Bo's sweatshirt.

"Hold on to this, sweetheart, will you?" Mal said with a wink and took off before I could say a word. I looked down at the sweatshirt and then, because I had this weird feeling I would feel safer if I wore it, I shrugged it on. I looked toward Bo again, and he gave me a nod of approval or acknowledgment. The gesture warmed me as much as the material of the sweatshirt. The clean male smell of him surrounded me, and I felt a little more at ease.

There was no time for more nonverbal communication. The bookie announced the fight was on, and Bo and his opponent, Skull Man, advanced toward each other. There was no desultory greeting in the middle. Instead, the two danced around each other, sizing each other up. I wished I knew more about Skull Man, but I wasn't getting anything out of Phil. I leaned back into the crowd, hoping to catch the threads of other conversations. About two feet behind Ellie, I honed in on two guys arguing about which of the fighters was better. I took a step back to hear better.

"Randolph's got a wicked left."

"That's all he's got, though. Parker nearly beat him last time, and his corner tapped him out too early."

"Randolph's too hamstrung by principles. Parker's willing to put several hits to the back of the head if that's what it's going to take to bring Randolph down."

The conversation wasn't making me feel confident for Bo. I glanced over to the fight ring but couldn't see well. The crowd had closed the void I'd made when I moved backward. Despite being relatively tall for a woman, I was still too short to have a complete view and could only see some of the fight when the two guys moved into a small viewing space. I tried to push my way forward but was repelled by the crowd. The fighting had lit a fever and the crowd pushed closer in toward the ropes. The top of Ellie's hair was just visible to me, but she was engrossed in the fight. Phil was actually talking to her from time to time.

I slid over to the side so there was only one person between Ellie and me. I peered through the shoulders and saw Bo ducking and weaving and backing away. His movements were more graceful than I'd imagined. He could skate backward on his feet without losing balance and then press forward with a short kick or a blow with his fist.

"Randolph's ducking more. That blows." I heard the two chatty ones. They were disappointed there wasn't bloodshed already.

"Fuck. This isn't a polka. Someone get hit already."

The fight was like a choppy film reel with images being shuttled in and out of the frame. I moved from side to side to get a better view. Bo stalked forward and Skull Man circled backward. They moved out of sight and the crowd roared. When the two came back into view, I saw a stream of blood down one side of Skull Man's face. Skull Man moved forward with a flurry of punches and one seemed to rock Bo backward, and he retaliated with an elbow. Bo caught Skull Man around the neck with his left arm and punched Skull Man with his right fist four or five times in rapid succession. Skull Man returned a few glancing punches, that caused Bo to release him. When Skull Man stumbled backward and appeared dazed, the crowd began chanting "Don't tap. Don't tap."

Blood was everywhere, down Skull Man's eye, nose, shoulders, and even down his back. Skull Man gathered himself and rushed Bo and the two rammed each other headfirst. The collision of the bodies caused the crowd to shout its approval. The fighters grabbed each other by the neck, and it appeared that Bo was trying to slip behind Skull Man's back. Skull Man twisted in Bo's grip.

They separated and circled. Sweat, blood and who knows what else dripped to the floor. In a blur of movement, I saw Bo rush Skull Man and pull Skull Man's head down into the triangle of Bo's right arm. With his left arm, he pulled down on his right bicep.

"The Anaconda choke," I heard the man in front of me say in approving tones to his friend.

"Yeah, cuts off the blood flow on both sides of the neck." Clearly this was a good move, but it sounded terrible.

Bo squeezed tightly, his muscles straining with the effort. I glanced down at Finn, who looked almost bored. The opposite corner all wore worried looks and for a moment, I thought someone in Skull Man's team would throw up the white flag. But they didn't.

Bo must have been waiting for it, and when it didn't come, he shoved Skull Man away with a disgusted gesture.

"See, he's got a weak stomach," chatty Cathy in front of me said. "It's why he's not in the UFC with his buddy Noah."

"He's got fists like iron, though," replied the friend.

"He'll need it against Parker. Parker's got a head harder than granite."

Bo shuffled backwards, allowing Skull Man to gather himself. Skull Man shook himself like a dog and then threw himself, fists first, toward Bo.

I wanted to look away, afraid the next injury I'd see would be Bo's, but I couldn't. The blood sport unfolding in front of me, frame by frame, was arresting. With each blow, it seemed like the crowd felt it, rocking back on its heels and then from side to side. Bo advanced with a flurry of punches, but Skull Man wouldn't go down. He was like an automaton. I held my fingers to my mouth. I wanted a bell to ring or something to pause the fight, but this wasn't an event taking place on Pay Per View with referees and officials. This was some illegal underground fight club with no rules and someone was going home tonight hurt badly. At this point, I just wanted it to not be Bo.

The crowd parted, momentarily, and I shot forward to grab Ellie's hand. She turned to me and pulled me forward, which displaced a couple of guys at the rope line. One of them was unhappy and a push in my back toppled me into Ellie. Her movement and mine, along with the crowd's push from behind, forced Phil off balance. With that infinitesimal opening, the crowd surged forward, making the fighting area even smaller. Pushing and shoving began to occur within the crowd and Phil, realizing that he'd lost the line, pulled Ellie and me close to him as he maneuvered toward the back of the room. The fighting in the crowd began in earnest after a huge roar erupted. Elbows were flying, some being thrown by Phil himself.

"Fight's over," Phil said, explaining as he was pulling us backward. "Everyone's a little chippy at the end of the fight."

"Who won?" I yelled. Phil ignored me and Ellie merely shrugged her shoulders.

Phil lifted Ellie and then me onto a barrel similar to the one that we'd been sitting on when Bo first walked in. This time we stood to avoid Phil from crushing our legs. He planted himself in front and repeatedly diverted the crowd by pushing them away.

"Was it like this when you and Tim were here?" I yelled at Ellie above the din. She grinned madly and nodded.

"Crazy, isn't it?" It was crazy. Adrenaline was an airborne drug here. Everyone was affected, and I wasn't exempt. I could feel it coursing through my body, making me think of things—want things—that I shouldn't. I could feel it in my fingertips, my throat, and that ever-dampening place between my legs. I squeezed my thighs together, but I wasn't sure if it was to increase sensation or make the feeling go away.

Bo's coterie stood at the edge of the lighted ring. It looked like the bookie was handing him something, probably money. Then the music that had been playing suddenly stopped and the dimly lit bulbs all brightened. The sudden lack of a soundtrack and the bright lights acted like a bucket of cold water and the mini squabbles that had broken out seemed to die down immediately. People began to be herded out the door.

"Where does everyone go from here?" I asked Ellie.

"Usually to the downtown bars, only Tim and I had to go home." She waggled her eyebrows at me.

"Why did you ever break up with him?" I shook my head at her. It seemed like fight night and what came after ranked among Ellie's college highlights.

"One can't live on sex alone," Ellie quipped. This made Phil turn his head to look at Ellie, and she leaned down to pat his shoulder. "No matter how hard you try."

"Maybe you aren't doing it with the right guy?" Phil offered.

"Is that an invitation?"

Phil's response was delayed by a long look up and down Ellie's body. Then his lips curved upward into what should have been a grin, but maybe rusty from disuse, it looked more like a sideways grimace.

"You look like a lot of work to me."

"Everything worth having takes time in the acquiring." Phil made no verbal response, but the two stared at each other for some time.

"What about Ryan?" I whispered to Ellie.

"He's a laxer." She glared, but I thought I detected a hint of dejection.

Phil's attention was diverted by his phone. In response to a text message, he turned around and pulled us off the barrel, almost pushing us out into the back alley where people were dispersing fairly rapidly.

"Can you guys go wait in Continental?" Continental was a bar next door.

"What about my money?" Ellie asked.

Phil grunted, texted someone a message, and then replied, "Someone will bring it to ya at the Continental."

Ellie nodded before I could formulate a response and dragged me off. Inside, we found a table at the back of the bar and sat down with our drinks.

"How long are you thinking of staying?" I asked.

"What? Until closing time." Ellie looked miffed.

"Really?" I was coming down off an adrenaline high and wondered what exactly I was doing wearing Bo's sweatshirt and ostensibly waiting for Bo and his crew to come in. Reason was creeping back in and telling me to get out. Now. Sensing my agitation, Ellie grabbed my arm to keep me from fleeing.

"What's so wrong with giving Bo a try?"

"I'm just not ready for that kind of hurt, Ellie." I lightly shook off her grip and traced my finger in the pool of condensation formed from our beer glasses. My impulse-driven behavior in the dark of the basement seemed unwise now.

"Don't be a fatalist. This could be amazing."

"How?"

"You could date him, sleep with him, go back onto campus with him on your arm."

"Like I'm a big game hunter? Do I mount the condom on my backpack?" I mocked. "Or I could sleep with him, have him blab it all over campus, thereby ensuring at least a decade more of therapy."

"You can't live like every guy at Central is going to run naked down the campus yelling that they've just bagged you."

I shook my head slightly. "I'm not living like that. I just don't think that the first time I take my training wheels off, I should get on a motorcycle."

"I still think you should give Bo a try."

"I agree." I heard a voice behind me say. A large male hand appeared next to mine and my eyes traveled up the corded muscles to the cuff of a gray T-shirt. Bo.

I wrenched my eyes from the arm and glanced at Ellie, who just rolled her eyes at me. A rustling noise made me look around. Bo's friends were gathering chairs and carrying a table back to us.

A number of people were following them. The little back room of Continental was soon swelling with people slapping Bo on the back if they were male or trying to sidle closer if they were female.

The guy with the inky black hair came and sat next to me, reintroducing himself as Finn O'Malley. He lived with Bo and three other guys.

He handed some cash to Ellie. "Phil told me I owed the cute chick with the braids some money."

Ellie waved the money in front of me. "We can fund our drinking tonight."

"Go hustle the guys at the pool table." I laughed and pushed her toward the front where pinball machines lined the wall next to two pool tables. Turning to Finn, I asked, "So you all live together in some mansion in the suburbs?"

I was wildly curious about this infamous party house. The Woodlands parties had been going on since the summer before and were gaining near-mythic status on campus due to their exclusivity. A select few Central students, mostly girls, attended parties out there. Rumors abounded about what went on there. Some said that they hired strippers and people just had sex on the pool loungers and in the kitchen and on the dance floor. It sounded more like an underground sex club at times than a party house.

"Yeah, my dad is a developer and someone skipped out, just walked away from the house, so the guys and I finished the house with a little help and took over the mortgage."

"That happens even in the richer neighborhoods?" I asked with some surprise.

Finn nodded, drained his bottle, and waved for the waitress to bring another. "Why haven't I seen you out there?"

"I tend to stay away from campus events," I admitted.

"We aren't campus events. We're townies. Except for Noah and Bo. They're transplants and solely responsible for all the coed strange that wanders out to our little abode."

"Is Finn trying to con you into coming to our house?" A new voice broke in. "Noah Jackson. I had Advanced Economic Theory with you last semester." He stuck out his hand. If Bo was the god of northern thunder, Noah was his dark opposite. I could see why yoga class was full during prime dinner hours if Noah and Bo were in a neighboring room, flexing and sweating.

"AnnMarie West." I tucked a strand of my hair behind my ear. "Didn't you come to the fight?"

Noah grimaced. "Can't. If I get caught there, I might be suspended from the UFC."

Finn explained, "Noah's fighting professionally. Can't be caught at an unsanctioned event, let alone an illegal fight."

"Why is it illegal if both guys agree to be there?"

"The fighting isn't exactly illegal; it's the betting that goes on around it."

"So we could all go outside right now and Bo and Noah could fight and no one could arrest them?"

"Maybe for public disturbance or something, but not for assault."

"So what's with the 'first rule of fight club is that there is no fight club'?"

"Because *Fight Club* wasn't just about fighting, it was the reclamation of self. There are still fight clubs around where they don't allow spectators. If you come, you come to fight." This was from Bo. He came up behind me, lifted me out of my seat, and sat, pulling me down on his legs.

"Gee, if you wanted my chair, I could have moved."

"Who said I wanted your chair?" He tipped back a bottle of beer and drained about half of it. These guys made beer bottles look like baby bottles with how fast they downed the alcohol. I was tipsy just from all the fumes.

"Where's Grace tonight?" Bo directed the question to Noah, who fiddled with his beer.

"She's studying. I'll meet up with her later."

"Friday night?"

Noah just shrugged, sidestepping the question, and asked his own instead. "How'd the fight go?"

"Guy was a bleeder. I hit him above his eye twice and he started gushing all over the place, down his face and onto his shoulder. I was skeeved out. Worse, he wouldn't tap out. Had to put him down after that," Bo said matter-of-factly. "What'd you think of it, Sunshine?"

What did I think of it? "Primal and brutal."

"That sounds about right." Bo pulled my body closer to his even as I tried to place some distance between us. Sitting on his rock-hard thighs was doing crazy things to my nervous system.

"Can I get you something more to drink?"

Unsure, I nibbled on my lip. I already felt intoxicated, and I wanted to avoid doing something crazy, like attacking Bo in the bar. "How about water?"

He slapped a hand on the table and said, "I'll be right back." He lifted me off his lap, stepped aside, and set me back down, like I weighed only two ounces. I'd be lying if I didn't say that the show of strength wasn't a total turn-on. God, everything about him was a turn-on. I needed to put some space between us. With concerted effort, I dragged my gaze from Bo's back as it disappeared into the crowd. I turned to see Finn wiggle his eyebrows at me suggestively.

"Finn O'Malley is a really Irish name." I looked over his dark hair and creamy, freckle-free complexion.

"I'm actually more Welsh than Irish, which accounts for the black hair, but I still have the propensity to burn if I'm outdoors for more than five minutes. But I do have these vampiric good looks." He waved his hand down his fit body, the tight shirt showing how nice the goods would be without the cotton covering.

"So why would your party be better than a house party over at Central? Lots of wild shit goes down there." When I first got to campus, I spent three nights a week partying hardcore with Ellie. There was everything from three-story beer bongs to human chess games. We came home smelling like we had bathed in the refuse at a brewery.

"I like to think we have a more elevated form of bacchanalia," Finn quipped. "You should come see for yourself."

"What special events will occur if I do?" I smiled. The banter with Finn was easy and nonthreatening.

"Me, of course. Once you've seen my delectable form in my natural habitat, every other guy will look dull and unformed to you." Bo's hand appeared heavily on Finn's shoulder. "Especially this guy."

"Are you poaching on my territory?" Bo squeezed Finn's shoulder.

Finn leaned toward me. "Bo's still stuck on level three of the evolutionary scale."

"I have biology with him three times a week. I know this."

Finn grabbed the pool cue Bo was holding. "I'm just keeping your seat warm."

Bo had apparently had enough of this banter because he shoved Finn off toward the pool table and handed me the water he'd fetched for me. He sat down in the recently vacated seat and placed one arm across the table. The way he positioned his body, I could barely see the rest of the bar. He had, effectively, culled me from the herd.

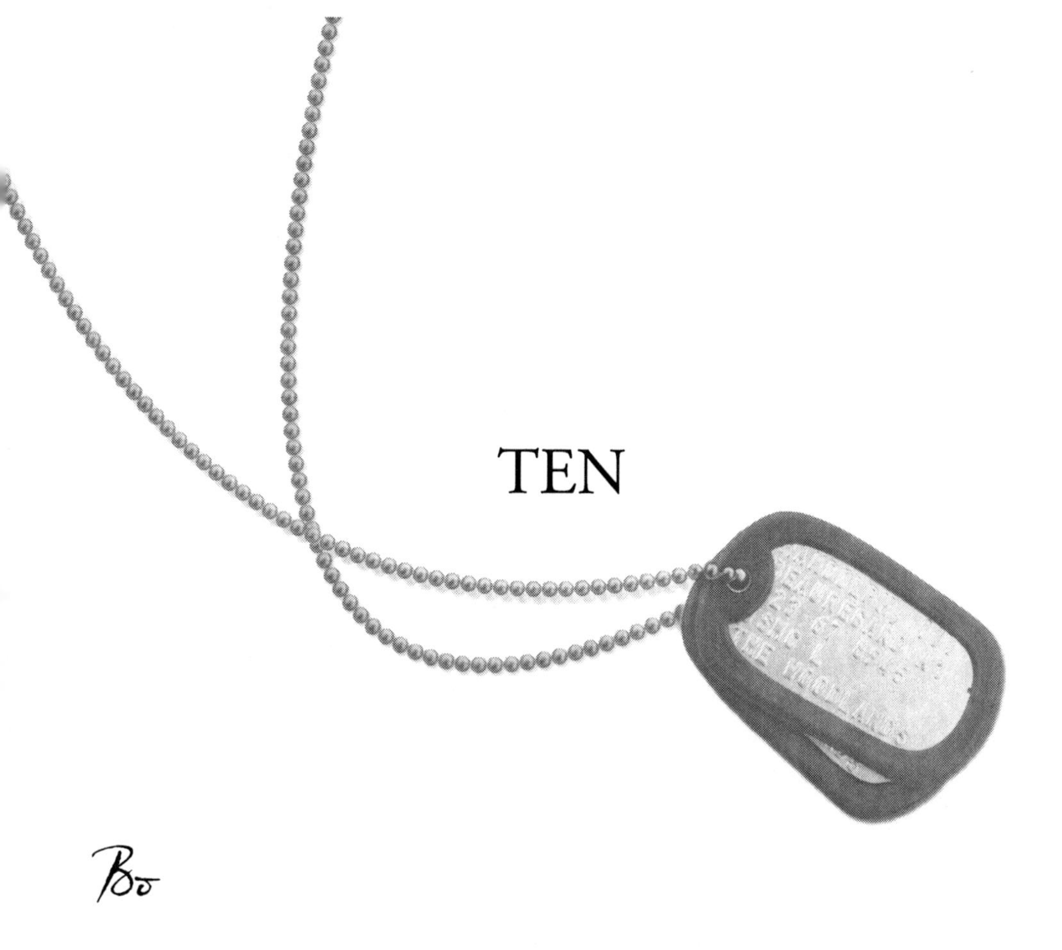

TEN

Bo

AM LOOKED READY TO BOLT, and while I appreciated Finn keeping her occupied, something rebelled in me when I saw the easy banter between the two. Finn would never break the bro code, so it was ridiculous to feel like I needed to piss a circle around her. But I wanted to, and the squeeze on Finn's shoulder might have been overly tight. In biology, I felt like I had AM to myself, all cozy in the front at our end of the table. But unlike my previous interactions with the opposite sex, I felt uncertain about how to approach AM without her thinking I just wanted sex. Because I *did* want sex, but I was pretty sure I wanted more than that. How much more, though, was a mystery to even me.

"Did you enjoy it?" I leaned my elbow on the table so that AM could see only me. Given our closeness, I was glad I took the time to take a sink bath. I didn't want to drip sweat or blood on her while trying to convince her I was worth her time.

She sucked in her lower lip, and I had to grit my teeth to keep a groan from escaping. Was there any non-crass way to tell her I could suck on that for her? Probably not. It was a good thing she wasn't still on my lap or she'd realize that my mind wasn't on what she thought of the fight but on how I'd like to test out the theory of how she'd look in my bed, her brown eyes heavy lidded with after sex happiness and her chocolate-colored hair in a tangle from my fingers. I tightened the grip on my beer bottle and drained it.

"It was exciting. How'd you get started?"

That was a loaded question and not one I was ready to answer truthfully, so I lied and said, "When I met Noah in seventh grade."

"This should be good," she said, propping her elbow on the table. She rested her head on a bent hand and looked at me as if the whole world was centered right in front of her. I felt something shoot through my body and this time it wasn't arousal. I knew what it felt like to get hard. This was different, better than ordinary sexual excitement. Her concentrated gaze made me feel not just wanted, but, well, *good.* Somehow I knew if I screwed this up with AM, I'd regret it forever. But she had to know me and what I was made of, so I took a deep breath and began to tell her about the first of my flaws.

"My momma drove me to school, but Jackson rode the bus. I remember him getting off the bus that first day of junior high looking like a badass motherfucker, and I didn't like it. I was the baddest guy in school. So I went up and punched him in the gut."

"He didn't say anything to set you off?" She shot a glance around me at Noah, who shook his head.

"Nope, not a word," Noah said.

"He looked at me wrong," I explained. "But he punched me right back and pretty soon we were rolling around in the dirt, like two pigs fighting over an old corn cob, dirty and snorting like animals. We were separated and sent to detention. The teacher made us sit next to each other. Jackson was tapping his pencil against the desk and it was pissing me off, so I grabbed it and snapped it in half. He looked like he wanted to snap me in half. But he couldn't, not with the teacher sitting right there. So he grabbed the pencil back and tucked the broken halves away and didn't say another word to me."

"It was my only pencil," Noah offered.

"Right, so not only had I been a dick, but I'd broken this kid's only pencil. I was lower than the pig I'd been acting like, so I apologized and Jackson nodded. When the teacher left for some errand, Jackson leaned closer and said, 'You know who really needs a beatdown?' 'No,' I said. 'Ricky Cartwright.' Ricky and Jackson had attended the same elementary school, and Ricky had a bad habit of trying to pull down girls' skirts and shorts and expose their underwear.

"I told him, 'Now you're talking.' So we got Ricky Cartwright, beat the living snot out of him, and told him if we ever caught him within five feet of a girl, he'd be singing tenor in the swing choir forever. He scuttled around for the next five years. Not sure what he's doing now."

"He's still afraid of us, but now he's working at the gas station," Noah confirmed. "When I went home over Christmas with Grace, Cartwright nearly pissed his pants when we stopped to fill up the truck. I asked him if he was treating the girls right, and he nodded but couldn't speak."

"Good job." I held out my fist to Noah for a dap of congratulations.

"Wow, avenging the ladies even during the precocious preteen years," AM said, her tone light but mocking. It didn't take a rocket scientist to guess that AM thought that guys standing up for girls was a thing rarer than an eclipse. "Who are you avenging now?"

"No one," I told her. Noah started to interject, but my glare shut his mouth.

Throwing a ten-spot on the table, Noah stood. "I'm out of here. Glad to see you aren't too battered."

Noah had the right idea. The stray bits of wet paper from my makeshift clean up in the bathroom stuck to my back. I was desperate for a real shower, but I wanted to make sure that no one else in the bar would sweep in and convince AM they had a better offer than me. "Come on, Sunshine, I'll drive you home." I pulled AM to her feet. Noah looked at us for a moment, trying to read me, read my intentions. Feeling serious about a girl was foreign to me, so I wasn't surprised Noah couldn't figure it out. Neither could I. It was uncharted territory.

AM must have picked up on the unspoken words between Noah and me. She looked at me hesitantly and then, in a tiny motion, took a step closer to me as if declaring her allegiance. I gathered AM close to my side and over her head I saw Noah give me a nod of approval. This was a keeper, he was saying.

"I need to talk to Ellie," AM protested as I tried to hustle her out the back door.

I held back a sigh and said, "I'll get her. Stay here." I took off before she could protest. I spotted Ellie hanging out with Phil and Finn at the pool table. "Finn, can you take Ellie home tonight? Make sure she's okay?"

"No problem," Finn said. "That okay with you, Ellie?"

Ellie took a moment to look me over, as if measuring my worth. I must have passed some internal barometer, because she nodded her agreement but cautioned, "Take care of my girl."

"Always," I replied. Her eyes flared wide at my use of the word, but I didn't correct whatever assumptions she'd made. They might have been right. Something in me had shifted when I saw Finn talking to AM. They were just laughing and joking, but I realized that I wanted to be the one to make AM laugh and feel at ease.

Always. Maybe I wasn't so uncertain. The question was whether I could overcome AM's reservations.

ELEVEN

Bo

I RETURNED WITH A MESSAGE. "Ellie says I should take care of you."

"No woman left behind, you know?" AM said awkwardly.

"No explanations necessary. It's smart," I reassured her. "Finn will make sure she gets home safe."

I put one hand on her lower back as I guided her through the crowd to the bar's rear entrance and held open the door with the other.

"Shit, did you bring a coat?" I pressed the remote starter on my car and hurried us to the vehicle. Even though it wouldn't be heated fully, inside the car was warmer than out here in the cold.

She shook her head and pulled my sweatshirt tighter around her even as she asked, "Do you need this back?"

"No, I'm fine." I wasn't, actually. My Texas blood wasn't well suited for the cold. But there I was in the frozen Midwest, ass-deep in snow at times, with a coat in my closet made of the wool of at least five sheep and wearing two pairs of socks at a time inside my old Marine boots. I once saw some dude tromping in the snow wearing shorts and boots and wanted to go punch him in the face. Wearing the wrong gear in bad weather doesn't make someone look tough. It makes them look stupid.

"What is this car?" AM asked, trailing her fingers across the smooth hood of my sports car. I followed behind and opened the passenger door for her.

"Audi TTS. Three-sixty horsepower. V-eight. All-wheel drive." I ticked off the important components of the car as she swung herself into the seat. When I climbed inside, she was taking deep breaths and stroking the soft leather.

"It feels very luxurious."

"Drove this puppy all the way from San Diego. Got three tickets, got out of three more."

"How'd you manage that?"

"Still had my Marine Corps sticker on the back. Some of the state troopers either were former Marines or knew someone who was and let me go with a warning. Still, insurance is a friggin' bitch."

"Hmm. I may have you drive me everywhere from now on." Her voice had a dreamy quality to it, like she was imagining something really good.

I wondered if AM had any idea how suggestive that sounded. I was guessing no, but if she didn't stop stroking the leather seat, I might have to pull over. Changing the subject before I proved to her that I *was* only one step above the pig I'd described myself as, I asked her, "You ever get in a fight? Learn some self-defense moves?" I wanted to know exactly how the rumors about her had started, if she'd been attacked or something, so that I could figure out how slowly I needed to take things with her. And who I needed to hunt down and destroy.

"Not really. I know they offer some on-campus classes, but Ellie and I have never gone."

"Do you know what a pressure point is?"

"Maybe."

"It's a weak point. Place pressure on it and a girl like you could take down someone twice your size. Like Zhang Zhi."

"Who?"

"Chick from *Crouching Tiger, Hidden Dragon*." At her blank face, I added, *"House of Flying Daggers?"*

"I never would have pegged you for a Chinese art house film buff."

"I'm not. I'm a fight film buff. Chicks throwing down? Even better."

"So I could bring down a guy your size if I knew pressure points?"

"Right. Like this Clay Howard the Third."

At his name, a silence filled the car and I could only hear the muted roar of my 360 horses eating up the pavement between the bar and AM's apartment.

"How do you know his name?" she finally asked. I didn't tell her I'd wrung it from Mike along with her address. Dude did know everything.

"I heard that he hurt you."

"Do you think that Clay *raped* me?" Her voice sounded far away, and I snuck a quick glance in her direction. AM's face was averted, looking out the passenger side window.

My muscles tensed at the word and the image it evoked of AM helpless under some guy's power. "Did he?" I asked through clenched teeth. At the thought of it, I wanted to crush his head between my hands until it popped off.

AM's reply was a short humorless laugh. She said nothing else the entire drive, preferring to look out the window. The smallness of the car's interior placed her close to me, but it felt like we were yards apart. Despite the heated interior, a chill hung in the air—much like the tiny crystals of ice formed on the window by the condensation from her breath. I swung into her apartment complex and parked the car in the farthest back corner, where the lights couldn't reach us. I wanted to hear the truth from AM's mouth because until we had it out, she was never going to let me in.

I didn't turn off the engine and AM didn't jump out like I thought she would. I'd been prepared to chase after her.

"No." The reply was succinct.

"Can you tell me what happened?"

"Why are you scratching at this?" She was upset, her brow furrowed and her mouth pressed in a thin, tight line.

"Because I want to know you," I said.

"What do you think is going to happen if you know the truth? You going to punch everyone at Central who says one bad word about me?"

I'd like to, I thought, but that wasn't the right answer. I struggled for a better one. "You aren't going to give me a chance if I don't know it all."

She knew I was right, but the question was whether she *wanted* to give me a chance. I was asking her to do more than reveal a painful memory. I was essentially asking her for something more than a random one-night hookup. I wanted her to *trust* me. I wanted her to be more than just a lab partner, more than just another warm body between the sheets. I wanted to matter to *her*. These were foreign desires to me, but sometimes my gut was entirely right. Trusting in my instincts had saved my life more than once in Afghanistan.

As the silence hung in the car, my breath seemed to stall in my chest. I feared any movement might startle her into bolting from the car. The quiet became oppressive, and I was afraid it would topple down like a boulder of snow and suffocate us. Maybe the weight of it was too much for AM as well, because she took a deep breath and began to talk.

"I don't remember much about the night. I was invited to the Delta Sig rush party by one of the Thetas. I was thinking of rushing with them. I drank. A lot. I remember taking some guy home with me to my dorm room. I told him it was my first time. We had sex. I don't really remember it. The next morning I was sore. He was gone. There was a tiny bit of blood on the sheets. It wasn't what I'd thought it would be.

"I was so drunk, I didn't know who he was. Only that he was on the lacrosse team. I don't understand why I don't remember him. Maybe I just intentionally blocked it out."

I tried to regulate my breathing, promising myself I would beat the shit out of someone or something later. Getting angry now was only going to scare her.

"I just figured nothing would come of it. It was a drunken party event, and I chalked it up to college. You know?"

She was crying now. I don't think she noticed, but there were tears leaking out of the sides of her eyes, running down her face. The silent but tangible proof of her pain made my heart clench.

"Yeah, I've done my share of stupid things while drunk." My voice was hoarse and raspy. She didn't notice, wrapped up in the torment of her memories. And I'd led her down this path. I couldn't tell her to stop now, that it was too painful to listen to.

"Right." She absently swiped at her tears, dashing them away as if they were nothing more than a pesky mosquito that had landed on her cheek.

"A month or so later, I was walking home alone from a Greek Street party. Ellie had wanted to stay longer, and I was tired. I told her another girl on our floor was going to walk me home. I didn't think, you know, that anything could happen. I got near the Health Center. It's dark there. Clay was coming from the opposite direction with a couple other guys. He stopped me and the other guys went on.

"I didn't know him very well. He backed me up to the brick wall of the Health Center. I can still feel it. The brick was rough against my fingers." She clenched and unclenched her hands. I had to touch her, to pretend like I was providing some kind of comfort. I placed my hand gently over hers, and she collapsed into me.

I breathed a huge sigh of relief, unhooked her seatbelt and tossed it aside, and dragged her over the console and onto my lap. Releasing my seat so it moved as far back as possible, I tucked her face against my chest and wrapped my arms around her. I wished I could enfold her entirely into me and absorb her pain.

"He backed me up," she repeated, as if she could barely believe it had happened. "I'm not sure how he even knew who I was. We didn't have classes together. I don't think I'd even ever met him before. But he said he'd heard I was loose. He stuck his hand on my leg. I had shorts on. He pushed his hand up.

"I pushed it down. He asked me what was wrong. His breath was sour, yeasty, as if he hadn't brushed his teeth that day and tried to wash away the stink with a dozen beers. He tried to kiss me, and I turned my face. He laughed at me and said he didn't know why I was pretending, because his buddy had told him that I was loose. I wasn't a virgin, he said, because I was too loose."

Her face burrowed harder against my chest, and her legs curled up. It was like she was trying to crawl inside me. As I rubbed her back, I cursed the sense of helplessness that rode over me.

"Did he hurt you?" *What a dumbshit question*, I thought. Of course he'd hurt her. But she understood that I meant physically and replied.

"No, his buddies called for him. I don't know if he expected me to have sex with him against the wall of the Health Center or he was waiting for an invitation to my room, but I said nothing and he left.

"So he didn't rape me. He didn't do anything invasive. I actually feel guilty about that," AM confessed. "Like I didn't have a reason to be upset or fearful because nothing really happened. But after that, the whispers started. I didn't realize it at first. I went to class, the library, and parties all fall without realizing that everyone thought I was a slut. It wasn't until someone wrote 'lacrosstitute' on my door in permanent black marker. Someone had pulled the plug in the dam, and after that, I heard it all the time. I couldn't go to a party without some guy trying to feel me up. I was like, meat, or something. Like a cup that they could just pass around."

"Christ, AM, why didn't you leave?"

"I couldn't tell my mother. What would I say? Everyone thinks I'm a slut at the school where Dad's entire family went, so I need to transfer?

"It wasn't the losing my virginity in a drunken stupor. It wasn't being creeped out by a laxer in the dark. It was the lies. The rumors and lies. And you can't combat them. Every guy I spoke with thought I was an easy mark. Every girl thought I was a tramp trying to steal their man. I wasn't good for anything or anybody."

She was full-on sobbing now. Her words were punctuated by catches in her breath as she struggled to get out her story through her cries. I ground my molars together to stop myself from shouting in anger. I wanted to leave right then and there and go to the D-Sigs where most of the lacrosse players were and beat the ever-loving shit out of them. I'd shove their dicks so far up their assholes that they'd only be able to fuck themselves for the next four years.

My muscles were aching from holding her so carefully that she didn't know how much I wanted to bend a steel bar in half. But I wouldn't have let her go for anything.

Pressure points. Fuck me. Of course she knew about pressure points. To hide their shame or their own insecurities, those two lacrosse players had pressed on her weak points and everyone else's and turned the Central campus into a house of horrors for AM.

"Do I win for most embarrassing story ever?" AM's voice was rough from her storm of tears, but her willingness to joke about this only made her more precious to me.

"No," I said immediately, wanting to kill any idea that she should feel ashamed about what happened. "You haven't heard all of mine yet." And never would, I hoped. Blood pounded in my temples when I thought about some of my high-school exploits that I hoped would never reach AM's ears.

"Unfair," she said, nose burrowing into my chest. Her body had lost the stiffness from earlier, and she felt almost pliant in my arms as if she *did* trust me. I shifted her slightly backward so she wouldn't feel my inappropriate arousal and that made her sit up. I felt like an ass and tried to draw her back into my arms but she resisted. Looking around the car, she asked, "Tissue?"

We looked in every crevice but only found one forlorn napkin. "Would you accept one unused but crumpled napkin?" I dabbed her face gently with it. AM allowed it for a second before taking the cloth from me and holding to her nose and sniffing like a kitten.

"I need to go inside anyway," AM said.

Instinctively, I knew that if I let AM out of this car alone, that was it for us. Embarrassment, shame, resentment would all pile up and she'd refuse to do anything not related to our class together. Deciding that I wouldn't let her say no, I opened the door to let her out but grabbed her purse, which was lying on the floor of the passenger side. She wasn't going anywhere without that and, therefore I hoped, without me.

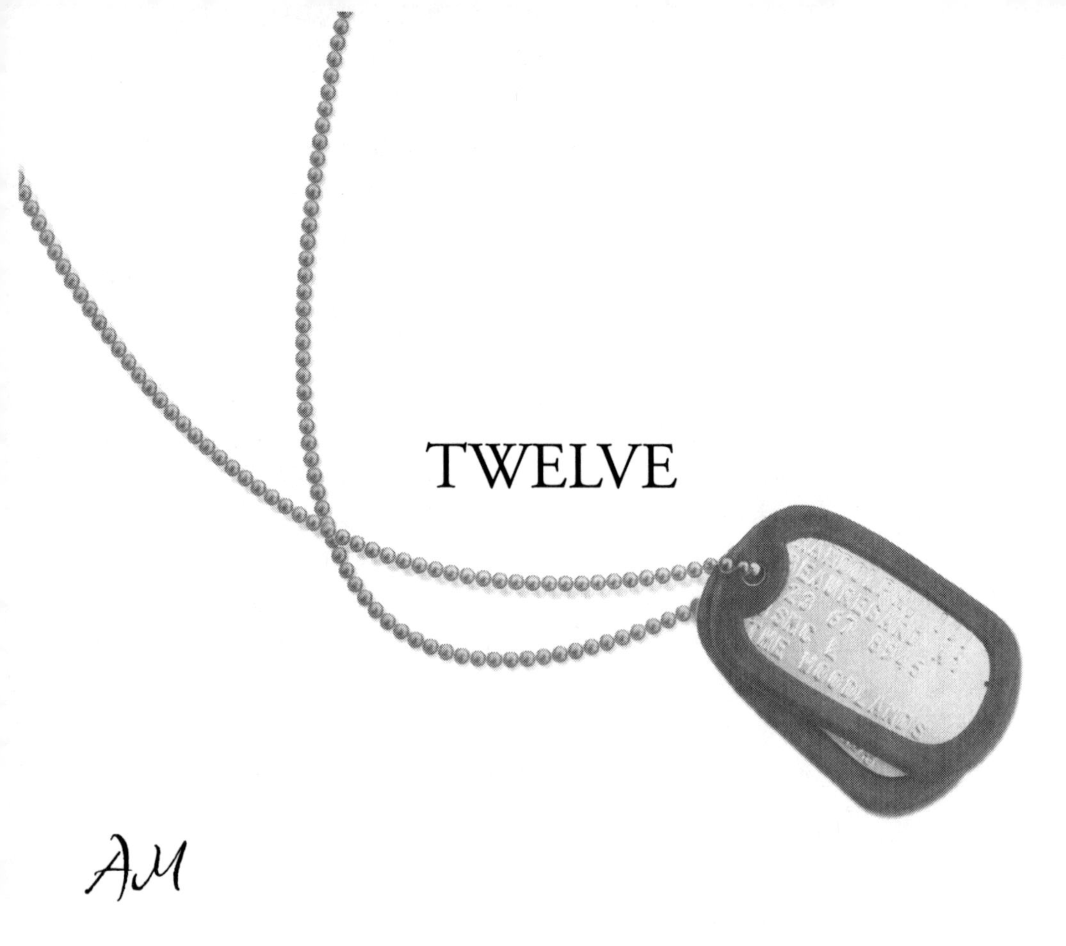

TWELVE

AM

I WAS SO EMBARRASSED BY my breakdown in the car with Bo, I couldn't bring myself to look at him. I wanted to go into the apartment and hunker down and hide for about ten years, until everyone here had forgotten who AnnMarie West ever was. I rushed to the apartment complex entrance, but when I got to the locked door, I realized I'd left my purse in Bo's car. I turned and bumped into his broad, immovable chest. The one I'd just spent the last twenty minutes unleashing a hurricane of tears and snot into.

"Looking for this?" Bo held up my purse. I tugged on it, but he wouldn't let it go. "I'm seeing you upstairs." His voice was implacable.

I frowned, but truthfully, I was feeling so bleak that I didn't want to be in my apartment alone, and I didn't want to ruin Ellie's night out either. Bo held the purse in his firm and unrelenting grip while I rummaged in it to find my keys.

Unlocking the door, I led the way up to my second-floor apartment. I was mentally cataloguing the interior. The living room was mostly clean, as was my bedroom. I might have a few things I needed to toss into a closet, but for the most part, there was nothing in there that would make me cringe. It was silly to even contemplate that some random bra left on the floor could make me blush after what I'd just gone through with Bo.

He followed me upstairs without a word. Once inside, he took in the space with a single gaze and turned back to me. "Couch looks comfortable. Uglier than the backside of a steer, but comfortable."

It was, but I wasn't sure what he was getting at. At my questioning look, Bo enlightened me. "I'm not leaving you alone tonight. I'll sleep on your couch until Ellie gets home, whenever that is."

God, I *was* going to have to call Ellie and interrupt her night out, because there was no way I was getting any sleep with Bo lying out here on the sofa. My intentions must have been clear on my face because Bo made a tutting noise with his tongue. "No, Sunshine, I'm not going anywhere tonight. I want to be here with you, and the sofa is just fine for me."

I could see by the set of his jaw that his mind wasn't going to be changed. Throwing up my hands, I stomped into my bedroom and slammed the door behind me.

I was drained, emotionally. I had no reserves to fight off my own attraction. I couldn't think of an argument to make Bo leave, mostly because I didn't want him to leave. The moment he'd shifted in the car and I drew back, I felt a hundred times worse. I opened my mouth and in the darkness, it had all spilled out. It *had* been embarrassing to cry and to tell him how I'd lost my virginity and how I felt victimized by the toad. But I'd also felt protected and safe, resting my cheek against his marble chest and feeling his arms around me like bands of steel.

I wanted that feeling back right now, but I wasn't prepared to give anything else tonight. I was wiped out and felt less sexy than I did on the first day of my period. Discomfited, I disrobed and got out my nighttime attire, which consisted of a pair of men's boxers, small, and a large men's Central College T-shirt. I pulled out an extra set for Bo and held them up. There was no way he was fitting into the boxers and even the T-shirt might be a stretch for him.

I changed, washed my face, and looked around for a spare toothbrush. I found a travel one my mother had likely stuck in my bag. Setting that out with the T-shirt and shorts for Bo, I opened the bedroom door. He'd shed his shoes and was lying back on the sofa with the TV on. At the sound of the door opening, he sat up and gave me a smile, which, as he took me in, turned to a frown.

I looked down and realized that I had the worst type of sleepwear. He was probably used to satin and lace and other sexy stuff. I plucked at my shirt.

"That's a guy's shirt," he accused.

"No, it's my shirt," I corrected.

"Whose shirt was it originally?" he demanded.

"Um, mine? I bought it at the Bookstore." Immediately his tense shoulders relaxed.

"You bought shirts in sizes that don't fit you?"

"It's comfy." I defended myself.

"As long as it didn't belong to some other guy," he muttered.

"Okay," I said, confused by why the shirt's origins made any difference. I had washed it a million times. There weren't any cooties on it, not even mine. "I've laid out some things for you in the bathroom." I extended my hand into my bedroom to point the way. My bathroom was accessible only via my bedroom. As he advanced, I felt unreasonably nervous. I hadn't ever had a guy other than Brian in my bedroom before, and he really didn't count. The two other guys I'd hooked up with had taken me to their places.

Unlike when he first came into the apartment, Bo took his time looking around my bedroom. My mother and I'd tricked it out with bright pink and green and white linens. I had several throw pillows that never quite made it on the bed and matching curtains. The bed itself was my childhood bed, a double that was quite big for me, but Bo looked like he'd only be comfortable in a king-sized bed.

He looked at the hastily made bed for what seemed like an eternity, then turned his back on me as he walked to the bathroom. The door closed, and I thought I heard a groan.

I rushed over and gave a little knock, "Um, you okay?"

A heartbeat and then a cough. "Yeah. Just dandy."

I went out into the living room to give Bo some privacy but I could still hear the faint sounds of water running and cabinet doors opening. I struck my hand against my forehead. Bo might want to shower. He had, after all, fought tonight. He hadn't smelled sweaty at all, only a musky, manly smell. Delicious and comforting at the same time. I rushed to my closet and pulled out a big bath sheet, thanking my mother silently for splurging on a couple of huge towels.

I knocked again. "Hey, do you want to shower? I have a towel here."

The door opened immediately, and I stumbled back a minute at the sight of Bo without his shirt on and his jeans unbuttoned and unzipped. What had Sasha said about him? My ovaries weren't clenching. They were doing a celebration. Every nerve in my body awoke and reached for him. I swayed a little on my feet, and Bo put out a hand on my shoulder to brace me.

"You okay, Sunshine?"

"Just a little lightheaded," I confessed.

"You get into bed," Bo ordered. I did as he said. There was no resisting his Nordic power at this point. It was like he'd struck me with the mythical thunderbolt. I climbed into bed and he pulled the covers over me. Bending over, he kissed me on the forehead and murmured, "I'll be two minutes."

I lay there dazed and listened to the water of the shower flood on. The shame I'd felt earlier was chased away by the images of Bo flexing and turning in the shower, running his soapy hands over the hills and valleys made by his muscles. I thought of the light hair that dusted his upper chest and the darker trail that arrowed into his jeans. There was a large mark on his back that looked like a tattoo of a winged creature. I wanted to explore it with my fingers and tongue.

I was getting out of bed to get a glass of water to cool me down when Bo came out, shirtless with loose-fitting boxers hanging precariously off his hips. Those weren't my boxers. The light briefly illuminated his fit body, from the wide shoulders to the tapered waist and his powerful thighs. Even his knees looked manly yet attractive. Who thinks knees are attractive?

We stared at each other, the sexual attraction arcing and rising between us like a living, palpable thing. Bo came over, draping the towel around his shoulders. His hand curled around the back of my neck and tilted my head upward.

"How'd you feel if I just held you tonight? No funny business."

Oh, the idea of being held all night by Bo filled me with delight. *This* was the temptation that was too enticing to resist. Zzzzap goes the moth.

"Would that even be fair?" I asked.

He shook his head a couple of times, and I felt tiny drops of water flit across my skin like little fairy kisses. "AM, you don't owe me anything. I *want* to be with you, but only so I can hold you. I'm wrung out from tonight."

"The fight?" I asked, unsure of what had gotten to him.

"Right, the fight," he said, but I think he meant something else. I wasn't brave enough to ask. Instead, I ducked under his hand and moved backward on the bed, lifting the sheets in invitation.

"I'd like that," I admitted reluctantly. "To be held by you."

"Good." He gave his hair another pass with the towel and stepped back into the bathroom. He came out with the extra T-shirt in his hand. "You buy this, too?"

I nodded.

"It's a little on the small side. You mind if I go without?"

"No, it's fine." I curled my nails into my palms. Snuggling only, I reminded myself. Suddenly all my tiredness was chased away, and I felt wired, full of ten cups of coffee on my way through an all-nighter. I'd caught my second wind, being stirred up by lust or something. How was I ever going to sleep?

"I like to sleep near the door, if you don't mind." Bo sauntered over to the bed and climbing in. He slid all the way under the covers and when his leg brushed mine, I jerked. He immediately apologized.

"No, it's all right. It's just been a long time," I confessed. I'd actually slept with my two previous partners less than a handful of times. This was still foreign to me. I debated how I would lie next to him, where I should put my arms or legs. But Bo just slid one arm underneath my neck and pulled my head onto his shoulder. He reached down and pulled my top leg over his and then kissed me on top of my head.

"Done rearranging me?"

"Yup," came the nonchalant reply.

"We haven't even kissed yet, you know," I told him. "It seems weird to sleep together."

"We're not ready yet."

I liked that. It wasn't just that I wasn't ready but that he wasn't either. He may have been blowing smoke up my ass, but I liked the sentiment. I thought I'd lie awake all night, but the comfort and warmth of his body relaxed me and the emotional tumult drained that sudden burst of energy. I fell asleep almost immediately, cocooned in the safety of Bo Randolph's arms.

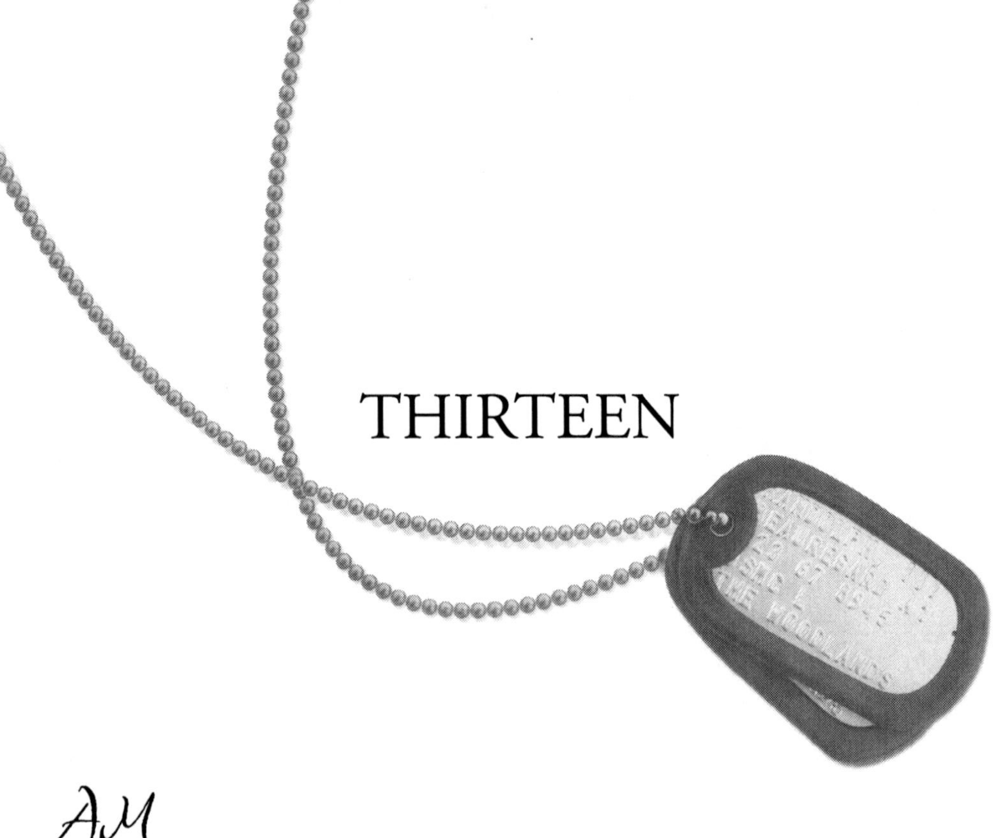

THIRTEEN

AM

Bo left early the next morning, whispering in my sleepy ear that he was going for a run. Later that day, he appeared, showered, changed, and ready to fulfill one of our lab requirements. I spent the time apart embarrassed by the revelations I had shared and confused about our status. We dating? Hooking up? Just friends? I didn't even know exactly what I wanted from Bo, so when he treated me with such normalcy, I didn't bring the subject up. My anxiety over the previous night's events only lingered for a moment, but my bewilderment over *us* only increased.

"Would you help me open this?" I handed him a jar of spaghetti sauce. I'd agreed, somehow, to make dinner for Bo tonight, ostensibly because we needed to study, but mostly because being around Bo and being the subject of his light flirtations actually made me feel good. I deserved that once in a while, I told myself.

He deftly twisted off the top and handed the bottle back to me.

"You know a man would never ask that. That's a difference between men and women."

"What?" I was incredulous. "You would never ask for help to remove a cap from a bottle?"

"You might ask for a bottle opener, but you'd never ask for help to remove the cap itself," he clarified.

"But how does that make you more manly?"

"Men don't need help opening jars."

"Are you telling me that every jar is openable for you?"

"If it's not, then it doesn't need to be opened."

"Not being able to admit you need help is manly?"

"Asking for help is a woman's thing," Bo said, ducking my point. "We don't ask for directions, and we don't need help opening bottles."

I shook my head. "I don't believe you. I think you're just a Neanderthal." I could tell he was egging me on, but I had to see how far he would take this.

"Real men never ask for help." Bo leaned forward, his arm across the counter. "In fact, this could be our lab."

"You're on." I slapped my hand on the table. "Where do we hold the lab study?"

"My house. We'll superglue a mayonnaise jar shut and we'll see if any of my roommates ask for help. I bet none of them will."

"You're on."

"Great. We'll do it Monday, unless you have another class after?"

"No, why do you think that?"

"Because you always run out of there like the hounds of hell are chasing you." He leaned even closer so that his arm brushed mine and his mouth was almost touching mine. I didn't move an inch. "It's only me who's chasing you."

"I'm not running away from you."

He leaned back. "So you say."

Bo didn't sleep over on Saturday night or Sunday, either. After we ate on Saturday night, he hugged me good-bye, molding my body to his. I might be somewhat inexperienced, but I knew an erection when I felt it poking into my stomach. But he ignored it, so I didn't bring it up, either. Instead, I hugged him back, enjoying the physical contact. His hands stroked up and down my back, and I bit my tongue to suppress the shivers of need building inside me. When his hand swept into my hair and his nose was buried in the side of my neck, I couldn't keep back a moan of delight.

"I've got to go," Bo said, but his hand tightened in my hair and his other hand spanning my waist pulled me closer.

If I spent a rational moment thinking about it all, Bo was right. We weren't ready. I was still feeling vulnerable after last night, and I didn't really know where Bo's head was. That didn't mean I was going to turn away an embrace. As if he understood my reserve and the need to go slow, he released me with a sigh and tapped me on the nose.

"See you in class."

Longing filled me the entire weekend, and I was so anxious to see him on Monday I think I flew to class rather than walked. When I finally did see him lounging outside the classroom waiting for me, I felt a giddy smile light up my face. Bo didn't pressure me into making some declaration, but he made it known throughout class that he was interested by the way he found little excuses to touch me, throwing an arm behind my chair and letting his thumb brush my shoulder. In response, I leaned into him closer than necessary. Class seemed like one long, extended bout of foreplay, so I was glad that he kept the tone upbeat and neutral when we were done.

"I'm going to need directions to your house," I told him as we exited class. Instead of responding, Bo tugged at the strap of my messenger bag until I let it slide off my shoulder. He looped it over his head and walked off again. "Hey, wait a minute." I trotted after him and when we reached his car, Bo popped the miniscule trunk where I saw a gym bag and nothing else. He threw both our bags in and came around to open my car door.

I started to protest, but really, I loved this car. For the fun of it, though, I told him, "This is kidnapping," as he climbed in the other side.

"How? You agreed to come to my house."

"Forcing me into your car is kidnapping," I replied, primly folding my hands into my lap and tucking my legs to the side looking as innocent as I could.

"I held the door open, and you got in willingly."

"It was coercion. You wouldn't tell me your address."

"I'm okay with coercion, but let's get our felony counts correct." He grinned at me. I just shook my head and looked out the window in order to hide my smile.

"What if I wanted to shop afterward or get dinner or something?" Hassling Bo was like foreplay, too. I suspect he thought the same.

"I can take you," he shrugged.

"Oh sure, you'll go shopping with me at the mall."

"Why not? It'd be interesting."

"How so? And I thought real men didn't like to shop."

Bo grinned wickedly. "Oh, real men enjoy shopping for some things."

I knew he was going to make some reference to lingerie or guns so I just said as ominously as I could, "We shall see."

Bo must have taken this as tacit permission because he started the car and peeled out of the parking lot like a teenager with his first car. Bo played music that I'd never heard before, a kind of punk rock with a big band sound. A distinctive male voice bellowed out the lyrics, singing that I was the one who told his secrets, the one who let him down.

"What kind of car is this again?"

"See, that's another thing. A guy would know."

"Who cares what car it is?"

"You asked," he replied glibly.

"I was making small talk! It's not like I peruse *Car and Driver* every day. I may not have any interest in cars, but there're plenty of girls who do, so it's completely sexist to assume a guy would be more likely to know what kind of car this is whereas a girl would not. There are girl mechanics. I've seen them on TV."

"Sounds like we have the basis for another lab study. We can run it after the mayo test and before we shop for shoes or whatnot."

"Even Pixar put a female in their lineup during the movie."

"She wasn't a race car."

"There's a car hierarchy?" I raised both eyebrows.

"In the movie, McQueen was top dog."

"A hot dog, you mean."

"Are we really arguing about animated cars?" Bo threw back his head and laughed. "AM, this is why we should be spending more time together."

I didn't reply to this out loud even though all my girl parts were yelling "Yes!" Instead, I asked him, "Tell me about your place."

"It's in a gated subdivision about twenty miles west of campus."

"I would think that real men wouldn't need to live behind the security of gates."

"Well, you may be right, but real men are interested in a good deal."

"Are you kidding? Women love deals. Retailers know this. Men's clothing is never on sale because they know you're easy marks."

Bo shrugged. "I never said that men were superior. Only that they were made differently."

Bo handled the vehicle confidently, his large hands resting lightly on the wheel and shifting smoothly from one gear to the other. He looked just as powerful in this sedentary position as he did sitting in the classroom or striding across campus. Bo was a head turner. When he walked into a room, people noticed. He seemed to suck up the void.

When you engaged with him, you realized that whatever fantasy construct you had created in your mind wasn't even remotely close to the interesting creature that he really was. Which, I supposed, only added to his mystique. He was funnier than I thought he would be. More self-deprecating. And maybe even bolder.

"I can feel you staring at me, you know," Bo remarked.

"What else is there to look at?"

"Are you saying I'm the best-looking thing in the entire city?"

"If you need the praise because you can't operate without a certain amount of adulation, go ahead and interpret my comment in the way that makes you feel the best," I said soothingly.

"I'll just assume you're too shy or embarrassed to admit your adoration of me."

"I'll just assume you're so insecure that you turn random comments into compliments."

"We're getting to know each other so well," Bo said cheerfully. "This bodes well for our future."

"Should we stop for superglue?" I asked. "We'll need that to seal the cap on the jar."

"No, every real man has superglue, duct tape, and a power drill in his house." Bo added, "Women should have superglue in their house. Or a man who's going to buy it for them."

I scoffed. "Well, I not only have duct tape, but I have a superior form of an adhesive that has displaced superglue. Women, you see, are looking for efficient and multipurpose products that are full of advancement while you men are stuck in your caveman superglue ways."

Unthinkingly, I went on, "Maybe after this, you can get an invitation to see my superior home improvement idea. It's moldable rubber." As the words came out of my mouth, I realized how suggestive they sounded, but rather than come back with a super salacious comment, Bo looked at me and burst out laughing.

I got out of the car with a huff. "It's a product that dries into flexible rubber. It's very cool." I didn't reveal that I had some because Brian had given it to us.

As we were walking in through the side door, Bo leaned down and said, "You stick with me, sweetheart, and you won't need moldable rubber anymore."

"Took you five minutes to come up with that reply, did it?"

Bo howled with laughter.

We went straight to the kitchen and Bo proceeded to open the refrigerator and make us two sandwiches. He whispered to me that this was going to "prime the pump."

After finishing the sandwich prep, Bo put everything away except the mayonnaise, which he glued shut, and then proceeded to place our sandwiches and bags on a long wooden table that separated the kitchen from a large, open-spaced entertainment center. Two guys sat on the sofa with their backs to us, playing a video game on a giant flat-screen TV. Bo gestured for me to sit and I did. We sat at the table with a clear view of the kitchen and then Bo picked up his sandwich. At the same time, he pushed his bag off the table so it made a loud thud on the floor.

The sound made the two guys, Mal and Finn, look up and one of them zeroed in on Bo's sandwich.

"Hey, is there meat left?" Mal asked.

Bo nodded, his mouth wrapped around the sandwich. Mal got up and went into the kitchen.

"You guys remember AM," he said. "She, like me, failed to take the science requirement her first year and agreed to be my lab partner."

In the fading light of the afternoon, Bo, Finn, and Mal looked like they were readying for a men's cologne or underwear ad. Finn and Mal were contrasts, pale skin against darker skin, but both sported blinding white, perfect smiles. I wondered if there was a dentist in one of their families. Finn was the more conventionally beautiful of the three, but Mal was hot; his dark eyes seemed to promise all sorts of naughty things. Looking at them, remembering Noah, I realized that the real draw at the Woodlands wasn't the parties, but the hosts—and the hope that you could spend the night upstairs with one of these guys.

Mal interrupted my reverie. "Leave it to you to find the hottest girl in class and make her your lab partner."

"Nice to see you again, Mal," I grinned. "I can tell I'm going to like you a lot."

"Hey, hey," interjected Finn. "I think you're hot, too."

"You'd never guess from talking to Bo that he would have such charming roommates," I teased. Bo spread out our books and we pretended to study but instead watched surreptitiously as Mal walked into the kitchen and proceeded toward the sandwich makings. For at least a minute, Mal attempted to open the mayonnaise jar but failed. He finally slapped together bread, meat, cheese, and butter, making two sandwiches, and grabbed both to return to the living room where he handed one to Finn.

It was the sorriest sandwich ever. Finn must have agreed because he took one bite and said, "What the hell is this?"

Mal said "butter" as his mouth engulfed his own sandwich. Finn got up and stomped into the kitchen. Once there, he tried to open the mayo jar. Finn worked on the jar longer and in more creative ways that Mal. He used his shirt and tapped it against the counter but with no success. Bo was trying hard to keep from crying with the laughter he was swallowing back.

The tapping sound alerted Mal because he yelled out, "The mayonnaise jar is broken, asshole, or I would have put it on."

Finn cursed a bit and put the jar back into the refrigerator. He ate his sandwich but was clearly unhappy about it.

I watched this whole debacle with open-mouthed amazement. Bo had to cover his mouth with his arm to prevent his snickers from giving him away.

"Two more," Bo said to me and pulled out his phone. He texted something to someone and when I heard his phone ping, I knew he'd received a reply.

"Mal," Bo called, "where's Adam?"

"He's playing."

"Wait, speak of the devil," Finn said as another roommate came strolling in through the French doors separating the patio from the living space.

Bo introduced us and Adam, all tattoos and wild hair, wandered into the kitchen, where he proceeded to make another sandwich. Adam's efforts to open the mayo were brief. A few twists and the defective jar was returned to the refrigerator shelf. He ate his sandwich in about three gulps and disappeared from whence he came.

"One more," Bo said, sounding confident. Noah came in with a pretty girl with long brown hair. Noah introduced her as his girlfriend, Grace, and handed Bo a grocery bag with a small mayo jar.

"Thanks," Bo said. He got up and took the old jar out, put it on the counter, and put the new jar in the refrigerator.

Noah picked up the tampered jar of mayo and held it toward Bo. "What the hell? This thing is totally full. Why'd I have to get a new jar?"

Bo shrugged and said, "It's broken."

Noah gave him a questioning look and Bo elaborated. "No one could open it."

Noah shook his head in disgust, and I think muttered something like pussies or pansies under his breath. He took the jar and proceeded to try to twist the top off. Noah, like Bo, was ripped. His muscles have muscles, and they all stood out in relief as he twisted the jar cap. Finally he gave up and threw it in the trash.

Bo turned to me. "Four out of four."

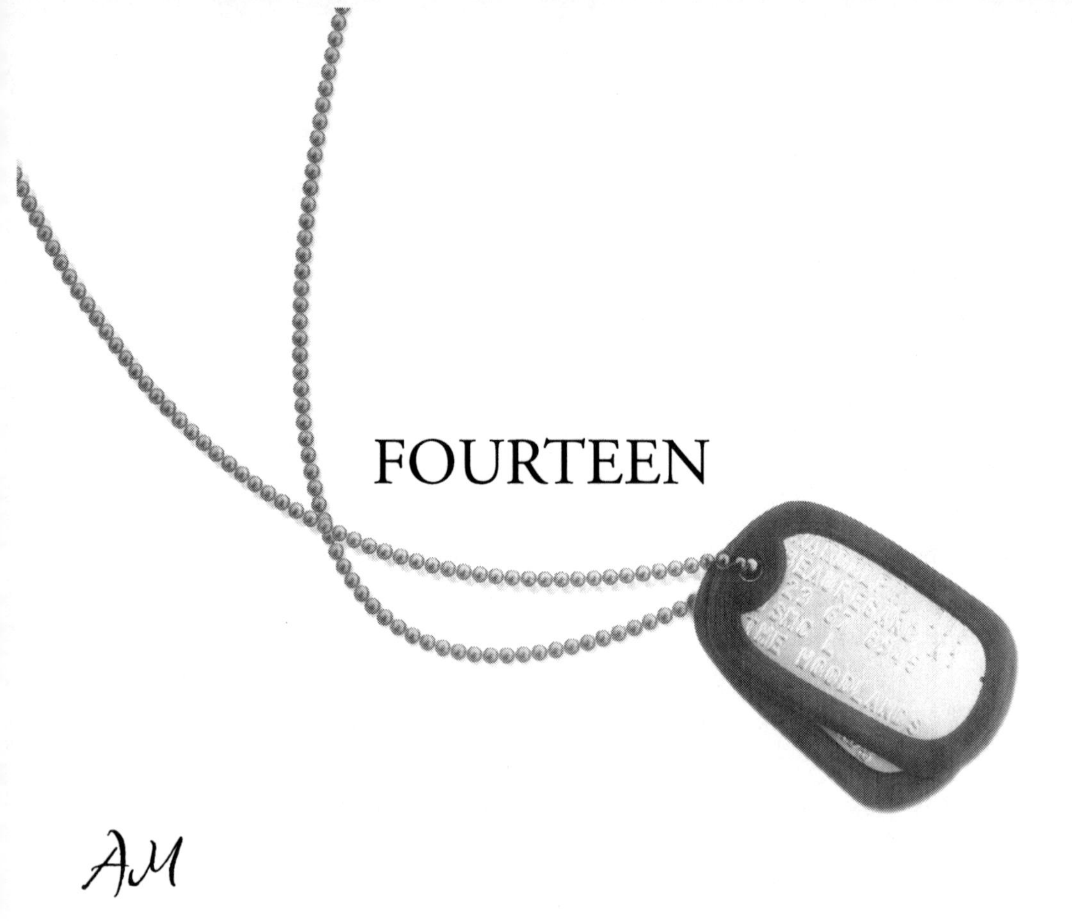

FOURTEEN

AM

THE NEXT DAY BO AND I made plans to meet at the museum to start the second lab experiment. The time we were spending together was intoxicating. The ride home from his house after the mayonnaise experiment was fraught with sexual tension. If his long game was getting me so worked up that I'd attack him, it was a good plan. Part of me wanted to rip his clothes off right there in the parking lot. Another part wanted desperately to invite him up to my bedroom. I'm not sure how I got out of the car without so much as a kiss.

Our sleepover seemed like a distant memory, and I was confused about what was going on between us. I knew he enjoyed spending time with me. We hardly went a day without seeing each other or e-mailing. Bo would even text me, despite his previously mentioned distaste for it.

When he suggested the museum, the "yes" came out of my mouth so fast that I think it surprised us both.

On my drive down to the museum, my phone rang, and I answered it. "What's up?" I'd turned down a ride with Bo, afraid of what I'd do to him if we were alone in his car once again.

"AnnMarie, are you driving?" my mother said reprovingly. The background noise of the road must have seeped through the phone.

"You called me," I pointed out.

"I'll make this short because you shouldn't be driving and talking on your phone. Are you driving with one hand? You know that's unsafe."

"You're extending my unsafe period by continuing to talk to me," I teased.

"Yes, yes, well, I spoke with Ellie's mother at the supermarket today and she mentioned that Ellie and you are planning a trip over spring break. Is that true?"

I grimaced. I knew what was coming, and it was the very reason that Ellie and I were planning on doing something this year over spring break, but I wasn't ready to discuss the issue with my mom.

"It's too early to think about spring break," I lied, ignoring the tug on my conscience.

"Darling, you know your father wants to see you. He mentioned something about Italy this year, and you know he didn't get to see you much over the holidays."

"Whose fault is that?" I couldn't keep the bitterness out of my voice.

A small pause skipped by as my mother swallowed whatever retort she wanted to make and instead replied gently, "I'm sorry."

I immediately regretted my lack of restraint. It wasn't my mother who deserved my venom. She'd suffered enough, and she didn't need me to add to it.

"No, I'm sorry," I apologized. No one can make you feel lower quicker than your mother. "But I plan to spend spring break with my friends this year." I could almost hear her biting her lip in dismay. "I'll come home the weekend before, though. You can tell Roger that."

I'd never called him Dad, and he'd never asked me to. My mother took all her cues from him, and for the most part, so did I. Roger's appearances in my life were infrequent albeit regular, a week after Christmas, around spring break, and a few weekends in the summer. I hated upsetting her, and any harsh word against Roger upset her. She would never say this out loud to me. Instead, she would gently urge me to take what little scraps of affection he threw out, like she did.

By the time I'd reached the Natural History Museum, my mood was bleak. I sat in my car for a few minutes in the parking lot, leaning my head against the headrest with my eyes closed.

Mom had stayed with Roger because she loved him, but maybe if she hadn't had me, she would have discovered the courage to leave him and find a new and better man to love. Saddled with a kid, she stayed, and because of that she'd provided me with a stable home life and a free college education. I had to respect and appreciate that. Of course, telling myself to feel appreciation was one thing. Actually feeling that way was entirely different.

I loved my mother, but I had a hard time understanding her decisions. We both deserved better, and even if she was content being the "other" woman, I was going to find someone who would love me and only me. I had my doubts that it was Bo. All of the reasons that I shouldn't be with him flooded in. He was a Central student. A jock. He had a reputation for multiple conquests. Did I really want to be another statistic?

Having allowed myself a five-minute pity party in the toasty warm car, I killed the engine and stepped out into the cold afternoon. Snow was piled up in small hills against the sides of the parking lot, making it seem like a fortress. The once-pristine white mounds were discolored with engine exhaust, rubber refuse, and dust, making them the color of dirty socks—dingy and gray.

I was grateful for my rubber-soled and lined boots. They were ugly but serviceable, keeping my feet and calves warm and dry. But my skinny jeans weren't much proof against the chill wind, and so I scurried inside as quickly as possible, clutching my notebook to my chest.

I paid the admission fee and asked for directions to the North American plant life and was instructed to go up to the third floor.

A text message alert chimed, and I pulled my phone out to read it.

Where are you?

At the entrance, paying.

Get your ass upstairs. I NEED YOU.

The museum wasn't terribly crowded. There were a number of schoolchildren, but few of them were on the third floor by the plants. No surprise, though. Who wanted to look at plants when there were dinosaur bones and wild animals or even bugs?

When I got into the North American botany section, I noticed that it was completely empty save for Bo, who was seated with a notepad in his lap, and a museum employee, who stood over him talking animatedly with her hands.

My entrance wasn't noisy but something caused Bo to jerk his head around. Even from here, I could see the wild expression in his eyes. I swallowed a laugh and tried to school my face to show no emotion. Clearly Bo felt like the hunted here, with the museum employee playing the role of the predator. My earlier depression flew away, and I felt my pulse kick up as he rose from the bench.

He called out rather loudly, "Sunshine, I thought you'd never get here." By the end of his greeting Bo had reached me, his long legs eating up the room one lengthy stride at a time.

The honey blond museum employee followed behind, almost running to keep up. Bo's hands pulled me close to him, and I could feel the notebook he still held in his one hand pressing into my shoulder blade.

"Um, hey," I smiled weakly to the museum employee whose look of dismay was clearly etched on her face. Apparently she was hoping that Bo might be interested in some private tutoring. I snuck an arm around his waist and leaned my head against the side of his chest. It was firm and broad and lovely. If I were in the shoes of the museum employee, I'd be offering things to Bo, too, all sorts of things. But her attraction to him was a reminder of how many women were at the ready for Bo.

The young lady bit her lip and glowered.

"Thanks for all your help, Marissa," Bo said, offering his hand. "Really appreciate it."

Marissa took it and gave him a sloe-eyed glance, one that said clearly that she had more assistance to provide if only he would ask. "Any time," she said, taking his hand and squeezing it with both of hers.

When she didn't immediately release Bo's fingers, I took pity on the both of them and pulled Bo's captured appendage out of her grasp and said in my best jealous, affronted girlfriend voice, "Let's go, honey buns."

Marissa wisely decided that she should move on and gave us a little finger wave as she walked past us to the exit. I turned to watch her leave and, as if sensing this, Marissa put a little extra swing in her hips. I had to hand it to her; looking sexy in khakis was tough to pull off, but she kind of had it going on.

Bo, on the other hand, did not watch Marissa's show but was intent on pulling me toward the exhibit he'd been sitting in front of. We stopped at the bench he'd previously occupied and he gestured for me to sit.

When I did, he dropped down close beside me and stretched his legs out, throwing his notebook on the floor. His large thigh was only a palm's width away. I knew the exact measurement because my hand was resting on the bench between us, and if I moved my pinky just slightly, I could be stroking the denim covering his leg. His hands were braced on the back of the stone bench, giving him a lazy, comfortable appearance, as if he was lounging in the grass instead of on a stone bench. "Thanks for saving me."

I glanced at the empty doorway through which our resource had disappeared. "Aren't you supposed to be pumping a worker here for information for our lab project?"

Bo rubbed his forehead. "I'm all for doing the least amount of work for the most amount of gain, but I'm not up for selling myself for a good grade."

"Was that what was on the table?"

"I think we were headed there before you got up here. I barely was able to text you my SOS message."

"What's our plan now?" I asked.

"Don't know. I spent my time fending off Marissa."

"I've some ideas." I opened my own notebook. "Professor Godwin is into disasters. Last year he had people write about weather-related apocalyptic events. This year he started class with a lecture about how we're all going to die."

"So we do some crossbred plant that would be a hardy food source and maybe something that would be a tradable commodity, like a sugary substance." Bo offered. He smiled approvingly at me. "We do think alike."

This time it was my turn to rub my forehead, but I was doing it to hide my surprise. Bo's attention to this project was serious.

"You're surprised, aren't you? Why?" Bo asked, nudging me.

Because you're too good-looking to be a serious student, I thought but didn't say out loud. Instead I gave him a vague truth. "It doesn't fit the image I have of you, I guess."

"Think about me a lot, do you?"

I hoped I wasn't blushing because I *had* thought a lot about him; I'd fantasized about him. Although my cheeks remained pale, my silence gave me away, and Bo's response was a wicked grin. He winked and said, "Probably not as much as I've thought about you."

This response did send blood rushing to my cheeks. I mentally slapped myself. Lots of guys thought about me, I'd learned early on, and none of it was good. Mercifully, Bo did not mock me further but instead reached down and picked up his notebook and flipped it open.

"So stevia and soybeans are both plants that grow well in the Midwest. Together they'd provide a filling bean that could be ground for its sweetness." He showed me a sketch in progress of two plants, one leafy and one with bean pods.

"You draw?" The sketches were in fairly good detail.

"Again with the shock and awe." He shook his head at me. "Anyone can draw a leaf, Sunshine."

"What's with the sunshine?" He kept using it like he didn't know my name.

"What's with the honey buns? You couldn't think up a better nickname than that?" He gave me a sideways grin. "Besides, I thought I was Thor?"

"Like sunshine? How many girls have you called that?" I scoffed.

"None." His expression turned serious.

"Oh."

"There's an art to nicknames," Bo began.

"And you're going to teach it to me?"

"Can't really be taught. It's just an innate skill. Although yours is so obvious I can't believe no one else has called you that."

I shrugged. "AM is my nickname. Short for AnnMarie."

"I know, but the logical extension is sunshine because AM is a good time—" Bo stopped and then corrected himself. "AM is a time designation for the morning."

"Were you going to say 'good time in the morning?'" I shook my head at the brazenness of his explanation.

Bo gave me a wry smile and replied, "I think you'd hit me if I told you what I was about to say, and you'd probably be justified in doing so."

It was a clear warning, yet I thoughtlessly charged ahead anyway. "I thought you were a fighter?"

My poke was met with a slight widening of Bo's eyes. His face took on an expression I couldn't decipher, but I thought might be excitement.

"Since you put it that way, I'm just making an assumption here because I don't know you well enough. Are you a good time in the morning? Because that's one of my favorite times of the day."

"By the speed at which you left the other day, it seemed like you weren't interested in seeing how I looked in the morning." It was a reckless reference to our sleepover.

"If I'd stayed, I'd've wanted to do something to you that you might not have been ready for."

Bo's response made me squirm on the bench. This was a dangerous game, and I knew I should stop, but the idea of Bo imagining the two of us in bed together doing something more than just sleeping was too much for me. A dozen images flitted through my mind. Bo above me, our sweat-slicked bodies moving in unison. His mouth licking my neck and down the valley of my breasts. I squeezed my thighs in response to the pressure that was building.

My previous fantasies had been so tame. I might have played out a few scenarios of Bo and me in my head during last semester's class, but none of them ever included him asking me what times of the day was I best in bed. I'd envisioned Bo would wash a car with his shirt off. Or maybe he'd help me move a sofa and I'd stare at his ass or see a sliver of skin between his jeans and his T-shirt. He'd stand with his arm over my head as he leaned down to press his lips against mine. Realizing I wasn't equipped to trade sexually-charged banter with Bo, I tried to steer the conversation back into safer territory. "What's the art of the nickname?"

Bo gave a deep sigh and shifted restlessly beside me, but he gamely accepted my change in topic.

"Nicknames need to be descriptive enough to identify a unique trait of the person, but different enough that they're meaningful to the individuals using them."

"Like baby or honey?" I asked, fascinated by this obviously thought-out position on nicknames.

"Babe, sweetheart, darling aren't nicknames. Those are throwaways. So my buddy Noah is Jep, short for Jeopardy. He liked to read trivia books while deployed and would likely kick our collective asses in *Jeopardy*.

Another guy we were deployed with had a hard-on for Skittles. He'd take every bag he could get his hands on and make these disgusting sex noises when he ate them so we called him Skittle-tits."

"That's a terrible nickname," I informed him.

"So is honey buns."

"I was on the spot," I protested. "What's your roommates' nickname for you?"

"You'll have to get to know me better before I reveal that." Bo looked slyly out of the corner of his eyes at me, as if he were was throwing out another lure. I wanted to pick it up, but I was afraid. Flirting with Bo would only make my nighttime dreams a little more feverish and my daytime fantasies intolerable. I couldn't go around living with an unrelieved ache in my lower body. Assuaging *that* particular ache would likely lead to a more serious one in my heart. Again, I moved the topic away to something more benign.

"Tell me your story then, Thor," I suggested.

"Thor, by the way, is a far better nickname than honey buns. Let's go with that from now on." His grin was knowing and wicked. "What do you want to know?"

Everything, because you fascinate me. And nothing, because I think you'd burn me up and leave me empty.

"How about your most embarrassing story?" I blurted out instead.

"I usually require at least one bottle of tequila before these types of confessionals." He shook his head in mock sadness.

"Forget I asked." I waved my hand. "Let's just get our project done."

"No, no." Bo grabbed my hand and pulled it to rest between us. The stone bench felt cool, but his hand covering mine was warm and dry, like a shelter. I realized I could get addicted to holding hands with Bo Randolph. Somehow, just that simple touch made me feel better, as if his hand were an IV of personal strength. "I'm in, but you have to agree to share too."

"I've already told you one."

Bo opened his mouth and then closed it. He turned away to look into the display that portrayed long wavy grasses, a fake pond, and a few trees in the background. A stuffed fox peeked through foliage, almost hidden by the leaves and ground cover.

"Not so eager once you're the guy being asked to spill secrets," I mocked.

Bo shook his head and replied. "All my embarrassing stories are kind of raunchy, and I'm not sure you'd want to hear those."

"Likely excuse." I shrugged and pulled out my phone. His hesitation gave rise to my fear that he thought I was easy and my refusal to capitulate was confounding him. Perhaps he thought I'd just drop my jeans and ask him to take me here in the museum, a natural, just because he smiled and complimented me. This was good, I told myself. Placing him with all the rest made his attractiveness fade, his shine dulling with exposure to the air like old silver.

Standing up, I bent over the display and took a photo of the information sign that described the scene in front of me and took another of the display itself. I went around the room, snapping photos of what I could. Later I'd magnify these on my computer and take more notes. At the far end was a tiny dark room with a video screen playing something on a loop. I stepped in and was about to press the button to start the sound when the light from the room that had spilled into the entryway was blocked out completely.

"I met this one chick at a concert," Bo said, his nearness startling me. "We both ended up near the fence line making eyes at each other. After the concert was over, we were just standing there, like the whole event was prelude, right?"

"Right," I said shortly, surprised he'd followed me into the dark room. His size swallowed up the space, and I felt like we were in junior high, about to make out in the closet. Only instead of kissing me, he was regaling me with a past conquest in graphic, profane detail. I hated this girl already. But then I *had* asked for this.

"I can't even remember her name now," Bo admitted. "Or quite what she looked like. We went back to her hotel room. She was sharing it with four other girls. I do remember the room. It looked like some mall had thrown up in there. There were clothes everywhere and only two beds. I guess it was two girls to a bed.

"We fell on that bed and started making out. She stopped me to tell me she'd never had an orgasm. So in my mind this was a challenge. I was going to give her the best damn orgasm ever, but I failed. She's lying there, bored out of her mind. Maybe she was thinking of the last book she'd read, maybe she was counting sheep. I don't know.

"She leaned over and asked me if I wanted anything, but I was dead from the waist down. Not only could I not get her off, but I couldn't get it up. I pulled on my clothes and ran out of there like her dad was standing over us with a shotgun. Hell, I would have welcomed that."

As Bo recounted this experience, he leaned against the far wall of the dark alcove, but there was very little space between us. I could almost feel the rise and fall of his chest as he spoke and breathed. The darkness and the small space lent an intimacy to the setting. But even in the dimness, with light from the other room outlining the doorway, I could sense his self-deprecation. He wasn't at all concerned with how it may have made him appear or how humorous it sounded. He just did *not* care. I wanted to borrow his attitude and wear it like the fox in the weeds wore his coat, blending in with his surroundings and belonging.

"I haven't told you the worst part," Bo went on. "For a month afterward, my equipment didn't work. Every time I felt like I was getting wood, I'd think of that room and that girl, and my dick would climb into my sack in shame."

I choked back a giggle.

"No, it's funny," Bo encouraged. "No need to try to hold back your laughter."

I started laughing, then, and couldn't stop. "How old were you?"

"Seventeen. I thought I was doomed. I tried looking up porn and everything, but nothing worked. I thought I'd be the only under-eighteen patient to have to take Viagra."

"What cured you?"

"The cure was even worse."

"Oh no, you didn't." I placed my hand against my lips to hold in my laughter.

"I sure did. My father had a bottle of those beauties. I took one and chased it down with about a fifth of his Scotch. Had a beauty of a beating from that—the Scotch, not the blue pill," Bo clarified. "He didn't realize he was missing one of those."

"What happened?" I managed to gasp out between the fits of laughter.

"So if you aren't actually having problems downstairs, you end up getting a nonstop hard-on that you can't get rid of. I rubbed as many out as I could, but then my dick became so sensitive I couldn't touch it anymore.

So I had a nonstop hard-on that was too painful to relieve. Eventually it wore off, but I thought I would never have sex again."

"So the next day, then?"

"Ah, you're getting to know me so well. Yes, the next day and then the next and the next. I was on a tear. Both jubilant that my dick actually worked and that I didn't need pills, but also a mental reproof to the girl I couldn't get off. How about you."

"I've already shared," I protested.

"What happened to you wasn't an embarrassment to anyone but the dickheads who assaulted you and then tried to boost their egos with lies," Bo said fiercely. "*You* have nothing to be ashamed of."

His words choked me up a little and for a moment I couldn't speak. Maybe when he told me we were on the same team that first day in biology class he meant it. His verbal support felt so good.

"There's a whole block of restaurants and stores that I can't shop at anymore," I confessed. When he made a protesting sound, I barreled on. "I met Mark at a bar with my roommate. He was really good-looking, but kind of dumb. But he seemed like he knew what he was about."

"Like how?" Bo sounded disgruntled. Kind of like how I felt hearing about how hot he was for some other girl even though I'd told myself I wasn't going down that path with him.

"I don't know. He just looked the part. Tall, attractive. I guess I thought because he was strong and handsome that he'd know what he was doing in bed, and I'd just come off a really crappy experience."

"Did he?"

"Yes, but my first time wasn't so good, obviously, so pretty much anyone who knew where my girl parts were was going to be better than the first time."

"I'm not sure where the embarrassment comes in. Did you break his dick or what?"

"No!" I exclaimed and then stopped for a moment. "Can that really happen?"

"Yup. There, there was an MMA fighter whose girlfriend broke his dick while doing reverse cowgirl or something."

I wondered how that worked. She must have gone up too high and then slammed down. When I felt Bo's hand cover mine and heard him trying to suppress a laugh, I realized I was trying to act out the scene with my hands. I pulled my hands out of his and stuck them under either side of my legs.

"So you were saying." Bo motioned me to go on.

"So I, ah, felt good with him, and I kind of began to have feelings for him."

"How is this embarrassing? That's normal." Bo sounded a little peeved, although at whom or what, I wasn't sure.

"I'm getting there, impatient Patty." Taking a deep breath, I rushed through the rest. "After a few weeks, he stopped calling me. I texted him and called repeatedly, but he never responded. I started stalking him, driving by his apartment, going to where I knew he liked to order out. I ate a ton of fattening and bad lasagna for like a month. The waitstaff started recognizing me and would shake their heads as if saying, 'Here comes that fool girl again, she can't take no for an answer.'"

Bo remained silent for a while. He rubbed his hand across his chin and his lips were sort of pursed, as if he was thinking.

"What? You scared of me now?"

"No, I just don't get how that is embarrassing. You fell for the first guy that made you feel good. He was a dick to you."

"How is stalking my hookup not embarrassing?"

"Because it just isn't. I feel like I deserve another story."

"That was a good story," I replied, miffed he didn't appreciate the confession I'd laid out. While it didn't involve Viagra, it was mortifying to me.

"If you were with the right guy, it wouldn't be stalking," Bo mused. "It'd be flattering and even welcome."

"Yeah, well, it wasn't flattering or welcome. After the third visit to the dive where he ate Italian food, the waitress told me she didn't think he was interested. Trust me, it was embarrassing." I turned my head away, not wanting to see his expression or for him to see mine. "You ever see that girl again?"

"Yup. I saw her later my senior year at a party. She was with some guy, and when she saw me she turned fire engine red, like that was the most humiliating night of her life. She took off before I could say anything." Bo cleared his throat. "I just want it to be clear that all my equipment is in working order."

"Thanks for the update." I smirked.

The silence fell again. Whatever plans I had for getting an early jump on our lab assignment were over for today. I moved toward the exit, not interested in hearing the video. The strange spell that the dark and the close space had held over us seemed to dissipate when I stepped outside into the still abandoned hallway of botany with Bo following close behind. I felt embarrassed that I'd revealed something so personal to him yet again.

"Let's go have dinner," Bo invited, placing his hand on the small of my back and leading me toward the bench where my notebook and his sketchpad rested.

Taken by surprise, I could only answer dumbly, "Dinner?" I hadn't realized it had gotten so late, but when I looked at my watch it seemed that Bo and I had spent quite a while sitting, sketching, and telling embarrassing stories to each other.

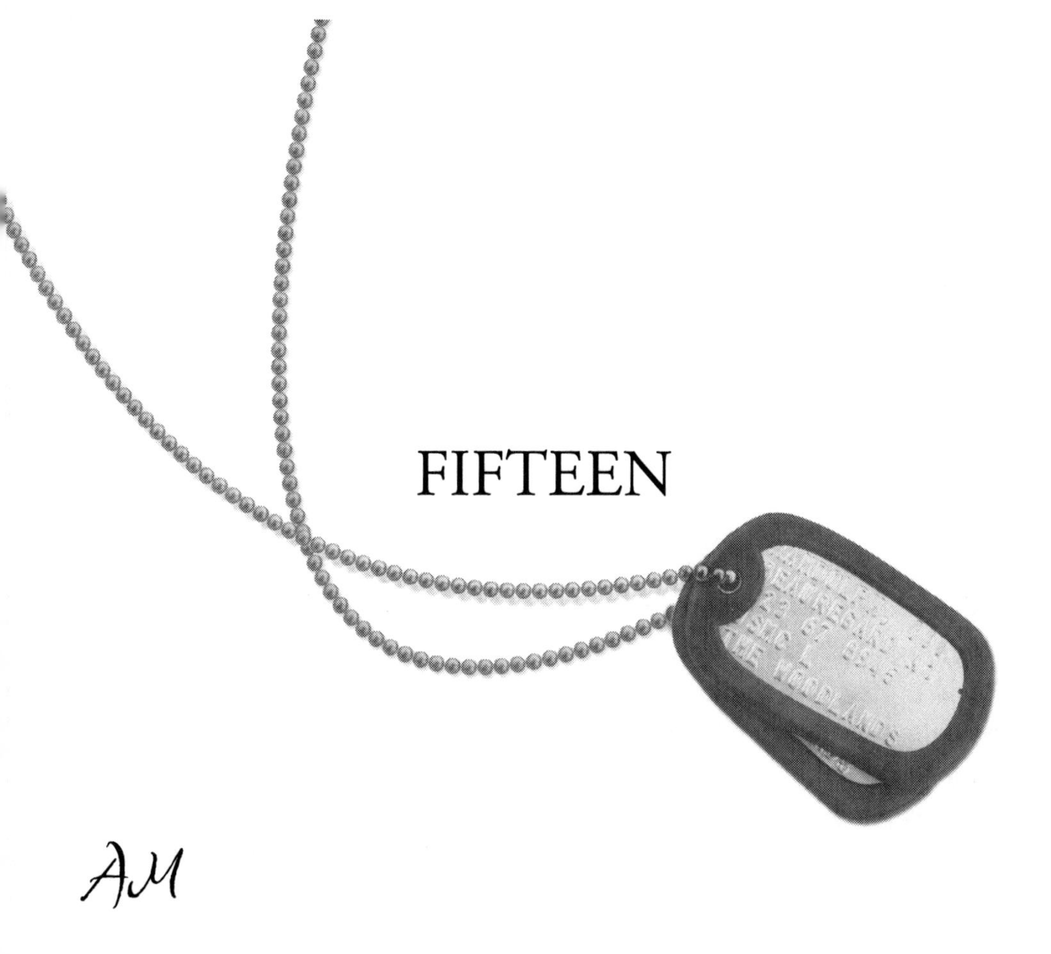

FIFTEEN

AM

As I stood next to Bo in line to order a bowl of chili at a deli about two miles from campus, I wondered if Bo had magical powers. My list of reasons why I should remain aloof, which I'd enumerated on the way to the museum, seemed to have been left on the marble floor.

He did provide a reasonable justification. We could talk about the lab projects and how we would finish them. It was a flimsy excuse, but I held on to it like it was the last tissue available during allergy season.

"I'm paying for my own meal," I told him after we had both placed our orders and moved to the cash register with our trays. He gave me a slightly amused glance and shook his head.

"I asked. I pay." He leaned past me and handed his debit card to the cashier. "You ask. You pay. But thanks for offering."

Short of causing a scene, there was nothing to do but accept the free dinner. The cashier goggled at Bo's tray, laden with three bowls of chili and two bottles of milk. You'd think he was working hard labor, given the amount of food he planned to put away.

"It's difficult for the male to navigate the waters," Bo complained as we sat down. "Do I hold the door open and stand until you're seated?"

"Why not just treat women like you'd treat a guy? You don't ever hold a door open for a pal, do you?"

Bo contemplated this for a moment, untwisting the top of one milk bottle. "I have, but generally my momma taught me that you stand when a woman enters a room, you open her door, you carry her bags. I'd have wrestled the tray away from you if I'd thought I could've gotten away with it."

"Good thing you didn't try. I'd have stabbed you with a fork."

"This is why I like you, AnnMarie. You speak the same violent language." Bo gave a shout of laughter, drawing the eyes of the patrons nearby. I saw a couple of older ladies' eyes linger on Bo's expressive face. I wouldn't blame them if they were thinking naughty thoughts about him. Bo looked like a walking sex machine. He had large hands and muscular arms that looked like they could hold you up against the wall, if you liked that sort of thing.

His whole face was engaged when he talked. That damn indent on the left side of his mouth deepened when he laughed and I itched to press my finger against it. I wondered if you hit the right place, you could jack into that smile and capture the owner of it. But for all his easy smiles, sometimes his blue eyes would flatten out and the ocean there would look stormy and dangerous. Those moments were transitory, but they were part of the package that mystified and intrigued me.

"How old are you, Bo?" I asked, suddenly realizing how little I knew about Bo outside of class.

"Twenty-three," he said. "You?"

"Twenty," I replied. "Where're you from?"

"Is this twenty questions?" He shifted uncomfortably in his chair. Asking where he was from was out-of-bounds? I raised my eyebrows at him. He sighed. "Little Oak, Texas. If we're playing the get-to-know-you game, I can hurry it along so we can get to the good stuff. I'm twenty-three, born August fifteenth, of Beauregard the Second and Sarah Beth Randolph. I'm an only child and said to be a sore trial to my momma. Your turn."

I twisted my lips up on the side and contemplated asking another question, but Bo shook his spoon at me. "Don't be a welsher."

"I never agreed to anything," I protested.

"It was implicit, now go."

"Fine," I huffed with mock indignation. "I'm twenty, only child, born June tenth, of Roger Price and Margaret West."

"Your parents divorced?" Bo asked.

"No," I said with finality. I didn't want to talk about Roger and my mom's relationship.

Bo nodded at me and didn't press, for which I was grateful.

"What else do you want to know?" Bo asked. He leaned forward. "You can ask me anything."

"Would you rather fight one hundred ducks or one horse-sized duck?" I asked, determined to keep our conversational topics as light and impersonal as possible.

"One horse-sized duck. He might be big, but he'd be ungainly. A hundred small cuts could take you down better than one large one," Bo answered promptly.

Didn't I know it. It wasn't one big scene that had driven me into off-campus exile. It was the culmination of weeks' worth of insults, both whispered and baldly stated. Mostly it was the general feeling that I wasn't safe half the time when I went out after dark, as if I had some sign saying "open, all hours" on my back.

"How come you aren't on campus much? Ellie says you're a campus vampire."

"Meaning do I drain the blood of coeds? Because that only happened once and it was totally an accident," Bo quipped.

"You drank the blood of some chick even by accident? Does Health Services treat for that?" I gaped at him.

"I'm not sure what Health Services offers and I didn't realize I drank her blood. I said it was an accident."

"I can't keep up." I shook my head in disbelief. "You really drank some girl's blood?"

"It was an accident. I keep telling people that, but no one believes it."

I must have had a horrified expression on my face because Bo hurried to add, "I'm joking. I know that there're any number of rumors out there, so I make a few up, just to see how far they spread and how many people believe in them."

"Really?"

"Yup."

"I'm disappointed. I thought this story would include alcohol, maybe a broken beer bottle or a tequila body shot gone wrong."

"Sounds like you could make up a story that's better than any real event that could have occurred."

"I disagree. When there's accidental blood-drinking involved, surely the potential for hijinks is enormous."

"Sometimes rumors start from the most mundane events and what was actually drinking a Bloody Mary the morning after homecoming becomes drinking blood from a co-ed at midnight during a fraternity orgy."

Yup, the germ of a rumor was like the magic beans in the Jack and the Beanstalk story. Planted at night and by morning, the stalks of the plant reached the heavens.

"Still disappointed."

Bo laughed and threw his arms wide. "You make up whatever story pleases you. Spread it around."

"Don't tempt me." Resentment was starting to overtake the want. It was so unfair that Bo could be so casual about *his* reputation, because no matter what the rumor was—whether it had to do with how many women he'd slept with or that he sucked blood from some chick's neck—he was always, always the hero. I knew it was wrong of me to be angry at Bo, but he made a big and convenient target.

"Oh no, I can't promise that. Tempting you is becoming a new interest of mine." Bo didn't even look at me when lobbing that grenade. His delivery was perfect. Throw out an incendiary statement and act perfectly nonchalant. I adopted his mien and pretended that he hadn't meant anything by it.

"Be prepared for disappointment when your temptations go unnoticed," I replied.

"Ah, a challenge. I like it."

"I think at this point I could act the clingy, needy woman, and you'd still give me the same response," I sniped.

"Probably." He appeared unruffled by my tone and my rejections.

"I'm not a challenge, Bo. I'm just your lab partner and your classmate. Nothing more."

He simply shrugged again, as if my protestations were meaningless. They probably were. After all, we had slept together. That seemed to have created some sort of intimacy even if it hadn't been repeated.

"Besides," I said, "I've heard you'll nail anything that moves."

A flash of something flickered across his face, an expression that on anyone else I might have interpreted as hurt. But this was Bo. Rumors about him only made him more appealing.

"While my reputation as a good-time guy isn't all wrong," Bo replied slowly, "I'm surprised that you would buy into it so readily when the rumors about you have been so inaccurate."

Shame flooded me. God, I had been doing what I hated most about my classmates, imputing characteristics and behaviors based on things I've heard.

"AM, ask me *anything,*" Bo invited again.

"Do you nail everything that moves?" I said quietly, still not looking at him, still upset at myself but wanting desperately to know what his intentions were toward me.

"I'm not going to lie to you, AM, so yeah, I've had my share of hookups. All the girls I've been with have wanted the same thing that I was looking for—a temporary hit off the endorphin bong. I'm pretty sure that's not going to be enough for me anymore. Not since I've met you."

I did finally look up at him, and he stared back steadily, not hiding from me, willing to expose himself, or at least part of himself.

"Rumors are the very devil, aren't they?" I said, avoiding his opening. Bo looked disappointed, and this time I read the emotion on his face correctly. It *was* hurt. I'd patted myself on the back for being so strong that I could withstand the rumors at school but I wasn't, not really. I was soft and weak inside. I was too scared to take a chance with Bo even though he was opening himself up. I wanted to take up his offer. I wanted to so badly, but I couldn't. Not right then. Maybe not ever.

"Tell me this. Is Clay Howard the Third the only laxer who spread the rumor?" Bo asked.

"What does it matter?" I wanted to leave. I had ruined the evening, and if Bo even talked to me after this, I'd be lucky.

"It doesn't, really, I guess." He polished off his first bowl of chili. He leaned toward me. "I just want to make sure that when I make it so the guy has to eat through a straw for the next two weeks that I've got the right person."

BY THE LOOK ON HER face, my last statement caught AnnMarie by surprise. I was frustrated that she wouldn't let me in, but someone—maybe it was Clay, maybe it was someone else—had hurt her, and she was scared.

I didn't know how to break through to her. Maybe if I could eradicate this one problem on campus, she'd be ready to trust me.

"I don't think violence is the answer to everything," AnnMarie muttered finally.

Aggravated, I barked, "You threatened to stab me in the eye with a pen and skewer me with your fork."

She shrugged her shoulders. "Like you said, it's not like I was going to be able to actually carry it out."

I slid back in my chair, the tension easing out. I was in combat for years, and I had learned to sniff out weaknesses. AM was grasping at straws, throwing up every barrier she could, because she was *thisclose* to not only admitting she wanted me but actually taking me up on the offer I'd laid on the table earlier. *Patience*, I counseled myself. For AM, I needed more patience. "Do you want to have a philosophical discussion on violence and civilization?"

"No, no—" She shook her head but I interrupted her.

"Because I'm perfectly fine with that. I'll even go first. Fighting in some form has been a mainstay of every society, even in some of the most civilized, like the gladiators in Rome or dueling in the refined historical England. It's a natural event seen in most predatory species, many times around mating. Ancient texts include references to physical brutality, including the Bible and the epic poem Gilgamesh."

"Wow, you've given some thought to this." She looked surprised once again.

What was with these girls thinking I had less than two stones rubbing together in my head? Did I look like a caveman? "I go to college, just like you."

She grimaced, then said, "Whatever our historical relationship to violence is, I don't think beating up any of the lacrosse club members results in anything positive for me. I'm just here to get my degree and get out." There was a tone of finality to her voice.

AnnMarie suddenly displayed a fascination with the placement of the kidney beans in her chili, scooping each bean individually and placing them on top of each other. A girl had never expressed so much disinterest in our conversation and me with so little volume. Her obviousness made me want to grin. I was really getting to her.

When I realized that AnnMarie was going to continue to act as if her food were more interesting than anything, I broached the most important question she'd left unanswered.

"Why not leave, AM?" I asked gently. The insistence on staying seemed masochistic, like she enjoyed the notoriety. But she didn't come off as someone who got her rocks off on being a hot campus topic. None of it fit for me.

"Why should I be the one to leave?" she shot back fiercely. "Like you said, I didn't do anything wrong."

"But at a new school—" I began, but AnnMarie leaned toward me with a glint in her eye. She looked so militant that I was afraid I'd pegged her wrong. Maybe she *could* stab me in the eye with a pen.

"I did nothing wrong." Every word was said slowly, a puff of breath emphasizing the pauses between each one, as if the spices from the chili had impaired my mental acuity.

"Okay," I said in reply. "But I think there's more to the story than that."

Her non-reply was answer enough.

"You know that the only guys who brag are the ones who aren't getting any," I told her.

Rattled, she said, "I don't disagree, but why?"

"Because then you aren't talking about actual exploits, you're playing telephone, trying to gain social power by being in the know. And then it becomes one person trying to top the other. It isn't even about the subject of that gossip anymore. It's a power play."

I knew all about power plays. It wasn't until I was a teenager that I understood that half of my father's actions were because he was a small man, not physically, but mentally and emotionally. His father was an overpowering figure, and to compensate, my old man was mean.

In boot camp, the sergeants enjoyed fucking with the newbies or "grunts" by waking us up at 2 in the morning to run with our rucksacks in the muddiest, dirtiest, most uneven ground on the base. It was their way of asserting their power over us. If they could have teabagged us every morning, I was convinced they'd have done that too. So I understood the *why* that led to *what*. I'd never been able to figure out how to terminate the action other than to walk away. That's what I'd done.

"Why does it matter to you?" AM asked softly, her head bent so I couldn't see her eyes.

"It matters." I replied firmly. AM wasn't weak, but she needed me. Or maybe I needed her. I felt boxed in here at Central, like I was living in one of those tiny houses Finn was flipping. Maybe because I recognized something of myself in AM, I felt like I could relax with her. I wanted to spend more time with her, and yes, if I was honest, I wanted to spend time *inside* of her.

As if my internal intentions had shouted to her, AM's eyes shot toward mine. Whatever showed through my eyes made her flush, color blossoming in her cheeks like someone took a brush and painted it on. But she didn't look away. Our verbal confidences had been personal, but they were nothing like the look we were exchanging. The clatter of the café around us diminished. I could see the pulse in her smooth, pale neck start to pump faster. I understood the vampiric instinct here. Bite and mark. Bite and mark.

There was no blood to rush to my cheeks. It was all lower now, much, much lower. I could hear my own breath turn harsh, like I'd run several miles at top speed. As one, we stood to get the hell out of the restaurant. AM might be running to get away from me, but I was leaving quickly because I was afraid I was going to jump across the table and start mauling her.

The cold outdoor air cleared my head momentarily as I held the door for AnnMarie to exit, but her body brushed mine and I felt all my muscles strain toward more contact. *Down,* I commanded, and I could feel my muscles bunch at the effort of not grabbing her. I wanted her. She wanted me. Now I just had to figure out how to get her to admit the latter and accept the former.

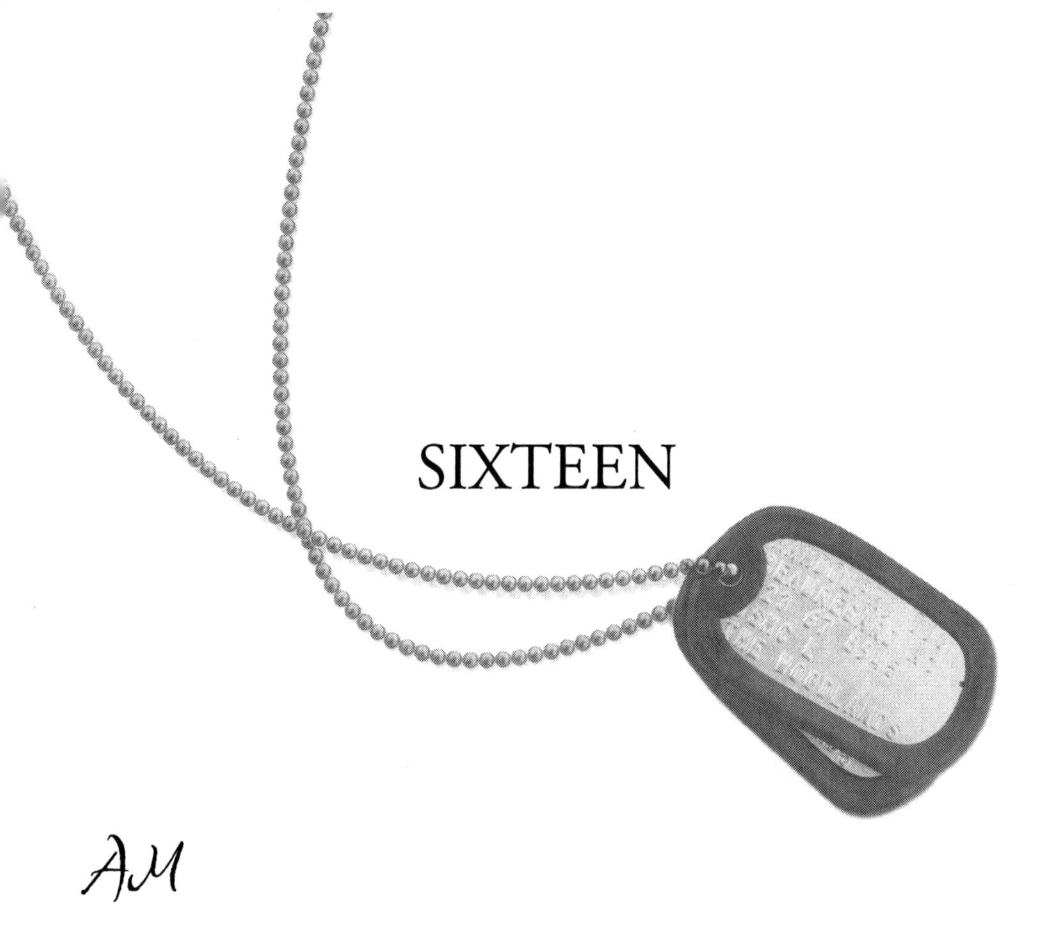

SIXTEEN

AM

“It’s me.” I heard Sasha’s muffled voice at the door.

“The Garden is having an underwear party Wednesday night,” Sasha announced, flopping onto our sofa. The news made both Ellie and me perk up.

“Open?” I asked.

“No, but I have four invites. Want two?” She waved two pieces of beige cardstock in front of us. Ellie snatched them out of her hand before they could make a return trip past our faces.

Gleefully, Ellie waved them above her head with a triumphant, “Yes!”

Sasha leaned toward Ellie. “I hear you’re one of us now.”

Ellie rolled her eyes. “Creeper McDouche the third sure has a big mouth.”

“Big mouth, small dick.” I offered Sasha a cup of hot cocoa, which she took with a grateful smile.

“I wouldn’t know, but that makes sense,” Sasha replied, taking a sip of the cocoa. Waving her cup in the air, she said, “You know I only come over here for this."

"If all it takes is peppermint hot cocoa to get tickets to the Garden so we can ogle hot gay guys in their underwear, I can deal," I joked and handed another cup to Ellie. Settling in between the two on the sofa, I leaned over to look at the details on the invitation.

"Who're you taking? Victoria?"

Sasha made a face. "No, she's being too hormonal. Last week she accused me of being too aloof because I didn't want to snuggle while we watched *The Bachelor*."

"I don't get why you watch that show." I shook my head.

"AM." Sasha heaved a huge sigh. "How many times do I have to tell you? There are hot, dumb women on that show. They're just my type."

"I agree that there are hot and dumb women on the show. I don't agree that that's your type," I argued. "Victoria's premed!"

"I know, and we aren't together, are we?" Sasha countered. "Speaking of big mouths and new people, the Central rumor mill has placed you in the same proximity as one notorious Bo Randolph. What happened to your No Central Guys Ever motto?"

It was my turn to make a face. "He's just my lab partner."

Sasha made a humming noise and took a sip of her cocoa. At my glare, she fessed up. "Martin Sommersby was at Palmer's Deli with his boyfriend and saw the two of you in a serious discussion. He said your faces were this far apart"—she held up her thumb and forefinger to display a minuscule distance—"and that the sexual tension was so thick it was like a force field."

With my cheeks burning, I replied as nonchalantly as possible, "We were a polite table distance apart."

"Good thing you're the math major," Sasha said to Ellie, "because this chick has major problems with measurement."

"Measuring isn't really a math thing," Ellie said mildly, having my back as always.

"Come on," Sasha cajoled. "Bo Randolph is interesting, even to this lesbian." She paused. "Maybe to all lesbians. He should be my plus one. It'd drive Victoria nuts."

"It's nothing," I insisted. "We're lab partners. I was hungry. He offered to pay. What sane student passes up a free off-campus meal?"

"If that's the way you want to play it." Sasha rolled her eyes.

"Let's talk about what we're gonna wear," Ellie interjected. I shot her a grateful glance, which she acknowledged with a wink. Sasha rolled her eyes again at our obvious ploy.

"I'm doing the bra and panty look this time," Sasha told us. "I got a new set at Agent Provocateur the last time I was in Chicago. It's a black widow getup with a spiderweb detailing in the butt area."

"I'm going corset," Ellie announced.

I shrugged. "I only have the one set that's acceptable to wear without clothes."

"I'm sure it will be hot, babe," Sasha said. She finished her drink and set the mug on the coffee table. Standing up, she waved the invitations at us. "Shall we cab it down around ten?"

Ellie and I nodded our agreement, and Sasha left.

"So this is a good thing, right?" Ellie looked at me.

I nodded. "Very good. We get to trick ourselves out, ogle some man flesh, and dirty dance with some gay guys and hot lesbians until our feet bleed and there isn't a brain cell functioning in our bodies."

"Bo is that much of a temptation?" Ellie said knowingly.

I fell back against the sofa. "You have *no* idea," I admitted with relief.

"Oh I do," Ellie said ruefully. "Ryan sat next to me in class yesterday and again in lab today. He smelled delicious, like baked apples. I wanted to lick his neck."

"Did you?"

"No, but I fantasized about him last night. A lot."

"Did that help? Because I dreamt about Bo, and when I woke up, I was more frustrated than before," I whined.

Ellie shook her head. "Do we need to watch *Magic Mike*?"

"No," I groaned. "That would only make it worse."

"You know we've got it bad when a naked and gyrating Channing Tatum can't solve our problems."

I rolled my head against the back of the sofa to smile at Ellie. "Take two CTs and call me in the morning."

"If only." Ellie slapped me on the knee and said, "Let's go make ourselves irresistible."

My one respectable set of underwear was from Agent Provocateur, too. Ellie and I had both bought a set when we were in the city. I'm pretty sure my mom would have died if she'd known that I spent some of my graduation money on this, but it seemed naughty and adult and fun. The bra was white with embroidered lace flowers with scalloped edges along the top of the cups. The straps were made of pink satin and were sewn to my exact size. It was a service that the store offered for free. Custom tailoring for underwear. I could hardly believe it when I bought the set.

The panties were made of the matching lace with the scallops dancing across my butt and along the v of my thighs. Pink satin laced up the sides and tied at each hip. I wore my hair down, curled, and hairsprayed. At the Garden, everyone seemed to wear makeup, from the gay boys to the cross-dressers and the lesbians. No amount of eyeliner was too much, and no color of lipstick was too red.

I shuffled out into the hallway with a pair of spike-heeled sandals unbuckled on my feet and a pair of wedges in my hand. Ellie was fluffing her hair and pulling at her corset. I held up the wedges with a query in my eyes. "Wedges are more comfortable," I said, knowing what Ellie's response would be.

"But the stilettos are sexier," Ellie pointed out.

"Stilettos it is." I dropped the wedges to the floor. Ellie turned and lifted her hair. She needed help fastening the corset. I hooked the laces and pulled a bit, finishing it off with a bow at the base of her spine.

We posed in front of our hallway mirror. "We look good," Ellie said, drawing out *good* so that it sounded like three words.

"Let's go, ladies," Sasha called from the hallway. Ellie pulled on her long puffer coat and I wore my trench. It wasn't even close to warm enough but it was the longest coat I had. I grabbed my clutch and double-checked that I had the invitations. Sasha pounded on the door. "COME ON."

"Hold your panties," I yelled. In the hallway, Sasha was standing with a hand on her hip, tapping her foot. The placement of her hand drew back the jacket so we could see the red and black webbing that made up her ensemble.

"Girl," Ellie whistled, "you look amazing."

Sasha winked at us. "So do you. Let's get down to the Garden and dance our bows off."

The Garden was one of two bars in the warehouse district. The other one was a dance club called Mustangs, a hiphop/techno dance club despite the country-western name. None of us were sure why it was called Mustangs, but it was a well-known meat market. Both guys and girls went there, primarily to find a hookup. Dancing was the mating call. I know this because I've had my own Mustangs hookup. I'm pretty sure almost everyone has. The Garden, however, was known for its awesome themed parties and cage dancers. Because it was targeted at the GLBT population, it was rare to see a straight guy inside, which made it a safe place for straight girls to come and let their hair down.

The undies parties were legendary, but I'd never attended one before this. I knew you were only allowed to wear underwear or pajamas.

Sasha, Ellie, and I spilled out of the cab and presented our IDs and invitations. Once inside, we stood and waited in the foyer as people took off their boots and overcoats. Ultraviolet light washed the nightclub, and bouncers were marking people's shoulders as they passed out of the coat check area into the main club.

The hardbodies were out in full force. Acres of ripped and glistening abs stretched from one side room to the other. Special Magic Markers sat on tables and people were drawing on each other, the black lights in the ceiling and in the spotlights making us look like glow-in-the-dark cartoons.

Men and women walked around the bar with trays that hung around their necks. Jello shots, slippery nipples, and Jager Bombs were offered for $5 a pop. Getting drunk at the underwear party wasn't cheap.

Sasha dragged us through until we found a table to prop our purses on. Cash, credit card, and ID we stuck in our bras. The phones and makeup were left in the purses. Some guys wore long fluorescent tube socks that held their gear. Others had cute fanny packs with the pouches resting at the base of their spines.

Every guy's package looked alive.

"Cock rings," Sasha whispered to me.

"What?"

"The cock ring makes the penis stand up. No guy wants to look like he has a sad package here."

Ellie waved over a waiter and paid for three slippery nipples. We gulped them down and perused the room. The webbing in Sasha's bra and panties were traced in thin strips of safety tape and in the dark, it made her look nearly naked. She'd make Victoria sorry in this getup.

"Oh my God," I heard Ellie gasp and she grabbed my arm, hard.

"What?" I asked, reacting to the panic. She lifted her free arm and pointed across the room. Following the path of her finger, I saw an equally shocked Ryan Collins, dressed in what looked like red board shorts. Even at a distance I could see his mouth was slightly open. I wasn't sure if he was shocked to see us or struck dumb by how gorgeous Ellie looked.

"Goddamn it," Ellie cursed. "Is he gay? Was he trying to get me to be his fucking beard?"

I didn't know what to say.

"What's going on?" Sasha asked. I quickly filled her in.

"Mohawk guy across the dance floor was hitting on Ellie."

"No way," Sasha said.

Ellie dropped her arm. "Yes, way." She looked furious. She pushed her way around me. "I'm going to confront that motherfucker right now."

She started across the dance floor looking fierce. Sasha and I glanced at each other, our eyes wide, and raced after her.

Ellie stopped right in front of Ryan and pointed her finger against his chest. "What're you doing here? If you think I'd be your beard for your stupid fucking lacrosse team, you've—"

Ryan grabbed her finger and pulled her against him, flush against his body. With her heels, she came up to his nose. The sudden and unexpected action shut Ellie up. Ryan dipped his head down slightly and pressed his mouth over Ellie's and began eating at her lips like he hadn't had a good meal in a week. His hands tangled in Ellie's dark, coarse hair, holding her tightly in his grasp. Sasha and I just stood there, dumbfounded. I think the entire crowd in a five-foot radius was watching with breathless anticipation. It was a Telemundo soap opera, acted out in real life.

Ryan let her go, and Ellie stumbled back. She brought her hand up to her lips, and I saw it was trembling.

"I'm not gay, honey," Ryan said and then placed his hand on his crotch. "And this is all for you."

Ellie raised her hand. For a moment it looked like she was going to slap him, but then she turned on her heel and stomped back to our table. Sasha followed her immediately, but I paused. My attention was arrested when

Ryan's face tightened as he watched Ellie walk away.

"Fuck," he muttered and hit his fist hard against the table, making it rock on its pedestal. A dark-haired guy with washboard abs walked up wearing tight green underwear with a fluorescent band and dollar bills poking out of the waist. He was carrying a mixed drink in one hand and a beer in the other.

"What'd I miss?" he asked, directing the question toward me but handing the beer to Ryan. Ryan took the beer and swallowed about half of it.

"Just me, fucking it up," Ryan said, swiping a forearm against his mouth.

The stranger held out his now-free hand to me. "Erik. Ryan's roommate."

"AnnMarie. Ellie's roommate." I jerked a thumb over my shoulder in the direction of our table. Erik peered past me.

"The goddess from geology?" Erik asked. Both Ryan and I nodded.

"She thinks Ryan's gay and was asking her out to be his beard," I told Erik, avoiding Ryan's gaze.

"Why'd she think that?" Erik asked.

"Lacrosse connection," I said. "She doesn't like them."

Erik raised his eyebrows at this and tilted his head questioningly toward Ryan. Ryan just put his head in his hands.

"She has good reason," Ryan mumbled, but loudly enough so that we could hear. "The lacrosse club is filled with a bunch of assholes." He lifted his head and looked at me. "I'm surprised you're even standing this close to me."

I shrugged. "I don't know. You don't seem like an asshole to me."

"I'm not," Ryan said, standing up and looking at me. "I swear it, and I'm not trying to have a beard."

"It's true," Erik piped up. "Not gay. I can tell."

"Dude, *everyone* can tell he's not gay," another guy next to us leaned in to say. Yep, we had quite the crowd.

"It just took Ellie by surprise," I said in her defense. "Plus you did act all caveman on her."

This made Ryan put his head down again. "I know. I can't think right around her. She messes me up bad. I'll probably be the only one to ever fail Rocks for Jocks because I can't focus on anything but her."

"I'll, ah, go put in a good word for you," I offered. A few people clapped.

I turned to go and then swiveled around. "Just out of curiosity, how do you all know he's not gay?"

"Oh my God, girl, did you see the hair on his chest? It's obviously not manscaped." Erik said this with obvious horror at my ignorance. I looked at Ryan's chest but saw nothing wrong with it. I met Ryan's eyes, and he just shrugged as if he didn't know what was wrong either. Soon we were all staring at him, and Ryan, for all his amazing confidence, became flustered and dragged his hand across his upper chest. The motion made me giggle a little. The whole scenario was kind of hilarious if you thought about it.

"I'll be right back," I promised and headed toward my table. This time, a small entourage of interested people, led by Erik, followed me. Ellie stood by the table, throwing back another shot and glaring daggers back toward Ryan.

"Ellie, this is Erik, Ryan's roommate," I introduced them. Ellie reluctantly held out her hand.

"I'm sorry you have to live with him," she sniffed.

"Me, too," Erik replied. "I was hoping for a gay roommate who'd either fall totally in love with me or go trolling for men with me. Instead I got a sporty lacrosse straight dude who likes to read Shakespeare and won't wax his chest."

"You're a pretty awesome wingman," I said to Erik after the recitation of Ryan's assets.

"I know," he said, without any faux modesty. Ellie's pissed-off look turned to uncertainty. As she nibbled on her lip, one of our entourage piped up, "Why don't you give the poor boy a chance?"

"Yeah, just a dance," another voice said. Pretty soon the crowd was chanting *dance, dance, dance*. We all looked back to Ryan who, buoyed by the crowd support, no longer had his head in his hands but was walking toward us. Ellie threw her hands up in surrender and pushed through our crowd. Halfway across the dance floor, the two stopped a foot away from each other. The music spun down and there was a lull. Someone else yelled out, "Now kiss!"

Ryan placed his arm around Ellie's waist and waved his other arm in the air, gesturing for the DJ to spin up another song. He yelled out, "Play that funky music, white boy."

The crowd erupted in cheers, and Sasha and I dissolved into laughter.

The dance floor was mobbed as everyone moved toward it to revel in the little drama that had played itself out. Sasha and I threw ourselves into the crowd, pushing until we found Ellie and Ryan draped around each other like they were trying to absorb each other. We pulled them apart and danced, jumping and grinding and swaying to the strange mix of K Pop and hard rap. As the night wore on, Ryan and Ellie became inseparable. Erik and Ryan had abandoned their table and taken up residence at ours. Sasha's ex showed up, looking magnificent in pink, her hair teased out and standing a good four inches in a halo around her head. Victoria must have had her own invitation, as Sasha's fourth went unused. Brian was off with some girl tonight, the opportunity to get laid by one girl outweighing hundreds in their underwear. One shake of Victoria's hips and Sasha was back in her arms. It seemed like everyone was pairing up.

Despite the sweat streaking down my back and the press of the bodies on the dance floor generating enough heat to warm the entire apartment complex, I suddenly felt cold. Chills warred with the sweat and dizziness hit me. I stumbled off the floor toward the table holding our clutches and drinks.

I looked around me. Everyone was laughing and shouting at each other, throwing back drinks and designing black-light illuminated tattoos on each other. I tried once more to enter the fray on the dance floor, but after one song, I knew I had to go home because the crowd was only accentuating the stinging ache of loneliness.

I grabbed at Sasha to let her know I was leaving. If I told Ellie, she'd demand to go with me, and I didn't want to ruin her night. Sasha waved me off and said she'd make sure Ellie got home safely.

Out in the entryway, I retrieved my coat and shrugged it on, the cotton canvas sticking to my sweaty body. I plucked at it, knowing that in a moment the material would be a worthless barrier to the chill of the winter night.

"Need a cab?" the bouncer queried.

I nodded my head. He picked up a phone and made a call. "Ten minutes," he told me, hanging up his cell phone and tucking it into his pocket.

"I'll wait outside." I needed a few moments of alone time. He gave me a dismissive nod, his head turning back to ogle the crowd inside.

I took a step outside and inhaled the crisp night air. Initially the cold felt good. It cleared my head, and the quiet of the night, as opposed to the loud pounding of bass from the dance music, was a huge relief.

Only the relief and clearheadedness didn't last. The ache of being alone crept in again, insidiously, like smoke curling in and around the base of the floor and climbing the walls, silently and menacingly. I wanted Ellie and Ryan to work out because as tired of being ostracized as I felt, I didn't want Ellie to feel that way. I needed to stop relying on her so heavily, to push her back onto campus and not allow her to regret that her college years were spent in exile with me.

I rubbed my hands along my face. Feeling sorry for myself was worse than feeling lonely.

SEVENTEEN

Bo

THE SITUATION WITH AM WAS confounding me. Given her past, I knew I had to let her make the first move, but exchanging lighthearted banter when I wanted to peel her clothing off with my teeth was wearing what little self-control I had down to a nub. Noah suggested heading down to the old zipper factory. A group of guys met to fight on Wednesday nights—a hump day celebration or something.

There were no crowds there, and if you showed up, the expectation was that you wanted to fight. There were around ten of us there. We could have done this down at the Spartan Gym, but I supposed that Paulie wouldn't want it to get around that we were trying to beat the shit out of each other instead of "training" or "working out." But none of us wanted to be the best at exercising. We just wanted the opportunity to whale on each other for five minutes without interruption or judgment. I never asked why any of the other guys were there, and they didn't ask me. It was bare knuckle fighting. Not everyone was even in very good shape. One guy had a tub in his belly but an iron jaw. My knuckles bore witness to his immovable facade.

Regardless, my two-hour stint there left me feeling relaxed and good-humored, even if my ribs did ache from the blow delivered by the Pillsbury Doughboy. Who knew those guys were so hardy?

I slowed down on East Second as a couple of guys clad only in what appeared to be jocks and jackets skipped across the street and disappeared into a bar. On the sidewalk, next to the entrance, I saw a dark-haired girl who looked somewhat like AM. I shook my head a little, knowing I had her on my mind, but when she moved to the side and her face was illuminated by the light, I realized it *was* AM.

I slammed the brakes on, grateful I was almost at a stop and didn't ram into anyone. I deployed the down button on the passenger window and leaned across the center console.

"AM," I yelled. She looked startled and came over to stand next to the car.

"Bo?" She leaned down to peer inside.

I reached over, pulled the door handle, and gave the passenger door a push. She gripped it indecisively for a moment and climbed in, but didn't shut the door.

"I was going to take a cab home," she said, biting the side of her mouth.

"You don't need one now," I declared. She shot me another glance and looked at the empty street.

"Guess not." She swung her legs inside and shut the door. I engaged the locks and took off.

"What are you wearing under there?" I tilted my head toward her trench coat. A trench coat seemed an odd choice for club attire. Even in the dead of winter, girls seemed to be impervious to the cold with their miniskirts, high heels, and see-through tops. No one wore jackets. It was like she was on a top-secret mission smuggling booze.

She shifted uncomfortably next to me, blushed, and looked out the window, which only heightened my curiosity. I glanced back at the bar she had been standing by and the two guys in their underwear flicked through my head. I shook it. *Nah,* that couldn't be right. AM wouldn't be wearing just her panties underneath that jacket.

I tried a different tactic. "Where were you?" It came out hoarse, like I hadn't drunk water for a week, but I couldn't help it. All fluids in my body were pooling below the waist at the thought of her attired in nothing but a bra and panties. Thank God it was dark.

"The Garden," she said, unconcerned. Likely she'd not a clue as to what was swirling through my head.

"What's that?" I hadn't heard of it before.

"Gay bar."

And that's the reason why. I saw no reason to go to a gay bar to drink. If I had to move it on the dance floor, it was for the express purpose of picking up a girl. But that would explain the two guys in jocks and, no, wait, it did *not* explain the guys in their underwear.

"I saw two guys go inside with some briefs on. What's that all about?"

"Special invite-only party," AM mumbled.

"What's that?"

"Underwear party."

I clearly didn't hear that right.

"Underwear party?" Out of the corner of my eye I saw her nod her agreement. I took my eyes off the road and looked at her jacket. Would that I had X-ray vision right now.

"Hey," she said, her hand coming over to the steering wheel. I'd veered off into the gravel and was perilously close to the curb. I took the next two lefts and ended up in a low-lit parking lot. The bustle of the downtown was two miles behind us and the campus a few miles in front of us. It was a no-man's land of closed businesses here.

I put the car in park and turned in my seat. "Underwear party?" I repeated.

"Why are we stopped?"

Did she think she was making sense? Because she wasn't. "You just said underwear party. I almost drove off the road at those words."

"I won't talk about it," she promised.

"I still can't drive. It's not safe for either of us."

She rolled her eyes at me, but I was thinking seriously of our safety. Did she honestly believe I could drive knowing that she was wearing underwear under her trench coat? Did she not know that this was like every guy's fantasy from the age that guys could have fantasies?

"Fine," she huffed. "It's an invitation-only party. You go in your underwear."

"Everyone?"

"Yes."

"All these gay guys get to look at you in your underwear?" I was outraged.

She nodded.

"How do you know if they're gay? Shit, I'd lie two ways to Sunday that I was gay to get into a shindig like that."

"I don't know. And there are straight guys there. Ryan Collins was there."

That sneaky motherfucker. How did he get in there? We were going to have a talk after tonight, he and I.

"Can we go home now?" AM said impatiently. "I'm kind of cold."

I bit the inside of my cheek to yell back that of course she was cold. She was wearing her fucking underwear and nothing else. Instead, I shook my head and got out of the car. I did a few deep knee bends, tried to lift the car, and then rested my head against the roof, battling back all sorts of images in my head.

I vaguely registered the car door opening and closing. Then felt the heat of AM's body as she stood next to me.

"Ah, what're you doing?"

"I have poor impulse control, AM." I refused to look at her. Did I really think she needed to make the first move? How illegal was it if I just kidnapped her and locked her in my bedroom until she agreed to my demands? *Very illegal, Bo*, I counseled myself sternly.

"What does that mean?"

"It means, I'm not ready to get back into an enclosed space with you," I huffed. Could she not just go back into the car and pretend I wasn't out here?

I felt her soft hand on my arm. "Is everything okay?"

I stood up and looked down at her. Even in her damn fine heels, she didn't come up much higher than my neck. "I fought some guys tonight. A friendly workout to release some tension. I bruised my knuckles." I showed her the scraped backs of my fingers. She hovered her hand over one of them but didn't touch. "I got hit in the face." I pointed to the reddish bruise forming at the top of my cheekbone on the right side. "I've got a helluva bruise on my ribs." I pulled up the side of my shirt to expose the killer shot from Mr. Tubby. I heard her sharp inhale. "But I can't feel even any of that because all the blood is in my shorts at the thought of you standing in front of me, all wrapped up quiet in that tan coat of yours, wearing some kind of crazy getup underneath, like a hidden surprise at the bottom of a Cracker Jack box."

I was breathing heavily at this recitation. AM's hand was a hair's-breadth away from my exposed ribs and everything in me wanted to lean into it and make contact.

Her hand crept closer, and my stomach muscles contracted in anticipation. But then she curled her fingers into her hand. I allowed my shirt to drop down and heaved out a big breath.

"Come on." I gently took her arm and steered her toward the passenger door. I helped her inside, shut the door, walked slowly around the car, and dropped into the driver's seat. "Sorry."

"I'm just," she started and paused. "I don't date guys from Central, and even if I did, you've already told me you're a hookup-only kind of guy. I don't want that."

God, when did I say that? I reviewed my conversations with her. But she wasn't wrong. I was a bad bet. I hadn't had a real relationship ever. Unlike Noah, who had always seemed to know he wanted his girl, Grace, I spent my time being the best in the moment because I was pretty sure I didn't want or couldn't sustain anything longer.

"But it'd be good, AM."

She gave a laughing huff and replied, "That's what worries me."

"What's that supposed to mean?"

"I'm not really good at separating the physical and the emotional aspects of things, and even though we're young, I guess I just don't want to have a series of casual hookups." She said this like it was an embarrassing confessional, like it was somehow wrong to want something stable and loving. The embarrassment should have been mine.

The trip to her apartment was too short. I pulled in and found a parking space toward the back, in a dark corner. Subconsciously perhaps, I was trying to get her to stay with me, alone, for just a few moments longer.

But she made no move to get out of the car either. *Yes, Bo* were the words I wanted to hear from her mouth. Will you let me remove your jacket? *Yes, Bo.* Will you allow me to lick you from the base of your neck into the valley of your breasts? *Yes, Bo.* Will you let me remove whatever delectable pieces of lace and satin you have on and let me warm you with my body? *Yes, Bo.*

Her mouth never opened. Instead we sat in charged silence. My hands curled around the steering wheel and her fingers fretted the end of her belt.

"AM." I broke the silence. "I have a lot of things stacked against me, but—"

Before another word could come out of my mouth, AM leaned over and kissed me squarely. My mouth opened in surprise and her delicate tongue poked inside, almost hesitantly. Immediately, my hand went up to the nape of her neck and pressed her more insistently against me. I stroked her tongue with my own, confidently, and she moaned into my mouth, the vibrations sending a shiver of desire from my mouth to my toes. I had waited for this moment for what seemed so long, since last semester when I first winked at her.

I hadn't realized how much I wanted her kisses until her lips were moving softly against mine. I wanted to drink her down and eat her up until I'd devoured every inch of her. I pressed my mouth against hers harder. The slickness of her tongue, the wet sounds our mouths were making, everything was making the tightness in my jeans nearly unbearable, but I couldn't stop kissing her.

I palmed her head in my hand and angled her so that I could penetrate deeper. So that I could taste every inch of her. She returned my kisses with the same fierceness, making tiny moans of pleasure that made my cock stiffer with every sound.

Nothing else made contact between us. Her hands remained in her lap. My other hand gripped the steering wheel, lest I end this moment with any sudden asshole moves.

She pulled back, and initially I fought it, but then I released her. We were both breathing heavily. I leaned toward her and pressed my nose against her neck and this time felt her body shake in response. I wanted to beg to come inside, but she issued no such invitation.

I took a deep breath and pushed away from her. Pulling myself out of the car, I stopped for a moment and adjusted myself. AM had gotten out of the car before I could move around to her side.

"Hey, I get to do that for you," I protested.

"What? Open my car door?"

"Yeah."

Her only response was to shrug. We were both at the ends of our ropes, I thought. Maybe tonight was a bad night for anything, even a hookup.

I walked her to the door and she pulled out her security card. My arm shot out, almost an involuntary reflex, and stopped her before she went inside. "Maybe I could be more than a good time."

She hesitated, and I thought for a moment, my heart pounding so loudly that I swear she could hear it, she'd agree.

"It's the maybe that scares me," she said and walked away. The pang I felt was indecipherable. I recognized only that it was strong and connected to AM. She didn't look back. Not when she got to the interior door and not when she hit the apartment complex hallway. I'm not sure how long I stood there holding the door open, but it was long enough that my fingers turned blue from the cold.

Until I realized this: *she had made the first move.*

AM

"I NEED A POSTGAME RUNDOWN," I informed Ellie when we met for lunch again. This time we were having fancy ramen noodles.

She smiled a bit sheepishly. "I'm just glad we don't live in the dorms anymore."

"Why didn't you bring him home?"

"Dunno!" Ellie exclaimed. "Erik went home with someone else, so the room was empty."

"Did you do the walk of shame, then?"

"Nah, I left early in the morning so I could shower and get to class."

"So now what?"

"I'm not sure." Ellie ran her finger around the top of her glass and looked around our apartment pensively. "He's not someone I think I can hook up with and then leave behind. He might make a mark."

"Would that be so bad?" I asked quietly.

"I don't know. What's stopping you from hooking up with Bo?" she challenged.

"Me," I admitted. "I'm afraid that he's only good for a short-term fling, no matter what he might say in the heat of the moment. You know how attached I get. I don't think someone gets a crush on Bo Randolph and comes away unscathed."

"We're a couple of sad sacks," Ellie said. "So what now?"

"Now I wish I'd switched classes with you in Rocks for Jocks," I said glumly. "But I guess I'm just going to have to learn to be friends without developing some huge crush on him."

"We need condoms for the heart." Ellie got up and refilled her water bottle.

"So you aren't jumping into anything with two feet either," I said.

"At least I'm putting my toes in the water."

"Traitor," I mumbled. Because I didn't want to spend another hour going around and around about why Bo was a bad bet, I left to study in a coffee shop downtown. Only Ellie knew I liked to study there. It was perfect and private and secret.

Which was why when I arrived there and Bo Randolph was ensconced in one of the chairs, I stood mutely with my mouth agape for a good minute. Perhaps it was only a few seconds, but it felt like a long time. Bo simply sat and smiled at me. I wanted to hit him. No, I wanted to hit Ellie. The only way Bo would have found this spot was with insider knowledge.

"How'd you get here?" I threw my bag on the floor and dropped into the chair that sat at a right angle to Bo's. Our legs were far closer than I wanted once I'd sat down, in part because of the chair placement and in part because Bo's legs were just so damn long.

"Can I plead the Fifth?" He held up his hands in mock surrender.

"I actually don't think this is funny. Are you stalking me?"

"If I say yes, will you report me to the Honor Code Committee?"

Again with the flippant response. I had an urge to fling my heavy messenger bag across his face. "Spill."

"I saw your roommate earlier today and asked her where you were. She said you'd be studying here."

I scowled at him. There was no way Ellie would have revealed my off-campus study place to him based on a simple request.

"What else?"

Looking contemplative, he steepled his fingers under his chin as if he were weighing what information to reveal.

"I want to hear all of it. And if not from you, I'll get it from Ellie later."

Bo sighed and dropped his hands to clasp them loosely between his spread legs.

"I told her that I needed to see you about an important lab issue and that I wanted to apologize. She said, by the way, to tell you that you need to be more open-minded."

Goddammit. Ellie was always trying to meddle, as if she were some kind of hippy fairy godmother or, probably in this case, some kind of Cupid. I needed to talk to her seriously about the *Beauty and the Beast* folk story where there's no happy ending and the Beast gets slain by the mob of townspeople.

"Since I know that what you told Ellie is a lie and you've already apologized, what's your real reason for stalking me?"

Bo shifted, bringing his one leg closer to mine, and I drew away from him, slipping my legs to the side and moving into the opposite corner of my chair. The recoil was instinctive, but it caused Bo to flinch a bit, his eyes darkening.

"Do you think I'm going to hurt you?" His voice sounded lower, almost raspy.

"No, why do you ask?" I lied.

"You're about as skittish as a newborn foal."

"I'm not an animal, and I'm not afraid of you. You're just always invading my space." I had to keep my annoyance levels up because I was doomed if Bo ever figured out how attracted I was to him.

"I'm not, you know." Bo shifted again, moving his legs away as much as the small space would allow.

"Not what?" I was staring at Bo's legs. Even through the worn denim, you could see his muscular thighs flex as he pushed to give himself more room and to make space for my legs. His hands, which had originally been loosely clasped between his legs, were now resting on said thighs. They were big hands with long fingers. I wondered how they would feel on my face, holding my hand, cupping me around my waist. *Safe*, I thought. *You'd feel safe inside the circumference of his arms.* But then I reminded myself that he'd only be good for a roll in the hay one time and then he'd be off to another conquest.

"What do you want from me, Bo?" His face was unreadable.

"I like being with you," Bo admitted. "You keep me occupied." He tapped his head.

"We're always arguing."

He waved his hand. "That's not real arguing. We're just having fun, and you know it."

Reaching across our chairs, he placed one of those large hands on my own. "Don't be mad at Ellie. She didn't reveal this information easily."

"She still sold me out." I stared at that hand, wanting to clasp it in return. Instead, I withdrew it. Bo wasn't going away any time soon, so all I could do was ignore him. I pulled out my textbook and settled in to study, only to be interrupted a few seconds later.

"You an economics major?"

I closed my book with deliberate slowness, keeping one hand inside as a bookmark. "Yes."

Bo shifted again, the living embodiment of the Newton theory of physics. I looked him over with some thoroughness, taking in his bright blue eyes, down past his muscular chest, to the unopened math book in his lap. He was holding a pen that he flipped through one finger and then under the other, making it dance on his knuckles. Yes, Bo was a body in motion, constantly moving.

"I bet you drove your Mom crazy."

This statement elicited a short laugh. Bo leaned forward, resting his elbows on his knees. It brought his face up close and I could see the long, light-colored eyelashes that framed his upper lids. A scar ran from just under his hairline on the right down to his temple. I hadn't seen that before. My fingers itched to trace the path. I pressed my free hand on top of the book, to keep them both trapped. I shouldn't be touching Bo's face, ever.

Here was the secret of Bo's success. The outward package drew you in and the layered complexities that seemed at odds with his flighty persona kept you engaged. I wanted to pull back those layers to find out what made him tick.

"I was a troublemaker. I don't know who was more relieved when I enlisted. My momma or the town."

"I'm sure it was neither."

Bo opened his mouth as if to disagree and then shut it. "Do you know why I only do hookups?" His sudden change of conversation topics surprised me.

"No, why?" I sighed.

"Because relationships require work and introspection. I don't like to spend time inside my head. It's not a good place." He fisted his hands and then splayed them out wide. "All any girl has ever wanted from me is to make them feel good for a short time, and I can do that. I want to do that. I've fucking perfected that. But the rest—having something real and lasting in my life? No."

"I got that message over dinner. You're only here for a good time," I recited. "But you know, Bo, I've heard that you put a lot of effort into romancing the girls, if you want to."

"What story is this?"

"That you serenaded a sorority girl last year after winter formal."

"Shit, you must be kidding. The guys at home won't let me open my mouth when the music is on."

"So what happened?" I challenged.

"The TKE winter formal was held at a hotel adjacent to a bar where we were drinking. We kind of crashed it. Adam took one of the band member's guitars during a break and we all sang along."

"What? That wasn't what I heard at all. That version is pretty lame, if you ask me."

He laughed. "Tell me what you heard."

"I heard you drove over to the TKE house and played 'If You Love Me' on a loop from your convertible until the sorority girl came out, with her white dress billowing behind her. Maybe there was a glass slipper left on the stairs. I can't remember."

Bo was laughing at this. "First, I don't have a convertible and wow, I sound like a total douche bag. How is this rumor helping my reputation?"

"It's not a douche bag move." I took a sip of my coffee. "It's totally a Lloyd Dobbler, *Say Anything* move. John Hughes could have scripted that."

"John Hughes?"

"You know, the moviemaker from the eighties."

"You weren't born in the eighties."

"They're still teen movies!"

"If I say you're hot when you're angry, will you hit me?"

I motioned that I would throw the cup of coffee in his face, which only made Bo laugh more.

"Okay, okay. Sorry. Tell me why this is appealing, because it sounds kind of pathetic to me."

"I can't believe you haven't seen *Say Anything*." I shook my head in disbelief.

"I'm pretty sure I was too busy killing people in *Call of Duty* to watch that movie."

"In *Say Anything,* Lloyd Dobbler stands outside his love's window and holds up a boombox that's playing their song. In the rain. It's very romantic." I held up my arms to mimic the gesture.

He looked at me skeptically.

"It's a sign of his true love," I argued.

"I think true love is signified by more than some dippy guy standing outside in the rain playing music for a girl."

"What's an act of true love, then?"

"Throwing your body on a grenade so your buddies don't become pieces of shrapnelized flesh."

"My God, did you do that in the war?" I was shocked. I'd seen Bo without his shirt on and didn't recall seeing any marks. Maybe I'd been blind? I shuddered at the thought of him being hurt.

"No," he sighed, "but I know a guy in a different unit that did."

"Okay, but that's not something you could do for a girl here." I frowned.

"True love means that you'd be willing to sacrifice all for another person." That was pretty profound. Bo believed that?

"So maybe Lloyd was sacrificing his ego for Dianne in the movie," I countered.

"Possibly. Still seems like a passive, weak-ass move." Bo rubbed a finger across his chin and relaxed back in his chair.

"What should he have done?"

"To express his love?"

"Yes!" I exclaimed, leaning toward him. My hands were planted on my legs and I felt poised to jump him, either in frustration or desire.

"Actions speak louder than words. Or singing, as the case may be."

"He was out there, in the rain."

"But he wasn't doing anything. You show a woman you love her by what you do for her, from opening her door to making sure that bumps in the road of life are smoothed out. That she wants and worries for nothing. That when you think about sex, it's her face in your fantasies, her body you're touching, her lips you're kissing. That every day you remind her that she's the first thought in your mind when you wake up and the last thought before you drop off to sleep."

"Oh." To hear Bo express something so romantic in his own way made me kind of delirious. I could only manage a sound of acknowledgment. This wasn't the sentiment of a guy who wanted only a series of emotional physical encounters.

"Yeah, oh." Bo straightened in his chair and the humor of the moment seemed like a long distant memory. He held out his hands in supplication. "I'm a bad bet, Sunshine, but if you're willing to give me a whirl around the ring, I'm yours. Because you've got me so twisted up inside that I barely know if up is down. I'm so inside my head that I'm coming out of my asshole. Have mercy on me."

I took a shaky breath and stared at him. Maybe he was *too* good at persuasive speech, but all my reasons for saying no seemed to have evaporated. Right there in the coffeehouse, I melted into him and his arms came crashing around me so tight I thought he might squeeze me until I burst. But what a way to go. His embrace was like being folded against a tree, strong and straight and rooted deep. The winds of winter could buffet us, but Bo would keep me warm and protected.

"Holy shit, Sunshine. Your hesitation was about two seconds too long," he breathed into my hair.

I giggled. "I didn't even pause."

"You did. But that's okay. I'm going to make it so good for you," he promised.

"You better. All those stories you've told and I've been told about you—they're giving me big expectations," I sassed.

"They were all practice for the real thing. You."

"That's a pretty good line," I told him, uncertainty creeping in again.

"I'm going to tell you something." Bo reassured me, as if sensing I was tottering on the edge again. "I'm scared, too, but neither of us are going to get what we want if we don't take a chance."

"I want to take this chance with you," I admitted.

I'd just done either the stupidest thing in my life or the smartest.

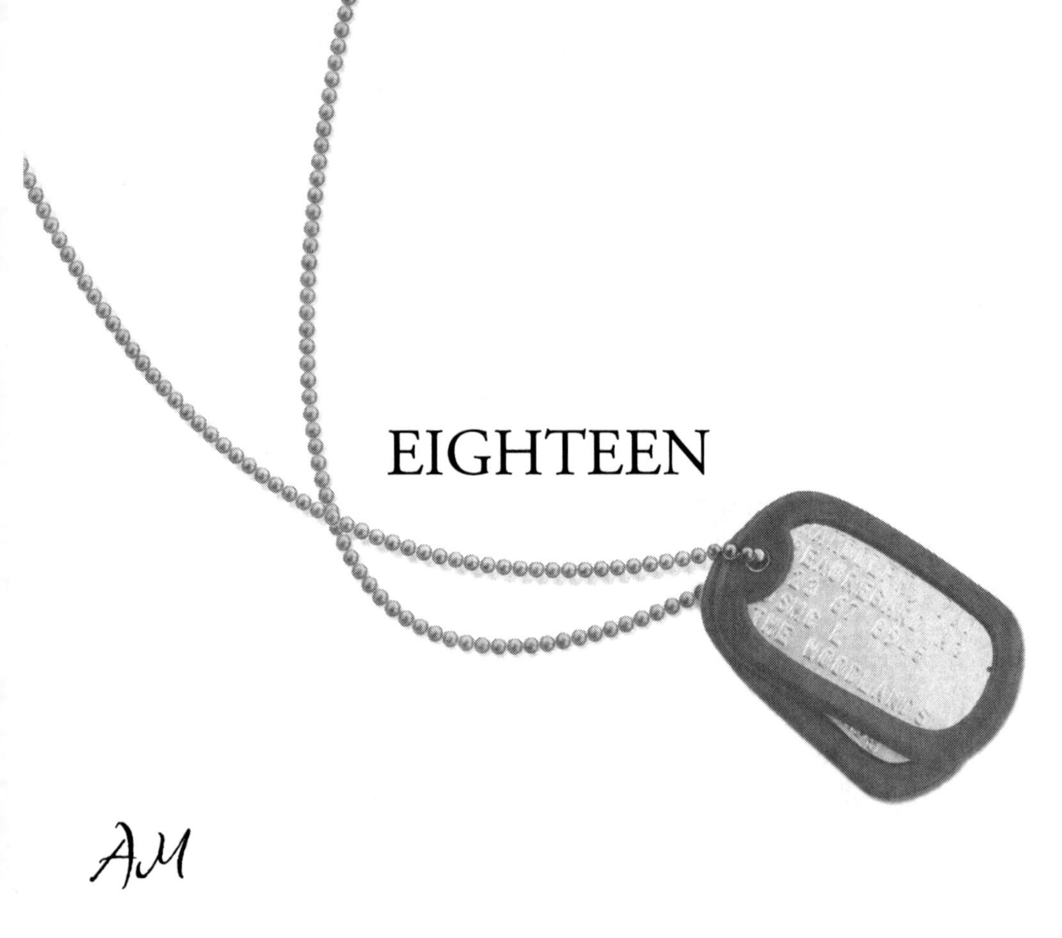

EIGHTEEN

AM

We drove straight to my apartment for the sole reason that it was closest to us. Bo told me not to talk and to sit on my side of the car with my hands in my lap.

"If you touch me, I'm pretty sure I'm going to wreck the car," he explained, after giving me my orders. I didn't tempt him because I wasn't sure that if I started, I would care if the car was wrecked.

Once we were inside my bedroom, his lips were on mine before I could open my mouth. Every kiss I'd experienced before had been innocent compared to this. From the first lick of his tongue against my lips, this kiss conveyed bone-deep want. Bo's mouth was hot and wet upon mine. He ravaged me, biting and sucking on my lips, his tongue seeking out every crevice and surface until I felt as if he were consuming me.

Bo lifted my legs around his hips, and I wrapped myself around him. With one hand under my butt, he used his other to push up my shirt up to expose my bra. The sheer strength it took to hold me up like this took my breath away and shot a bolt of excitement straight to my core. I whimpered with need.

He shushed me and bent his head to lick between my breasts, pulling down one lacy cup with his teeth to suckle hard on my nipple. I clutched his head to my chest so tightly I was sure I was suffocating him, but I didn't care. By the way he pressed in tighter, he didn't seem to mind.

My legs were splayed open, but I wasn't getting enough relief. I canted my hips upward and wiggled against him, trying to find relief for the ache between my legs. In answer, Bo's hand left my breast and went to the juncture of my legs. Through the denim and the lace of my panties, I could feel his hand, but this sensation only made me want a closer, stronger touch. Bo undid my snap and my zipper, grunting his disapproval.

"You should wear a skirt, always," he instructed, lowering me onto the bed and pushing my jeans down just far enough so that he could insert his hand between the denim and my flesh. He braced one hand on the side of my head and held his body suspended over mine. I didn't reply. I was too busy feeling. Feeling his mouth, his stroking tongue. Feeling his hands, his seeking fingers.

There was only one thought in my mind: *How can I get closer to him?*. He began rubbing me in circles, and I pushed up against his hand, frustrated by the restraint of my jeans. His fingers dipped inside me, and I couldn't stop a moan from escaping me. "Oh God. *Bo.*"

"I love that you're so wet for me."

I shivered, the pulse of my blood drumming so loudly in my ears I could barely hear him. He pressed the heel of his palm hard against my pelvis bone and his two fingers began a slow thrust inside me. I was dying, one infinitesimal centimeter at a time.

"So hot. Tight. Can't fucking wait to be inside you." Bo's words were more grunts than complete thoughts. I understood. I had no ability to form complete sentences either. My sole focus was on the slick between my legs caused by the movement of his fingers thrusting in and out and the abrasion of his palm, rough and calloused against my sex. "I want to stay inside you for hours. Live here."

All my nerve endings reached for something and then, like an explosion, sensation rushed down to my center and detonated. I was grateful to be lying down, because my legs felt like noodles, and I could only see sparkles of light.

Bo kept his hand firmly against me, drawing out as many shudders and shocks from my body as he could, and when I finally came down off my high, he withdrew his hand. He wiped his fingers on the sweatshirt that he'd discarded upon entering the room and applied soft soothing kisses on my lips, cheek and jaw. The hand that had caressed my core now moved in long strokes up and down the side of my body. I drew him down on top of me, wanting to feel his delicious weight press mine into the mattress.

As I felt his insistent erection against my stomach, I knew I wanted to give him the same pleasure, have him under my thumb just as he'd overpowered me with emotion and need. Bo pushed upright and lifted the heavy fall of my hair aside as I slid off the bed to kneel in front of him. "You don't need to do this."

I pressed my hand against his thighs and stared up at him. "I want to."

The button had already come undone and I unzipped his jeans. Underneath he was completely nude, and his heavy cock fell forward, free of its constraints. I pressed my face into his hair and rubbed my cheek against the soft skin of his erection. It bobbed against my cheek. He smelled of male sweat and musk. I licked his skin between his leg and crotch and tasted the delicious salty flavor. His leg buckled, and Bo readjusted, bracing one knee against the bed, one hand hard against my shoulder. With his free hand, he stroked my hair tenderly.

I rained soft kisses down the hard length of him and licked the top softly. There was a spot of liquid on the tip and I lapped it up. Bo groaned, and the hand in my hair turned to a fist as he tightened his hold. His hips moved forward, as if wanting to be deeper inside, but he asked for nothing, waiting for me to set the pace.

I'd never enjoyed this in the past, but with Bo it felt natural and good. I inhaled his smell, felt the crisp hairs against my nose as I bent forward. Everything about this felt right. His shaft was thick on my tongue. I could hear him panting; it seemed as if he were breathing harder now than he had during the fight. I ran my tongue over the ridge as I mouthed him.

Bo reached along my arm and grabbed my hand. He brought it up to his shaft and wrapped my hand around the base. He moved his hand in short, hard movements, in the same rhythm as my mouth. It was unbearably exciting to have him touching himself over my hand. Under my hair, his other hand palmed the back of my head, providing support. When

I'd gotten the gist of the movement he wanted, he brought his hand up from his cock and stroked my cheek, feeling the hollows as I sucked and pumped.

I could feel his balls tighten against the back of my hand as I twisted and pumped like he showed me. As I could feel his release coming, Bo pulled out of my mouth.

"Don't you…"

"No, I want to finish inside of you."

I dabbed my finger on the tip and tasted his pre-come.

"Jesus." He gave a small rueful laugh. "Are you trying to kill me?"

"It doesn't taste bad. Kind of salty." I looked up at him. "I wouldn't have minded if you came in my mouth. I thought that's what guys like."

He drew me to my feet and kissed me hard and full on the lips for a long time. "It felt great, just having you touch me. If you want to try this later, and you want to swallow, great, but we aren't going to do that without you telling me you want to do it before we even start. Anytime we do anything, I want to know that you're fully into it, not in the heat of the moment because you think I like it. Besides," he flashed a quick grin at me, "I'm going to like everything with you. Now I need to take off your clothes and continue to debauch you."

We looked depraved with both of our jeans unbuttoned and unzipped. My bra was half on, half off. Yet I didn't feel an ounce of shame. The pleasure in Bo's eyes only made me want to preen.

Bo pressed me back to the bed and pulled his shirt over his head in one motion. He paused, dumped what sounded like a thousand coins on my desk, and dropped his jeans. His cock was rock-hard, and it tented the cotton. I licked my lips, remembering the taste and feel of him in my mouth.

"Sunshine, if you keep looking at me, pretty sure I'm going to come prematurely, which my fragile ego might not be able to deal with."

"I think that'd be kind of hot," I admitted with an arched eyebrow.

"You're not helping," Bo growled, pulling me into a seated position.

Bo's hands reached for the bottom of my t-shirt, and he swept it up and off. Another swift motion disposed of my jeans. He took a moment to give me a sustained look and dragged one long hand down my front, starting at my neck, ending at the core of me he'd played so expertly before. My panties were wet from my orgasm and my renewed arousal.

When I reached behind me to unclasp my bra, he stopped me.

"Let me," he said and he undid the back clasp and pulled the straps down slowly, first one arm and then the other. Goose bumps covered me.

"Bo, please, now," I urged him. I ached so much. I needed him inside of me.

He bent over, his large body covering mine, and licked the tip of my nipple lightly.

I hit him in the arm lightly. "Don't be a tease."

"So greedy," he murmured, sucking at one nipple and then the other, the sensation causing my back to arch. I wanted more pressure, hard and now.

I reached between us and caught his heavy erection in my hand. His shaft pulsed and jerked against my palm. I rubbed him like he had taught me and he moaned.

"Yes, I am really, really greedy," I whispered. This time I felt *him* shudder.

"What're you greedy for? This?" he asked, pressing into my hand.

"Yes, Bo." I tightened my hand around him and he growled his approval. But he pulled himself out of my grip, and I let out a mew of disappointment at the loss of the weight of him in my hands.

But my sense of loss was soon diverted by the attention he was lavishing on my breasts. His tongue dipped around their swells, in the valley between them. Every part of my chest was marked by his lips, tongue, and teeth, from the upper curves of my breasts to the hardened nipple points to the sensitive sides and the tender skin underneath.

"You ready?" he asked, looking up at me.

I wiggled my hips. Yes, I was ready. I wanted the touch of his flesh against mine more than anything. But instead of rising above me, he moved even lower. He pressed his face right between my legs and took a deep breath. Before I could even be self-conscious about our positions, Bo's mouth was between my legs, his hands on my inner thighs, urging them apart.

"I want to live down here," Bo said, stroking me lightly. "When you're running your own business, I'm going to come into your office every noon and eat you."

My choked laughter turned to moans as he began tonguing me in earnest. Flattening his tongue, he licked me in long slow sweeps. He worked one and then two fingers inside me, scissoring them, rubbing them against the front wall of my core until he hit a spot that made me jump away and cry out, but his other hand grabbed my hip and held me firm against his mouth. He began plunging his fingers inside me, rubbing against the small spot of flesh that was so sensitive, and I jerked with each movement. His tongue flicked my clitoris, and I could see his cheeks hollowed out as he sucked hard on my flesh.

The sensations he was drawing out were too strong, too powerful. I heard harsh gasps of breath in the air and realized it was *me*. My body was quivering and building toward something, a physical release that was so pleasurable it was almost painful. I could feel my inner walls spasming and I tried to draw away, but Bo wouldn't let me; his tongue and mouth and fingers held me firmly as he drank down my orgasm.

My body felt boneless, and when Bo slid out from between my legs to kneel in front of me, I could only move my eyes, and even that felt like too much of an effort.

"Fucking delicious," Bo said. His mouth was glistening from me but instead of wiping it off, he brought the fingers that he'd had inside of me and licked them clean. That dirty movement made me so hot that I felt a surge of energy. "I'm gonna want to do that for at least an hour next time."

Dazed by the second orgasm so close on the heels of my first, I gripped Bo's biceps and leveraged myself into a sitting position on my knees so we were face to face. His hands slid to my waist to steady me. I applied myself to mapping out more of Bo's body, memorizing every hill and valley of skin and muscle and sinew and bone. He shuddered when I ran my fingers over his nipple, and as his hands tightened on my waist I pressed my tongue against him. With each lick and press of my mouth and fingers, Bo gave me sensory and auditory feedback. I learned what he liked and where he liked to be touched. What parts were sensitive and what parts were just nice. His sides were sensitive. His breath caught when I licked behind his ears. His knees were ticklish. When his cock bobbed up for attention, I looked up at Bo. "Let's hope you know how to use that monster."

He threw his head back and laughed with pure pleasure and happiness. "I do. I promise."

He took charge then, leaning over to shake a condom from his jeans.

He rolled down the rubber and then dipped his fingers between my legs to gather some of my natural lubrication. I watched in fascination as he rubbed his fingers over his erection and then as he guided himself between my legs.

"This is an amazing sight, isn't it?" Bo whispered. I nodded in agreement. It was incredibly erotic. His body was braced over mine, the veins in his big arms standing prominently against the skin. A film of sweat covered his upper torso and arms. Everywhere I looked, I saw Bo's hard, straining body around me. Above me, beside me, and between my legs.

He slowly eased into me, the wetness of my two orgasms and the sweat of our bodies making his path smooth and slick. I drew up my legs so that he could seat himself even deeper and he groaned his approval. "Fuck yes, Sunshine. Take me deep."

His words made me even hotter and wilder. He hooked one arm under my knee, and I brought my leg up to rest against his shoulder. I was totally spread for his penetration. The thick length of him rubbed against every internal nerve. I could feel my body tightening as the now-familiar signals told me yet another orgasm was soon upon me.

His hips began to pump against me in a faster and faster rhythm. I hung on to his neck, pulling myself up against him. His hand dug into my ass as we strained to get closer, closer. His mouth dropped to my ear, and he growled, "Are you there?"

"Close, so close," I panted. He reared up onto his haunches with barely a break in his rhythm and began hauling my hips in short up-and-down movements as he rocked inside of me. His thumb touched the top of my clit, and it felt like he had pushed a button to release the top of my head. At the sound of my scream of release, Bo let go and slammed into me, his balls touching my ass with every deep, fast, hard stroke. He shouted out his own release and then collapsed on top of me. I stroked his back, smoothing my hands down the sweat-slicked skin.

"When I said that I wanted you to give me a chance, I didn't mean have sex," Bo mumbled against the pillow.

"I know," I replied. "It's a perk."

Bo's big body rumbled against me in amusement. A light streamed through from the hallway, and I noticed we hadn't even closed the door properly. I hadn't heard Ellie come in, but an elephant could have been rampaging through the apartment and I wouldn't have noticed. All I could do was laugh in rueful embarrassment.

"Don't ever laugh after you've had sex," Bo mumbled into my neck. "It gives us performance anxiety." He rolled over onto his back and then off the bed. He hitched up his jeans, closed the door, and went into the bathroom. I heard the faucet turn on, the toilet flush, and a little rustling. When he returned from the bathroom, he was completely nude. If I'd had an ounce of life left in me, I'd have been excited, but Bo had pretty much screwed me into a state of extreme lethargy. I crawled under the covers and held them up, and he climbed in beside me.

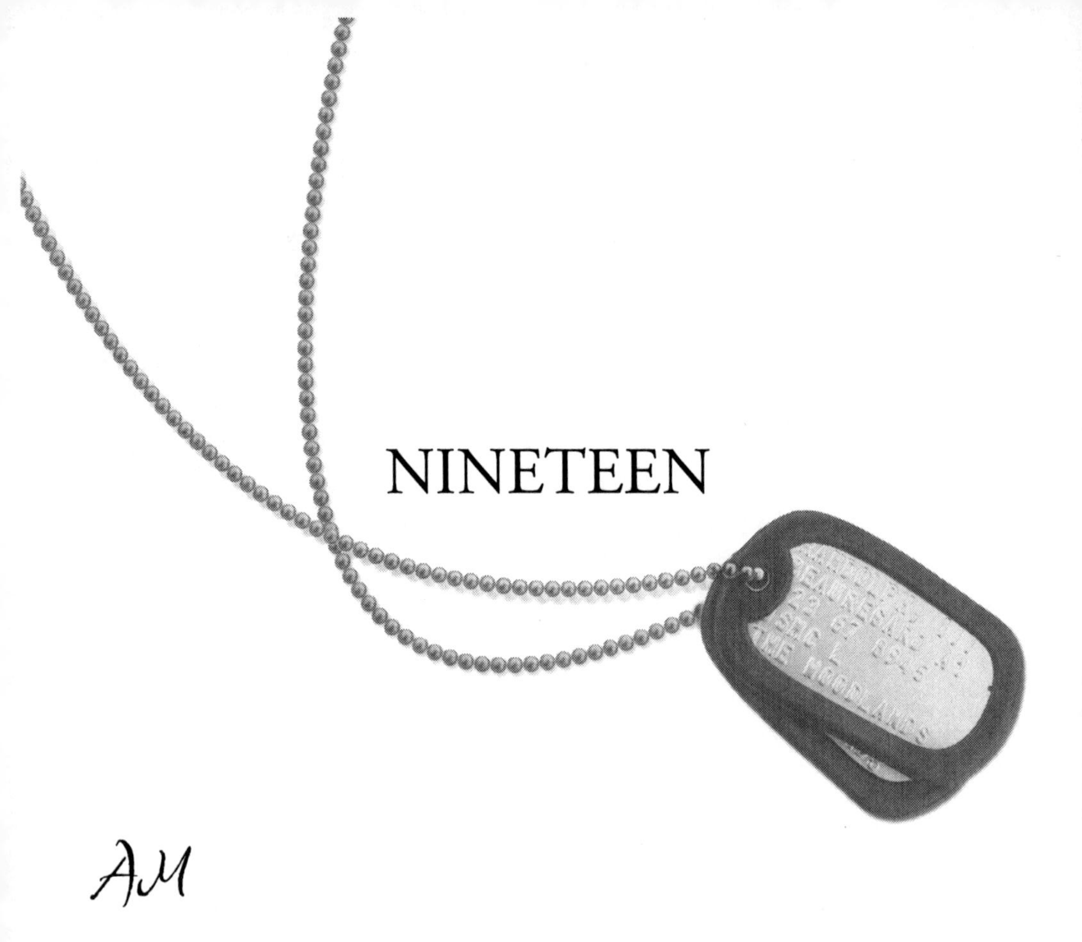

NINETEEN

AM

SLEEPING WITH BO SEEMED TO change everything. It spurred Ellie into moving things along with Ryan. "If you can take the plunge, then I will, too," Ellie declared when she came home to see Bo dressed in my ill-fitting boxers and nothing else, making mac and cheese. I hustled him into the bedroom to dress while he and Ellie laughed at my bright red face.

Of course Bo wasn't embarrassed that Ellie had seen him almost nude. I was the one who couldn't think about it without looking like a tomato.

"Don't worry, Sunshine," Bo whispered in my ear as he passed out the bowls of pasta. "I get it. You don't want to share me."

In anticipation of Valentine's Day, a day both Ellie and I despised despite actually having the potential for dates this year, we arranged to watch *Magic Mike* on Friday night. Bo and Ryan insisted on staying over. The apartment seemed crowded with two rather large males roaming about. Add in Sasha and Brian and I felt like we were hosting a Super Bowl party or something.

Bo was convinced that all of the cast were gay, as no straight man had any decent moves. Ryan then put on a little performance in the living room, both by shaking his booty and then kissing the hell out of Ellie until she was the one red as a fruit.

When we all went down to the Garden that evening, Bo showed off a few moves of his own, which proved that he was once again yanking our chains just to see our reactions.

On Saturday, we ran a few more mayo experiments in one of the houses Bo was helping Finn flip, using people we'd pulled off a Craigslist ad Bo had posted a week ago. The results were largely the same. The women asked for help and the men usually went without. There were deviations, of course. Whether this was the result of social conditioning, however, was something we couldn't figure out.

We spent all Sunday in bed because the newness of our relationship made us so horny that being in public was actually a dangerous activity. Sasha had had to pull us off the dance floor earlier that week, stating that even at the Garden, some propriety had to be observed.

"You look *very* good in the morning," Bo said Sunday morning. He looked edible himself, with his hair mussed from our late night and early morning activities. I stroked a hand over it, more to just enjoy the soft springy feel than to smooth it down.

"What do you want to do today?" he asked, leaning over to kiss my forehead. He tenderly brushed the hair out of my eyes and smiled at me like I was the best thing he'd ever seen.

"I don't want to move," I admitted. "Or put clothes on. I just want to stay right here and touch you."

"Great minds think alike," he whispered, pulling me on top of him. I felt his cock growing hard against my thigh and felt my own body dampen in response. His palms rested on my hips, repositioning me until our centers were pressed hard flesh against softness. I rocked against him, but his hands kept me from slipping that delicious firmness inside me. Instead he dragged me up and down his length, all the while running his hot, open mouth along my neck.

I curled my arms around his shoulders and held on as he slowly rubbed against me, like we were teenagers in the backseat, and I'd only agreed to over-the-clothes touching.

"Are we sixteen?" I gasped when his cock's head hit a particularly sensitive part.

"If you were sixteen, you'd be jailbait. But," and he paused for a second, "I'd still want to be all over you. And inside you."

"Come inside me now, then," I pleaded. I tried to wedge a hand between us so I could guide him right to the spot where I needed him.

"Shhh, we've got all day," Bo said.

With that, I tamped down my impatience and allowed myself to be swept up by Bo's desire.

CLASS THE FOLLOWING WEEK WAS particularly difficult. We couldn't keep our hands of each other. The professor didn't say a word, but I felt like he caught us a time or two.

I had to be the good one, because Bo claimed he had no self-control. What he really meant was that he had no desire to exert it now that we were together.

His hand crept onto my leg, higher and higher. It wasn't that I didn't want him to touch me. Rather it was that I responded to him too easily. He'd absently rub his fingers against the inseam of my jeans, and I'd get wet and have to sit there trying to take notes while aroused and uncomfortable. It wasn't easy.

"Can you *not* place your hand on my leg," I hissed at the beginning of class on Wednesday. I'd barely made it out of Bio on Monday without having an orgasm from just his hand resting on my thigh.

"Will you place yours on mine instead?" Bo bargained.

"No, I won't." I frowned at him.

"I'm glad I'm a lefty. Makes it easier to take notes and stroke you at the same time." Bo looked smug, as if he had willed himself into being left-hand dominant for just the purpose of being able to multitask with his girlfriend during class.

"I'm trying to concentrate, and you're making it too hard," I complained.

"Lord, I'm the one who's hard all the time." Bo smiled perversely. "But I like it." Suddenly his mood turned serious. "Am I really bothering you? Because I'll stop."

His blue eyes filled with worry. He was always so concerned about how I felt: whether it was good for me in bed, if I had the right kind of food; if should he carry me over the snow-covered walk so my boots wouldn't get wet. I cupped his cheek and gave him a sweet kiss. "It's all good."

I did love his hand on my thigh or around my shoulders. His near-constant attention and his need for regular physical connection made me feel secure and desirable.

We traded our schedules, but apparently Bo knew all of mine already.

"Mike," he explained with a touch of chagrin.

I shook my head. I barely knew who that was, but I didn't care. Bo worked out early in the mornings and then met me at the apartment to take Ellie and me out for breakfast, if we wanted. Sometimes Ryan even came, and Ellie and I shared a small smile of pleasure at seeing both guys get along so well despite their five year age difference. Ryan was an old soul, I guess.

"Is your nickname because you like to do Easter dioramas with Peeps?" I asked one evening we were having dinner together. Bo had finally confessed, after I subjected him to much pulling of his chest hair, that the boys in his platoon called him Bo Peep.

"Easter what?" he asked, his forkful of spaghetti hanging suspended halfway between the plate and his mouth.

"Dioramas, you know, the little scenes made out of candy?"

"Nope. And I'm going to have to see pictures of this. Is this like the duck face? Because I haven't recovered from that yet." He proceeded to shovel the food in his mouth like he hadn't eaten in a month, when I knew for a fact he'd had a foot-long sub sandwich after biology class.

"Maybe I don't want to tell you. You might not respect me in the morning." His tone was semi-serious.

"Don't say that. It's not funny."

"I know it's not. That's why I don't want to share with you." Bo set his fork down and reached for my hand. "I want you to continue in your deluded state believing that I'm good enough for you."

I gave him a dour look and gave up. "Do you want me to walk you to the gym before class?"

"On campus?"

"Yeah, I heard you put on quite the show." I pulled my hand back and picked up my fork.

"Nah, I went back to Paulie and abased myself. Promised I wouldn't fight, and he allowed me back into Spartan."

"Why there instead of Central?"

Bo shrugged and took another big bite of his dinner. "Where else can I flip tractor tires?"

"A farm?" I teased.

"I'm an oilman, not a farmer, Sunshine," Bo drawled.

"Are you?" I asked curiously. Bo didn't share much about his past.

"Well, Pops was," Bo referred to his grandfather affectionately. "He had a couple of wells we thought were dried up on the back of some property but ended up having a little left. Leased the mineral rights for a lot of money, gave some to his son and put some in trust for me."

"What are you doing at Central then?"

"Didn't have anything better going on." At my stare, Bo grinned. "That's the real reason. I couldn't think of anything better at the time when Noah announced he was coming here. I've been following that boy since we were seventeen. I figured that if I spent two more years in school, maybe I'd figure out what I wanted to be when I grew up."

"I've always known," I admitted.

"Insurance has always been your dream?" Bo asked skeptically.

"Not insurance, but being able to support myself and my mom," I explained. "I know from other people's experience I can make a good living in it. And it's something that's kind of recession-proof. I need to be in a career with a lot of security."

Bo nodded gravely. He understood that I needed stability in all aspects of my life, including the parts where he was taking root.

If I had an evening class, Bo showed up to walk me home, and he often spent the night. I was grateful that Ellie didn't mind the company.

Afternoons and weekends we studied. Or tried to, at least.

"I'm bored," Bo said, throwing his pen down on his notebook. "I hate class."

"This particular class in general or all of them?" My nose was still buried in my notebook.

"All of them," he grunted and rolled onto his side so he could trace the curve of my spine as we laid side by side on the bed. It was Friday night, two weeks after our coffee shop confessions. Bo didn't seem to mind that I wanted to work on school stuff instead of going out and drinking with his buddies. I'd even skipped a party at his house, although Bo went for a short time and returned a couple hours later complaining the party was no fun without me.

I turned my head to peer at him. "Why? It all seems to come so easy for you."

Bo had an amazing recall. I wasn't sure if he even needed to take notes or if he did so because it kept him occupied during class.

"I'd rather be doing stuff. Sitting for fifty minutes listening to some prof wank on about some dead topic is worse than walking patrol for eleven miles with our hundred-and-fifty-pound rucksacks on our backs."

"What about your trust?"

Bo gave a negligent shrug. "Dunno. Think it's controlled by the bank back in Little Oak."

"Do you have to be in school? Is that like a requirement of your trust?"

He shook his head.

"Then why even be here?"

"What else would I do?" Bo asked, perplexed. "Isn't that what people do? Graduate, get a degree. Work nine to five and then want to kill yourself at the end of the day from boredom."

"I hope not." I frowned. "If you don't see yourself wanting to be in an office, then you should look for something you do enjoy."

He glanced at me and rolled onto his back, settling his shoulders against the headboard.

"Come here." He motioned for me, and when I didn't immediately move, he pulled me on top of him so I straddled his legs.

"What's up?" I teased, my hair forming a curtain around us.

"I'm looking for something I enjoy doing" was his smart-ass comeback.

He pushed me lightly on my back so I would press harder against him. Looping my arms around his neck, I asked, "Is it biology or boredom that makes you horny?"

"It was philosophy, and no, *you* make me horny."

He moved his hips against mine, slowly rocking his hard cock against me. I couldn't hold back the corresponding movement, swaying to meet his gentle thrusts.

His hands cruised slowly up and down my sides, his blue eyes darkening to navy with want. He paused at the bottom of my t-shirt; a question lit his eyes. I lifted my arms in silent assent to his unasked question. Pulling my shirt up, he twisted it in the back so that the cotton caught on my braless breasts. Then he jerked the shirt up, and my breasts bounced from the quick release.

He laughed, low and delighted, at the movement. "I love your tits." He framed them with his hands, pushing them together, a thumb over each small nipple.

"Tits? Nice," I said a little breathlessly.

"What would you rather I call them? Breasts? Boobies?" His voice was muffled as he pressed his nose and mouth against the plumped-up flesh. "Tatas?" He licked one nipple and looked at me with a wicked, mischievous smile.

"More action, less talk." I pushed his head back toward to my breast as all thoughts of biology, careers, and class were chased away. He acquiesced and placed his mouth over my breast, sucking in the nipple, rolling it gently between his teeth. He moved from one breast to the other, the cold air replaced by his hot mouth providing a heightened response. I felt like every part of me was standing at attention as he licked and sucked and my body strained to offer itself up to his marauding mouth, tongue, and teeth.

I clutched his head against my chest and moved more quickly, rubbing harder and harder against his cock.

"Use me, Sunshine." He pushed up against me.

Releasing my breasts, he dipped one hand beneath my shorts. Feeling the wetness that had pooled between my legs, he groaned. "Fuck." He rubbed me with the flat of his hand, coating his palm and fingers with my desire. "Pull me out," he ordered.

I pushed down the thick elastic of his gym shorts. His cock was engorged, deep red, almost purple, and pointed straight up in the air. There was a pearlescent drop on the top, and I rubbed my finger across and then tasted the pre-come. Licked it right off my finger as Bo was watching.

Bo's groan was even louder, and the hand at my waist clenched more tightly.

"You're doing that on purpose!" he growled at me.

"What?" I tried to look innocent, but with my breasts bare and his hand down my shorts, that wasn't an easy feat.

"You know what."

"We really should be studying," I admonished. "We have midterms coming up."

"We'll study after," Bo said and rolled me under him.

Sheathing himself with a condom, he sat back on his haunches between my legs.

"I think this should be our biology study," Bo said absently. He held his cockhead at the entrance of my opening with one hand, rubbing the head in short movements up and down. I moved restlessly as he played with me, but his other hand held firm at my pelvis.

"What?" I gasped. My interest in discussing our class subjects had waned completely. I wanted him to slide right into me and fill me up. I pushed my hips up to hurry him along.

"We're supposed to write about the differences between men and women, right?" I wasn't sure he required a verbal response. With his attention fixed at the juncture between my legs, I wasn't sure I was capable of one. I made a "mmhmm" sound, and he went on. "I'm hard. You're soft. We both have nipples. I love sucking yours." He stroked the wet tender folds that surrounded him, eliciting a moan from me. "You're pink and I'm—" He groped for the right word.

"Plum-colored?" I offered breathlessly, as he teased and spread me open. I wiggled my hips a little to invite him to push inside, but he ignored me.

"Yeah, plum-colored," he murmured. Then he began pushing his broad head inside me, slowly stretching me, rubbing along my sensitive nerves. "Your body stretches to take mine in."

We both watched as he shallowly shuttled his cock in and out of my opening. He pressed down on my pelvis the whole time so that the pressure built swiftly between my legs.

The ache centered between my thighs spread outward until I was engulfed in a web of need.

"Bo, please," I begged.

"See our differences. How you're made perfectly right here for my cock?" He teased me some more.

"God, Bo, right now? Do we have to talk biology right now?" I groaned.

"Why, AM, is there something you want?"

I sat up and grabbed him by the shoulders to pull him on top of me. Wrapping my legs around him, I pushed my pelvis up. "Yes, I want you. Inside me. Now."

He laughed delightedly against my mouth and then kissed me hard. At my plea, he thrust in until he was seated to the hilt. He let out a low moan and stilled for a minute to allow us both to adjust to his size.

Then with one big hand, he lifted my hips off the bed and began thrusting inside of me. His other arm was braced alongside my head. I turned and licked the sweat and salt off his forearm. I widened my thighs, allowing him to sink even deeper, and wrapped my legs around his waist, resting my ankles on the top of his firm buttocks.

He dipped his head and sucked hard on my neck, his mouth moving frantically across my skin. He sought my lips and kissed me. His tongue moved in rhythm to his thrusts, stroking me hard and fast. I held on, sucking on his tongue, matching his rhythm as best I could. But soon the tension he had so skillfully wrought had me gasping, until all I could do was hold on to him as his hips moved more quickly and became more forceful.

My only thought was *more, more, more* until I just wasn't capable of thought at all. I bit down on his shoulder to prevent myself from crying out and locked my legs around him to keep all that delicious feeling in. Dimly I registered a corresponding moan in the pillow by my head, but I was too caught up in the whirlwind of fervid heat skittering across every cell in my body. As I floated down off my high, I reveled in the warmth and weight of his body pressed to mine. He made an attempt to detach from me, but I only clenched him tighter.

"I'm too heavy," he whispered in my ear.

I protested. I didn't need to breathe, but he rolled off instead, taking care of the condom by using his t-shirt and then rolling back to my side. "I take it back. Biology *does* make me horny," he huffed.

I stifled a laugh and looked at him. His eyes glinted with mischief, and I knew that the next time we were in class he'd be thinking about this, and I'd grow hot thinking about him examining me. And it'd be an endless feedback loop of lust, but I couldn't care less, so I grinned right back at him and let the love and lust I had for him shine right through.

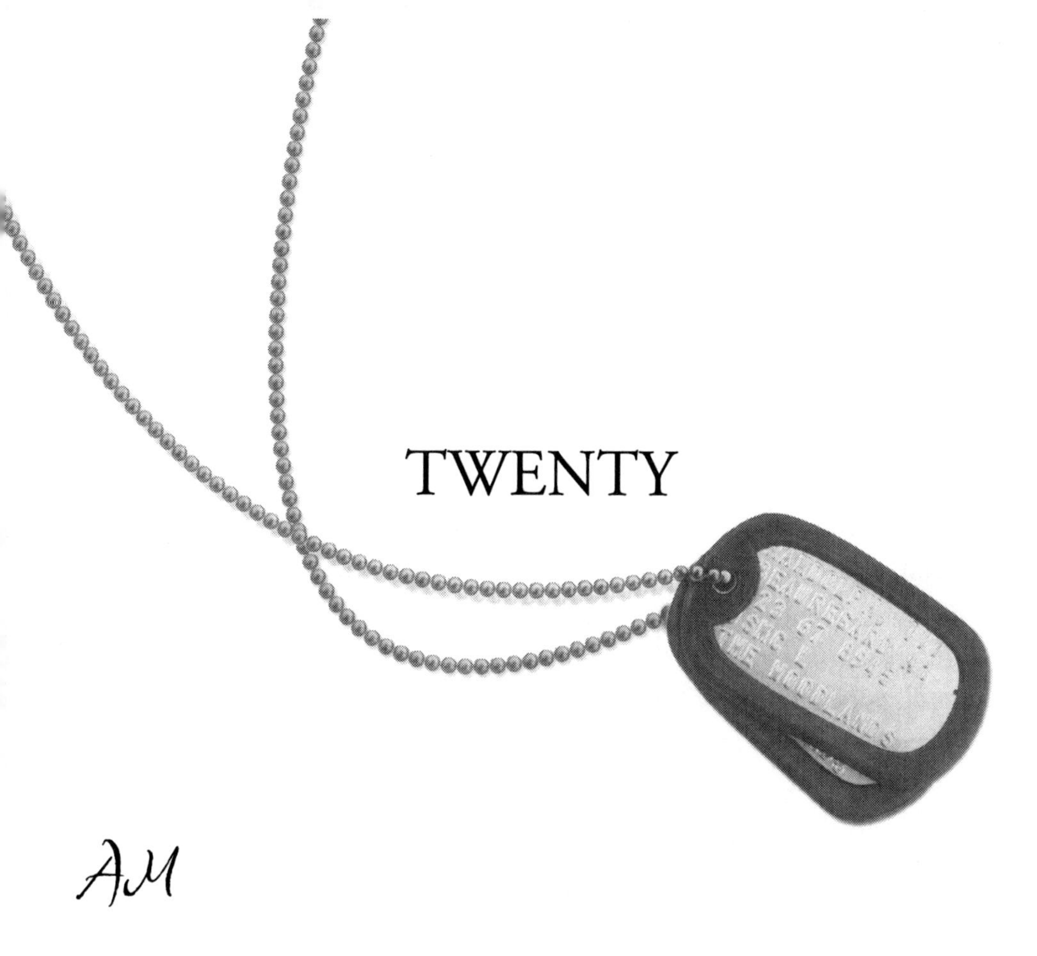

TWENTY

AM

WE DID MANAGE TO GET in some studying that afternoon, and Bo thought we should reward ourselves by going out.

Ellie and Ryan suggested going to the party house. The party house was a big house rented out by six or seven guys on the opposite end of campus near Greek Street. They charged a cover and made you pay for premium alcohol, but unlike the fraternities, there was no list to get in, so it was a good mix of Greeks and non-Greeks at any one time. The only downside, of course, was that you had to pay for decent liquor or be content with drinking really watered-down keg beer.

I hadn't been to the party house since freshman year, first semester, but emboldened by the large friendly crowd in my apartment, I capitulated. Bo looked worriedly at me.

"She's stronger than any of us," Ellie assured Bo, and I blushed as he nodded his agreement.

Bo reached over and kissed me on the forehead. "It'll be all good, Sunshine." I'm not sure if he was reassuring himself or me.

Ellie beamed at Bo's endearment for me, like she was my proud mother.

I WALKED INTO THE PARTY house with Ellie, Bo, and Ryan. We paid for the shots of Jager that they poured and made everyone drink as part of the admission. No one seemed to recognize me, and the ordinariness of it, along with the shot, gave me a false sense of security. The rear rooms of the party house weren't entirely full yet. The party seemed to be in its early stages.

There was no DJ mixing music, only a playlist of hip-hop, pop, and dance music cycling through. I guessed the DJ came later. We moved through the room toward the back deck and saw a few hardcore smokers blowing rings into the cold night air. I shivered just looking at them.

My back was to the room so I didn't see *him* approach, only heard him stupidly mocking me in front of Bo.

"So you're going for the easy pussy now?"

I turned and saw Clay in a long-sleeved t-shirt, faded Greek letters stenciled in artful decay across the front. Bo turned on him immediately.

"Did I hear you wanted to be sucking your own dick?"

I grabbed Bo's arm before it could jettison into the stupid asshat's face. It wasn't anything I hadn't heard before, and it was one of the reasons why I stayed away from the campus party scene. There were plenty of bars and other places to go that didn't involve everyone who thought they knew my business.

"Come on, Bo," I whispered. I wanted to get out of there before we were in the middle of a scene. God only knew what rumors would develop from a fight between Bo and Clay with me standing right here. Bo looked at me and flexed his fist. I silently pleaded for him to let it go. He unfisted his hand and mouthed, "For you." We turned to walk out.

"You know she's called Typhoid Mary, right," he called after us. "Because you never know what kind of disease she's carrying."

The girl next to him chimed in. "I bet your crotch could sustain a semester's worth of laboratory study. Is that why you took biology this year? So you could test out exactly what kind of diseases you have?"

My cheeks burned. The name-calling and jeering should've been expected, but it was just so humiliating and unfair to have the untruths half-shouted in a large room. I wanted to *leave*. Hot tears pricked at my eyes, but I wasn't going to let those motherfuckers see me cry. I stiffened my spine and walked determinedly to the door, not caring at this point whether Bo was with me or not. I couldn't see the cluster of people around me, only felt the quietude of the crowd, as if they were all settling in to watch a drama.

"Who are you?" Ellie advanced on the girl and got right up into her face.

"R-Rebecca." She shrank back despite the height difference. Ellie's ferocity made up for her lack of size. Rebecca wasn't so brave in the face of my tiny dragon.

"Rebecca who?"

"Anderson."

Ellie gave Rebecca a long look and spoke so confidently it was like she could see into the future.

"Rebecca Anderson, ten years from now you're going to look back on this year, and it will be the pinnacle of your life. You'll be married to some douche bag who's cheating on you with his secretary. You'll have no friends. Everyone who calls themselves your friend will be regaling each other with how you're being shit on by your husband, that your kids don't like you, and that the last plastic surgery you had done in Palm Springs was so botched it makes you look like you're wearing perma-surprise." Ellie's tongue was so vicious I was vaguely surprised Rebecca was still standing upright. She burst into tears and tried to get comfort from Clay, but he was too busy looking warily at Bo.

"You want to fight me, little boy?" Bo taunted. He had stopped next to by Ellie, and they were both trying to fight for me, but what was the use? Put out one fire and five more would pop up. It just wasn't worth it. "Put up. Otherwise, you're just some blowhard who tries to compensate for his tiny dick by making girls who've turned him down feel small."

I closed my eyes. The whole situation was spiraling out of control. Bo strode toward me, and this time instead of feeling protected, I felt like a target. I had no doubt that Clay would be making good on all his threats. Roger would be getting a phone call this weekend about the fact that his daughter was the campus whore. I choked down the bile climbing the back of my throat.

"Come on, Bo, he's not worth it. No blowhard is."

"Ah, honey, I'll fight even dickheads for free, and frankly we both know he's all talk and no action. I'm thinking the only time he forms a fist is to jerk it at pictures on the Internet."

Perhaps if there hadn't been so many people around, if the taunting wasn't so public, Clay would have been able to leave the challenge unmet. But with all the avid eyes and ears here, there was no doubt that this would spread like wildfire across the campus; he had to accept.

"No problem, bro," he said, faux swagger front and center. "I'll take you right here."

Bo took a giant step from me and held out his arms. "Come at me then, *bro*." Clay launched himself at Bo, but even though they were about the same height, he didn't have the experience fighting that Bo did.

Bo didn't step to the side. No, he leaned forward and as Clay was bringing up his right arm to swing at Bo, Bo blocked it with his left, brought his right fist up and rocked it into Clay's face. Bo followed up the crack to the cheek with an uppercut left under the jaw and one more right punch.

Clay's head snapped back and he stumbled, trying to grab for something to hold him up, but the crowd, even Rebecca, stepped back. His cheek looked like it had caved in, and he fell to the floor. The music had stopped and the sound of Rebecca's screams were about the only thing I could hear.

I took one look at the scene and ran out of the room.

TWENTY-ONE

AM

Bo followed me back to the apartment, but I didn't stop. He kept saying I shouldn't run, that it made me look weak.

"I'm not weak. I don't need to be saved from anything," I yelled at him.

"You aren't standing up for yourself," he yelled back.

"I'm still here, aren't I?"

"What did you call me, the campus vampire? You're the campus ghost. That's not standing up for yourself. That's hiding."

"Just because I'm not in everyone's face, punching their lights out whenever they piss me off, doesn't mean I'm not standing up for myself."

"You're running away."

"I am not!" I screamed.

"I know all about running away. I've been doing it for years." Bo's suddenly quiet tone broke through my madness and my anger. "Why don't you just fucking transfer, AM? I'll go with you. I hate this fucking place anyway."

My anger gave way to frustration, and the tears I'd battled all night spilled out. "I didn't do anything wrong. Even if I'd slept with the entire lacrosse team, I still deserve to go here without a bunch of assholes calling me names."

"You live in an utopia. This is the real world!" We were back to screaming at each other, the tension of the night overwhelming me so much I couldn't control my tears, my hurt. I couldn't keep it in one minute longer.

"Running away doesn't solve anything," I yelled.

"You're so wrong. It does. Sunshine, let me take you away from here." He'd switched from shouting to cajoling, but I wasn't having any of it.

"I don't want to go anywhere." I wasn't just hurt or humiliated. I was damn angry. I was angry at myself for being so stupid in the first place, for allowing the rumors to fester. I'd been wrong to stay off campus and let the lacrosse team control my image. I was angry at the other students for not standing up for me. And I was angry at Bo for not understanding all of these things.

Bo let out a bellow and turned and smashed his fist into the plaster right by the front hall closet. The sudden shift from calm to violent action shocked me. For a moment there was no sound but our heavy breathing. He looked at me, and then his hand, as if he couldn't believe what he'd done. When he slowly pulled his hand from the wall, plaster pieces fell to the floor, creating a tiny plume of dust. White chalk or dust coated his fingers and when he uncoiled his fist more detritus fell to the ground and onto our jewelry and makeup.

His gaze swung from his fist to my face, and his expression made me catch my breath. My palm went to my throat as my anger was subsumed by the pain and horror in his own face. I reached out my other hand but Bo whirled and left before another word could be said, the door swinging open behind him.

I hesitated a moment too long and by the time I'd reached the door he was gone. Sasha's door was open and she and Ellie stood in the doorway with Brian hovering behind them.

Brian spoke first. "Dude, that was some argument."

"What happened there?" I asked, knowing they couldn't give me an answer. They tumbled into my apartment and took in the mess.

"He didn't hit you, did he?" Ellie asked anxiously.

I shook my head. "No, he'd never hit me."

"That's some hole," Brian said, poking a finger at the edges and making more plaster tumble to the floor.

"You're only making it worse." Sasha grabbed his hand and pushed him away.

I went into the kitchen to grab a broom and proceeded to clean up the dust and drywall on the floor. "Guess we'll have to fix this before the landlord sees it." I sighed.

Ellie brought over the wastebasket. "I've always wanted to see the inside of a home improvement store. Maybe hook up with a handyman."

"What about you and Ryan?" I dumped the stuff in the wastebasket and brushed my hands on my jeans. I realized I hadn't even taken off my coat yet.

"He should've stood up for you," Ellie snarled.

"Was he even there?" I asked. At the end of the confrontation, the faces of the other students had just been a blur.

I walked over to the sofa on unsteady legs and threw myself into the soft cushions. "Maybe Bo's right. I've been a fool to hide my head in the sand. I left the field totally open for Clay and his crew to say whatever they wanted about me. If I had fought back instead of hiding out here, adopting the pretense that I could ignore everything that was going on around me, maybe it'd be different."

"So now what?" Sasha asked. She handed me a glass of orange juice I hoped was liberally laced with vodka. I took a sip and shuddered as the alcohol hit my tongue. Inside, I saw a few gummy bears.

"What are these?"

"My emergency stash of frozen gummy bears soaked in vodka."

"Really?" I rolled one in my mouth and nearly broke my tooth trying to chew it.

"Yup, I only break them out in dire times."

"Hey, when I was dogged by Tim a thousand times last semester, I should have gotten one of those," Ellie exclaimed.

Sasha rolled her eyes. "Not every dating disaster warrants frozen vodka-soaked gummy bears, or else they wouldn't be special."

"Are you saying we have too many dating disasters?" I joked lamely.

"Besides, I have to get these giant gummy bears from a special candy store at home, and they aren't cheap." Sasha ignored my comment but she did ask me, "Are they making you feel any better?"

"Not sure if it's the gummy bears or the vodka, but I am feeling better." I smiled at her.

"How are you still able to generate a smile? If it was me, I'd be in a fetal ball in the corner, sobbing." This came from Brian.

"What? Didn't you see the ugly crying and shouting I did in front of Bo?" The tears had washed away my anger and shame and left only regret behind. I regretted making my friends have to stand up for me. I regretted allowing Clay to have so much control over my life. I had told myself I was being so strong, but I hadn't ever stuck my neck out. I had made so many mistakes, and letting Bo storm out was only one of them. I sighed and took another sip.

"Who says that shit to someone else's face, though?" Ellie asked, disgust evident in her voice.

"People say stuff like that to other people. Why is it so shocking when it's said to the target directly?" I argued. I didn't know why I was defending these people. The things that were said were vile and hurtful, and maybe I was in shock, but the surreal nature of the whole situation was getting to me. "I guess because I'd envisioned something like this happening…when it did it was almost déjà vu. I'd already lived it, and I kind of felt like all these people and their assumptions and their time spent making up stories about me must mean either I'm super interesting or they're super boring." I'd remember these things tomorrow and the next day and weeks from now and I'd feel awash with mortification, but for tonight I just wanted to pretend it would be okay. Fake it until I could make it so. The thing that was making me sick in my belly, though, was my mother. I got up and went into my bedroom and pulled out the notes that Clay had sent me.

"I'm worried about my mom, Ellie." My voice cracked a little as I handed the pieces of paper to her. Five in all.

"What the hell are these?" she asked, reading them and then passing them over to Sasha and Brian.

"Part of the reason I stayed away from campus was because of these," I confessed.

"How long have you been getting these?" Ellie demanded.

At Sasha and Brian's questioning looks, I explained, "Clay's dad knows Roger. I'm afraid that if Roger knew about the rumors he wouldn't support my mom."

Sasha carried the bottle of vodka over. "We're going to need a lot of liquor to carry us through this shit."

"I got one every time I returned from break, whether it was summer, fall, or Christmas, one of these would be on my windshield."

"He was fucking terrorizing you. These are an Honor Code violation." Ellie was enraged and shook the pieces of paper at me.

"Maybe they were, but what was the point? It wasn't like I wanted to go back onto campus, hook up with the Central social scene. Do you think I *liked* what went on tonight?" I cried.

This sobered everyone up and Ellie said, "No, sorry, but why wouldn't you share this with me?"

"Because it was too damn embarrassing. I am still so embarrassed," I whimpered. Ellie drew me into her embrace, her tiny body trying to suck out the pain from mine. I felt the stroke of Sasha's hand on my back and a warm cheek on the top of my head. Within the cocoon of love made by my friends, I allowed myself to release a little of the shame I'd carried for so long. I hadn't even realized that I'd felt like I'd deserved it. Oh, I'd said all the right things, telling myself and Ellie and anyone else that it didn't matter what anyone said about me. But deep down, guilt ate away at me. Guilt for drinking too much. Guilt for giving away my virginity like it was nothing more than a kiss. Guilt at allowing myself to be victimized. So much guilt that I avoided Central because the whole campus and all of its students had become the witnesses to my shame.

"You don't have any reason to be ashamed," Ellie whispered into my hair.

"I know that in my head, but it's hard to convince my heart," I confessed.

"AM, you are the strongest, most amazing chick I know," Sasha said, adding, "I'd have folded like a house of cards."

"I'm like my father, you know?" I said.

"My God, you're not," Ellie protested.

"I am. Roger hates conflict. He'd rather go on conducting a double life than face making a decision and dealing with the fallout. And I'm the shameful product of his own failings." I realized then how deep my hurt ran. I'd pretended that I didn't care what Roger thought of me and that the love of my wonderful mother was enough. But the two of them had taught me that hiding and secrecy was a normal way of life.

I just didn't want to live like that anymore. I wasn't sure why Bo ran away from me, but he was right. I needed to stand up for myself.

I sat up and wiped my eyes with the heels of my hands. Taking a deep breath and giving my friends a watery smile, I said, "I'm not going to play ostrich or victim anymore. I'm going to go on campus and, eventually, they'll all be tired of talking about me and move on. When I made myself scarce, it became too enticing for them to make up stories. When they see me doing normal things, like studying in the library or eating in the cafeteria, it won't be such a production. I mean, how much longer can that story be of interest?"

"We're totally with you," Sasha said. Brian nodded his own affirmation, and Ellie wrapped her arm around my shoulders.

"With you."

All these months, I'd felt alone, but that was a misery of my own making. I had wonderful friends and, if I could fix it, a pretty amazing boyfriend.

TWENTY-TWO

Bo

I COULDN'T CATCH MY BREATH. I ran like a five-year-old at his first Halloween, scared at the sight of a *Scream* mask. The look of shock in AM's face was the only thing I could see whether my eyes were open or closed. I'd made her scared. After being so careful, I'd hit something in front of AM. I hadn't hit her, but was this how it started with my dad?

The fear that had haunted me my whole life. The demon that chased me from Texas to Afghanistan. The very reason I hated thinking instead of doing was threatening to rise up and swallow me.

I ran, trying to leave it behind me. I ran, trying to outrace my past. I ran from AM's fear, from my fear, from everything until I realized running wasn't my answer.

Panting, I pulled up and jacked a number into my phone.

"Yes?"

"I need a fight. A big one. Someone who legitimately stands a chance at beating my sorry ass. Do you have someone like that or do you just trade in little girls dressed up and pretending to be men?" I snarled.

"Come to the Casino. We'll hook you up."

"Twenty minutes," I confirmed.

I ran back to my car, which I'd left in AM's parking lot. I tried to think only of the lights of the Casino, the raised boxing stage, the springy mats. I envisioned the type of opponent I would have and how I'd feint and jab. Do a power kick.

I sped out of the lot as fast as I could, thinking that distance would help me forget her, but all I could see was her hair spread across my pillow. Her lips swollen from my kisses. Her body flushed with arousal. Her face white with fear. *Fuck me.*

My hands twitched with the desire—no, the need—to get back to AM and throw myself at her feet so I could beg for forgiveness. But I forced myself forward. I was too afraid to go back. Too afraid I was going to use my fists on something other than the wall. I ignored the pain in my gut, the coin burning a hole in my pocket, and the wetness on my cheeks to prepare for the fight ahead.

The lights of the Casino blinded me as I pulled into a reserved spot for employees near the rear entrance. I pulled out my gym bag out of the trunk and unzipped it. There were shorts, a wife beater, and some wraps. No shoes. I didn't need shoes. Grabbing the bag, I went to the staff entrance and pounded. It opened immediately to reveal Noah, Finn, Adam, and Mal. The four of them wore thunderous looks.

"What the hell are you doing here?" I barked.

"That's the same damn question I have for you," Noah spat back.

"Isn't it obvious? I'm here to fight." I lifted my gym bag.

"You look like you were in a fight already and lost it," Mal observed, his nonthreatening voice making the words seem all the more disheartening. It was Mal's connections that likely brought them all trooping out here. Either that or someone from the fighting community ratted me out to Noah.

I rubbed a hand down my face. On top of everything, I didn't need a lecture from these guys, who were supposed to have my back.

"Am I five?" I asked Noah.

"No," he replied.

"Then I get to make my own decisions. I'm going in to fight, and either you guys are with me or you go home." I waited, arms crossed. Noah and

I stared at each like gunfighters in the old west, but finally he gave in and moved aside.

"I've got your back, always," Noah said as I brushed by him. "It's just that sometimes that means keeping you from danger instead of running behind you into it."

"We were Marines. We laugh in the face of danger. We *lean* the goddamn whole way into danger."

"If we're smart Marines, we avoid it until we have a plan to defeat it."

"I'm trying to defeat it right now, Noah," I told him tiredly.

Noah sighed. "Okay then. Let's go beat the shit out of danger."

AM

THE BUZZING WAS INCESSANT. I thought it was my dream, but then I realized it was someone downstairs wanting to come up. Ellie wasn't responding. I dragged myself out of bed and answered the phone in the kitchen.

"Whosit?" I mumbled.

"Noah Jackson. Can you let me up? It's urgent."

"Um, yeah." I pressed the access code. I was barely awake, and Bo's roommate and best friend was bringing urgent business to my apartment at a godforsaken time in the morning. I peered blearily at the microwave. The clock said it was two in the morning. A knock, more like a pounding, woke me from my reverie. I walked like a zombie and opened the door. The sight at my doorstep jerked me out of my stupor.

Noah and Finn held a beaten, nearly unrecognizable man between them. Noah immediately muscled his way inside, pushing me aside. "Sorry," he said, but he wasn't sorry at all. "Which bedroom is yours?"

I pointed numbly down the hall. None of my synapses were firing here. I couldn't really process this scene or having a half-bloodied man being dragged into my apartment and put on my bed. "Is that Bo?"

"Yes," was the clipped response from Noah.

The sounds of our voices must have roused him because I heard noises coming the battered and bruised face. I crept toward the bed.

Bo's eyes were both swollen shut. He had cuts above his eye. His nose was taped. There were abrasions on both cheeks and a cut on his right cheek. His upper lip was split and swollen.

I leaned down because I couldn't make out what he was saying. "I'm sorry, AM," he breathed against me. "So sorry." I didn't realize I was crying until I saw tears drip down on top of his cheek. He winced slightly, a tiny drawing up of his cheekbones. Even that small pressure was painful. My heart clenched.

"What's going on?" I hissed at Noah, trying to keep my voice low so that I wouldn't wake Bo again if he passed out.

Noah avoided my question, but instead gestured for me to help me him undress Bo. The jeans were bloodsoaked in spots, particularly on the thighs. Noah unsnapped the shirt that was thrown over Bo and pulled it out from under him. Each movement made Bo wince and moan. But Noah got Bo down to his boxer briefs, and I threw a blanket over him, not wanting to look at the desecration made of his body. His hand crept out from under the blankets. I looked at it but made no move to take it. Noah knelt down and grabbed the hand.

"I'm here, buddy. What do you need?" His tone was almost motherly, soothing.

"AM," Bo groaned.

I came over and knelt down beside Noah. He removed his hand, and I laid my head on Bo's outstretched palm. It was the one thing on his body that seemed to be unhurt. I pressed my cheek against it and turned my head to the side. "Shhh. I'll be here when you wake up." This promise seemed to settle him. He pulled his hand out from under my cheek and placed it on top of my hair, tangling his fingers in the threads of my messy bed hair.

Noah had dragged my chair up to the bed and pulled out his phone. He propped his feet up on the edge of the bed. He fiddled with his phone and then dropped it on his lap. I hadn't even noticed that Finn had left.

"What's going on?" I asked again, unmoving. Bo's hand lay warm but firm above me. When I shifted, his hand tightened and he moaned in distress. "Shh," I tried to soothe him, stuffing down my anger.

"Why haven't you taken him to the hospital?"

Noah's breath gusted out, like it was some big ordeal to tell me what the hell had happened to Bo.

"I can't. Bo's condition would place the whole fight ring under scrutiny. No one would allow him to fight again, and a lot of people would get into trouble. Besides, I had him checked out by someone I trust."

"Maybe it would be a good thing if he doesn't fight again," I whispered furiously. I was trying to keep my voice down, but it was hard, given how much I ached to yell at Noah, throw some things around, and just generally shout out my unhappiness. This was insane.

"He's been in worse conditions."

"Where? In Afghanistan, where you were fighting insurgents and dodging bombs? I mean, really, Noah, why can't you leave that behind?" I stood and started pacing.

"Itemize his injuries for me," I demanded.

Noah dully starting listing them off. "Possible concussion. Multiple contusions on the face, over the eye and cheekbones. Nose surprisingly not broken but damaged. Possible rib fracture, definitely rib bruising. Then just more contusions on the thighs and legs."

"Contusions? Speak English."

"Bruising and swelling. Superficial injuries."

"So the worst is the ribs?"

"Yeah, but without an X-ray, we won't really know. The fact is, for rib injuries, it's just a matter of staying stationary until you heal. Like a tailbone. Nothing you can do about it."

"You know a lot about injuries."

"Can't fight and not know the consequences. Bo knew the consequences. He wanted those consequences and given that he would not stop bothering me to come here, I'm guessing you had something to do with that."

"Me? Bo and I are—" I started to explain but I didn't know what we were. Before tonight, I would have said we were dating and now, with a hole in my wall and one in my heart, I wasn't sure what the hell was going on. I was worn out emotionally and couldn't think straight.

"Whatever." Noah was just as angry as I was, I realized. He was angry at Bo, but he didn't want to be angry with his old friend, so he redirected it at me. I was angry with Noah for the same reasons, because it seemed wrong to direct my ire at Bo while he was lying prone and defenseless and looking like a battered rag doll. I wanted to soothe his wounded brow with a soft cloth and then beat him with it when he recovered.

"AM, why don't you try to get some rest, perhaps in your roommate's room?"

Bo grunted a "No" and his hand reached for me again.

"Okay," Noah said, trying for a placating and patient tone. "No one's trying to take her from you. I'm only looking out for her, like you'd want." Noah turned his attention to me. "I need to wake Bo every two hours. Since he may or may not have a concussion."

I shook my head. Bo had moved silently to make room for me on the bed. I hadn't heard him make a sound even though I knew it must have been excruciating. I sighed and climbed into bed next to him, leaning against the headboard. Bo grunted his approval and laid a hard, hot hand on my thigh. My presence on the bed seemed to settle him, because his breath evened out.

"So Bo got in a fight tonight? Or got hit by a car? And you guys like to play doctor, so he's here in my apartment and not in an emergency room?"

Noah eyed me contemplatively, probably deciding how much truth and how much fiction I should be given. I cleared it up for him.

"I want the whole story. You owe it to me."

Noah grimaced. "Right. Look, I only know that Bo wanted to come here so badly that he practically wrecked us in the car, fighting to get me to bring him here. So here I am."

"That doesn't tell me why Bo looks like he was an extra in *Rocky*."

"Bo went to the Casino looking for a fight. He took one, and then challenged the crowd, asking for anyone with a set of balls to stand up. He knocked the next guy down and then the next, but with each bout he took a ton of hits. Finally, and I don't know why but I suspect it's because of something to do with you," Noah accused, "he picked the biggest fucker in the room, someone who blew out his knee or he would have played professional football as a lineman. A pro athlete. And then Bo didn't even try. He poked at him, taunted him, basically drove the lineman into a rage and then suffered a beatdown like none other. I kept yelling for him to tap out, to wave the white flag, but he kept going back in. Now we're here. What's your side of the story?"

"My side?" I was furious that Noah wanted to blame this debacle on me. Furious and feeling terribly guilty.

Noah sighed and ran his fingers through his hair. "Sorry. I'm just frustrated. I don't know what happened tonight, and I wish to fuck I did."

I wasn't going to tell Noah that Bo and I had fought over the frat party debacle or my refusal to transfer. I ached that my own wrongheadedness was what had driven Bo crazy. If only he'd waited just a few minutes longer, I could've told him I was going to confront all those things he rightly pointed out that I'd been avoiding.

"Oh, Beauregard, always trying to make things harder on yourself."

"You know why Bo isn't a professional fighter even though he's far more naturally skilled than me?" Noah asked out of the blue. This seemed like a random question. Maybe they'd both suffered a knock on the head. When I shook my head, Noah continued, "Bo lacks discipline. He was constantly getting in trouble, just little things, when we were enlisted, but he's so strong and capable and so damn brave that his little infractions were smoothed over. We needed every able-bodied person willing to step up, and Bo was willing to do all the things that were dangerous and scary and unwise. We all covered for him because every guy in the unit loved Bo. How could you not?

"But the rigidity of the unit helped him. Out here, he's just a crazy-ass motherfucker waiting for the right person to piss him off. You need to get as far away from him as possible, so you aren't hurt by the shrapnel when he takes one for the team."

I struggled to understand all this military speak and how this applied to me. All I knew was that Bo was hurt and that made me hurt too. One argument shouldn't have led to this. "You don't have to stay. I can wake him up."

"I can't. Bo would never leave me." Noah shook his head adamantly.

"What's going on in his head, Noah?"

"Dunno." Noah dropped his own head in his hands. He spoke to the floor. "Why don't you get some sleep?. I'll watch him for the next couple of hours, and you can take the next shift."

I looked at Bo reluctantly. I didn't want to leave him, but Noah was right. I eased myself carefully off the bed, went into Ellie's room, set the alarm on my phone, and fell asleep on her bed almost immediately, emotionally tapped out.

When I woke, dawn was breaking through the windows. I looked at my phone to check the time. I'd slept for five hours. I jumped out of bed and ran into my bedroom. Noah was in the same position as I'd left him. Sitting in the chair and contemplating an unmoving Bo.

"You didn't wake me up," I hissed at Noah. He seemed unsurprised by my presence. I guess he heard me get out of bed.

"You didn't wake up to the alarm. I've stayed up for far more consecutive hours than this."

"How is he?"

"Fine. I don't think he has a concussion. He responds normally whenever I wake him."

"He can hear you just fine, too," I heard from the bed.

Bo

"GODDAMMIT, BO." AM EXPLODED WHEN she heard me speak. My entire body ached like it hadn't ached since Basic. I wanted to get up to take a leak, but every time I tried to sit up, the pain in my ribs made me dizzy.

"Come 'ere." I gestured for AM to come closer. I needed her closer. "I'm sorry, Sunshine. So sorry."

My apology broke a dam of tears she must have been holding back, and she ran over to the bed, collapsing to her knees. I stroked her head as best I could with my mangled hand. "No, I'm sorry," she sobbed. Noah cleared his throat. He looked more pained than if he'd taken the butt of an MK19 machine gun to his gut. He pointed to his watch and held up two fingers. He wanted me to check my signs every two hours.

"AM, stop crying. You're breaking my fucking heart."

"I'm breaking *your* heart?" Her head shot up and her eyes glittered, part with rage and part with fear. I understood everything she was feeling because that was exactly how I had felt last night.

Between her crying and my aching body, I felt lower than an ant's belly. Broken and bruised, I wanted nothing more than to sink into AM's bed and have her soothe me, but now that I was here, I realized what a stupid mistake that was. I had to get out of here before I did more damage to AM. For the first time in my life, I wanted to think. Somehow I managed to sit up and signal for Noah to help me out of there.

AM's face went still at my movements.

"Don't look like that, AM. I shouldn't have made them bring me here." I struggled to my feet. "It was wrong. I've done you wrong." Noah threw a blanket over my nearly naked body. There was no way I could bend over and put on clothes. Noah bent down to help me put some shoes on, but I shook my head no. There was a limit, and I'd reached it. I stood up as straight as possible and looked at AM. "This is wrong," I repeated.

"No," she cried.

I tried to shut out the sounds of her choked sobs, but they tore into me with more force than any of the fists that I'd endured last night.

TWENTY-THREE

Bo

NOAH GOT ME HOME AND the four guys took turns calling me names at every two-hour mark. Douche bag, asswipe, dickwad, fuckstick. Noah gave me a Vicodin, and I soaked in the jet tub installed in the bathroom attached to Finn's bedroom. The heat of the water and the pain killers eased the pain.

After I'd proven to Noah that I didn't have a concussion, I went over to AM's apartment, but she wasn't home. I had no idea where she was. I weaseled my way inside the security door by flirting with a resident and then popped AM's disgustingly easy locks with a credit card.

After inspecting the hole I'd made, I called and asked Finn to bring over supplies for repair.

"Your fist?" Finn asked when I let him into the apartment.

"Yup."

Finn shook his head. "They just don't make walls like they used to." He set down a bucket that contained a bunch of tools and pulled out what looked like a tiny saw. "Do you want to learn to do this or do you just want me to fix it?"

I looked at his tools: knife, hammer, power drill. "Is this a joke? Of course I want to fix it." Not only would I get to use tools but I'd be able to brag to AM about it if I could bring myself to face her again. After running away like a chicken this morning I realized I had a lot of groveling and explaining to do. I was a mess, wanting to be with her and knowing that if I stayed I'd end up breaking her heart or worse. Patching this hole up was the least I could do. Whatever rip I'd torn between us wasn't reparable.

Finn looked at my bruised and swollen fingers and shrugged his shoulders.

"Cut the hole into a square with this knife and then cut a square of this drywall to make the patch," Finn instructed. He handed me the knife, which I clumsily grasped, and I went to work. The sheetrock crumbled as I sawed my way around the hole I'd punched. Bits of it clung to the back of my hand and other pieces fell to the ground to dust my boots and the carpet.

"You enjoy flipping houses, Finn?" I asked as I finished creating a square in the wall. I'm sure Finn could have fixed about ten houses by now but he stood patiently while I fumbled with the tools. I held up the partial piece that Finn had handed me and marked the sides with a pencil.

"Yeah, it's okay. Here, score the front and the back and then just break it off," Finn told me, running the knife down the pencil line I'd made. I broke the shorter piece off.

"This is cool," I told him. "You go to school for that? Is there like a construction school?" I repeated the cut on the other side.

"The 'on the job' school, you mean? I went to State and got my business degree and worked summers at my dad's construction company." Finn leaned against the wall and watched me construct my little square patch.

"Why aren't you working for him?" I asked, lifting the square to see if it fit into the hole. Perfect, I thought.

Finn didn't answer and I looked over my shoulder to see him peering at his boots. "Flip?" I asked him, using the nickname that one of my other roommates had used once in jest.

"Why do you and Noah never go home to Texas?" Finn answered.

"Gotcha." I turned back to the wall. Those were things filed under "don't want to talk about it." "Now what?"

Finn pulled out a sheer tape that looked like it had little fibers running through it. "Tape the patch to the wall with this, and then we'll mud over it."

As we were putting on the final touches of white plaster, or what Finn called mud, I asked him, "You ever feel like hitting a woman, Finn?"

Finn sighed, knelt down, and started packing his tools away. "Is there any beer in this joint?"

"Why?"

"We gotta wait until the plaster dries, and then we have to sand it smooth."

"Oh, okay." I went over to the kitchen and opened the refrigerator. It was filled with diet soda and juice. I started going through the cupboards and found a bottle of vodka. "How about a screwdriver?"

Finn's look clearly conveyed distaste and resignation. "Vodka on the rocks?" I offered as an alternative.

"Whatever." He walked over to AM's ugly sofa.

"Are these chicks color-blind?" Finn asked as he stood next to the monstrosity.

"Not that I know of." Finn sat down and looked like he was swallowed inside the cushions.

"Goddamn," I heard him moan. "This is the most comfortable sofa ever."

I found two glasses and pulled some ice from the freezer. Poured two large fingers of vodka and a splash of OJ.

I handed a glass to Finn as I rounded the sofa and sat on the other end. I sank down deep, as if embraced by an actual goose. "There's something wrong with those girls for not covering it. Looks like snails are leaving a blood trail behind them." But given AM's penchant for not running away, I guess it made a perverse kind of sense.

Finn laughed and took a long draught of the vodka. "Yeah, I have thought of it."

It took me a minute to track back and remember what question Finn was answering. "And?"

"My mother."

"Dude, what?" I choked on my ice cube. I had kind of asked the question half-facetiously so Finn could tell me I was fucked up and that I belonged a thousand feet away from AM at all times. Finn fell firmly in the decent guy category, but he was just as fit as Noah or me. His muscles were developed from hard work rather than the gym. He carted around boards and pulled down walls. A blow from his fist would probably level a woman.

"She cheated on my dad with my dad's brother." He took another drink. "Worst part, my dad and uncle are in business together and still are. Which is why I flip houses instead of build them with my dad like we'd always planned."

"That's..." I didn't know what to say. It wasn't a story I'd ever heard before. It was like something you'd see on a daytime drama and that you'd think was all made up and shit.

"Unbelievable? Incredible? Disgusting?"

I just nodded.

"When my mom finally confessed, my dad looked devastated, and I wanted to hit her. Make her feel even a portion of the pain she'd caused us."

"But you didn't?"

"No. I went outside and chopped a tree down in our backyard. It was her favorite. Took me an hour." Another sip and an evil grin appeared. "Damn, that felt good." He rolled his shoulders as if remembering the pain of the effort and appreciating it.

"She cry?" Finn might have hated his mom about as much as I hated my dad.

"Her little lower lip trembled, but she heroically kept her tears in," Finn said grimly.

"Damn. But I hear you."

"So you're worried that you're going to hit AnnMarie?"

"Or someone," I admitted and tossed back half my glass. There wasn't enough liquor to smooth the passage of my story so I just vomited it out. "My dad beat the shit out of my mom all the time while I was growing up. I begged her to leave, but she just refused. Said that she was married to him and she wouldn't leave him. That I didn't understand." I drank the rest and slammed the glass on the table. "I didn't understand. Still don't.

"But I want to fight sometimes. I enjoy the violence, the danger. I like my fist driving into someone's face, hearing the crack of the bone, feeling the flesh give way. I like imagining it's my dad's face each and every time."

"You've got issues," Finn said.

"I know," I replied glumly.

"You should talk to Lana."

"What?" Lana was Grace's cousin and a psychology major. I guess talking to her was better than not seeing AM ever again.

"That girl's scary. Hot but scary," Finn went on.

"What makes you say that?"

"Last party we had? I said something about how those 'your momma' jokes are like a documentary of my life, and Lana leaned over and said 'Oedipus, huh?' I had to look it up."

"And."

"He's the original mother-fucker."

"Ouch."

"I'm hoping there's another Greek character I can be patterned after."

"Ask Noah. He's read *The Odyssey*."

After we'd sanded the patch smooth, Finn pulled out a jar of white paint that I applied over the patch. When we were done it didn't look half bad. I swept up all the debris until the place looked like we'd never been there. Could it be as easy fixing things with AM? I doubted it, but because I was a dumb impulsive ass, I left a Post-it note on the mirror in the front hall.

AM

Sorry about the hole in the wall. And everything else.

Bo

TWENTY-FOUR

AM

BO SKIPPED MONDAY CLASS. I kept his note in my backpack the entire time. I didn't know what to make of it. The minute I had read it, I texted him back that I was sorry, too, but silence was the only response.

Instead, I had to take the one phone call I was dreading. At 6 in the evening on Monday, my phone rang and the caller ID showed an unknown source with the Chicago area code. It could only be Roger.

I swallowed hard and answered it. "AnnMarie here."

"AnnMarie, it's Roger. Roger Price." I rolled my eyes. How many Rogers did he think I knew?

"This is a surprise, Roger." I enunciated his name carefully so that he was clear that I knew exactly to whom I was speaking.

"Yes, well," he cleared his throat, "I've received a disturbing phone call from an old Central College classmate of mine."

I decided to go on the offensive because at this point, what did I really have to lose? "Clay Howard's calling his dad to spread rumors about me now? I knew he took my brush-off hard, but this is kind of ridiculous, don't you think?"

"Hmmph," he said. I held my breath as Roger processed this. "Is this some kind of bad prank?" he finally asked.

"Like a fraternity prank? I'm not Greek, Roger." I emphasized his name again petulantly. "But if it is a prank, it's in really poor taste."

"I think we both agree on that," Roger said. "AnnMarie, are you trying to act out to get my attention? As I explained to your mother, I'm sorry we couldn't spend more time together at the holidays but my, ah, other obligations were pressing. I'd like to take the two of you to Italy during your spring break this year."

Unbelievable. Roger, the narcissist, thought it was all about him. I wasn't even sure that he cared if I was the college slut. He only cared whether I was engaged in some post-teen rebellion that might reflect badly on him. I didn't know what my mother saw in him.

"Do you love Mom, really love her?" I asked.

The question must have caught him off guard because he didn't have an immediate response. When he answered, his words were measured, his voice cautious. "Our situation may be unconventional, but yes, I do care for your mother deeply."

Just not enough to leave your wife, I thought. Not wanting to antagonize Roger more, I simply replied, "I hope so."

"Well, then, thank you for taking my call, AnnMarie. I'll be sure to tell Clay Howard just exactly what I think of his son making up stories simply because he was rejected. Very ugly flaw in his character. I hope everything else is going well?" Roger's voice turned formal again.

"Swimmingly, Roger, just swimmingly," I said.

"You'll call if you need anything? You can reach me by this number," Roger offered, ignoring my sarcasm.

This time the pause was on my end. Roger had never offered me anything before.

"I thought you preferred not to receive my requests?" It was more question than statement.

"And I, AnnMarie, thought that your frequent avoidance of me meant that you preferred that I didn't exist," Roger replied bluntly.

"Huh, I guess we were both wrong," I sighed. Roger made me repeat the phone number to him before he hung up.

I stared at the phone in my hand with disbelief. Was it possible that Clay's threat was actually going to mend a rift between my father and me? It's not like we were immediately going to fall into a father-daughter relationship, but perhaps we could actually sit in the same room together without being overwhelmed with animosity.

Speaking of animosity, Ellie sat in the living room staring blindly at the TV. She'd fought with Ryan, but over what I wasn't sure. What was it that she expected him to do? It was almost comical how it had all gone south so quickly. One night you're watching naked men together and the next no one was talking to each other.

Maybe I couldn't fix Bo and me tonight, but I could help Ellie. Ellie didn't even move as I walked over to the coffee table and picked up her phone. "I need to text myself from your phone. I'm worried my texts aren't going through. Bo hasn't responded at all."

All true, but that wasn't why I was using her phone. I was stealing Ryan's number so I could meet up with him. And I was going to do it on campus. Maybe even in the library, and if Clay was there, all the better.

You still care about Ellie? – AM

My phone pinged immediately.

YES! I screwed up again but not sure how.

Meet me in 15 at the library?

Library?!? U sure? Sat. night was rough. Sorry! We can meet elsewhere.

Am fine. Don't care about what ppl are saying. CU soon.

OK.

Before I left, though, I threw Clay's notes away. They had no hold over me now.

"Ellie," I called over my shoulder. "I'm going out. My phone works now."

"Okay," she mumbled.

Ryan was sitting on the third floor near the O-P-Q section of the fiction books in the library. Perhaps he'd had some hope that Ellie would be with me because when he saw it was just me, a half-hopeful smile turned crestfallen.

"That's a sad look," I teased weakly.

Ryan snorted and then put his head in both hands. "God, what happened Saturday night?"

"That's what I want to know," I replied. "I didn't even see you."

"I got a text from Ellie that she was going to the party house with you guys. I told her I'd meet her there. I came in at the point when everyone was rushing out," Ryan declared. "I didn't know what had happened until like a half hour later."

"What did happen after we left?" I'd been so caught up in the drama playing out in my apartment that I hadn't given a thought to what had gone on back on campus.

"The party kind of broke up. I don't know if people left because they thought someone was going to call the cops or what," Ryan said. "A couple of my teammates and I carried Clay home."

"Is he going to press charges?" I worried that Bo would get in trouble for this.

"Nah, we talked him out of it. Told him it would make him look like a pussy," Ryan said and then grimaced. "No offense."

"Whatever." I couldn't care less about his pejorative use of gendered words right now. "Why is Ellie moping around?"

"She saw me as she ran out and thought I was standing around, just listening." Ryan looked down guiltily. "And I guess I was. I mean, I knew since the incident at the QC Café that Clay was behind those rumors. You aren't the only one, you know."

"What?" I gasped.

"Yeah, the lacrosse club has a book of girls that they want get back at. It's like revenge porn, I guess, but instead of putting up nudes of their exes—which they totally do by the way—they spread rumors about the girls that turn them down. It's their way of taking the girls down a peg or two," Ryan confessed.

"And you knew this for how long?" I frowned at Ryan. Maybe he wasn't the good guy I thought he was.

"Just last night. After we brought Clay home and dumped him in his room, I asked what the hell was going on. One of the younger guys caved and confessed. It'd bothered the shit out of him, but he'd been reluctant to confront Clay about it." Ryan huffed a deep sigh and leaned back in his chair, seemingly relieved to get it all out. "After all, what could he have done?"

"Who are the girls?" Were they freshmen? Could I have done something to put an end to this? The shame I'd tried hard to disperse was creeping back in.

"Not sure. My friend said some of the girls transferred or graduated." Ryan grimaced. "I think you were their new pet project."

I shuddered. "Great."

This wasn't what I was expecting when I'd asked Ryan to meet up with me. Pushing that aside for a moment, I said, "You need to just be persistent and tell Ellie the truth. But not about the revenge rumors. Okay?"

"She won't answer her phone. How am I supposed to be persistent?"

I handed him my keys. I owed Ellie one. "Don't make me regret this. Go now and sweep her off her feet."

Ryan snatched the keys up and was out of the library before I could even stand up from the table. One problem down. A million more to face. I laid my head on the table and wished I could start over.

AS I STARED AT THE heavy brass knocker of Lana Sullivan's door, I wondered exactly what I was doing here. Lana was a second-year psych major with an eating disorder. What possible help could she give me?

I shifted my weight restlessly from side to side and turned to leave, but before I got even halfway down the steps, I heard the door open and her voice call out, "Running away already?"

Christ. Hot but scary.

I turned back and leaned against the wall of the stairwell, not yet committing to returning to Lana's pop-up psychology tent. "No, just wondering why the world doesn't make sense for me."

"Age-old question. Existentialism. Do I make sense in a fucked-up world?" Lana pushed open the door and walked away, not even waiting for an answer.

I followed. Damn, maybe she knew what she was doing. Closing the door behind me, I noticed she was making herself a drink. Fizzy pink lemonade went into a glass followed by a generous dose of vodka.

"I'll take one without the fruit."

"Vodka on the rocks, coming up."

"Do all therapy sessions involve alcohol? Because if so, I see why it's popular."

"Nope, only mine."

She handed me a large tumbler with ice cubes and what seemed like a fifth of vodka.

"Do you think I'm that fucked up that I need an entire bottle of vodka to fix me?"

Lana shook her long blond hair. "It's to loosen you up."

She led me over to the sofa, but I looked at it dubiously. I'd heard a lot of activity took place on that sofa. Lana huffed and pushed me into the chair next to it. "Is Grace still bad-mouthing this sofa?"

I nodded, taking a long draught from the tumbler. "Yes, she's warned all of us that the sofa's to be used only in the direst of circumstances because it was infected by Peter the Pumpkin Eater, as she calls him. I take it he's an ex?"

"Yeah. He's clean, as far as I know, though. But enough about Grace's sofa-phobia. What are you doing here? Trying to find the best way to break Noah and Grace up?"

"No!" I exclaimed. "What kind of jackass do you think I am? Is that what Grace thinks?" More importantly, was she saying shit like that to Noah?

Lana scratched delicately behind her ear, like a Persian cat, and contemplated me. "Nah, I was just testing you out. Although, Grace does still think you don't like her."

"I don't know her well enough to like her or dislike her," I said flatly. "But she makes my boy happy and that's enough for me." I didn't add the "for now," but Lana let it go.

"Why are you here?"

"Because Grace says you're always trying to give her advice."

Lana rolled her eyes. "What do you need advice about?"

"Stuff." Even sitting here, I was reluctant to share. I had held on to the secret of my dad's behavior so long, it seemed weird to say it out loud. I felt like I was admitting to some defect. Would Lana think I was a monster because my dad was?

"Stuff is a broad topic," Lana said mildly. She stretched her legs out, lifting her delicate feet and resting them on the stuffed cube in front of her chair, looking like she could wait me out all day long.

I opened my mouth and I told her everything I had shared with Finn. My dickhead dad. My confusion with my mother. My fear of hurting AM. Lana simply listened. Her face didn't change one iota. If anything, the longer I went on, the more bored she looked, as if my story was mundane and ordinary and not at all the source of nightmares.

"You could write stuff down in a journal. That's what every therapist liked to tell me. They're big into journaling," Lana suggested.

"Write stuff down? Like what?" I asked.

"Your feelings."

"My feelings?" I felt like a parrot—a dumb, uncomfortable one.

"You know, I kind of like having you here. It gives me insight as to how awful real therapy will be," Lana joked.

"Your bedside manner needs a lot of work."

"The point is, Bo," Lana said, finally sitting up. She leaned her elbows on her knees and pinned me with her blue eyes. "If you really think you need help, you shouldn't be here talking to me, someone who's had less than two years of psychology classes. I don't think my years of therapy are counted into my practicum."

"Do you think I really need help?"

"I don't know. I guess if how you express yourself is either with sex or fighting then probably, but I think those are just excuses."

"How so?" I held my breath and leaned toward her as if she was going to hand me the secret solution to every problem I had.

"You're a pretty disciplined guy. You work out a lot or you wouldn't have the body that you do. You're obviously very smart or you wouldn't be here at Central. You don't seem to be wrapped up in your appearance, given that you seem to wear the same ratty pair of jeans every time I've seen you and your boots, which I presume you wore in the Army."

"Marines."

"Whatever, it's all the same."

I opened my mouth to explain to her that it wasn't all the same, but she waved her hand to forestall any further talk.

"I don't really care about how it's different. You wouldn't have survived in the disciplined environment of the military without learning some self-restraint. So you have it and you're able to use it when you want."

"But what about my dad?"

"What about him?"

What did I want to say? I just blurted out, "He's a bad guy."

"So you think you're bad, too?" I didn't want to nod, I just looked at her.

"You can write your own story." Lana sighed softly.

"Like in the journal?"

"No, your life story. Write your own narrative. Be your own person. You want to be the guy who lives only to fight and possibly turn into someone hooked up to a breathing tube, breaking your girl's heart, or you want to be the guy who enjoys every day of his life? What's the best revenge against your dad? Do you really think he feels it when you pummel someone else? Do you really think that bothers him? Wouldn't the biggest thing that bothers him be you living well and being happy?"

I stared at her in amazement. She really was scary because yes, that would be the biggest thing I could do to bother him.

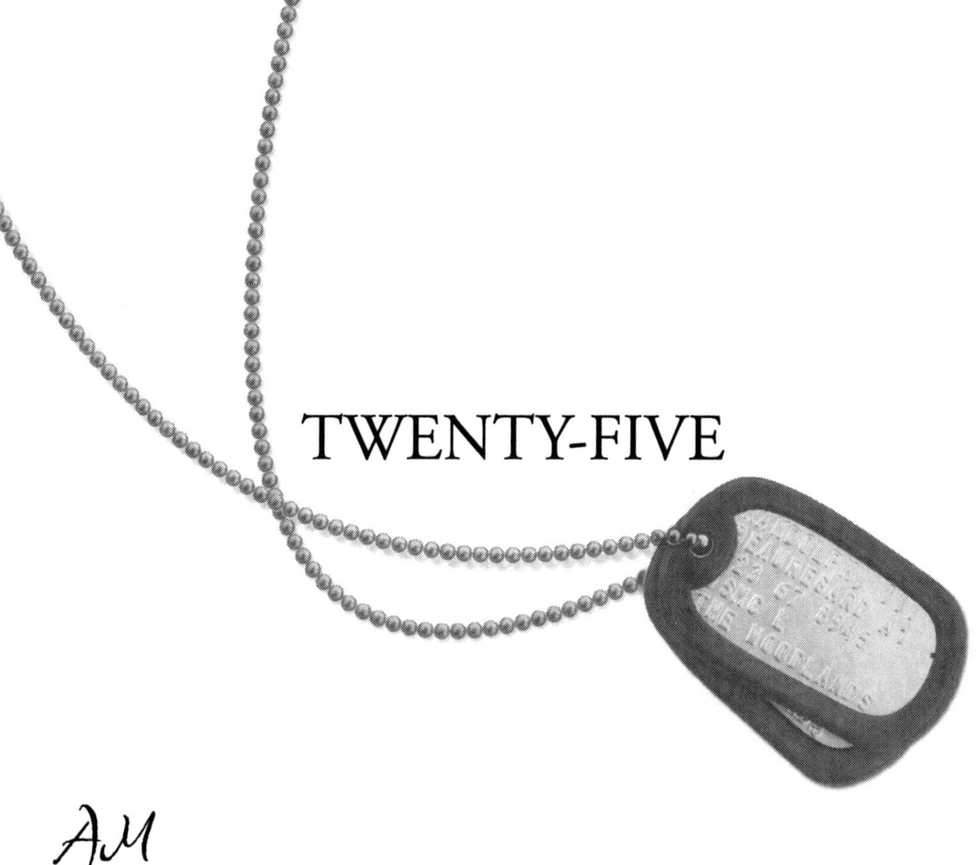

TWENTY-FIVE

AM

"WHAT'S THAT NOISE?" ELLIE EXCLAIMED.

The blanket was over my head as I lay on the sofa. Ellie and I had splurged on pizza and milkshakes to compensate for the hearts and flowers that seemed to pervade every retail establishment, left over from last week's Valentine's Day. Ellie and Ryan had talked last night about her fear of attachment and then we'd all discussed the issue of the laxers. I didn't know what to do about them, and I wished Bo would call me back, but the phone remained stubbornly silent. He'd missed class again on Wednesday. I wondered if he was going to drop out or transfer and the thought of Bo not being a part of my life seemed worse than attending a thousand parties with Clay Howard.

I pulled down the blanket at Ellie's proclamation and listened. It sounded like an animal was dying painfully underneath our balcony.

Ellie ran to the balcony doors and wrenched them open, the snow and ice making it difficult. She was out there for a minute, nearly motionless. The dying animal sounds stopped and then started again.

The sliding door creaked as she returned. "I think you need to go out there."

"What is it?"

"You won't believe it unless you see it," Ellie said. "I'm going to my room to call Ryan. Don't disturb me."

"Yes, ma'am." I rose and saluted her. Dragging the blanket with me, I stepped outside and realized that it wasn't an animal dying but someone singing. Someone singing really badly. I peeked over the railing and saw Bo and Adam sitting on the top of Bo's car. Adam was strumming his guitar and Bo was singing into a microphone hooked up to a portable speaker. The sound emanating from Bo's mouth distorted the lyrics, but I think I caught the words to Bruno Mars's "When I Was Your Man." Bo was singing that he regretted that he'd let his ego and pride get in the way of us being together.

It didn't make sense to me. I hadn't wanted him to leave, but I never got a chance to say so. Instead, Bo just disappeared. He didn't come to class. He didn't return my phone calls. But he kept on singing about all the changes he was going to make. Other doors or windows in the apartment complex opened and invectives were released.

"Shut up!"

"This isn't the place for losers to audition for *American Idol*."

"If you don't shut the fuck up, I'm going to come down and shut your mouth for you."

But still Bo wouldn't stop singing. I held up my hand and both the awful singing and the guitar playing stopped. "If I let you come up, will you stop torturing my neighbors?"

"I will," Bo said into the microphone.

"You'd better come inside then, or we'll get kicked out."

Bo jumped down off the car and held out a hand to Adam. They slapped their hands together, and Adam got into Bo's car and drove away. Instead of going to the front door like a rational human being, Bo vaulted onto the first-floor fence and swung his way onto the second-floor balcony and then the third floor.

"You're a crazy person, Bo Randolph."

"But you love me anyway?" He spread out his gloved hands in front of me, trying for innocent schoolboy but not quite pulling it off.

"I guess so." I sighed and turned to go back into the apartment. Inside, I felt all shivery. Love? Did he really love me? Bo followed me inside, locked the door, and pulled the shades.

"Your security here is really bad," Bo noted, trailing me into my bedroom.

"I don't think anyone else is going to scale the walls to get into our apartment," I said dryly.

"Still, I think it makes sense, from a safety standpoint, to sleep here every night."

"From a safety standpoint?" I asked, dropping the blanket and starting to help Bo out of jacket and gloves.

"Yeah, don't want the owners to get sued for unsafe premises." Bo allowed me to unzip, unbuckle, and unsnap.

"That would seem to be something that would jeopardize my lease," I agreed. "I like living here, with Ellie, and across from Sasha."

I pushed his jacket off and ran my hands across the uneven texture of his thermal shirt, lightly kneading the muscles underneath.

"No, we wouldn't want to do anything that would create unnecessary friction," Bo murmured, a hitch in his breath as I dragged my nails down his chest to his belt buckle, but before I could undo the fasteners, Bo grabbed my hand.

"We need to talk."

Four of the most hated words in the English language. I knew we should talk, but I didn't want to, which was why I was trying to undress Bo before either of us thought too long and hard about this. Was this a precursor to him telling me we were done? That he just wanted to be friends? That it was him and not me? I bent to grab the blanket and wrapped it around me like the fibers and threads could somehow prevent his words from hurting me.

"I was scared I was going to hit you," Bo confessed. His admission cut me off at the knees and I had to sit down.

"You wanted to hit me?"

"No!" Bo exclaimed. He squeezed the back of his neck with one hand and covered his eyes with the other. "After I struck the wall, I saw you look at me. With fear. Like I was going to hit you. And I ran away. I found a fight, or several, and I used those guys to beat out every ounce of feeling inside of me, but each time they hit me or I hit them, I kept thinking of you." He dropped to his knees in front of me. "I was afraid for you, for me."

"Because your dad hit your mom?" I guessed.

Bo reared back onto his haunches. "How did you know?"

"I didn't, but it was the only thought that made sense to me." I smoothed a hand over his shoulder. "I never thought you'd hit me. It was an emotional night. I was just taken off guard."

Bo rocked forward and dropped his head in his hands. "I'm so screwed up, AM. I don't know why you'd want to be with me. I'm not sure when dear old Dad started beating my mom, but I remember the first time I caught him doing it. I was at Little League and had gotten sick to my stomach. One of the coaches drove me home early. I came in and Dad was hitting my mom with his belt, across her arms, her chest, her legs. She was just sitting there, curled up in a kitchen chair. His face was red and each blow seemed to fire his rage hotter and harder." Bo's tone hadn't changed, but his breathing was becoming choppy, faster, as if he were reliving the moment. His eyes stared, unseeing. I kept stroking his shoulder even though I really wanted to hug him to me. I bit hard into my tongue to keep my tears from falling. If the ducts were unleashed, I was afraid I'd fill the room with my tears.

"I launched myself at him and felt the sharp end of the belt across my face for my efforts. I was bruised for days. I can still hear the whistle as the fucker swung the thing through the air." Bo lifted a hand up to his temple as if remembering the blow.

"What did they say, your parents?"

"Nothing. My dad sent my mom up to her room, like she was a disobedient child. Then he turned to me and said I wasn't to ever to come between them again like that. It was his right as the man of the household. What did I know? I was a motherfucking ten-year-old."

"Did he stop?" I knew he hadn't, or Bo wouldn't be so torn up by this, but I asked anyway, hoping.

Bo shook his head. "No. I didn't see it often, but I could tell by how my mother moved, tenderly, cautiously, if she'd had a beating. I don't ever know what she did to deserve it."

Nothing. But Bo knew that, I'm sure. I stroked his head, smoothing down the strands of his hair.

"I've never felt like you'd ever hit me, Bo, but maybe you've got to stop letting physicality be your first response, no matter how instinctive it is."

"Yeah, I know. That was some bullshit I spouted to you, wasn't it?" Bo leaned his head against my leg, as if in need of comfort.

"Violence *is* part of history, but I understand that you don't want it to control you."

"No, that's right." Bo sighed, and allowed more of his weight to rest against me.

"I won't transfer because my father went here and his father before him. It's the only legacy I have of him." With this, Bo drew back away from me and I felt the ache I'd been battling with tears, liquor, and ice cream invade me once again.

"This is the first time you've ever spoken to me about your dad."

"He's not really my dad," I explained. "He's just my mother's lover. She's the 'other woman,' you see." At Bo's look of incomprehension, I said, "My mom's his mistress. He has a legitimate family with two perfect and legitimate children. They're about ten years older than I am. They were Central alums, too."

The more I spoke, the more Bo understood, compassion flooding his expression.

"He pays for me to go here, but I felt like he'd rather I didn't exist. My mom has never held a job for as long as I can remember, and she survives on the gifts he gives her. I was afraid that if he knew of the rumors about me, that he might just cut me off or, worse, cut her off."

"Your dad might rival mine for the Darth Vader award," Bo said.

"What's that?"

"Worst dad ever," he explained. "You aren't afraid anymore?"

"No, I don't think so. He called me just the other day and we kind of talked for the first time." Even I could hear the wonder in my voice. "My mom's convinced that if we just spend some time together, we could get along better."

"Sunshine, I wouldn't want to spend time with him either. It's a wonder you don't hate all penises after what's gone on."

I shook my head. "When I was a kid, my mom always told me to be careful with my reputation. Never do anything that would call attention to myself. Keep my head down. As I got older, I understood better, but I never fully comprehended what she must feel like in our small town until

I came to Central. Leaving Central would be like giving up or something. I figured that even if Roger didn't want to acknowledge me, I'd take this opportunity to get a degree from a great college, and I'd be a success," I declared.

Bo took my hand. "I believe it. I believe you." He squeezed my fingers and bent to press kisses on the tops of my legs. "Do you know why I think we're going to make it when others don't? Because you don't let me get away with any bullshit, and I'll keep you from going too far into your own head. Plus I know all your dark secrets and you know mine and we still feel the same about each other."

"Is that right?" I said, almost giddy with his affirmation.

"Yes," he replied firmly. "And pretty much twenty-four-seven I'm thinking about boning you."

"Goddammit, Bo." I pushed him so he rocked back.

He laughed. "See—no bullshit." He slipped his arms around my waist and pulled me onto the floor with him. "You have no idea. Whenever I see something even halfway interesting, I turn to tell you, share it with you. Nothing makes sense unless you've seen it, too. That's how far you've crawled into me. I'm sorry for running away. I'm sorry for being afraid. I'm sorry your dad is a dickhead. But together, you and I, we can do this."

He stood and picked me up to carry me the short distance to the bed. He took off his shirt, pulling it over his head with one hand. His undressing was too hurried for my taste, but I liked to cut my wrapping paper off and carefully preserve it. I would have liked a slower reveal so I could savor the body underneath, all sinewy muscle. The bruises of his fight had purpled, but he moved like he couldn't feel them. Hard-edged hipbones jutted out over jeans, which rode dangerously low on his hips. His thighs were powerful and his calves lean. His abdomen was ridged and defined so sharply that I often wondered how I didn't cut my tongue on the edge as I swept it along the ridges and valleys. The light smattering of hair on his chest arrowed down to a single line of darker golden hair leading straight into his jeans and under his boxers.

I noticed his hands had stopped on his jeans, in the processing of unzipping them. I swung my eyes upward and met his. They were gleaming with amusement. But he said nothing. He didn't have to. I smiled a bit ruefully and waggled my eyebrows, acknowledging I'd been caught, but my gaze drifted down to his hands again and another time, maybe Bo would have played it up for me, grabbed himself. Stroked himself.

I remembered where he liked to be touched, remembered the day I'd learned. Sitting in my chair, with the afternoon light caressing him, he'd run my hand over his body, pressing lightly at his most sensitive spots and groaning audibly to let me know when he wanted my touch heavier, tighter. The vision of his head tipped back in pleasure was burned into my memory. I don't know that it could ever be excised. Or that I could ever have enough of him. I raised the blanket to invite him in when he'd disrobed, nude as always.

He slipped in next to me, sliding an arm under my neck and pulling my head onto his chest. The fingers of one hand stroked through my hair. The other he wrapped around my cheek and chin so he could tilt my face upward. He pressed his lips hard against mine, his tongue plunging forward. I gripped his shoulders and he dropped his hand from my hair, wrapping it around my back. I could feel the heat of his body, the protectiveness of his embrace. His mouth was wide and open, eating at my mouth, my lips.

When he finally pulled away, I felt dazed. Like he'd consumed part of me with that kiss.

Bo's hand traveled from my face and ran slowly down my arm, raising the flesh and making me shiver. He bent his head toward me, biting me softly between my neck and shoulder. He laved the bite mark and moved up my neck, alternating nips and licks. He slid a hand down the front of my jeans and pressed his fingers hard against my clit. His fingertips rested near my opening. He began to rub me, gently but with firm pressure. I could feel my body lubricating his fingers.

Our heavy breaths filled the night air. I was so close to succumbing. My nails raked up his back, and I could feel the play of his muscles responding to my attention. I wished I could see his body in the moonlight, watch the beams caress every dip and hollow.

We shoved my jeans off together, a mix of hands and feet until I was as nude as he was.

I pushed him backward and laid my tongue against his pectoral. I kissed and licked my way across the acres of moonlit skin. I rubbed myself against his chest, abrading my nipples against his chest. His fingers still stroked me, readying me for his intrusion.

He lifted his already-covered cock and positioned the tip between us. I lifted my hips to accommodate him and sank down slowly, allowing my body to accustom itself to his girth. Even though I'd had him before, my body still acted surprised and shy. He placed both hands on my hips and pushed upward.

I gasped.

"You all right, Sunshine?"

"Yes," I groaned out, "keep going," and I moved around on his shaft. He took over, pushing hard into me. I allowed him to control the pace, but it wasn't enough, and soon he'd flipped me underneath him, dipping a hand between the two of us and rubbing me hard while thrusting swiftly. His skin was pulled tight over his bones and he looked like a fierce hawk at that moment, the hard planes highlighted by shadows.

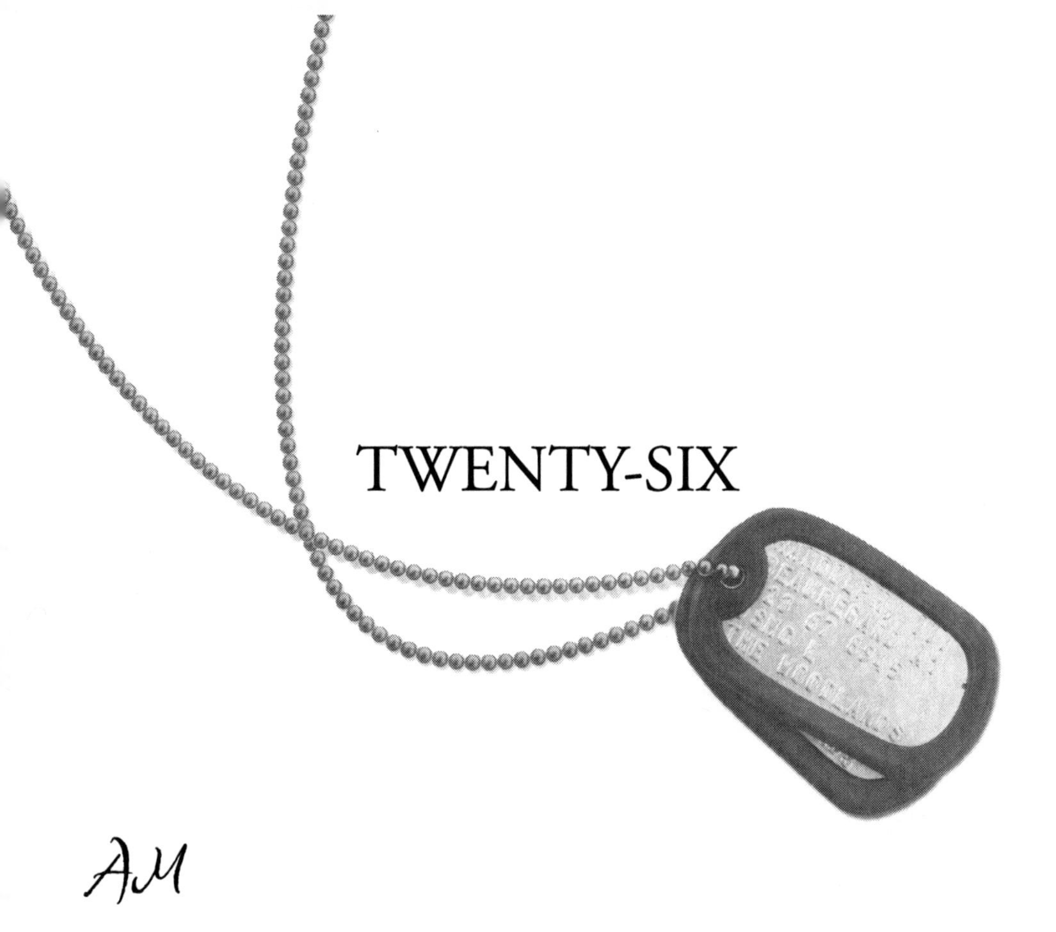

TWENTY-SIX

AM

"WHAT'S THIS?" I ASKED, PULLING a round, heavy object from the mishmash of coins, keys, and bottle caps that represented the contents of his pockets. He'd dumped it all on my dresser before pulling off his jeans, as was his regular habit. After taking a bathroom break, I wandered over to look at the collection.

Bo sat up and the blankets pooled around his waist, leaving his chest bare. The morning light peeked through the shades. I didn't even realize I was holding my breath, afraid he would disappear, until he threw back the covers and climbed out, uncaring that he was naked. I stared at his obvious arousal, a flush of heat and embarrassment mixing to bring color to my cheeks and the tops of my breasts.

Following my gaze, he looked down and then up to grin unrepentantly at me. Spreading his arms, he said, "What can I say? You turn me on."

"I think a stiff wind would turn you on," I mocked, trying to hide my own pleasure at this thought.

His arms wrapped around me, and I felt his erection press against my side. "This is all yours, stiff wind or no. You can't expect me to wake up in your bed, surrounded by the smell of us, you looking all rosy and hot, and *not* get a stiffy."

He sat on my chair and pulled me down facing him. As always, he arranged me to his liking. My legs over his, straddling him. The tip of his morning wood pressing lightly against me. I squirmed a little, the light pressure turning me on more than I thought it would. Had I thought it'd been good with old what's-his-name? I didn't know what good was.

Bo tossed the coin in the air a couple times as if considering its value.

"It's a challenge coin. A challenge coin is something that an officer or, I guess, anyone can have minted. It's given to people, usually in the military, to inspire. I was just finishing Basic and a guy comes up to me, really random, and hands me this coin. I could tell by the look of him that he's a BAMF. He has two prosthetics on his legs, from right above the knee down to the foot. "

"BAMF?"

"Bad ass mother fucker."

"Does every military acronym include a curse word?"

"Yes and if it doesn't, you add the F and it's all better." Bo pressed my head against his chest and resumed his story. I took it as a request to be quiet. "I didn't recognize straight off who it was or what I was receiving. I just saluted, and said, 'Thank you, sir.' With all the shit that was going on with packing up and returning home, I didn't remember the coin in my pocket until I was unpacking the dress blues at home. I pulled it out, and it has the Medal of Honor emblem on it. I knew immediately who it was then. I didn't know how to get a hold of this guy, but when I get to SOI, School of Infantry, I ask my commanding officer, who sends me all the way up to battalion command.

"I'm a POG, the lowest of the low in the Marines, and I'm nearly shitting my pants standing in front of the LT. He asks to see my coin. I hand it over. He fingers it for what seems like an eternity, then hands it back. Tells me I'm dismissed and doesn't say another word."

"So he doesn't tell you who it is?" I asked.

"Nope. At the end of the five weeks, we're at a bar, just off the Camp San Onofre base. In walks the battalion commander and every officer underneath him. They walk up to the bar. Pull out these coins and slam them down. Everyone else in the place rushes to the bar and slaps their coin, if they have one, on the table. LT looks at me and tells me to pull out my coin. I don't even know why I have it but I do. I carried it everywhere. LT passes the coin down and without a word everyone looks at it and passes it back. The LT calls for a round for the bar.

"Then he tells me about how this guy earned his Medal of Honor. He was on patrol and his squad comes under heavy fire. His squad leader falls. This guy covers the squad leader with his body, all the while discharging his weapon accurately and killing several insurgents. He single-handedly saves other members of the squad from being killed and pushes another out of the way of incoming artillery, the last action resulting in injuries so serious that it requires the double amputation of his legs above the knee.

"LT tells me that he contacted the MoH recipient and asked him why the hell he would have given one of his challenge coins to a sorry-assed Marine such as me. The response? That inspiration should be given to those who are trying as well as those who succeed.

"I wasn't the best Marine at that point or throughout my enlistment, but—" He fell silent. I left my head resting against his chest, enjoying the rise and fall against his chest as he took easy, even breaths.

"The guy who gave me the coin e-mailed me the next day and told me: *Do the Corps proud, both in uniform and out.* I haven't been living up to that out here," Bo admitted; this time his breath was deep and heavy. "But I'm trying."

"You're too hard on yourself." I rubbed my hand over his bare pectoral and smiled when I heard his breath hitch as my finger rubbed lightly over his nipple. I pushed up against him so I could look him in the face. "You're an incredibly loyal friend. You don't make assumptions about people. You fight hard for the people you care about. I think that all adds up to a pretty awesome Marine."

He brought his hands up to cup my face. "You still with me?"

"Yes," I said firmly. No hesitation in my voice. We'd weathered the storm, and I didn't want him to think I regretted any of it. Bo was more vulnerable than he'd ever let on. I plucked the coin from his hand and held it up. "It's nice that you have this, like a talisman."

Bo looked at me seriously for a moment, studying my expression. He pulled me down for a kiss, open-mouthed and wet. His hands dropped to my butt and drew me hard against his erection, which seemed harder and thicker than before.

My hands tangled in his hair, and I deepened the kiss, wanting to cement the personal intimacies with a physical one. He broke the kiss and reached behind me to pick something up. It was his dog tags, the chain and tags mixed among the detritus on my desk.

Bo turned them so the light caught the metal. "During Basic, sometimes you're so tired you can't even get up to piss. You're pushed beyond whatever limits you had set for yourself. You realize that your body can do things that you never imagined. But there are times when you don't think you can go on, and that's when your brother is there to lift you up and push you forward. He yells encouragement when the drill sergeant's shouting obscenities. You know that if you're ever caught by the enemy, your brothers will never stop looking for you. If you're hurt, they'll help heal you. The Corps is a unit of many, not one, but dozens, thousands even, who have your back. You can smite one Marine, but a thousand will rise up to avenge him."

His voice was low, almost hushed.

"That's not the romantic notion that's sold, but it's the one that keeps you going. You don't want to let your brothers down, and they won't let you fall, either. Ten years from now, I could meet a Marine on the street, and he'd buy me a beer and lend me a hand. I'd do the same for him."

He let the tags fall from his hand until he was holding only the chain. Slowly, he lifted the chain and slipped it over my head. Too stunned to move, I sat quietly as he pulled my hair out from under the chain and moved the closure to the back of my neck. He lifted the tags to his mouth and then let them drop, the weight dragging the chain between my breasts. My hand came up involuntarily to clench the tags. He closed his fingers over my fist.

"Now whenever you feel alone, know that I've got your back. No matter who's against you, know that a thousand others wait to avenge you."

"But I'm not a Marine," I whispered back, my voice catching on the tears threatening to spill out.

"You're a fighter, Sunshine. Plus, you belong to *this* Marine."

"What if you want these back?" I fingered the tags.

He gave me a crooked grin and shook his head at me. "I'll know where you are."

"Is that a threat?" I tried to joke, but the effect was ruined by the two big fat tears that rolled down my face and plopped onto our joined fists.

"A promise. You aren't ever going to be too far away from me." He lifted me again, as if I were weightless, and carried me over to the bed. When he laid me down, I heard the clink of metal as the tags jostled against each other. "I've got other promises to make to you."

He laid his mouth against the chain at my throat and followed the path to the tops of my breasts. My tears were lost under a wave of desire, just as he'd probably intended.

"With your tongue?"

"With this body, I thee worship," Bo said against my skin.

And I surrendered to him and my sore heart began to lighten as it absorbed all the unspoken promises Bo made with his mouth, fingers, and tongue.

TWENTY-SEVEN

AM

"RANDOLPH," BO BARKED INTO THE phone the following morning. I couldn't hear who it was, but as the conversation went on, Bo tensed.

He threw the phone on the nightstand and took in a deep breath.

"What is it?"

"Finn's dad died."

I gasped. "Oh that's terrible. What happened?"

"Heart attack. Dude wasn't even fifty. Shit!" Bo cursed and rubbed his face. "I need to get over to the house."

He quickly donned his jeans and shirt and shoved his sockless feet into his boots. I jumped up, gathered his books, and stuffed them into his backpack that Noah had dropped off the night before. Bo shrugged on his coat and pocketed his phone.

I held his backpack out to him and he ignored it momentarily, crushing me to him instead. "I'll call you later."

"No problem." I shushed him. "Go be with Finn."

Bo did call, much later. "Funeral's going to be in a week. Can you come?"

"Yes." I didn't hesitate. "How's he taking it?"

"Numb, I think. We're just playing video games right now to keep his mind off it."

Bo stayed over at the house the rest of the week and skipped Friday class as well, likely comforting Finn. We talked every night on the phone. They had taken Finn out paintballing, and Bo had helped demo and rebuild a house that Finn was flipping. They were trying to keep Finn as busy as possible.

I called my mom twice that week to tell her I loved her. On the second call, she confronted me and demanded to know what was wrong.

"You never call this often, honey."

I gave her the truth. "A friend's dad died. He was pretty young."

Mom made some sympathetic tuts. "That's too bad, dear."

"What would you do if Roger died?" I'd never asked the question before, always scared of the answer. How would my delicate mother, who had never worked before, provide for herself?

"Roger has taken care of me," Mom swiftly replied.

Ordinarily I wouldn't press but I had to know. "How?"

"He's given me a nice insurance policy, honey, and I've money set aside from him. We'll both be taken care of," she reassured me.

"What if Roger stopped coming by?" Once I had become aware of money and household payments, I recognized how careful my mother was with her money.

I learned not to ask for expensive jeans or the name-brand fuzzy boots every other girl in my class wore. I took care not to overspend at school, not wanting to be a burden on my mother and not willing to go to Roger for more assistance. Maybe I'd judged Roger unjustly and my mom was just really thrifty. The phone call with Roger made me look at everything differently.

My question generated a deep sigh from my mother. "I'll be okay, honey, don't you worry about it. The house is paid off and so is my car. I've got some money set aside just in case, but I'm not with Roger because of what he can provide, honey. We love each other."

They had been together, despite all the circumstances, for almost a quarter of a century. Roger supported my mother through all that time. I guess they did love each other. It might not be the love I wanted to experience, but I realized that part of growing up was accepting other people's versions of happiness.

Bo CAME TO PICK ME up a week later, on Thursday for the memorial service. He'd explained to the professor that there had been a death in his family, resulting in his absences. Bo didn't explain which family. Professor Godwin admonished Bo, but since Bo apparently had a good GPA, it would be overlooked. We were cautioned, however, to produce a stellar lab project.

"You look nice." He kissed me hard. "I've missed you."

"I've missed you, too," I said, wishing he'd hold me longer, but he hustled me into the car.

"The funeral was earlier today, and we're going to the memorial service now," Bo explained, maneuvering the car to the outskirts of the town until we arrived at an estate. I didn't have any other name for it. White fences butted up against the road, providing a barrier between the pavement and the rolling pastoral land. We followed the white fencing for at least a couple miles before we came to an archway of trees covering a long drive, the spring buds just sprouting on the ends of the branches. I imagined that when the trees were in full bloom, the canopy of leaves was amazing. Instead, the trees looked almost macabre against the backdrop of the gray sky. Skeletal fingers reached out from one tree to caress its partner across the blacktop divide.

I shivered and Bo reached over to clasp my fingers.

"I don't know what it's going to be like inside. Finn told me his mom cheated on his dad with his dad's brother," Bo said.

"Erm. That sounds terrible."

"No lie, so it might be awkward or something."

"That's likely an understatement."

"I'd like to say we won't stay long but—" He paused.

"You want to be there for Finn?"

He squeezed my hand tight and nodded, a sad smile of appreciation on his face. "Don't get me wrong, I'd love to stay outside in the car avoiding this."

Hiding and avoiding was something I'd perfected. It was no way to live, though, so I just squeezed Bo's hand back and waited patiently for him to open my car door. If I didn't, he always look aggravated, and today I didn't want to be a source of any unnecessary frustration. The house at the end of the drive looked like a farmhouse on steroids. The large, white wood-sided structure had a massive wraparound porch, and people were lounging on the railings, glasses in hand, making it look almost like a party.

Inside, Finn stood stoically next to his mother, greeting each arrival. His angelic beauty looked haunted and empty, from his hollow eyes to the pained smile he attempted when he greeted me. Bo dragged Finn in for a back-beating hug. They clung fiercely to each other for longer than most guys would have. Then it was my turn and Finn's arms wrapped around me, and I could feel the emotion in his rigid but tight embrace. Like always, I was without the right things to say. I could only murmur, "I'm sorry." Inadequate words at best.

He thanked us for coming and directed us to the living room, where a number of chairs had been set in groupings. It looked like a tasteful setting from Martha Stewart funerals. All the chairs had been swathed in black and tied with some kind of raffia. A tag in the middle said "In memorium of Matthew O'Malley" in swirling script.

Bo escorted me over to a small group by the front windows, where the crew from the Woodlands sat with a few girls. Noah and his girlfriend. And a blonde so beautiful that people on the other side of the room couldn't help but looking over at her. She was sitting between Mal and Adam, so I didn't know which one she was with, or maybe it was neither. A tall, Finn-looking guy stood behind the group, looking out the window.

He wore a white shirt, untucked and unbuttoned at the collar. A loosened tie hung around his neck, the whole effect broadcasting his disheveled despair. I hadn't ever attended a funeral or memorial service before, and already I knew I hated it.

Bo found me a seat next to Noah's girlfriend but refused to sit, preferring to press both hands down on the top of my chair with enough force I was afraid it would become permanently embedded into the floor.

"Callum, you guys need anything?" Bo asked, directing his attention to the guy standing in the corner.

Callum shook his head, "Not today."

"We're taking you on that fishing trip after classes are over," Bo informed him. A ghost of a smile whispered over Callum's face.

"You okay that with Finn?" Callum asked.

"It's all good," Bo replied, neither confirming nor denying that he'd checked with Finn.

"You going to catch anything this time, Peep?" Callum asked.

"Nah, I'm the keeper of the cooler. Someone needs to make sure we have enough to drink. Noah can filet 'em, so as long as y'all catch enough fish, we'll be good." Bo's drawl was accentuated.

Callum gave him a brief, pained smile and went back to looking out the window again.

"Hi, AM, Grace, remember?" I did, from when we ran the mayonnaise experiment. At my nod, she introduced the beautiful blonde I'd seen around campus. "And that's my cousin Lana."

Lana gave me a stiff wave. No one wanted to make small talk, so we sat there like the most miserable group of people ever, like we were all back in high school sitting outside the principal's office.

Finally Finn came over and said, "Anyone want a smoke out back?"

The stampede to the door almost knocked chairs over. The porch actually did wrap around the entire house, but Finn led us down a path that led to a red barn. We stood around a picturesque white fence that overlooked large swath of pasture land and a pond beyond. The smell of hay and manure from the nearby barn was ameliorated by the sulphur of the matches used to light the blunts. Finn's smokes weren't cigarettes, but on a day like this, who could blame him. Bo, Noah, Grace, and I abstained, but the rest shared a few that were rolled in what looked like grape leaves; Bo told me later that they were cigar wrappers.

I noticed as the blunt was passed around that Callum wasn't with us. "Where's the guy that looks like Finn?" I asked Bo.

He raised his eyebrows and shrugged. "I'll tell you later."

But Finn heard us. "Callum feels like he needs to avoid me because his father is fucking my mother."

Adam exhaled a stream of smoke and offered a succinct response. "Cousins."

"My family's fucked up," Finn said, snatching back the blunt from Adam.

"Mine, too," I said. "My mom's the other woman."

"My mom hates me," Lana chimed in.

"My mom's dead," Noah deadpanned, and for some reason the black humor of us one-upping each other about our shitty backgrounds relieved some of the tension of the day and we all laughed.

Adam went back to the house and dragged Callum out. Someone rounded up some beer and chairs. We sat outside for a long time, even when the night got chilly, staring into the land behind Finn's house. Bo's arms were wrapped securely around me the whole time.

He wasn't afraid of loving me despite his past, and life was so short that I needed to stop being afraid, too.

I AWOKE TO FIND Bo sitting at my desk and typing on my laptop, wearing his jeans and no shirt, impervious to the slight chill in the air. I lay there for a few moments and just enjoyed looking at his back, the one I'd spent so much time staring at during class last semester. Only now I got to look at what was under the near-transparent T-shirts he sported, and it was every bit as amazing as I thought it would be. He had a large black bird tattooed on his back, the wings stretching from shoulder blade to shoulder blade. On the right side, just above the wing tip, I could see an indentation, a little larger than a quarter but deep, like someone had carved out his skin with a spoon.

Looking around, I spotted his t-shirt lying at the side of the bed, discarded late last night. I pulled it on, as well as a pair of panties, the metal dog tags lightly brushing my skin as I moved. When I reached him, I traced the top of the bird pattern on his back, the part that I could see above the chair back, dipping a finger into the depression in his back.

"Bullet scar," Bo said as I ran my finger around the edges, feeling the scar tissue bumpy against my fingertip.

"My God," I gasped. "Someone shot you in the back?"

"We were on patrol and came under some fire. People scattered. They think the bullet may have ricocheted off a vehicle or something, because if it had hit me directly, I wouldn't be here."

Fear swept over me, and I leaned down to kiss it. "It looks so painful."

"I'm not going to lie. Hurt like a bitch, but not when I was shot. Then I was too hopped up with adrenaline. It was later. Then I was pissed because

I was sent home to recover." Bo recounted this experience as if it was no different than picking up a latte at Starbucks.

"Just a normal day at work, right?" I said, and then I didn't want to talk anymore. I kissed along his back, this time tracing the wings and head of the bird with my tongue and lips. His muscles bunched in response to my attention.

Bo maintained a constant level of activity, whether it was sparring with me verbally or working out or driving too fast. He had to be doing something. I didn't really understand why he was so afraid of stillness or quiet, but I knew he said provocative things in hopes that I'd provide some tart response to distract him. Or, as I had been doing for the last few hours, that I'd distract him in many wordless ways.

With a growl, he swiveled in the chair and lifted me to sit on his lap, my legs hanging on the outside of his. With one hand placed on my bottom, he pulled on the dog tags' chain until I was close enough to kiss. His wide mouth covered my own, his tongue rubbed along the top of mine, lapping at me like he was trying to capture my entire essence and swallow it. Other parts of his body brushed mine, and even though I felt sore from the overuse of parts that hadn't seen this kind of workout, ever, I couldn't stop myself from pressing down against Bo's groin, stroking myself against the hard ridge of his erection as it pulsed with need between us.

I pulled away, panting. "Ellie said she broke up with her last boyfriend because their sex was too good."

Bo's response was to pull me closer and kiss me again. His hands swept my back, under the t-shirt and around the sides of my breasts, teasing me. This time he broke the kiss. "I always thought Ellie had a good head on her shoulders. I see now that I'm completely wrong."

"Yeah, she's pretty deceptive. I think it's because of her small size." My words ended in a moan as he mouthed his way up and down my neck, giving me small bites and soothing them with his tongue and lips. Just when I thought he would pick me up and carry me back to bed, Bo leaned back. He dropped the dog tags under the t-shirt.

Patting the tags, he said, "Regs require the tags to be under the shirt at all times."

"All times?" I teased.

"Yes." He turned the chair toward the laptop, and I saw that he was researching flights from here to Texas. I wondered if that was where he was going for break. Despite all our grand plans at the beginning of the year, Ellie was going home and Brian was taking Sasha skiing with his family. I'd actually been considering the invitation to Italy.

"I want you to come to Texas with me this weekend," Bo said, tapping his finger on the screen. I swung my legs up and curled into his lap. I didn't want the idea of meeting Bo's family to thrill me so much, but I couldn't suppress my internal shivers of delight. I tried to act unaffected.

"I'll have to see what my mom says," I told him.

He placed his jaw on the top of my head, and I could hear his jawbones crack as he kneaded the top of my head with his chin. "Tell her I've already bought you a ticket."

I pushed against him. "You did not."

Bo nodded.

I KNEW AM HATED WHEN I acted like a presumptuous ass, but I couldn't go home without her. She was like the living embodiment of my challenge coin. Every time I looked at her, I realized I wanted to be better, do better than I was. There was no way I could face my past without her. But that also meant telling her the whole truth, and I wasn't prepared to do that either.

I just wanted to lie on the bed and pretend that nothing existed outside of the cocoon we'd made of the sheets. Although at this point the cocoon was mostly on the floor. Looking at the wreck we'd made of AM's bed made me feel smug as fuck, but the feeling faded quickly when I thought about all the crap I'd have to tell her. I rested my head against her side as she peered at the laptop screen to see the evidence of my ticket purchase.

TWENTY-EIGHT

Bo

The trip to Little Oak, Texas, was far shorter than I wanted, even though we'd traveled half the day. AM told me about her conversation with her father, Clay's threats, and the whole lacrosse house's shitscapades on the flight down. I felt even dirtier after hearing it all and wanted nothing more than to eat, shower, and spend the entire night screwing AM's brains out. I did not want to see my old man or my mom. I didn't even want to be here. My crappy attitude permeated every one of my actions the closer the rental car got to Little Oak, and this did not escape AM's notice.

"You sound like the wolf from the 'Three Little Pigs,'" AM told me. At my quizzical look, she blew up her cheeks and released a big stream of air.

"I'm full of hot air?"

"You are, but no, you're huffing and puffing like you want to blow something down."

"Shit. I think this was a bad decision."

"Then let's go home." Home. Right, home wasn't Little Oak, Texas. Home was, well, I wasn't sure where it was, but I figured if I could stick with AM, I'd be okay. An icy hand grabbed me by the balls. After this visit, I might not have her. Not after she saw my old man, my mom, and how I ran from all of this.

"Don't tempt me." I clutched the steering wheel a little harder. AM was right. My body felt tighter than a tick on a bull's balls. If this went on, I'd end up twisted into a pretzel and starting fights with random strangers to let off stress. This was not the way to convince AM I was worth staying the course for.

I unclenched the wheel with one hand and fumbled in my pocket for the challenge coin. Going home, facing my demons, was the only way to look forward.

AM

LITTLE OAK, TEXAS, WAS A town so small that it almost looked fake. I made Bo drive through the middle of town, which was arranged in an actual square, four blocks of storefronts facing a park and a big stone edifice that I assumed was the courthouse. Some jokers had defaced the post office so it read S OS AL ICE, instead of US Postal Service, the missing metal letters lying against the building like discarded noodles from a can of alphabet soup.

"Who's Alice?"

Bo squinted through the windshield and his lips tipped up in the first smile I'd seen all day. "No idea, but I'm glad to see the grand tradition of punk-assed miscreants is being continued."

"Does the park have your last name on it?" I pointed out a recently-painted sign proclaiming that the postage-stamp-sized lawn was "Randolph Park." This time Bo's response was a bittersweet smile.

"After my Pops," Bo admitted.

"Big-time stuff, huh?"

"Little oil well."

"Big enough to get a park named after you."

"After my grandfather."

I could tell by Bo's insistence on credit being given to his grandfather that he considered the elderly man to be the last decent Randolph around. I'd bit my tongue a million times, wanting to ask Bo about why exactly we were going back to his hometown. I only knew he felt it was important and that he wanted me to come. I knew he'd reveal something at some point, and I counseled myself to be patient. We drove aimlessly up and down small streets peppered with equally small houses. Finally, we crested a hill to see a large, stately brick mansion, probably three or four times larger than all the others we had passed, staring down over the town like a disapproving dad. Bo pulled the car over to the side of the road and killed the engine.

"If your father came to Parent's Day, what would he talk about?" Bo said, not looking away from the house.

"First, he would never come to Parent's Day for me. But if he did come, with one of his other kids, he'd probably talk about his great times with his fraternity and how successful they all are now. Why, what would your dad talk about?"

"Which coeds he'd like to bone."

That was kind of a disgusting thought. The idea of leering dads at Parent's Day, saying how they'd like to test out a newer model than the old car they had at home, was creepier than fuck. I didn't say this to Bo. He already knew it, I could tell.

"My dad would always ask me what girls I was banging. Who had the sweetest snatch. Which cheerleader put out the most."

Bo's recitation was made all the more chilling by the matter-of-fact way he was telling it, as if he were reciting the weather report for the day. "I fucked my way through high school. Slept with the whole goddamned drill team. It was like a challenge for me."

"All of them?" My voice sounded small, even to my own ears. The self-loathing in Bo's voice made me ache. I forced myself to sit still and not throw open the door and run away screaming.

"Every last one," he said grimly. "You want to know how I got my nickname, Bo Peep? Guys from my platoon said its because the girls supposedly follow me around like sheep. I'm not entirely proud of my past. You know why it didn't matter to me about whether the rumor about you and the lacrosse team was true?"

"Um, no?" I offered tentatively, a bit mortified that he was bringing the issue up.

"It's because I've done everything a thousand times worse. I don't care if you slept with the whole lacrosse team. Maybe you did and maybe you didn't. It just didn't matter.

"Thinking it was some flaw in me that was causing Bobby, my dad, to lose control with Mom, I tried to fashion myself into whatever *thing* Bobby wanted. The football player. The guy who could get all the pussy. The academic. Whatever. I tried it all until I realized that nothing I did was going to change him. And somehow, he knew. He just knew that hitting me wouldn't cause me any pain. I wanted it. I goaded him as I got older, and then I learned to shut up when he would hit my mother or burn her with the iron if I didn't just *shut the fuck up.* Finally, when I was about fourteen, my dad starting talking about girls in a way that—" Bo paused, searching for the right words. "In a way that wasn't right, but I thought, maybe if we can bond this way, he'll get off my mom's back. I was such a stupid fuck. He drank my stories down. Some I made up, but when I realized that I could lose my mind, forget what was happening around me when I was with someone, I started doing it for myself. Using them. I cut through that dance line like a butter knife through a hot fresh biscuit.

"I'm telling you all this because my past is so gross and sordid that nothing you could have ever done would have ever turned me off. So what if you slept with fifteen or fifty guys? It doesn't define you."

"If you think that about me, then why can't you cut yourself slack?" I cried.

"Because I can't unsee all the shitty things I've done. Just sitting here looking at that *house,*" Bo spit out the word "house" like an expletive, "only serves to remind me what an asshole I was. And still am. Do you know that I've not called my mom once since I left? That I've ignored her attempts to contact me? I just wanted to forget all of this." Bo threw up an arm over his eyes, as if he was trying to block out that mental image of him doing whatever unsavory acts he now despised. "Maybe I'm not supposed to be with someone like you."

"I think that's kind of a shitty thing to say." It sounded like he was trying to ditch me again. "You're going to decide for me what's best?"

"What?" Bo dropped his arm and faced me for the first time. "I'm not trying to tell you what to do. I'm trying to warn you off."

"You're saying that you shouldn't be with me because you aren't good enough for me, but that's like saying that I'm too dumb to make decisions for myself. Don't I get to decide what's good enough for me?"

"Yes, but—"

"You'd best be quiet now before you dig yourself a deeper hole," I huffed.

Bo stared at me, slightly open-mouthed, then burst out into laughter. "Goddamn, AM. How'd I ever get so lucky to find you?"

"You must've done something right," I sassed. Somehow I knew that Bo needed me to show no sympathy, no pity, even though inside my heart was breaking into a thousand pieces for the confused and traumatized boy he'd been. I wished I were a mythical Norse creature so I could hurt Bo's father, as if that would somehow make up for the horror of his childhood.

"Am I feeling sorry for myself?" Bo asked, a rueful smile playing around the edges of his mouth.

"Yes, and if you act like this any more, I'm going to start calling you Edward."

"Wow, is that the insult we're using instead of pussy?"

"It's the male version. Essentially, the same thing. Now put this car in gear, and let's get this over with."

BEAUREGARD RANDOLPH II WAS THE same height as Bo. Had the same hair, although his was longer, shaggier than Bo's, like he hadn't had a haircut, a decent one, in years. And even though they were clearly stamped from the same cloth, this man looked smaller. His shoulders were rolled slightly forward, making him look shorter. He shuffled down the hallway, whereas Bo always strode.

The house itself smelled of rotten food and disuse. Flies buzzed around the rooms, alighting on what looked like old spills on tables and counters. The sun that shone in through the big windows at the back was hazy, the dust so thick that it created a fog inside the house.

We followed Bobby back to the kitchen, a large room dominated by a huge center island. At one time, this place would looked like it belonged in a magazine. The counters were made of marble and the appliances were industrial-grade stainless steel. The setup showed signs of serious money, but the counters were filled with unwashed dishes. The flies that had buzzed around the front living areas were more plentiful here and the smell worse.

I pretended to be unaffected, but I tried not to touch anything.

The look on Bo's face had changed from stoic indifference to shock. Obviously he'd never seen it like this either.

"Sit down, sit down." Bobby Randolph gestured toward the table. I sat down gingerly on a chair but kept my arms tucked close to my sides to avoid touching something and contracting a disease. Bobby took out the chair next to me and sat too close. Bo stood like an angry Thor by my side, ready to smite Bobby for any wrong move. His muscles tensed when Bobby leaned forward.

"You're a hot—" Bobby's voice cut off when Bo let out a noise that sounded suspiciously like a growl. I leaned back so my head was resting against his thighs. Bo placed a hand on my shoulder and leaned forward.

"This is my girl, Bobby, and you treat her with respect or we're out of here. Now why don't you tell me why this place looks like it's been abandoned for months. It smells rank and looks twice as bad."

Bobby sat up and tried to bluster. "You aren't showing me much respect, soldier."

"I was a *Marine,* old man. Answer the question." Bo had never appeared more commanding and in control, but his hand bit into my shoulder hard, so hard it kind of hurt, but I would never, ever let on. At the direct command, Bobby deflated like a popped balloon.

"Maybe we can talk alone, man-to-man, for a minute." Bobby looked at me expectantly, hoping, I guess, that I'd take the hint and leave, but I wasn't going anywhere unless Bo wanted me to and his firm clasp told me I was staying.

"We don't have private business ever. Where's Mom?"

Bobby shifted uncomfortably in his seat. "I've been wondering what you're doing with your trust."

"You need to borrow some money?"

Shooting me another uneasy glance, Bobby said slowly, "Just maybe a little bit, to fix up the house." He waved his arm around the room.

"Where's Mom?" Bo leaned over farther, looming over both of us. Even I felt intimidated.

"Your old lady moved out years ago," Bobby sneered.

Bo released my shoulder and pulled my chair back, away from Bobby. For a moment I wondered if Bo would hit his father. Instead, Bo tugged me to my feet and started toward the entrance. I heard Bobby's chair scrape backward and winced at the thought of the scratches the chair was making on the once-beautiful hardwood floors. Bo picked up the pace and we walked faster, as fast as we could without appearing like we were running.

"Now wait a minute there, son," Bobby called out. Bo whirled around.

"I'm not your 'son' and haven't been since I discovered you're a lowlife piece of shit that gets off on beating a woman half his size while jerking off to fantasies of his kid's conquests. I don't claim you, old man." Bo spat at the floor. "I only came back here to see Mom, and since she isn't here, I'm gone. Don't speak of me. Don't even think of me. You can rot here with the spoiled food and the spilled beer."

I squeezed his hand hard, trying to convey every ounce of nonverbal support possible. He squeezed back, and we turned and walked through the door. Bobby was calling something out behind us, but we both ignored him.

The sun was setting, turning the horizon on fire. I heard Bo take a deep cleansing breath, and I did the same.

Bo

RELIEF. I'D FACED DOWN MY old man. I didn't know if AM understood how fucking scared I had been of this moment. She got me, so it was likely she knew without me verbalizing it. I hated appearing weak in front of her. The old man wouldn't approve, but I was determined to stop measuring myself by those standards, the ones that *he* had defined. I didn't even realize I had been until I stood in the house, remembering all the directives about what a real man did or did not do. A real man got a lot of pussy. A real man didn't pick up after himself. A real man showed a woman her place.

A real man? Bobby looked like a broken-down and abandoned car. Unwanted. Ugly, inside and out. I looked down at the top of AM's dark brown hair, the setting sun making it look blue in some areas, more mysterious. I loved pulling my fingers through her long hair, wrapping the strands around my fingers like I could tie her to me with some spell. If there was a higher entity out there, I had to thank him or her for AM. I'd be lost without her.

I wanted to pull her into my arms and show her exactly how much she meant to me. I could express myself so much better when we were alone, in bed, and naked. But I also didn't want to expose her to the unsavory lusts of my father, so I hustled her into the car.

"See how fucked-up my past is? Still want to be with me?" I asked, trying to joke about it but failing.

"Yes, Bo. As long as you don't try to keep pushing me away."

"I'm trying hard to hold on to you."

"Don't doubt it," she answered with no hesitation. "Where to now?"

"I need to find out where my mom is. How about I drop you off at the motel, and you can get us a room while I go and ask a few questions," I suggested. I suppose I could have asked my father, but I didn't want to spend another second with him. In a town as small as Little Oak, even Ricky Cartwright at the gas station would know.

I KNOCKED ON ROOM 214, and AM let me in. I noticed the two double beds and scowled. "Why two beds?"

AM shrugged and closed the door. "The clerk kind of weirded me out. Asked me a bunch of questions, so I figured two beds gives you plausible deniability."

"Christ, AM, I'm not embarrassed to be sleeping with you." I threw our bags onto one bed. "I'm damn proud of it. Plus, everyone's going to hear you scream with pleasure tonight anyway." I picked her up and threw her onto the empty bed, joining her there immediately. She wiggled underneath me until my head was resting between her breasts.

"You find your mother?"

I didn't answer right away, enjoying her fingers running through my hair, lightly scratching my scalp. It was both relaxing and arousing. "Yeah. She's living in a house over on Betsy Ross Road."

"Betsy Ross Road?" AM said, and I could feel the gurgle of laughter in her chest and belly. I smoothed my hand over the belly, enjoying the feel of her amusement.

"We're real patriotic down here. I went to Daniel Boone Middle School and Liberty High School." I traced her belly button and followed the line straight down to the top of her jeans. Pulling on the button, I popped it open. AM's laughter had died out, and now I could feel her increasingly shallow breaths.

"Do you want to have dinner with her?"

"No, Sunshine, I don't. Not right now." I pulled down the zipper and ran my finger under the white lace of her polka-dotted panties. "Are these the ones with the elastic that runs down the crack of your ass? I love these panties. They frame your ass perfectly."

AM smiled. I couldn't see it, but I could feel it. "Why don't you find out?"

I turned her over and pulled off her jeans, her hips rising to help me. I sat back on my haunches, smoothing my hand across her ass, making the fabric even tighter, I admired the way the dark blue cotton hugged her cheeks. She wiggled slightly, either in invitation or anticipation.

I bent down and kissed the inside of her right knee and then her left. I licked and kissed my way up to her sensitive inside thighs. She tried to close her legs, but my body was too solid to be moved. I had her right where I wanted her.

"I've never seen anything so delicious," I told her, pulling aside the panties and exposing her deep pink pussy. I rubbed two fingers up and down either side and then pressed my thumb against her little button. Her cry of pleasure only made me smile wider. I needed this release right now. I needed to show AM how much I treasured and loved her. I bent over her then, lifting her hips into the air as I dragged her panties down. She moaned when I began tonguing her, pressing the broad flat of my tongue against her clit and then licking her in long strokes. "You taste so good," I murmured against her skin. "And you're so wet.

"Press your elbows against the bed," I instructed. When she did, her ass came up even higher. I pushed her legs farther apart with my shoulders, exposing more of her to my gaze and my tongue. As I worked her, I held her steady against my mouth, refusing to let her go. I drank her down like she was the sweetest liquid I'd ever had the pleasure of tasting. I feasted, and my tongue and lips left no space unexplored or unloved. I could feel her legs tightening against me, her pelvis contracting and then she began moaning and shuddering in my arms. I felt like the god she sometimes teased me about being.

"You okay?" I asked her when her quakes were dying down. I rolled her over and her eyes were big and luminous. Her arms reached up around my neck and pulled me down, kissing me hard. Eating me up with the same delight I'd exhibited feasting on her. I felt her hands grabbing at my shirt, so I sat back and pulled the t-shirt off my head with one hand and quickly shucked my jeans. Pulling the condom out a pocket, I wiggled it at her. She nodded.

And then I was pushing inside her, her come lubricating my entrance. "You feel so big," she moaned.

I laughed, my voice rough. "Talk like that and it'll get even bigger."

I looked down to where we were joined, my cock pumping in and out of her gorgeous pussy. I groaned. "God, you look amazing. So hot." And then there were no more words, only the sounds of our bodies moving against each other until I could no longer see or hear. Pleasure blurred my vision and blocked out every sound but the rush of blood in my ears. My whole body shook until I became undone.

In the aftermath, we lay naked on the covers with the ceiling fan lazily circling above us. AM's head was resting on my chest, her finger tracing patterns on my skin.

"What happened with your mom?"

"I hate telling you these things, AM. I keep thinking that one more sad tale about me and you'll figure you've had enough of my bullshit."

She tugged on my chest hair. "Don't make me hurt you, Bo."

"Okay, okay." I hugged her, appreciating her fierceness. "Mom apparently moved out a couple of years ago, about the time that I separated from the Marines."

"Why didn't she call you or connect with you?"

"She did at first, but then when I didn't respond, she said she was…"." I paused.

"Ashamed?" AM filled in.

"Yeah, how did you know?"

"Well, I mean, I never suffered what she did, but I can kind of understand how you feel like you're at fault for the bad things that happen to you. You feel dirty and guilty. It's sometimes easier to accept the abuse."

I tipped my head back and breathed heavily through my nose. "And I'm such an asshole."

"No, you're not," she chided gently. "You're as much a victim as your mother. Don't let this poison what you could build with her now."

I didn't want to think of all the times I'd thought my mother weak. What did I know, after all? I stuck my nose into the crook of AM's neck and burrowed deep, taking comfort in her body and her scent, which was becoming so familiar and dear. "If you're still worried about your mother, maybe you'd let me take care of her. I could take care of both our moms. We could move my mom to live next to your mom or vice versa."

"Maybe they could both live in Chicago by Lake Michigan," she added excitedly. "Wait, you have enough money for that?"

We'd never talked about the extent of my trust. I'd only told her that I wasn't too concerned about what I was going to do after graduation, that maybe I'd work in the mailroom of the insurance empire she planned to build.

"Yeah. Why do you think it's taken Bobby a lifetime to spend his money?" I chuffed. "It's in a trust, too, so he wasn't able to waste it all at once."

"What do you think he spent it on?"

"Hookers and blow."

She punched me lightly. "No really."

"Really. At least the hooker part. Maybe alcohol instead of cocaine."

"I don't want you to waste your money."

"It wouldn't be a waste to take care of the moms." I licked her neck to taste her sweetness. "Besides, you can take care of the money for us, right?" I stared up at her with my best puppy dog eyes but held my breath. I was a tiny bit scared that AM would tell me hell no, she wasn't making plans for the future with me. But her next response was immediate, as if it was a foregone conclusion that we'd be living together, wherever we might be.

"If you want me to," she said coyly, but I could tell by the excitement in her voice that she was thrilled I'd trust her with something like this. I'd have to take her over to the bank and introduce her before we left.

"Oh I do," I said. "I want you to take care of all of me." I pushed my hips against her slightly so she knew exactly what I was talking about.

"So your dad needs a loan from you? Is that why he was asking you about the trust?"

"Exactly. And he'll get that over my dead body."

"What if he sells the house or some of the land?" AM's voice sounded drowsy, as if sex and the emotional roller coaster of the day had done her in.

"I guess I don't care. It's not like I've got good memories there. AM," I said before she fell asleep. "I need to leave. I can't hang around here for another minute. I know I still need to work things out with my mom, but I'm too raw right now. Will you come to San Diego with me, and we can hang out with some of my enlisted buddies until we have to get back to class?"

"You bet, Bo."

TWENTY-NINE

AM

"YOU DON'T MIND THAT I spend the day with the boys?"

"For the forty-eight-thousandth time, no." Bo had been asking me this question on and off since we left Texas.

"I just feel bad about dragging you here and then leaving you." Bo nuzzled my neck as I was picking through our luggage for something to wear. It was slightly colder here than it had been in Texas.

"Go. I'll be fine. I have a book I've been wanting to read. I'm going to call my mom. The shopping place you told me about sounds fun."

"Do you want to come with us?"

"What will you be doing?" I was curious what Marines did on their day off. Go to the shooting range? Spend all day in the strip clubs?

"Fishing, maybe. Surfing."

"No and no. I'm going to this mall. I'd like to buy my mom something." Every time I'd talked to her, I felt guilty. I needed to buy a gift to make both of us feel better. Or maybe just me. It wasn't like she was alone. Roger was there with her.

"Bought you a hire car for the day."

"What? Why?"

"Because I don't want you to be driving around by yourself in a strange city. This way you'll have someone with you. And I can be sure I paid for it." He looked smug.

I rolled my eyes. "God, it's a good thing that you'll have me around to manage you. You'd be bankrupt in a year."

"I like you managing me," Bo growled against my neck, kissing the sensitive space along my shoulder and raising shivers as he went. "I hope that later you'll manage me right out of my clothes."

"Is that all you think about?"

"No. Sometimes I think about food." He smirked. His hands crept under my shirt to rub my belly and moved upward to cup my breasts.

"I thought you had to go?" I said breathlessly as he began to drag his thumbs across my suddenly-sensitive nipples.

"Not until I've had some breakfast." Bo dropped to his knees, pushed my shirt up with one hand, and pulled my panties down with the other.

After a heated morning encounter, Bo left me lying drowsily on the bed. I was in no hurry to rise and instead simply rolled over to my side to watch him get ready, my eyes already at half-mast. "Why don't you go back to sleep?" he suggested as he kissed me good-bye. "I texted you the number to the driver. Call him when you're ready to leave." I nodded and rolled over, tucking myself under the downy comforter and drifted off.

How much longer?

I'm still shopping. I want to have the perfect outfit for tonight.

Stop me the next time I say I have a great idea.

I thought you hated texting?

Then you know much I want you here. Now.

Be patient.

Send me a naughty pic.

So you can share it with your Marine buddies? Forget it.

Those fuckers don't get to see you like that. For my eyes only.

Here.

Oh shit. Buy the black ones!

My lips curved up into a sly smile. So Bo liked black lace. I picked up the black lace panties and matching strapless bra from the pile that had served as my text picture. "I'll take these." I told the sales attendant. She winked at me.

"Got a positive response, did you?"

I couldn't keep from flushing, but I smiled happily at her. "Yep."

The hire car was waiting for me when I exited the shopping complex. The instantaneous availability of it was luxurious, but I reminded myself not to get attached to living like this. My mother's frugality was too deeply ingrained. Back at the hotel, I primped myself like I imagined a bride would before her wedding night. Every part of me was buffed, shaved, and lotioned. I spritzed myself with a light perfume from a sample the fragrance counter had given me. It smelled like the ocean and reminded me of Bo's eyes when he was happy and at ease.

I pulled my clothes on layer by layer, shivering in anticipation at the gleam in Bo's gaze when he saw the black lace undergarments I'd bought. I realized my sexual appetite for him had become voracious, but he seemed not to mind. In fact, he reveled in it.

I knew he loved that I wanted him and that I couldn't wait to rush home after class and throw him down and ravish him. He encouraged me to do it; he encouraged me to explore sex in ways that I thought I'd be too shy to do before I met him. I loved going down on him, feeling his thickness in my mouth, feeling him shake helplessly when I brought him to climax. I enjoyed his lavish attention to my body. While the morning quickies were delicious, it wasn't anything like the nights when he took to exploring every inch of my body.

The thoughts of Bo and I rolling around naked in my bed, his bed, this hotel room bed, carried me into the bar on a wave of anticipation. I saw Bo's eyes alight on me almost immediately when I stepped out onto the patio where he sat with what seemed like a whole platoon of Marines, all except one sporting their distinct haircuts, which Bo had told me was a "high and tight."

He didn't wait like a potentate for me to come to him, running a power play in front of his friends. He got up immediately and came over to kiss me, not a social peck on the lips but an open-mouthed one that smeared my lip gloss all over the both of us. Breaking the kiss, he drew a thumb across my lower lip, wiping off the last of the gloss. I ineptly tried to rub the shiny substance off his mouth, but without a wet napkin, his lips looked glossy.

Bo didn't care, even though the table hazed him when he sauntered back, one arm wrapped around my waist.

"Boys, this is AM. AM, the One-Ten."

A round of glasses and bottles met at the middle as they toasted in unison, "The Death Bringers. Ooorah!" Then they drained their respective drinks and slammed down the containers as if one. I guessed they were. Bo pulled out an empty chair next to the one guy whose hair had grown out slightly, as if he'd somehow skipped out on the last trip to the barber. When I sat, Bo reclined next to me.

"What does One-Ten mean?" I asked.

"First Battalion, Tenth Marines. There are thirty-eight battalions in the entire Marine Corps," Bo explained, handing me a bottle of beer from the large bucket of ice in the middle of the round table. He turned and signaled a waitress for a refill of the bucket. "And it just kind of signifies where we're stationed, who gets to order us around. That sort of thing."

"You're all, um, enlisted?"

"Your girl doesn't know much about the Marines, does she?" the longer-haired guy to my left interjected.

"She knows all about me, and that's all that matters," Bo replied.

"I'm Gray," he said and stuck out his hand. I shook it.

"What's your nickname stand for?"

"That's not my nickname, sweetheart, just my name."

"His nickname's the Fog, because he's a quiet motherfucker," another guy at the table contributed.

Bo pulled me close to him so he could whisper in my ear. "Did you buy the black panties?"

"Yes," I replied as nonchalantly as possible, as if he wasn't asking me what I was wearing under my dress with all these guys sitting around staring at me as if I were the first female they'd seen after ninety days of isolation at sea.

"Will you take them off so I can put them in my pocket?" he whispered again.

"No," I told him, biting my inner lip to keep my cheeks from betraying our conversation.

"Knock it off, Lothario. Thought you came to see us," Gray joked.

I pushed Bo away and silently chastised him, but as always he was irrepressible and I couldn't stop my own lips curving up in a return smile.

"You still fapping to Wilson's sister, Hamilton?" Bo said, without tearing his gaze from me, wearing a grin as big as Texas.

"Damn right. Miss February still hangs in my locker," replied Hamilton.

As if on cue, a guy with dark hair and a thick neck pushed back his chair and towered over the one called Hamilton. "That's not my fucking sister." The table cracked up, and Gray and Hamilton reached around to give Bo high fives.

"Wilson's sister posed for *Playboy,*" Bo explained.

"That's not my goddamned sister, you sick fucks. That's someone else. How many times do I have to tell you this?" Wilson shouted at the laughing table. This only made everyone laugh even harder.

Another member of the table whose name I didn't know piped up. "I can tell you some shit on Bo, AM."

Bo's body tensed next to mine, but I figured this was just more of the same. "Puritan," Bo warned, but I shushed him with a wave of my hand.

"Sure," I encouraged.

Puritan, or Jerry Purdy, proceeded to tell the table about of several insane things that Bo had done in high school. Puritan was two years behind Bo and Noah and had followed them into the Marines. From the bored looks on the faces of the guys around the table, they'd all heard these stories before.

"You put *cows* in the school?"

"They can walk up but not down," Bo explained. "And they're cattle in Texas, Sunshine, not cows."

The stories made Bo sound vaguely like a hoodlum. I wasn't sure how many beers Jerry had managed to down during the recitation of Bo's many sins or before I arrived, but it was clearly quite a few. Jerry had dragged his chair around so that he could see me better, or so he proclaimed. He seemed to lean closer with each tale, and I kept moving away. Pretty soon I'd be sitting on Bo's lap. I squirmed a little in my chair, but that seemed to invite Jerry even closer.

"Want to know why Bo's called the Baker?"

"Puritan, no one calls Bo the Baker, you dickhead. That's your own shitty nickname," Gray interrupted. "Bo and Noah went to grunt school—

that's a good thing, by the way—but Puritan didn't get in. He's held a grudge for a while now."

"I didn't want that anyway," Jerry protested.

"Jerry," Bo cautioned. He'd been fairly quiet since we sat down, not interjecting or protesting any of Jerry's stories. "I don't think AnnMarie wants to hear any more of my high school exploits. They happened a while ago, and they're in my *past*." Bo emphasized the last word and placed his beer on the table, the one he'd been nursing since I'd arrived. It had to be warm by now.

"Because he loved to eat cream pies." Jerry snickered, ignoring Bo's warning. I looked uncertainly at Jerry and then Bo. Bo's easygoing attitude disappeared in a flash, and everyone at the table, other than Jerry, seemed to stiffen.

"There's nothing wrong with liking dessert," I told Bo. "I love pie myself." This set Jerry off into gales of laughter. I looked around the table and the other guys had pained expressions. None of them were looking me in the face.

"What?" I asked and turned to Bo. He sighed, scrubbed a hand over his face and then drew me onto his lap, far away from Jerry. Jerry had been leaning in so close that my absence nearly caused him to tip over, in part because he was gasping for breath from his laughter.

Bo whispered in my ear. "Not the food kind of pie, honey."

I felt my body flush hot with embarrassment. Of course not that kind of pie. I felt like a fool.

"Stop being an asswipe, Jerry." Bo curled his arms protectively around me and pushed my head onto his shoulder. He kicked Jerry sharply in the leg.

Jerry sputtered a few times and then managed to catch his breath. He wiped a few tears off his face. "Man, your face, AnnMarie, so innocently talking about liking pie."

Bo didn't like this; I could feel him stiffen around me. I pressed my hand on his tense thigh to prevent him from kicking Jerry even harder this time.

"Shut up, asshole." The disgust in Gray's voice was evident to everyone but Jerry, who looked bewildered that anyone would take offense to his story.

"Just roasting Bo, man," Jerry complained.

Even Wilson, who had been the subject of hazing earlier, chimed in. "Not cool, bro, not cool."

"Why don't we talk about something else," Bo said, his voice as hard as his frame. Jerry was determined, however, to tell one more story, and I regretted egging him on. I hadn't realized that Jerry wasn't really an old friend, but someone who was eaten with jealousy over Bo's exploits. This last story of Jerry's, the one he was desperate to tell and had been building toward since he started, was the *coup de grace*. Whatever slight Bo had done to Jerry, imagined or real, Jerry had been waiting to repay him.

"See, Bo here, with his love of bets and pie, couldn't resist his buddy Noah's bet that Bo here couldn't fuck the entire drill team, all twenty-seven of them." Jerry nodded affirmatively. "He fucked them all, some of them two at a time, his senior year."

I felt Bo's arms tighten around me, afraid that I was going to jump off his lap screaming. Maybe I would have, before, but not now, after all we'd been through.

"Yeah, I'd be a little leery, too, of what kind of things ol' Baker's carrying around on his person. Why don't you come sit on me?" He patted his knee. It was a disgusting offer. I got the sense that the only reason Bo's fist wasn't in Jerry's mouth was because I was in the way. But I didn't want Bo to get upset. That would only feed into Jerry's narcissistic plan. I relaxed against Bo and pulled up his arm snug against me, right under my breasts. His grip was almost painful. I kept one hand on his arm, and the other I dropped down to stroke the side of his thigh.

"No, thanks. I'd rather sit here. At least I can be confident that Bo knows what he's doing."

Jerry looked confused, as if he couldn't believe I wasn't totally disgusted by Bo's whorish behavior.

"But, did you hear me? He was called the Baker because he ate out all those girls," Jerry repeated, more loudly now.

I felt Bo starting to rise, getting ready to set me on my feet. His chest rumbled as if he were was about to growl something at Jerry, but I pushed back against him, hoping he'd stay seated. Getting a rise out of Bo was Jerry's goal. Jerry wouldn't like it half as well if Bo didn't react, which was why Jerry's stories had become increasingly disturbing.

"Like I said, at least he'll know what he's doing tonight."

Jerry looked like he wanted to try again, like I hadn't gotten his point, but Bo had had enough. He rose and gently set me aside and stalked over to Jerry's chair. Bo hauled Jerry up by his collar and frog-marched him out the door. The rest of us followed behind him. I wasn't sure what Bo was going to do, but nothing good could come from a private confrontation.

Jerry was protesting loudly, but Bo's friends formed a kind of circle around him so that other people couldn't really see. For all they knew, we were helping a really drunk guy home. Jerry stopped struggling once he realized that no one was coming to his aid. Whether it was the liquor or just a dogged pursuit of his agenda, Jerry decided to renew his attacks on Bo's reputation.

"What's the matter, Bo? You afraid your reputation's going to scare off your girl? Did you see her face when I told her the entire drill team?"

It was as if we weren't even there. It was just Jerry and Bo.

Gripping Bo's arm, I swung around to face him, and he pushed Jerry aside. I placed both hands around his face. "He's not worth it. You know who won this? You. You did before he ever showed up. He's eaten up inside with jealousy. His life must suck a thousand times worse than a Hoover vacuum because no happy guy tries this act without feeling so insecure that he hates himself for it in the morning. I bet he can't even look in the mirror without disgust. You've won, Bo, or you wouldn't even be a target. So walk away. Right now. Walk away with me," I begged.

I LET AM HOLD ME even though I could have broken away at any moment. In a flash I realized that this moment, more than any, would determine my future, because this was *my* choice, *my* decision. It wasn't my father being a shithead or my mother being victimized. This was all on me. Would I answer every provocation with my fists, or would I employ that self-control I had supposedly learned? I forced my hands to unclench and AM grabbed on and lifted them to press them against her lips. I looked at her when I said the words.

"Not worth it."

"What's that, Baker?" Jerry taunted.

"You aren't worth the effort," I said loudly.

"Puritan, you've always been sick in the head," I heard Gray say. He was backed up by murmurs of agreement from my other friends. Jerry Purdy wasn't going to have an easy time of it when he returned to base. There were a thousand little things that the other guys could do to make his life miserable, and he had to know it. There was a scuffling sound but I paid no attention.

AM's shining smile washed away the tension and filled me up. As I leaned in for a kiss, she glanced past me and her smile turned to a grimace before she shouted at me. I sensed him before I felt him, and twisted on the balls of my feet. He flew past me, and I gave him an extra push, which propelled him into the garbage dumpster. His body struck the metal with a loud clang.

"You ripped my fucking shirt," he bellowed. Facing him, I could see the flush of inebriation riding high on his cheekbones. His pupils were pinpoints. Maybe Jerry wasn't drunk; maybe he was high. I swung AM behind me, and I could feel the boys close ranks. "This was my favorite t-shirt, you asshole."

I turned my back on him, not just to avoid the spittle-laced curses, but to put this day to bed. I grabbed AM and pulled her into my arms.

"Still with me?"

"Like glue, baby."

"I thought I was Thor." I nuzzled her hair, filling my lungs with the fresh lemon scent of her shampoo. I began walking AM backward to the waiting hire car, holding her a few inches off the ground so she wouldn't trip and fall.

"Hey, Bo." Gray ran up beside me. "A minute?" I nodded and held the door while AM climbed in.

Gray swept a hand over his hair, only small remnants of his regulation haircut showing slightly in the back. "I'm thinking of getting out."

I gaped at him in total shock. Gray had a hard-on for the military. I thought for sure he'd be career. "I didn't see that coming. Why?"

"Now that the troops are drawn down, we're all just sitting around base and devising pranks. Guys are spending too much money and hooking up with boot chasers. There isn't much going on, and it's driving me crazy."

"What about going to Officer Training School, moving up?"

"It's either that or trying for one of the Spec Ops, but I've been thinking that maybe I should just do what you and Noah did and get out. How is it?"

This time it was me rubbing my head. "I mean, shit, man, I don't know what to tell you. If you had caught me before AM, I would've said I regret it."

"But now?"

"I lucked out there. Look, if you want to see what it's like, a little, come with me for the rest of your leave. You can bunk with Noah and me, go to some Central College functions, and see what you think," I said.

"What's Noah up to? He hunt down his girl?"

"Yeah, although it was no walk in the park for him. Damn amusing for the rest of us. He bought a yogurt franchise."

"A yogurt what?"

"A place where you go and get frozen yogurt and put shit on top. People love it. I think he's going to buy another one."

Gray scratched his head in wonder. "What're you going to do when you're done with school?"

"Thinking of throwing in with my man Finn. He flips houses, buys old ones and renovates them."

"No shit. You gotta have a four-year degree for that?"

"Nah, but I'm about three semesters away from graduating with a degree, so I might as well finish it out."

"Huh." Gray sounded intrigued and while I didn't mind shooting the shit with him, I wanted to take AM back to the hotel and remind her why she was still with me.

"Give me a call or just show up. We'll show you around," I told him and then climbed into the backseat with AM. "Tell the other guys I'll see them this summer."

Gray nodded and jerked his head toward AM's side of the car. "She's really it for you?"

"You know how it's all about God and country over there in Afghanistan." Gray nodded. "Well, when you find someone like AM, what you felt about the cause, about being a patriot, is like eating eggs from the MRE pack. Dry, tasteless, meaningless. It's nothing. I'd kill for her and," I paused, "I'll learn to walk away."

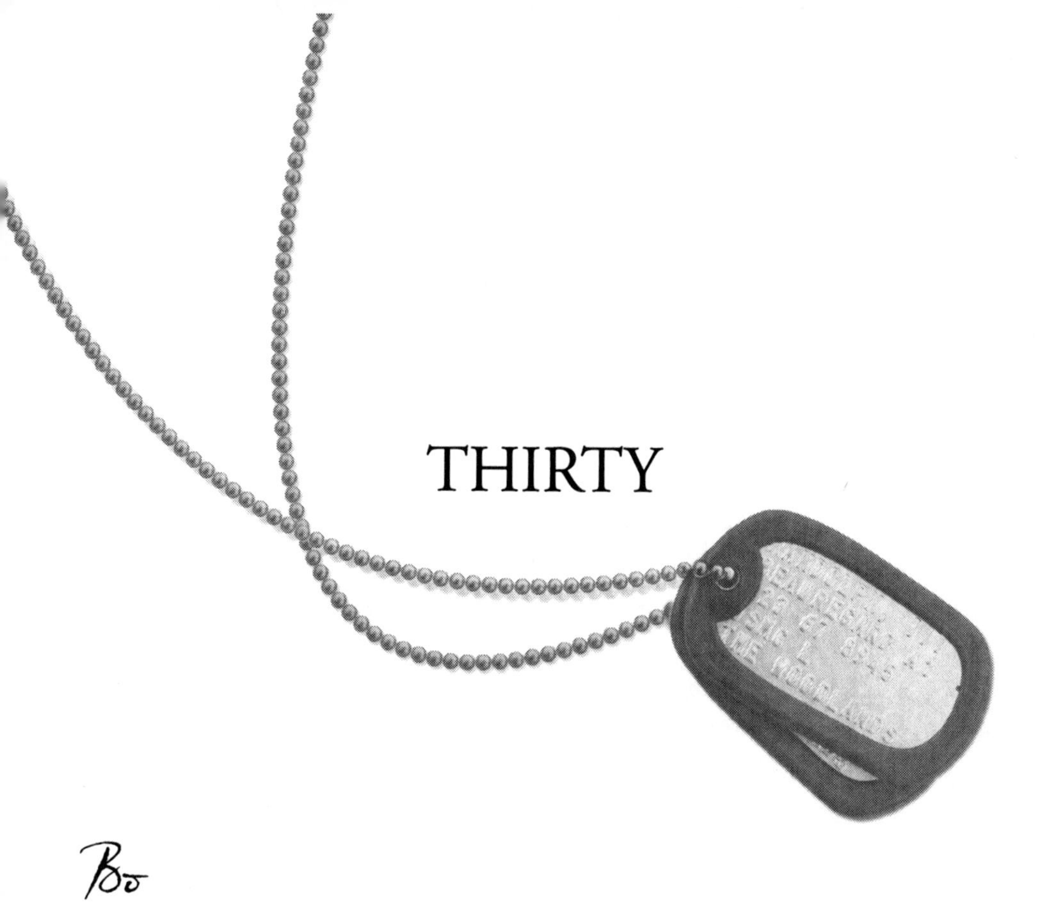

THIRTY

Bo

AM AND I WORKED OUR asses off to finish our labs after our midterms. The plant hybrid report generated by our theoretical study was completed by AM; she typed up our notes and I added a few sketches. AM declared my pencil drawings to be brilliant and was convinced they would give us an A. I tried not to look too skeptical, but I hoped our professor wasn't going to be simply won over by a few encyclopedia drawings.

"What's this?" AM asked, flipping through some carpentry books I'd picked up over the weekend. I hesitated to tell her, wondering if she would think I was a complete fool for taking my life in such a different direction. I knew that AM would run her own business someday. It might be small, but I doubted it. Her energy burned too strongly for that. Would she still be okay with being with someone who worked with his hands and not in an office?

I gave myself a metaphorical kick in the ass. It was a good thing I'd never fallen in love before. I wouldn't have been able to wipe my ass after all this second-guessing.

I pulled the books from AM's fingers and rubbed my fingers over the covers. "I'm thinking about working with Finn, flipping houses."

AM's face lit up with interest. "Oh, Bo, that sounds fantastic."

"Yeah? You aren't going to be bothered if I wear boots to work instead of a suit and tie?"

My question was met with a punch to the arm. Our propensity for physical violence seemed to have grown inversely, with AM increasing her nonverbal responses and me decreasing my fight instinct and talking more. Of course, AM's punches were like insect bites, tiny and barely noticeable, but I yelped like a dog so she knew she had my attention.

"Does this mean you can build me whatever I want? Like a new desk or a bookshelf or something? Wait, you won't sell your car to get a pickup instead, will you? I haven't even gotten to drive it yet." AM hopped over to pick up my key fob off the desk, the dog tags jingling like a little bell underneath the t-shirt she was wearing. Mine, of course. I'd taken all her pre-Bo nightwear and hidden it. Even though no guy had ever worn those T-shirts, I didn't like the idea of seeing her in a man's shirt that hadn't already been worn by me.

"Maybe after I have a few years in, I'll build us a house." I pulled her down on my lap, nestling her ass against my growing wood. She always looked so awesome wearing my shirts. I'd like to keep AM locked up in my room wearing only my old PT Marine t-shirt and nothing else, but I kept those thoughts to myself. After classes were out, AM and I were going to go on a little road trip together, first to visit her mom, then mine, and then back down to San Diego.

I'd promised she could drive the car, but I hadn't promised anything about how long she'd spend in the driver's seat. I might have mellowed, but some things would always be instinctive, like wanting to drive and carrying her things. And having sex standing up. She'd just have to learn to deal with that.

"Let's go to the party house this Friday night," AM said. The words flew past me as I rocked my hips against her, pressing her harder against my erection. I wasn't interested in any parties except the ones we would have right here in her bedroom. I pulled down on the collar of the t-shirt and kissed the base of her neck and shoulders that were exposed.

"Wait, what?" I asked as AM's statement registered. Instinctively I hugged her tighter to me. No one should go through that mess again. I'd resigned myself to AM not transferring and was prepared to buffer and shield her as much as I could, but going back to the party house seemed like trying to walk through a minefield without any testing equipment or field gear. At some point, you'd step wrong and the world would blow up. Last time, AM's wounds healed. Next time they might not. My whole promise to stop fighting would go down the drain, too. The memory of the lacrosse shithead with the big mouth lying in a pool of his own nose blood made me smile, which was definitely *not* the response I was supposed to be having.

"I'm tired of hiding out, Bo. I don't want to be afraid any more, and I don't want what's happened to me to happen to other girls."

AM sounded determined. I pulled her legs up so she was curled like a kitten in my lap. "I've got your back, then."

Later, while AM was showering, I called in reinforcements. The entire house needed to show up.

"Are we coming to help you lay waste to the crowd or to prevent you from losing your mind?" asked Noah. "I don't care either way, but Gray wants to know whether he should wear a new t-shirt or an old one."

"Let's play it by ear," I cautioned. Gray had taken me up on the invitation to come up for a visit, and I was glad to have him for backup.

"Foggy is hoping for bloodshed, so don't expect him to be the voice of reason."

"That's why Mal has to come, too," I said.

"Good call," Noah affirmed.

WE LEFT AROUND 10:00, AFTER making a half-assed attempt at a pre-party. Ellie spilled her drink on AM, which necessitated a change of clothes. Ellie apologized profusely for about ten minutes. Her neighbors were a train wreck, with the guy looking like a forlorn puppy at AM's lesbian friend whenever he thought no one was looking. Falling in love with a lesbian was like putting your nuts in a vise and asking for them to be crushed. Captain, may I have blue balls for the rest of my life? I kind of wanted to punch him in the face for being so stupid about it, but AM definitely wouldn't appreciate me hitting her friends.

Out of all of us, AM was in the best mood. While she wasn't bad at putting the brave face on, I didn't get the sense that she was full of tension. It was like she'd made up her mind to do something and regardless of the outcome, she was at peace with herself. I made a conscious effort to relax and swung an arm around her shoulders to let her know she wasn't alone.

"I love you, you know."

She smiled up at me, face as beautiful and shining as any star. "I know."

At the door of the party house, AM marched right up the steps and I was right behind her. One of the residents, Lance, I think, was wearing a t-shirt that said "Choking Hazard" and an arrow pointing downward. He placed his hand on my arm as I followed AM inside.

"Hey, man, we don't want any trouble tonight."

I looked at his hand and then at him, incredulously. "You don't take your hand off my arm, and we'll see what kind of choking hazard your cock makes as I stuff it in your mouth."

Lance jumped back and raised his hands in surrender. "Just saying. Blood's a bitch of a stain."

"Then you better not let things get out of hand," I warned, brushing by him. Unsurprisingly, Lance didn't stop me again, nor did his roommate, who was manning the shot table. Unwritten rules required a toll to get into the back parts of the house where the party and the other liquor was. I caught up with AM and laid a fifty down before she could pull out any cash. "For all of us." I gestured to the group behind me. He started to pour us all shots, but I shook my head no.

"Speak for yourself, soldier boy," Ellie said, muscling me out of the way. "I'll drink his and mine," she informed the bartender. He finished pouring the shots for Ellie, AM, Sasha, and Brian. Ellie downed one, and then picked up another and gave it to AM. "For courage."

"For fun," AM responded and tipped her head back to swallow the alcohol. She coughed a bit and pounded her chest. "That stuff is vile."

A commotion sounded behind us, and I turned to see the entire Woodlands crew tromping inside, even Finn. All tall, big, and muscled, the group of five looked suitably intimidating. Lance moved out the way without even attempting to give a warning. Reaching into my wallet, I pulled out another fifty and threw it on the table. "We'll take the bottle." The guy handed it over wordlessly, and I waved everyone through.

"Why are they all here?" AM hissed at me.

"They like a good party?" I said innocently.

She made a face at me and said, "This is my show."

"I know, Sunshine, but we want to make sure the response at the end of the show is appropriate."

"Whatever that means." She frowned.

"It means that sometimes a show of force can prevent actual fatalities or injuries down the road."

"It's not just that there might be an opportunity for a brawl?" she said skeptically.

"That, too," I admitted. You can't instantly change every instinct honed from a young age.

AM HAD PICKED THE RIGHT night to go out. The back rooms of the party house were packed with people spilling out onto the deck to enjoy the fresh air. Relief from midterms, I guessed. Wall-to-wall bodies filled the makeshift dance floor, and someone was spinning beats in the corner. At AM's signal, Noah and I walked over to the DJ corner and told them to cut the music. I might have included a few threats about broken fingers and equipment. My reputation for having a short fuse and a heavy fist caused them to cut the music without any bloodshed. Noah, standing by my side, looked faintly disappointed.

"Sorry. I promised AM I'd try to keep the hospital bills down," I said.

Noah just shrugged, and we walked back to the front of the room, where AM had climbed onto a table.

"You know what she's planning?" Noah whispered.

"Nope. I'm just here to catch her." And hold her, comfort her, and beat the shit out of anyone who made her cry.

Gray came up to stand on my left and the rest of the boys from the Woodlands fanned out in a semicircle in front of the table.

The chatter of the crowd quieted, and I heard whispers spread like a wildfire. A flash went off, and I raised my hand instinctively to shield myself.

"What the hell, Ellie?" I asked.

"You look like you're AM's big bad security detail." She tucked her phone in her back pocket and mimicked our stance—folded arms, feet hip-width apart, and the grim look. "You're only missing the suits and earpieces."

When AM didn't move and the music didn't spin back up, the crowd began to shift restlessly. AM cleared her throat. "I'm AnnMarie West, a sophomore and economics major. I have a three point eight-five GPA. Professor Quinlan gave me a B in her literature class. I didn't profess enough love for *Pride and Prejudice,* I guess." At this, a few people in the crowd laughed. This must be a well-known quirk.

"You may also have heard of me from your friend or study group partner or intramural teammate as Typhoid Mary or the Lacrostitute."

This statement led to titters, clucking of tongues, and snapping of fingers, but few laughs.

"I'm not really sure who started the rumor that I slept with the lacrosse team, but it become Central College canon before the end of my freshman year. It shouldn't be a surprise to most of you that the rumor wasn't true. I mean, when would I have time to do the whole team? Am I right?" She held out both hands, palms up to the crowd.

The whispers started to crescendo.

"The truth is that yes, I slept with a lacrosse player in a drunken stupor about a month after I came to Central."

"Erik Trenton," someone shouted. I turned around and looked back into the crowd to see who had spoken. I saw a couple of hands point to the top of dark head. Visually marking the guy's red t-shirt, I whispered to Noah, "One hundred fifty pounds, about five foot nine, dark hair, red t-shirt. About eight o'clock." Noah nodded and slipped into the crowd. Seconds later, I heard a thud and scuffle of feet. I presumed Noah had cuffed the guy on the head, covered his mouth, and was now taking him out back.

AM continued, her voice rising in volume. "I don't remember much about it other than it wasn't as painful as I thought it would be. It was my first time, you see. And then, I didn't have sex with another guy from Central after that, especially not Clay Howard the Third. He tried to feel me up, but I turned him down. I didn't want him. So in retaliation, he and his buddies and the rest of you started spreading rumors about me. You posted about it to the Central College bulletin board. You tweeted and Facebooked about it. I had to shut my Facebook page down because of it." She paused and looked around the crowd. I could see her start to breathe more rapidly and worried that she'd break down, which I knew she'd hate. I took a step forward but AM stayed me with her hand. I dropped back and she continued.

"You wrote on my door, you called me names. But none of it was true. And even if I'd slept with ten guys or a hundred guys, what goddamned business is it of yours? At first, I thought I'd just ignore it, but I couldn't. For some reason, because you guys have nothing better to do, you thought it would be fun to make me a pariah. Spreading rumors about me having a venereal disease. Telling all your buddies how easy I was. Some of you guys even lied that you had bagged me, but we both know the truth. You haven't been within a foot of my body. And maybe no one else's."

AM took a deep calming breath and this time, no one tittered, laughed, or whispered. The entire crowd was spellbound by her words, by their own guilt, by their shitty actions.

You don't know how strong she really is. I could hear Ellie's voice repeating her admonishment. And she was right; I didn't. I had faced down my dad. My fears. But AM was facing down her peers, people she saw daily, people she might work with, people she went to class with and would have school projects with.

That took some kind of bravery. My heart swelled with admiration for her.

"Goddamn," I heard Finn mutter next to me.

"Times a hundred," said Gray. Both of them were transfixed as AM laid out the hypocrisy of the entire crowd like a hunter doing a field dressing on a deer he's just killed.

"But I woke up and realized that I'm going to be here for another two years, and I deserve to have the same damn good time on campus as I've been having off of it. So I'm here to tell you that you're all full of shit. Guys, you're constantly running girls down for not putting out and when they do? You call them names. Is it any wonder you have to work so hard to get laid?" Her voice was mocking. The previous signs of nervousness had been completely banished.

"And girls, what the fuck? Why aren't you supporting your girlfriends? So she wants to get laid and you call her a slut and whisper behind her back? Who cares if she sleeps with one guy or fifty? Does it make her any less of the girl who'll help you with your homework, spot you money for a formal, lend you clothes from her fucking closet? Why are you judging her based on the number of men who've stuck a penis in her instead of all the other things she does for you? Grow the fuck up and start treating each other with some goddamn respect."

With that, AM jumped down and headed straight for me. Though she tried to hide it, I could see she was trembling with adrenaline—but not fear. Nope, AM wasn't afraid. She was just high on hormones.

Her speech might not make a big change on campus, but it'd be something these people would never forget. Never.

"Will you punch me if I tell you I that I'm totally in love with your girlfriend right now?" Gray muttered.

"Ordinarily, yes, but tonight, I'm giving you a pass." How could you not be turned on by the Valkyrie that was AM? This was a girl who wouldn't be put down by anything. She'd always fight, not only for herself, but for you and anyone in her circle. The natural, animalistic response was to claim her because this woman would make the best wife, the best mother, the best partner.

I didn't take a step forward like I wanted to. I waited until she'd come to me so everyone else could see the steel in her spine, but once she was within the circle of my arms, I couldn't resist telling the room silently that I'd spread the black plague on them if they said one negative word tonight. I hugged AM tightly to me and allowed her to lead us out of the party house, and the rest of the Woodlands guys falling in step behind us like they were the palace guard.

Ellie met AM outside the door of the back room and gave her a huge hug. "I want to be you when I grow up." Ryan, too, hugged AM and said she was an inspiration. As we walked through, hands reached out to pat AM. Murmurs of apologies and "preach it" were littered along her path. And with each step, I felt her trembling lessen, her steps become more firm, and her bearing more erect. Whatever changed or didn't at Central was of little consequence. AM would shape her own destiny with her beautiful, strong hands.

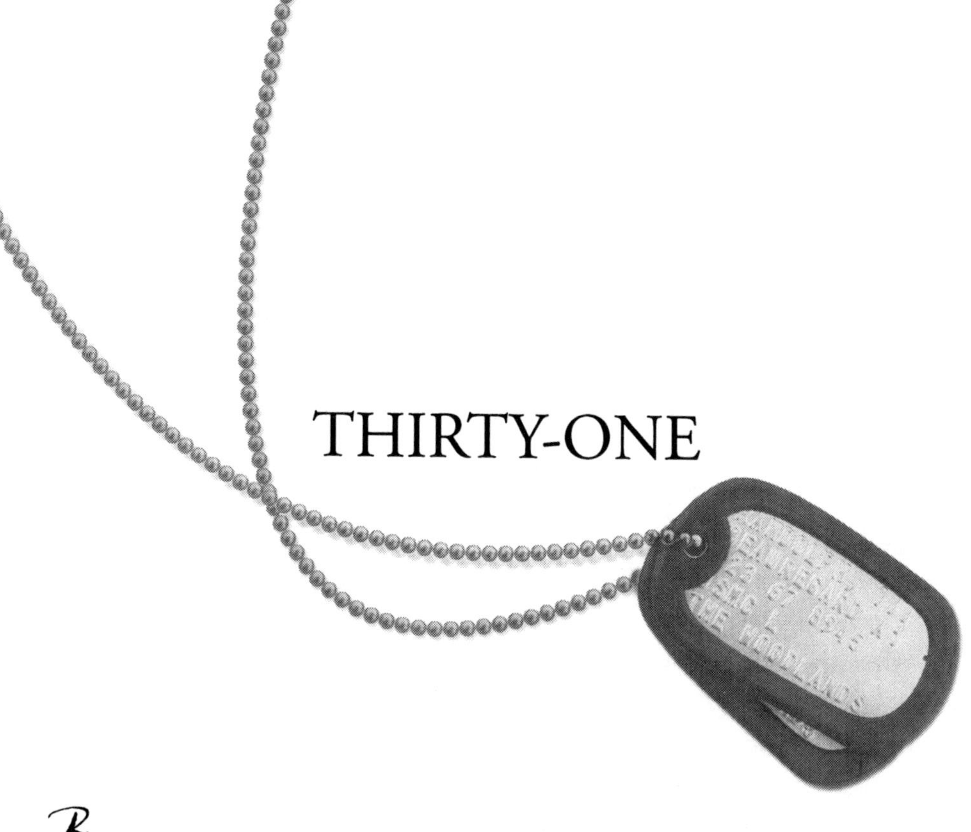

THIRTY-ONE

Bo

CENTRAL CHANGED FOR AM AFTER that night. Not everyone, of course. There were always going to be assholes, no matter what. But the next day at biology class, the room gave her a standing ovation as she walked in, and that seemed to embarrass her as much as the cruel whispers. She hid her face in my chest until the clapping died down. Professor Godwin frowned the entire time. We spent the weekend on campus, eating in the café and hanging out in the library and commons. It was incredibly boring and the food was bad.

"Promise me that we don't ever have to do this again," I said to her after eating some meat plate surprise. AM nodded her head in vigorous agreement. Apparently the wilted lettuce and defrosted vegetables from the salad bar weren't doing it for her, either.

Besides the food, however, was the dismal existence of the lacrosse club. While Clay Howard never approached while I was around, I couldn't be with AM every second of the day. At some point, Howard would corner her, and he'd want his piece of flesh in repayment for the humiliation that both of us had dealt to him—AM with her words and me with my fists.

He was a loose end that needed to be taken care of and in a way that would ensure he was never a part of AM's life again.

"Did you get it?"

Gray nodded grimly and held out a little vial with three pills. Mal, with all his connections, had helped Gray with this part of the plan. "It's too fucking easy to get these, and they aren't even very expensive. We outta shut that down."

"How many?"

"Enough so that when Campus Security gets the tip about the pot, the marijuana plants will seem like a nuisance charge."

"How will you get that stuff back?"

"After the charges are brought and the club dechartered, Mal and I will raid Campus Security, take back the pills, and destroy them. Campus Police stores everything in their office, which has a back door access and zero video surveillance. We cased it yesterday."

"When?" I wasn't ordinarily the planning type. I left that for Noah, but this was my show, and I wanted to make sure all the details were taken care of, including not introducing a bunch of date rape drugs onto the campus scene.

Mal folded his arms, "Gray and I will deal with this. You take care of your girl."

I got on the phone and called Ryan. "When's the meet?"

"Half hour."

"I'll be there."

Ryan had set up a meet with the president of the lacrosse club. I didn't know him very well. He was a senior and some kind of philosophy major. I had to wonder what kind of sociopath he was to take philosophy and not think for a moment about the repercussions of his actions. I hated philosophy classes for just that reason.

"So we're here to parlay." Brent Davidson rubbed his hands together in anticipation, as if we were playing a game of Risk. We had agreed to meet in the basement of the Alpha Phi house, which apparently violated a thousand sorority house rules, but Lana had decreed it was the perfect place. Neutral territory for both of us, or that's how she sold it to Davidson. We stood facing each other in a dank room, the water heater of the house not ten feet away.

I wondered if he thought that this would be some great chess game, with his wits matched against mine. I had a lot to accomplish in the next twenty-four hours, so I wasn't going to spend a lot of time stroking this guy's ego. Actually, I was going to spend zero time. Today was the day for a beatdown, and not one meted out by my fists.

"You're weak, Davidson," I informed the lacrosse club president. "That's why you're here playing a club sport instead of an Ivy out east. You lack real talent and suck as a leader. Your club is a cancer and needs to be excised."

My bluntly spoken words penetrated Davidson's backward baseball cap, and he looked about as pale as the color of his polo. He glanced nervously at Ryan, who stared back impassively. I continued. "Here's what's happening. There is no bargain. Your house is being searched right now, as we speak, by campus police. They will find in your kitchen pantry a grow light and ten weed plants. Now that's not so bad, right? A few recreational drugs aren't going to put you down, but in Clay Howard's room they're going to find a hundred grams of GHB. That's a lot of date rape drugs. See, either Clay's raping every girl on campus, or he's dealing. Which do you think it is?"

Davidson's mouth opened and shut like a fish sucking for air. I waited for his little brain to catch up. "No one's using GHB in the house."

"Is that right? I've heard it's already being called the rape house. Good ol' Central campus rumor mill is working extra hard today. Turns out that Clay keeps a little ledger next to his pill stash. There are initials in it, and a lot of those initials match the guys in the club. Initials like BRD. That wouldn't be you, would it?"

I didn't think that Davidson could have gotten paler than he already was, but the whiteness of his skin made his eyes look like they were going to pop out. I moved back a bit so that I'd have a decent amount of room to swing, in case it came to that.

"You aren't going to get away with this!" Davidson cried. "Everyone will know you're behind it."

"You mean everyone like the students? Because that'd be a good thing. They'll know not to fuck with me or mine. If you mean campus admin, how would they ever draw the connection? Unless you're going to admit to a violation of Honor Code ten, Section A, which says that if you knowingly spread false and malicious statements about another student, you'll be up for expulsion. BRD, dude, you're only a month or so from graduation. Do you want to jeopardize that?"

Whether it was because of the use of his initials or the threat of delaying his graduation, Davidson decided to stop protesting. I admired the effort he employed to keep from screaming at me. "What do you want?" he asked dejectedly.

"That ledger, which points fingers at over half the club, goes away if you agree to two things."

"I'm listening."

"First, you clean house." I handed him a piece of paper and, when he refused to take it, I reached over and picked up his listless hand. Shoving the paper into his palm, I closed his fingers over it. "This list contains the names of the girls who were the target of the revenge rumors. You have until tomorrow to file charges against the appropriate men in the house in front of the Honor Code committee. With the filed charges, you will have affidavits filled out from members of the lacrosse team speaking in favor of the victims and against the accused. If this isn't done by 5 P.M. tomorrow, the ledger stays with Campus Security and will eventually be transferred to the county for investigation by real detectives. You want them sorting through your e-mails and browser history?"

Davidson shook his head and shoved the list into his pocket.

"The second thing is that you forfeit the rest of your matches and you apply for a decertification for the club."

"No way, man, this is my senior year," Davidson protested.

"Hey, your funeral. Don't know how you'll play when you have the drug investigation hanging over your head, but I guess you'll deal."

"You're a fucking sociopath," Davidson snarled at me.

"Now I know you never paid attention in any of your classes. Sociopaths don't feel anything. I'm feeling a lot right now. Glee. Satisfaction. Also anger. Don't step wrong, or I'll punch you until every bone in your face is broken."

"What about Ryan, here?" Davidson shook his finger. "He's going to be taken down by this, too."

"Nah, see, Renaissance Man is beloved by a number of factions here at

Central. The sport factions, the GLBTQ groups, the Greek system. I hear he's being fought over by the sororities as to who gets to have him as a little brother."

Ryan smiled angelically as we both looked at him.

"Ryan's going to become the face of the lacrosse club. He will publicly mourn the loss of the club, but acknowledge that it was something that was necessary. Next year, the club charter will be reapplied for, by Ryan and a select few surviving members deemed by Ryan to not be involved in whatever disgusting shit you guys carried out during your reign."

"Why the fuss? AnnMarie had her say." Davidson had turned petulant now. His quicksilver changes of emotion were almost comical but showed what little spine he had.

"She didn't have a 'say,' she was doing some much-needed truth-telling. I'm not doing this for AM," I lied. Of course it was for her, but I wasn't putting her in the crosshairs. "I didn't put myself in harm's way for four years in Afghanistan so I could come home and watch a bunch of assclowns terrorize an entire campus of women. This is a fucking mess, and I don't want my years at Central to be tainted by it. You with me?"

Davidson nodded. "What about Howard?"

"You leave him to me. You've got a shitload of stuff to do before five P.M. tomorrow."

"Or what?"

"Or I guess you'll see how you like seeing your name in the *New York Times* connected with a date-rape drug. Bet that looks good on the old résumé."

With that, I signaled for Ryan and we left.

"What's your plan for Howard?" Ryan asked quietly once we were outside.

"Just a military prank." I squeezed Ryan's shoulder. "Why don't you go to AM and Ellie's apartment. Make sure they stay inside tonight. Rent some movies. I'll be by about ten."

At 9 P.M., I showed up at Karl's, a dive bar with about ten tables and cockroaches as dinner companions. People drank heavily for anesthetization both inside and out. Gray was sitting with Howard at one table in the corner. I pulled down my skull cap and flipped up my collar. No need to be too obvious. I sauntered over and sat down right next to Howard, stretching my arm across the back of Howard's chair.

"Having a bad day?"

He was gone. Blitzed. I could barely make out his words between the slurring and spitting. "You're behind this. I know you are, fucking asshole."

"Where're your friends?" I looked pointedly at the empty tables and chairs.

Gray looked at me, a twinkle in his eye, and answered for Howard. "We're getting acquainted. This guy says that he's been taken advantage of by some jackass with an ax to grind. You the jackass?"

I nodded. Gray was having far too much fun tonight.

"I'm here to make it up to you, though, Howard. We're going to have some fun tonight." But before we could do anything, his head dropped listlessly on the table and drool seeped out of the corner of his mouth.

"This is disgusting," I told Gray. "You were supposed to watch him."

Gray shrugged. "I was, but I couldn't keep him from drinking without sitting on him, and I figured that defeated the purpose of me being the one to babysit."

"Fuck, okay, let me think." I drummed my fingers on the table. I needed Noah, the plotter, because *my* plans all hinged on threatening Clay with bodily harm until he left. Hard to threaten a guy who was passed out face down in his own drool. Finally, I threw up my hands in disgust. "I can't do anything to him while he's drunk. It would make me no better than he is."

"Principles, schminciples," Gray scoffed.

"Don't encourage me," I said. "I'm trying to do the right thing. I have to be able to look AM in the face tonight. Let's just take the asshat home. I'll corner him tomorrow when he's hungover but sober."

We hauled the drunk and drugged Howard out of his chair and half-carried, half-dragged him out of the bar. Gray handed me a pair of plastic gloves, and I snapped them on. "Jesus, what size did you get? Extra small? The rubber is cutting off my circulation."

"You want to touch him or complain about the plastic gloves, Bo Peep?"

I shut up. Worried that Howard would get sick, Gray ran in and paid the bartender for a roll of plastic wrap. We lined his car and laid Howard in the backseat. Howard stayed unconscious even after we wrestled him out of the car and onto the porch of his house.

The next morning, someone texted me several photos of Howard, still passed out with his hand on the business end of a wooden steer. I didn't know if it was a sorority girl's revenge or the work of someone in the theater arts program, as the steer looked like a prop for a play. He'd be unable to go a minute without someone mooing in his face.

Mal and Gray took care of the drugs, and Ryan took care of the club decertification. I didn't have to hit anyone once.

THIRTY-TWO

Bo

I WAS WAITING IN THE library lounge for AM to appear after class. I'd stopped waiting for her outside of her classroom. She didn't like that. She'd eventually told me it made her look weak, like she needed someone to escort her across campus. I just liked to spend the time with her, but I understood her need for independence. It was one of the things that had drawn me to her in the first place, so I really couldn't complain. Instead, I waited in the lobby of the library. She'd meet me here and we'd study. Or AM would study, and I'd just drink her in, this miracle of a girl who saved me. All this time I thought I was saving her.

She burst through the doors, noisily, unafraid of someone noticing her. The tension I'd once seen in her shoulders while she moved through campus was no longer present. I felt my mouth widening in response to her apparent happiness.

"Finals canceled?" I asked.

She shook her head, but her eyes were dancing wildly with some suppressed emotion. I thought it was glee. She executed a little hop over to me, looking five kinds of adorable. I wanted to scoop her up and lick her all over, but I restrained myself.

She threw herself at me, and I was surprised. When I looked around, there were people milling about. I took advantage of her changed behavior and snugged her up close to my body. Her eyes widened as she felt my arousal hard against the swell of her belly, and her amusement turned to outright laughter.

It only made me want her more.

"What?" I asked her, rubbing my hands along her arms.

"Clay Howard has left school."

"Really?" I tried to look surprised, but she caught something in my tone. Her amusement faded away and was replaced by a suspicious look. With an effort, I smiled as blandly as possible. "Where'd you hear that?"

"It was all anyone could talk about in class," AM informed me, but she was searching my eyes, my face, for some sign that I knew something. I employed some of the discipline that I was working on and tried to project innocent interest. It must have worked, because her suspicious look dropped away and was replaced by excitement once again.

Stepping back, she pulled me toward the exit door. "Let's go home instead of studying here," she said. I went along benignly.

"Tell me," I urged her again. I wanted to hear what this end of the telephone chain sounded like.

"I heard he dropped out. And I heard some gossip that the lacrosse club was being disbanded, but I didn't figure that was accurate."

I only hmmmed. AM tried a couple more theories out on me.

When we arrived at the apartment, Ellie was there to greet us. "Guess what I heard!" she cried, throwing her arms wide as if throwing us the news.

"Is it about Clay Howard?" AM said, turning to shut the door behind me.

"Yes." Ellie's arms came down with a flap. "Already heard?"

AM nodded, but then she began jumping up and down and the two clasped wrists and hopped around the room like they had pogo sticks attached to their legs. I leaned against the hallway wall, not too far from where I had punched a hole, not too far from where my world fell apart and AM and I stitched it back together.

Someday I'd tell AM what I did and why. I pulled out my phone and snapped a picture of her smiling face. I'd show her this picture and tell her I'd do anything to make her look this happy.

I wanted to bask in that glow. She and Ellie pogoed their way over to me. I drew her into my arms and said, "See ya later, Ellie." I steered AM down the hall into her bedroom.

"What are you doing?" she asked, all coy and shit.

"Oh, I have a few ideas about how to extend your happiness at this moment." I smiled down at her.

"Did you have something to do with this?" she asked me, her suspicious look back. I couldn't lie to her, so instead I kissed her cheek and then her ear and then ran my tongue down the side of her neck until I hit that sweet spot on her shoulder that made her shiver. I bit down and felt a corresponding shake of her body.

"I love you," I whispered against her shoulder, pulling the collar of her t-shirt aside to gain access to more creamy skin. I mouthed the bone and skin and muscle until I felt her collapse into me.

THIRTY-THREE

AM

"AN A," I CROWED, TURNING the pages of the report we had just picked up from Professor Godwin's office. Bo and I had had the entire thing bound at the copy center, and it looked so professional with its glued edge and clear acrylic cover. "Is it incredibly nerdy of me to love this binding?"

"Yes." Bo smirked.

"Whatever." I stuck my tongue out at him. Bo grabbed my hand and yanked me tightly to him.

"Stick that tongue in my mouth, why don't you?" he teased. Who could resist that invitation? I pushed up on my tiptoes and gave him a wet, loud kiss. The unexpected nature of my public display of affection caught him off guard, and he didn't immediately respond. I was still a little reserved in public, and Bo had generally limited himself to handholding.

But then a wide slow grin spread across his face, until the bracket on the left side appeared, a sign of his true happiness. He leaned down and returned my kiss with a wet and hot one of his own. He gripped my ass with one hand and pressed me tight against his growing arousal, and he tangled the other hand in my hair, angling my head for an all-out assault on my mouth. In the distance, I heard some hoots, but this time, I hoped that they would gossip about me. That they'd go home and say that they saw Bo and AnnMarie making out in front of the Admin building. That they'd talk about how we always looked like we were one step away from tearing each other's clothes off. That they wished that someone would look at them like Bo looks at me, with unrestrained love and pride.

Realizing this was going nowhere, though, Bo pulled away. His face was flushed and his heavy lidded eyes were navy with desire. My entire body tingled in response. I gave him a little smile and waggled the project report between us.

"Good thing you didn't crush it." I dusted it off. "I'm keeping this."

Bo shook his head at me. "What's the point?"

I gasped with faux shock. "It's our first project together. I expect us to celebrate our important reportaversary."

He dropped his arm around my shoulders and kissed the top of my head. "Reportaversary?"

"The anniversary of our report," I said solemnly.

"Is that the anniversary of the start of the project or end of the report or when we got the grade? Because I need to mark that shit down in my phone." Bo's response was just as mockingly serious.

"It's all three," I grinned.

"If you say so." But I knew he was delighted that I cared so much about this. I flipped through the pages to admire the notes and drawings. When I got to the one showing the fully grafted plants, I noticed a small detail that I had missed previously. Bo had penciled our names, "AnnMarie" and "Beauregard," into the stems of the plant.

"Hey," I nudged him with an elbow, "this is really neat. Am I the stevia plant and you're the soybean?"

"Hell, no," Bo protested. "I'm the sugar. You're the substance." I peered closely at the plant, but I couldn't tell where the root of one plant started and the other stopped—which, I realized, was the point. Together, Bo and I were stronger, better people despite our differences. I felt tears pricking my eyes at his thoughtfulness and his beautiful vision of us as a couple. Lord, I loved him. I loved him so much. Now and forever.

Author's Note

There is no 1st Battalion 10th Marines, but because I'm telling a fictional story about fictional guys who never fought, I didn't want to diminish the bravery of the actual Marines. Instead, I made up my own Battalion, which could accommodate a couple thousand military heroes, although I'll never write that many.

Want more from the Woodlands? Don't miss Noah and Grace's story in* Undeclared, *the "sexy as hell"* debut from Jen Frederick...

**Craves the Angst Reviews*

UNDECLARED

A WOODLANDS NOVEL

Available Now in Print

ISBN: 978-0989247917

Amazon • Barnes & Noble

Also Available in Digital Format

Kindle • nook • iBooks • Kobo
and anywhere ebooks are sold

For four years, Grace Sullivan wrote to a Marine she never met, and fell in love. But when his deployment ended, so did the letters. Ever since that day, Grace has been coasting, academically and emotionally. The one thing she's decided? No way is Noah Jackson — or any man — ever going to break her heart again.

Noah has always known exactly what he wants out of life. Success. Stability. Control. That's why he joined the Marines and that's why he's fighting his way—literally—through college. Now that he's got the rest of his life on track, he has one last conquest: Grace Sullivan. But since he was the one who stopped writing, he knows that winning her back will be his biggest battle yet.

"A lovely debut book...a big fluffy pillow of a sweet love story. I wholly recommend you read it." —Nocturnal Book Reviews

About the Author

Jen Frederick lives with her husband, child, and one rambunctious dog. She's been reading stories all her life but never imagined writing one of her own. Jen loves to hear from readers, so drop her a line at jen@jenfrederick.com, or visit her website at www.jenfrederick.com.

Facebook: AuthorJenFrederick **Twitter:** @JenSFred

CPSIA information can be obtained at www.ICGtesting.com
Printed in the USA
LVOW07s1628230715

447374LV00007B/964/P